MW01178648

# Abuse of Power 4

§

*The Planters*

Special thanks to two classmates
of the Royal Military College of Canada
for their interest and help in developing this book.

3108 Arthur Beemer
3164 Paul Ruck

# Abuse of Power 4

§

## *The Planters*

By Bill Smallwood

Borealis Press
Ottawa, Canada
2005

Copyright © by Bill Smallwood
and Borealis Press Ltd., 2005

*All rights reserved. No part of this book may be used or
reproduced in any manner whatsoever without prior
written permission from the Publisher, except in the case of brief
quotations embodied in critical articles and reviews.*

# Canada⁣

*The Publishers acknowledge the financial assistance of the
Government of Canada through the Book Publishing Industry
Development Program (BPIDP) for our publishing activities.*


**National Library of Canada Cataloguing in Publication Data**

Smallwood, Bill, 1932-
    The Planters / Bill Smallwood.

(Abuse of power: Canadian historical adventure series ; 4)
ISBN 0-88887-281-X

    1. New England—Emigration and immigration—History—
17th century—Fiction. 2. Maritime Provinces—Emigration and
immigration—18th century—Fiction. 3. Great Britain—
Emigration and immigration—History—17 century—Fiction.
I. Title. II. Series: Smallwood, 1932-  . Abuse of power: Canadian
historical adventure series ; 4.

PS8587.M354P58 2005        C813'.6        C2005-903088-7

Illustrations by Eugene Kral.
Cover design by Chisholm Communications, Ottawa.

*Printed and bound in Canada on acid free paper.*

# Table of Contents

INTERMISSION

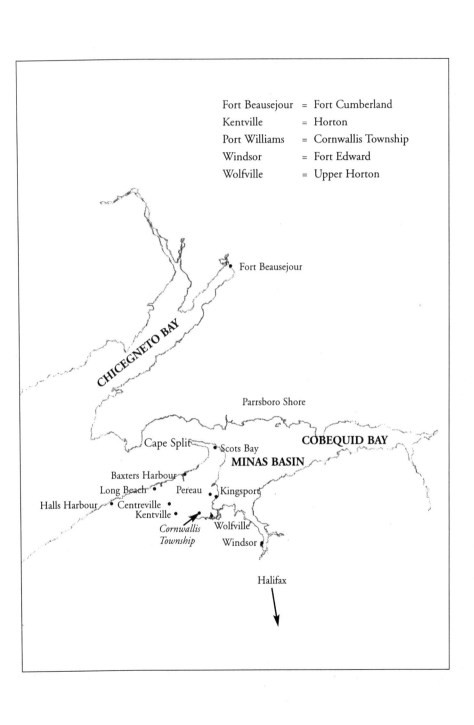

Fort Beausejour = Fort Cumberland
Kentville = Horton
Port Williams = Cornwallis Township
Windsor = Fort Edward
Wolfville = Upper Horton

Fort Beausejour

CHICEGNETO BAY

Parrsboro Shore

Cape Split
Scots Bay
COBEQUID BAY
MINAS BASIN
Baxters Harbour
Long Beach    Pereau    Kingsport
Halls Harbour    Centreville
Kentville
Cornwallis
Township    Wolfville
Windsor

Halifax

The Elizabethan word for colonist was planter; they were the people who planted colonies.

# Prologue

## 1585
## Tower of London

Ben looked out over the river. He turned to his companion. "Barge comin' downstream. Might be comin' here." Ben, the larger and older of the two, and Georgie, the new recruit, were standing guard at the Tower of London Traitor's Gate. In the moonlight, they could see that the swiftly moving barge had three occupants.

"Who'd be comin' this late?" Georgie asked.

They watched as the barge passed by and continued downstream.

"You don't know nothin' 'bout the Tower, mate. The Tower's been in the late night business fer a long, long time." Ben leaned his pike against the parapet and rubbed his hands together to get some warmth. "When you've been here as long as I 'ave, you'll know 'bout the Tower."

Georgie kept looking at Ben's pike which was leaning against the wall. Finally, he blurted, "The sergeant says we can't do that! 'e says it must be 'eld at the order or at the rest."

"Yeah, Sarge's right." Ben continued to rub his hands. "I 'member me old Sarge used t' tell about England and the Tower." He cupped his hands and breathed into them for the warmth and then began rubbing them again. "It's time you learned somethin' about what we're doin' here." He stretched out his arms and leaned against the parapet. He looked out over the river and spoke to the younger guard in a low voice.

"The Frenchies beat us at 'astings, not a battle Englishman can ferget. They kilt off our Anglo-Saxon overlords, family by family, and kilt the rest of us anytime we didn't speak French. The new Norman King, William—'e liked to be called William the Conqueror—'e built this place. 'e called it a Norman Keep; it keeps them's that's inside safe from them outside." Ben gestured at the river. "And sometimes 'e brings

1

them that's outside in and keeps 'em inside whether they likes it or not."

"What'cha mean?"

Ben stood back from the parapet and pointed off into the moonlit darkness. "See that one over there?"—indicating one of the dozen towers. "King William built White Tower to keep himself safe from us Anglo-Saxons. Then, when William was mad at somebody, 'e had them dragged through this gate and kep'em under there,"—pointing to the White Tower. "When 'e was through with them under there, 'e sent them up there." His thumb pointed to the heavens.

They stood in silence for several minutes and then Ben continued. "William and the French are gone. There wuz more of us Anglo-Saxons than there wuz of them and we sort of won out because they became just like us and spoke English. That's why we're Englishmen and not Frenchies; but the Tower still does business." Ben retrieved his pike. "Queen Elizabeth 'as Royal Chambers in the Tower and poor souls still come through this gate on their way up there," he said, nodding his head toward the sky.

George looked up, startled. "But we're Englishmen. We got laws and rights. The law is the most important thing we got. Everyone—even the nobles—must obey the law."

"You're right, m' boy. But religion is bad business. There are Englishmen helpin' the Queen's cousin, Mary, steal the English crown, an' Mary's a Catholic. If Mary becomes Queen of England, she'll force us to become Catholics." Ben spoke quietly. "Either be Catholic or be dead."

George thought about that. He stood up straight in his red and gold uniform. "I'm a soldier of the Queen. They'd better not try anythin' while Georgie is on watch." George performed a perfect port arms with his pike. He did a proper left turn and looked out over the river, scanning the water approaches to the Tower of London. With a nervous quiver in his voice he said, "Barge comin'! Barge comin' to our landin'!" Stepping back a pace, he whispered to Ben, "Quick, wot's the password!"

Ben whispered, "Rainwater."

George resumed his post and shouted, "Who goes there!"

"A sheriff on the Queen's business."

"Give the password!" George replied.

"Willow tree."

George whispered to Ben, "Call out the guard. We must defend the gate."

Ben snorted. "'old on, laddie." He turned toward the barge. "Say agin the password."

Across the water they heard, "It must be past midnight." In a louder voice came the reply, "Rainwater."

"Come ashore, friend." said Ben.

When the barge landed and the prisoner passed by, Ben recognized Sir Francis Throckmorton, a well-known confidant of Mary, Queen of Scots. Throckmorton was escorted through Traitor's Gate and disappeared into the White Tower.

* * *

Sir Francis Throckmorton had been locked up in a tiny cell for several days. He was tired, dirty, and very, very frightened.

With a clatter and bang, the cell door opened. Two guards lifted him off the straw pallet and hustled him down the long corridor toward a set of stairs going in both directions. Up, and Throckmorton might be able to see someone who could help him. They went down.

At the bottom of the stairs they entered a room where a big man with one ear missing stood smiling as if he were listening to a funny story with his missing ear. He motioned the guards to the other side of the room.

As soon as Throckmorton saw the long bench with the ropes and pulleys, he knew he was going to be tortured. He didn't resist when the guards threw him onto the bench. One Ear ordered the guards to pull the prisoner's arms over his head and to hold his feet tightly.

One Ear spoke softy as he did his work. "I won't ruin your 'ands, Sire. M'lord Walsingham gets angry when prisoners can't sign their names after they've been racked. Your ankles don't matter none; you won't be able to walk after you've been stretched but you'll be an inch taller!" He started to cackle at his own humour but, hearing the bolts and chains of the main door being worked from the outside, he silently finished his job. The door easily swung open on its well-oiled hinges.

Lord Walsingham entered with two henchmen. He dismissed the guards and, speaking to the largest of his companions, said, "Robin, a couple of turns on the rack just to get our guest's attention."

The man called Robin, obviously very familiar with his assigned task, quickly applied enough pressure to the spoke wheels to lift Sir Francis Throckmorton's body off the planks. Throckmorton made whimpering sounds as he felt the full weight of his own body on his wrists and ankles.

One Ear stepped closer to the prisoner, carefully checking the ropes on the wrists. "It'll do fine, m' lord."

Leaning over Throckmorton's face, Lord Walsingham said, "You have been accused of treason, of threatening our Queen's life with your Catholic intrigues."

Throckmorton denied any knowledge of a plot against Queen Elizabeth.

Walsingham then bent so close to Throckmorton that their goatees touched. "My agents tell me that you are recently returned from the continent. In Madrid you agreed to participate in a conspiracy called 'The Enterprise.'"

The body on the rack quivered but made no other response or acknowledgement.

Without moving, Walsingham said, "A generous turn of the wheel, Robin."

Throckmorton shrieked as Robin did as he was told. Walsingham wiped the spittle from his own face but was obviously gratified to see the pain in the other man's eyes. The rack was now as taut as the standing rigging of a ship and the chamber filled with the gasps from the suffering man.

Lord Walsingham stepped back and, in a conversational tone, said, "I know all your plans: King Philip of Spain expects the Irish will rise up against us when he sends them troops, the

French King will land an army in Scotland to encourage the Scottish Catholics to rebel, and, with the help of traitors like you, our Queen's cousin thinks she will steal the English throne." Raising his voice, he pounded his fist on the prisoner's chest. "But it bloody well won't happen as long as I am Secretary of State!" He leaned over Throckmorton's face. "What were you writing to Queen Mary when my men apprehended you?" Full of anger when Throckmorton refused to reply, Walsingham thundered, "What were you going to tell her?"

No response.

Walsingham stood there, breathing heavily. After several moments he turned to his companions and said, "There are two kinds of pain. The rack gives a pain that permits noble thoughts: Queen, Country, and Heroic Death. Well, let's introduce Sir Francis to another kind of pain: the pain that makes you realize there is only you and a dark pit of agony, nothing else." He took a dagger from his vest and delicately slit the fabric of Throckmorton's trousers revealing his manhood and a quivering thigh.

He gestured to One Ear, who then retreated to a corner of the chamber where there was a soft glow from a brazier. One Ear inserted an iron rod into the flames and worked the bellows to make the flame brighter and hotter.

"While we are waiting, Robin, put a bit of a turn on the wheel for Sir Francis."

After some clanking as the wheels were turned and the cogs held, there was a more basic, human odour filling the chamber.

"Dear me, I think Sir Francis has embarrassed himself," Lord Walsingham said with a short laugh.

The second of Lord Walsingham's companions spoke. "Please, Sire! Before more harm and degradation befalls this poor soul, may I have but a moment to speak to him?"

"Well, yes, Thomas, we are all God's creatures. Take a moment with him." Walsingham moved out of Throckmorton's view and a small, almost petit figure, completely engulfed in a monk's humble brown robe and cowl, shuffled to the prisoner's side.

The monk leaned over and gently placed a hand on Throckmorton's arm, the pressure of the hand firm and reassuring. Throckmorton could not see the face of the person called Thomas because the cowl was worn well forward over his head. Consequently, where Sir Francis might have expected some human contact or warmth there was only the occasional glint of reflected light, suggesting a pair of eyes somewhere in the cowl's oval darkness; however, the voice was pleasant and sincere as Thomas spoke of the nature of each man's journey from the warmth and safety of a mother's body to the death all must face. "Sometimes, the crossing is so difficult the soul yearns for release," he said. Then, Thomas lowered his voice to a whisper. "Make no mistake. Your time here will be extremely unpleasant at the hands of these men. You must realize that they will manipulate you until they obtain the truths they expect. Not until they get what they want will you be permitted to escape to the loving arms of God in His Heaven."

"Who . . . who are you?"

"I am Padre Thomas Bennett. I am permitted to offer God's grace to the prisoners of the Tower of London." The monk paused for a moment, lightly stroking the sweat and tears from Throckmorton's face. Continuing in a whisper, he asked, "Has your dear mother gone on ahead?"

More tears as Sir Francis nodded 'yes.'

"With her mother's love she will intercede on your behalf and ask our dear Lord to give you a merciful death." In a normal voice the padre said, "Dear son, tell these men what they must hear and end your torment."

There was some strength in the reply. "I cannot betray Queen Mary."

The padre stood upright over the prisoner and raised his right hand to make the sign of the cross. Sir Francis saw that the hand was shrivelled and twisted into a claw of flesh and bones. For the first time the light of the chamber allowed a glimpse of the sallow face and thin lips. Sir Francis could see that the right eyelid drooped and a pale liquid, like tears,

The monk leaned over and gently placed a hand on Throckmorton's arm;..."

dripped onto the monk's robe which was drawn in closely at the neck. "I will pray for you, my son. May you have . . ."

"That's quite enough, Thomas!" Lord Walsingham came from the far corner of the chamber with a white-hot, iron rod in his gloved hand. "Step back! I want to get on with this." Walsingham laid the rod lightly against the inside of Throckmorton's thigh. The hair over the prisoner's testicles smouldered and shrivelled as the skin on the thigh broke and the leg muscles seemed to melt.

"Damn! He's unconscious," said Robin.

"Look at 'is hands, my lord. It's time to loosen'em off."

Lord Walsingham threw the rod to the floor and stalked out of the chamber. "Have him here tomorrow for another session." He walked several paces down the corridor and waited as his two companions came out of the chamber. "He will break. He will break, tomorrow."

Robin nodded his head in agreement.

Thomas Bennett threw off the monk's robe and brushed the coarse, brown fibres off his black priest's habit. Adjusting his frock, he slipped a heavy gold chain and crucifix over his head. He smoothed his hair with his good hand. "A fine meal awaits us in the next Tower. A nice wine will go well with tonight's business."

Lord Walsingham shook his head negatively. "You are excused, Robin. Thomas and I must attend to some other matters."

Thomas Bennett looked disappointed but said nothing. He followed Lord Walsingham to Traitor's Gate where the Secretary of State's personal barge awaited them. They went down-river to the point of land near the lane where the Assistant Secretary of State, William Davison, had quarters. There was no pier so the two men had to scramble ashore. With wet and muddy shoes, they were in a very foul mood when they intruded on Davison. Although it was late in the evening, Davison was working with his aide, William Brewster.

Lord Walsingham made no salutation. He began the meeting by saying, "We have the traitor Throckmorton in the

Tower. He admitted nothing but tomorrow is another day. I say, have your man see to my boots, will you?"

Davison gave a small bow to his superior but the aide, Brewster, stepped forward and asked what evidence there was to place another Englishman, a prominent man like Sir Francis Throckmorton, in the Tower of London. Glancing at Thomas Bennett, he said, "I suppose some priest spoke against him and now he is a threat to the whole of England."

Lord Walsingham looked full into the face of William Brewster and said, "Our Queen has laws generous enough to allow religious dissidents like you to live in England and to prosper, but let me assure you"—here he paused to give emphasis to his words—"those laws do not give you licence to be critical of the Queen's actions against traitors like Throckmorton!" Walsingham turned his back on Brewster and spoke to the Assistant Secretary of State. "This fool will put you both in the Tower."

There was an uncomfortable silence. Bennett sat down on a bench near the fire and proceeded to scrub his boots. The other three men stood there, dressed remarkably alike, from the buckled shoes, black stockings, knee breeches, vest, and coat to the shoulder-length hair and goatee. Perhaps the only difference was in the richness of Lord Walsingham's adornments; his shoe buckles were the colour of gold, he wore a number of heavy rings, and he had a gold stickpin in his cravat.

The silence lengthened. Davison opened his mouth as if to speak but Walsingham took no notice of him. Davison remained silent.

Brewster, his face bright red, perhaps from the reflected glow of the fire, cleared his throat. "Your pardon, Sire."

Walsingham, turning his back to the fireplace, raised the skirts of his coat to warm his backside. He nodded his head.

Davison gathered up some papers from the desk. While Brewster held a candle over the pages, Davison began to read from the files. "We have a report from one of our spies on the continent that the Protestant Dutch King, William I, was assassinated under the orders of Pope Gregory XIII. The Pope plans to rid Europe of all of the Protestant leaders and has issued similar orders for the death of our Queen." Looking over at Walsingham he said, "Our spy was in the main audience chamber when Pope Gregory said"—Davison read directly from the page—"I look forward to that English Jezebel being done away with and, understand this, I would not only approve the murder of Elizabeth but if the murderer should be executed simply for killing her, I would consider him worthy of canonization!"[1]

The fire crackled and there was a shower of sparks. Walsingham stroked his haunches and legs to make sure there was no live cinder in his clothing, but otherwise maintained his position at the fire.

Bennett quietly commented, "The plot has an official name, The Enterprise."

Davison nodded in agreement. He continued the briefing. "There's more. Here's a report confirming a Papal Dispensation for William Parry to give him a clear conscience just in case he murdered Queen Elizabeth. He was a junior member of the Queen's Court so he had the opportunity to commit the deed. Fortunately, he was not clever enough and our officers captured him this morning."

"That's two of them: Throckmorton and now Parry," Thomas Bennett interjected. "They can be shown no mercy. They pretend to be members of the English Church while plotting with the Catholics . . ."

Lord Walsingham glanced at the priest with obvious displeasure.

Bennett stopped in mid-sentence.

Walsingham extended his hand. Davison gave him the file. By the light of the fire, Walsingham read the file. He selected a single sheet and held it up for the two gentlemen and the priest to see. "This piece of paper condemns Parry to be hanged." He returned the sheet to the file and handed the lot back to Davison. "Set up a hearing. Get the thing done quickly. Make it a public execution; if there is nothing more of importance, I think I will call it a day." He left, without ceremony, as quickly as he had come. Bennett followed.

As soon as Davison was sure that Walsingham and Bennett had actually departed, he sternly warned his employee not to be critical of the Church of England around Thomas Bennett.

"Walsingham is a very, very powerful man with a lot more to worry him than muddy boots or thoughts on religious freedom from a government official like you, but that priest, Bennett, is a real threat! He will remember what you said. He has the power, and if he should find the opportunity, he will make you regret that you spoke against the priesthood." William Davison sighed. "I love you like a son, William, but your ideas are not popular in this England of ours." He gestured for Brewster to return to the desk to resume their work.

Davison walked over to the hearth and lifted the skirts of his coat. "If Throckmorton is guilty of being a part of the Catholic Enterprise, he probably was in contact with Queen Mary. If Queen Mary is aware of The Enterprise, the English Parliament will demand her death." He rubbed his backside with both hands, enjoying the heat. "I wonder if Queen Elizabeth will be able to order the death of her closest relative." He allowed his coat to fall and turned to gaze into the fire. "Queen Mary will have to die." Then, almost to himself, "I wonder how Elizabeth will get someone to do it."[2]

Months later, William Brewster was to remember those words.

## Prologue

*1585*
*Amsterdam, Netherlands*

Assistant Secretary of State William Davison returned to Holland, where he was in charge of Lord Walsingham's intrigues on the Continent. It was pleasant enough duty for Davison, since William Brewster did most of the day-to-day work.

Brewster handled the correspondence concerning the second interrogation of Sir Francis Throckmorton. According to the file, Throckmorton was taken to the rack chamber, where he was unable to face the torture a second time. He confessed the plot, giving names, dates, and places of the invasions and uprisings. Sobbing, Sir Francis admitted that Mary, Queen of Scots was fully informed of the plot and was a willing participant. The file reported the traitor as saying, "I have broken faith with my Queen and I deserve to be hanged." A note, written on the last page of the file, stated that Sir Francis Throckmorton was, indeed, hanged at Tyburn.

When told about the report, Davison said, "So it begins. There will be a commission appointed but it is no longer a matter of what to do with the Queen of Scots. It is now a matter of the survival of England."

Brewster nodded. "If our Queen is killed, there will be civil war and the Catholic kings and the Roman Pope will take the opportunity to invade us. It would be the end of England."

Sounding very exasperated, Davison added, "Life would be simpler if Elizabeth had married and produced an heir." He smiled at the thought. "I can't imagine anyone man enough to mount that mare!" He looked out the window at the Dutch countryside. It was a grey day, a blustery kind of day—a good day to be inside. Davison turned back to face Brewster. "Mary will be executed. If Elizabeth won't do it then the nobles will."

\* \* \*

Over the months, William Brewster followed the events as he continued his work.

Davison was right. A commission was established to investigate the charges that had been laid against Queen Mary. Reading the file, Brewster thought that they hadn't given Mary much of a chance to defend herself: she had no counsel; the letters that were supposed to brand her as a conspirator were ambiguous and were only copies—the originals could not be found. It was no surprise when the commission found Mary guilty of conspiracy.

* * *

Back in London, Walsingham reported to the Queen on behalf of the commission. He met privately with her in the Royal Chambers. "Madam. Queen Mary was guilty of conspiracy and was an active participant in the plot to kill Your Majesty. Please, please, Madam, please act upon the recommendation of the commission. For as long as that woman is alive, she is a mortal threat to your realm, to your church, and to your person."

Elizabeth was loath to cause her cousin actual harm and said so.

Lord Walsingham took another approach with his Queen. "Your Majesty, I suggest you refer the matter to your Parliament for decision. Let them review the subject thoroughly so that we can be sure that, if we must act, we act in the best interests of England."

Walsingham knew his Queen. He didn't use the argument very often, but when he appealed to the Queen's genuine concern for the welfare of the English people, he usually got what he wanted. He was not surprised when the Queen agreed that the problem of Queen Mary should be presented to the English Parliament for review and for a recommendation. He also knew his countrymen. He expected that they would strongly recommend Mary be put to death, which they quickly did. The parliamentary recommendation to Queen Elizabeth was remarkably short and direct: "The only way to provide for Your Majesty's safety is by the speedy execution of the Queen of Scots."[3]

Queen Elizabeth thanked her Parliament. She made no decision, asked for no further recommendations, and, in a lengthy speech, left the matter of the disposal of Queen Mary in the hands of God.

\* \* \*

In Holland, Brewster read that the lawmakers did finally pass the death sentence for Queen Mary but there was a delay in the issue of a death warrant. Queen Elizabeth was the only one who could sign it; she delayed and delayed.

Davison's only comment was, "Walsingham must be having a fit!"

Throughout all of this time, William Davison was becoming more concerned as to who would be responsible for the death of Queen Mary. He explained to Brewster, "It certainly isn't going to be Queen Elizabeth. Elizabeth is not going to be held accountable for the death of her cousin, who is the legitimate heir to the throne of England."

\* \* \*

Toward the end of the year, Lord Walsingham was reported as being sick and confined to his home in the country. The Assistant Secretary of State was ordered to return to England to substitute for the missing Walsingham. Davison, accompanied by William Brewster, returned to England.

*Prologue*

*1586*
*London, England*

Davison was given an audience with the Queen soon after his arrival. Queen Elizabeth signed Mary's death warrant but, after the Acting Secretary of State had left the room, gave private instructions to several of her nobles as to the handling of the matter.

Stepping into the hall outside the Privy Chamber, Davison expressed his concerns to his aide.

"I believe that the Queen is still looking for a way to escape any blame for the death of her closest relative." He started walking down the hall, with Brewster hurrying to keep up. "The nobles are obliged to serve the warrant on Queen Mary, and Elizabeth probably wants them to proceed with the execution without the necessary final approval from the Queen of England."

Brewster asked, "Isn't a death warrant, signed by the Queen, all that is required?"

"A signed death warrant is enough for the likes of you and me to be executed without delay. Royals get one last chance before going under the axe; the royals don't like commoners killing royals out of hand."

They stepped into the courtyard. William Davison looked up and just stood there, soaking in the sunlight. "We'll just have to wait and see. I pray that it is out of our hands, now."

The matter did not proceed smoothly. For some reason, the selected nobles balked at their assignment. It was left to a meeting of a council of nobles to decide that, in the best interests of England, Queen Mary would be executed on the morning of February 8, 1587.

* * *

On that morning, as Davison completed normal business in the Privy Chamber, the Queen motioned for him to approach.

He stepped closer to his monarch and bowed his head slightly to listen.

"Prepare a letter of instruction to the nobles who are handling the Queen of Scots problem so that the matter may be dispatched."

William Davison, the Acting Secretary of State, was caught speechless. He looked around the Chamber. He was the only person in the Chamber who knew that Queen Mary was being executed within the hour. He stood there. The Queen waited.

"Your Majesty, I, . . ." He made up his mind. "Your Majesty, there is no real necessity for such a letter."

Elizabeth turned away for a moment. She returned her gaze to England's Secretary of State, who was standing there with his head slightly bent forward. He lifted his head and looked directly into the eyes of his Queen.

Queen Elizabeth waved her hand, saying, "You are dismissed."

\* \* \*

It was just a matter of time. Queen Elizabeth was informed of the execution of Mary, Queen of Scots. Reportedly, she was furious that her cousin had been executed without her knowledge. She said the warrant had been signed just to frighten Mary; Elizabeth would have rescinded the death warrant and Mary's life would have been spared.

Elizabeth was not to blame.

Walsingham was not to blame; he had been sick.

Davison was to blame; he had told the Queen that a letter to the nobles wasn't required. It was Davison's fault the Queen wasn't able to pardon her dear cousin in time.

In the dark of the night, William Davison was taken away.

\* \* \*

The next day, Brewster was denied entry to the offices of the Secretary of State. When he sought out his employer, William Davison, at his lodgings, he found that the place had been ransacked and all of the files and correspondence taken away; Davison himself had disappeared.

William contacted friends at the palace but no one would talk to him. Now he feared the worst, remembering Walsingham's words of warning to Davison: "This fool will put you both in the Tower." *Perhaps Davison is in the Tower,* he thought. *That little priest would lock me up too, if he knew about my congregation and our plans to purify the Church of England. We have been meeting secretly but Walsingham and Bennett have spies everywhere. We may have been discovered.*

Nevertheless, in spite of his genuine fear for his own safety, Brewster visited all of the officials who would see him and, eventually, learned that William Davison was a prisoner in the Tower of London.

* * *

When Brewster went to the main entrance of the Tower, the guard wouldn't speak to him. He tried another door; it was locked and no one answered his knocks and calls. He was walking across the Tower Bridge when he saw another entrance near the water's edge. There was an armed guard dressed in red and gold.

As William walked toward the entrance, the guard moved abruptly and raised his weapon. It was obvious that he meant to bar Brewster's approach to the door. William stopped. The guard remained motionless.

William Brewster was dressed in the height of fashion, looking every bit the gentleman he was. His hair was shoulder-length and tightly curled. His goatee was carefully combed so that it failed to hide the jewelled stickpin in his cravat. His outer coat was of blue brocade while the jacket was a rich chocolate brown. The buckles on his shoes shone like gold and the buttons at the calf of his breeches were shiny. He wore several rings on either hand. William carried a basket with a linen cloth covering the contents. The guard couldn't help but recognize quality when he saw it and there was a note of respect in his voice when he challenged the stranger at his gate

"What's your business 'ere, Sire?"

"I seek information about William Davison, who may be inside the Tower." Brewster's voice was a little shaky as he faced the blunt end of the Queen's authority.

The guard heard the quaver in the stranger's voice and decided on his course of action. "You have no business 'ere, Sir, and I must ask you to withdraw. Leave now," the guard firmly commanded.

When William didn't make an immediate move to leave, a voice from behind the gate asked, "Ask 'im wot's in the basket."

The guard stood absolutely still, with a strained look on his face.

"Ask 'im!" The hidden person prompted.

Brewster spoke in a louder voice so that the other person might hear him. "I have food and drink for William Davison, Secretary of State for England. I pray that I may learn about his condition and if he is in good health."

The hidden person sounded friendlier when he asked, "Wot kind of food and drink?"

"Cheese, a piece of ham, fresh bread . . ."

"Wot's to drink?"

"Some wine that . . ."

"Mister Davison 'as an apartment on the inner court; bright and comfortable 'e is. No questioning for 'im, nosiree. Good food. Good drink. 'is linen is cleaned for 'im and 'e bathes. Seen 'im take a walk in the inner court t'other day."

"May I see him?"

"No! No visitors! Leave the basket and be gone."

William stepped forward and placed the basket near the gate. The young guard flinched when Brewster stood up to turn and leave, since Brewster was a tall man, much taller than the guard. Then Brewster walked away. When he had taken several steps, he heard the gate open. He did not look around but the voice said,

"Well, what d'you think, Georgie? We got ourselves a fine supper!"

William Brewster smiled at that. A basket of food was a small price to pay to know that his friend was being fairly treated, although a prisoner in the Tower of London.

\* \* \*

For several months William Brewster tried to maintain activity as the aide to the Secretary of State but it became obvious that Davison was not going to resume his duties. Money became a problem and Brewster left London, returning home to Scrooby in Nottinghamshire, where his father, John, was Master of the Post and Bailiff for the Archbishop of York.

As tenant of the Archbishop, John Brewster lived at Scrooby Manor. He made space for his son in a wing of the manor house.

## Endnotes

[1] Concerning the plot to murder Queen Elizabeth, the Pope is reported to have said; "…know ye we do not only approve the act, but the doer, if he suffer death simply for that, to be worthy of canonization."

[2] Davison was of the opinion that Queen Elizabeth would not have her nearest relative, Mary Queen of Scots, killed.

[3] The report labelled Mary "by nationality a Scot, by upbringing a Frenchwoman, by blood a Guise, in practice a Spaniard, and in religion a Papist." It recommended Mary's just and speedy execution.

*Prologue*

*1588*
*Scrooby*
*Nottinghamshire*

Life was certainly a great deal quieter in Scrooby. There were no dastardly traitors or grand plans of invasions, but there were spies and intrigue because the bishops of the Church of England had the power, granted to them by Queen Elizabeth, to make life very difficult for those they felt weren't following the official state religion; they were particularly watchful of educated, articulate citizens like William Brewster. William Brewster bore watching.

William had many opportunities to make mischief for the clerics of the Church of England. He was admired and respected in the community as the son of John Brewster, a prominent citizen. Educated at Cambridge and a thoughtful Christian gentleman, William lived by the values of his religion, helping friend or stranger whatever the need. Consequently, when he said that the Anglican clerics in the area were not godly men and interfered too much in the daily lives of the people, his statements were echoed by a large number of the community. He felt that the clerics abused their powers and acted mostly out of self-interest and he said so, often. When laws were enacted making attendance at the Church of England services mandatory, William sought ways around the restrictions. William was heard to say, "Religious persecution that endeavours to drive a flock along a path is successful, as a rule, only with the sheep. It makes the goats unruly."[1]

At the death of his father, William became Master of the Post responsible for the maintenance of the system of relay horses for the Royal Mail. His other duties as the Bailiff for the Archbishop of York allowed him to participate in the selection of Anglican clerics, and it was in the performance of the latter duty that William used every bit of influence that his position, money, and personality could bring to arrange the selection of clerics sympathetic to Puritan beliefs. His actions earned him a visit from Bishop Bennett and two junior Anglican priests. The meeting took place in the receiving room of Scrooby Manor.

Bishop Bennett was seated on one side of the room, while William, accompanied by his eldest son, was seated facing him. The two priests arranged themselves near the table usually reserved for cloaks and hats. They were busily getting their files and papers in order as Bishop Bennett made some polite inquiries about the Brewster family's health and the effect the recent weather had had on the deliveries of the Royal Mail. He trusted that there had been no complaints raised that might have some impact upon the tenure of the present Post Master.

William half-smiled but made no reply.

The bishop continued, "You live well, here, as a tenant of the Archbishop of York." Bennett looked around the furnished room. "I suppose there are lists of chattels that belong to the property in the event that another bailiff should be quartered here."

Brewster replied, "You, as a bishop of the Church of England, have acquired an interest in the delivery of the mails and in chattel lists for the Archbishop's properties?"

Bennett looked up sharply and leaned forward. "I have developed an interest in the affairs of gentlemen who busy themselves in the appointment of my priests!"

Both junior priests popped open their inkwells and dipped their quills. Hands poised over the parchment, they waited for Brewster's reply.

"I perform my task as Bailiff conscientiously."

The priests began making notes. The room was very quiet. The only sounds were the scratching of the quills and the strong, clear voice of William Brewster.

"I interview every candidate with aspirations to be a priest in this diocese. I search for men who know the Bible and who are capable and willing to minister to our congregation and help the people any way they can."

Bishop Bennett held up his good hand to stop William. He accepted a list from one of the priests. "I personally spoke with all of these candidates before you saw them." He handed the list to Brewster. "They each had an excellent understanding of the Bible, the rituals and hierarchy of the Church, they each understood the authority of the priest," Bennett raised his damaged right hand as if it were the symbol of such authority as he emphasized his last point, "and they each had a great desire to enforce the rules regarding the use of the Common Book of Prayer, as approved by Queen Elizabeth." Bennett waved the claw in the direction of the list. "You failed to approve any of them."

Just then, the Brewster boy looked up at his father and asked, "What does Bishop Bennett mean by a Common Book of Prayer?"

Sensing the priests' anger that a youth should raise a question in such a discussion, William smiled at his son and, turning to face the bishop, explained. "I encourage my sons to ask questions about our daily approach to God." He patted his son's knee. "That's a very sensible question, Wrasling." William made a motion with his hand as if to include the priests in the explanation to the boy.

"Our Queen believes that arguments about religion cause great trouble because we have had long, terrible wars about religion. She will have no more fighting about religion in her England."

"That's why we have the Church of England?" Wrasling asked.

In a flat voice Bishop Bennett answered, "Yes. That is why we have the one church, the Church of England. Queen Elizabeth is the head of that Church and her priesthood must follow the order of service approved by her."

William lightened his tone of voice and ruffled his son's blond hair. "We, on the other hand, believe that trying to worship with a set of routine prayers is blasphemous." He paused. He wanted to put his next thoughts into terms the boy would understand and accept. "Elizabeth thinks it is good for

England if we all pray with the same words at the same time. We believe it is not good for our souls."

The bishop's face was getting darker and darker. The priests were scribbling furiously.

Wrasling, looking up at his father, asked, "What is so wrong about having words already prepared? The written words are probably much better than anything I can think of, Father."

Bishop Bennett nodded his head in agreement. "That is proper thinking, my good lad."

Brewster continued as if the bishop had not spoken. "My son, think of it this way. Using the prayer book is the same as greeting family members at the breakfast table by reading the salutation from a book."

The boy laughed.

Choking sounds 'welled up from the bishop's throat. He finally managed to say, "I can't believe you would challenge the decisions of your betters or the dictates of the Queen!" Bennett grabbed the arms of his chair and tried to thrust himself upright. His crippled right hand slipped and he fell forward to his knees.

William had a moment of concern for the bishop and reached forward to help the fallen cleric. The bishop struck Brewster's hands away, refusing any assistance.

When William saw that the bishop was unhurt, he gazed down at the kneeling figure. "We are ordinary, everyday people who accept the rulings of the Church of England in articles of faith." He again extended his hands to help the bishop. "But the priesthood should not be a distinct order. Priests have been given too much power over us. They have too privileged a position in spiritual affairs."[2]

Bishop Bennett was scrambling on his hands and knees trying to get out of the kneeling position and away from the feet of William Brewster at the same time. The result was that he fell over, prostrate at the feet of the larger man, who now leaned down and, again offering his hand, said, "The congregation must be able to vote to select its most godly members to be the leaders."

"I will have you locked up!" Bishop Bennett finally made it to his feet—clothing in disarray—his gold chains hanging over one shoulder. His face mottled with rage, he had the appearance of someone crying but only from one eye.

The two priests raced to give him aid.

"Get out! Get out!" he screamed. "Get out, get out!"

The priests hastened to obey, spilling ink, scattering files, and stumbling out of the room. The front door slammed and they could be heard running down the gravel walk.

"You are a threat to the Church!" He shook his clawed hand at the bigger man. Stepping back he shouted, "You are a danger to England!"

"I'm sorry that . . ."

Bishop Bennett turned on his heel and stalked out of the room.

The room was silent again. Wrasling, with concern in his voice, asked, "Did I do something wrong, Father?"

"No, son." William put his arm around his boy. "Men like Bishop Bennett are only interested in the power their position gives them."

"Will he cause you trouble?"

"Probably so."

"What will you do, Father?"

"As Christians, we must do what we think is right in the eyes of God. We believe that certain privileges and power can't be given to an exalted elite because all Christians—all of us—are priests and are equal before God. Those of us who are chosen by the congregation to be ministers have no right or authority to anything other than hard work, helping people."

The boy looked at his father with pride and understanding.

They could smell the rich odours from the kitchen. William rose and led his son in for the evening meal. "The bishop probably won't leave us alone, but we will continue to have our meetings. The most godly from amongst us will find a way to change the Church of England. God will guide us."

* * *

The first day of 1593 was cold and clear. Scrooby Manor was white with frost. Several of the chimneys were spouting white plumes of smoke when a horseman rode pell-mell across the lawns to the kitchen entrance. John Tilly, a member of the Puritan congregation, pounded impatiently on the kitchen door as Mary Brewster fumbled with the latches.

"Where's your husband, Mary?"

"He's in the parlour with a young couple from the village."

John walked through the kitchen and stood just outside the parlour. He could hear voices speaking earnestly but quietly.

". . . whenever a husband and wife engage in sexual intercourse for pleasure rather than procreation, then that pleasure befouls the sexual act." The young male voice continued, "The priest also said that a woman was a temptation. The sexual act was innocent in marriage but the passion that always accompanies it was sinful. He told us that it would be better if we were chaste than have lustful sex."

William's voice asked, "He gives advice like a Catholic priest. Is he Catholic?"

A female voice replied, "He is Anglican but his father was a Catholic priest."

There was a pause.

John turned to tiptoe away.

William said, "Married couples should engage in sex with goodwill and delight, willingly, readily, and cheerfully because God created people as sexual beings. There is true joy to be shared by . . ."

John was back in the kitchen. "Mary, in a moment or two, would you call for William and tell him I'm here with important news?"

When Mary called, William Brewster wasn't long in coming. He stood in the doorway listening to the excited John Tilly.

"One of our ministers has been arrested for speaking out against the Book of Common Prayer. Bishop Bennett sentenced him to life imprisonment! I also learned that Parliament will be passing a law that will forbid us from holding our own church services. Anyone who refuses to attend the Church of England for forty days and who goes instead to private meetings shall be committed to prison without bail until they promise to conform."

William sighed. He came into the kitchen, and took John's coat, hanging it on a wall peg.

"We knew when we formed into congregations separate from the Church of England we were bound to face persecution. Expecting to have trouble and then actually having the trouble doesn't make it any easier." He stood there, rubbing his chin. "I suppose the bishop waited until after Christmas because of his sense of Christian charity."

John shook his head, negatively. "No, the priests waited for Bishop Bennett to come up from London. Bishop Bennett executes the orders of the church in all matters dealing with dissidents in this area. They say he is particularly interested in the activities at Scrooby Manor."

William sat down at the wooden table in the middle of the kitchen. "I know the bishop. He is most unforgiving." Looking around the room, his eyes misting, he said quietly, "Men like Bennett make it almost impossible for us to follow our beliefs. Perhaps there isn't a place for us in England."

No one spoke for several minutes.

"I will talk to one of our ministers, John Robinson, and suggest to him that I go to London to see if I can get the sentence reduced or dismissed. I can't promise anything." With a wry smile he continued, "The last time I tried to help someone—although I tried mightily—I failed; my friend William Davison is still in jail. However, I will try to do something for our minister."

He looked directly at Mary. "Dear wife, continue with our work here. For the meetings on the Lord's Day, you have enough money so that you may entertain our friends in the usual way."

* * *

William returned from London several weeks later. His travel bags were still by the kitchen door when several of the elders and one of the ministers knocked to gain entrance. With his arm still around Mary's waist, William welcomed his friends and told them that he had been successful. The sentence of life imprisonment had been suspended.

There was a chorus of questions.

Mary kissed William lightly on the cheek and moved to the hearth, where she busied herself making some tea.

William invited the visitors to sit around the table. When they had settled down, he began to speak.

"Using my old contacts, I was able to arrange freedom for the man they called the Puritan troublemaker."

"He wasn't a troublemaker!"

"It was the priests who . . ."

William raised both hands to quell the surge of objections to the term "troublemaker."

"I must tell you, the Anglican clergy are so angry at our Puritan holier-than-thou attitude, they would gladly put us in jail and throw away the key."

He raised his hands again as they all began to speak at once.

"I was only able to secure the freedom of our minister by promising more moderation and discretion in our attempts to purify the Church of England."

Again, the men raised a ruckus.

"Now, now," he hushed them one more time. "We must be more humble in our dealings with the priests!" He smiled at his listeners. "Surely, we can be humble?"

There were mutterings but, eventually, they all nodded assent.

"The tea's ready." Mary poured the tea and passed the cups around. The men helped themselves to the short bread that she had placed on the table in easy reach. "I'm surprised that Bishop Bennett let our minister go," Mary said in the quiet moments as the men drank their tea and devoured every morsel of bread.

"He wasn't there," William replied as soon as he could get his tongue around the bread in his mouth. "Bennett had returned to London. I don't suppose he will be any more happy with us because of my interference."

One of the elders responded sharply, "It wasn't interference! You were just seeking justice for one of our own!"

"I don't think the good bishop will see it that way." Finishing his tea, William put his cup down and said, with a sense of finality, "I think Bishop Bennett will be watching us even more closely. He will cause us trouble if he has the chance. But, at least, we got our minister out of jail."

"This time you got away with it," Mary said. "I worry how long you can tweak Bishop Bennett's nose and expect to . . ."

William looked over at his Mary. "Some other good news, Mary!"

Mary looked at him expectantly.

"Our old friend and employer, William Davison, has been released from the Tower and is living on his country estate some distance from London."

Mary clapped her hands. "Praise be to God! Will he return to Court?"

"The Queen doesn't want him in London. He carries the blame for the execution of Queen Mary. William Davison is meant to remain on his estate and the Queen is paying him a very fine pension to stay there."

The visitors thoughtfully took these personal comments as a sign to leave and they gathered up their cups as they made their farewells and left by the kitchen door.

William and Mary stood at the door watching the members of the congregation cross the lawns to the village.

Mary, giving her husband an embrace, murmured, "I'm pleased for your old friend—pension and retirement rather than death or exile."

William, kicking the door shut, lifted her into his arms and carried her through the kitchen to their chambers. "We should visit him just as soon as we can. Perhaps the whole family can go."

Mary giggled as William blew in her ear.

* * *

Life being what it is, the trip to visit William Davison was postponed, first for sickness with the children and then because William was elected governing elder of the Scrooby congregation. Perhaps they might still have gone to see their old friend but, on March 24, 1603, Queen Elizabeth died in her sleep. Her death would have dreadful consequences for the Puritans.

The country mourned the loss of their Queen, but at least the royal successor had been determined without any bloodshed. James VI of Scotland, son of Mary, Queen of Scots, was invited to come south and be crowned King James I of England. That meant that Scotland and England were truly united for the first time under one king. The English quietly anticipated continued prosperity and religious tolerance under their new king.

Unfortunately, King James believed that he ruled by the divine right of God and he disliked Puritans. Laws that supported the concept of One Kingdom and One Church were rigorously enforced. Any hopes of reconciliation between the Church of England and the Puritans were laid to rest with Queen Elizabeth.

As elder of his congregation, William Brewster was forced to the conclusion that there wasn't a place for his people in England. Where could they go to live a Christian life and worship as they pleased?

\* \* \*

"Where can we go to live a Christian life and worship as we please?" With both hands raised in supplication, William was a striking figure as he stood at the front of the congregation. By this year, 1607, his shoulder-length hair was dusted with grey; his moustache and goatee had, as yet, no hint of anything other than its normal tawny colouring. Broad-shouldered and handsome, he lowered his powerful-looking arms and leaned on the pulpit, waiting for a response.

There was a general shuffling of feet but otherwise the congregation remained silent.

William made no move to continue. He waited.

Elder Miller broke the silence. "Bishop Bennett excommunicates anyone accused of religious dissent . . ."

"He's Chairman of the Court of High Commission. He's got the power!" John Tilly shouted.

"Hush. We are in the presence of the Lord." To soften his reprimand, William added, "I think He heard you, John."

That brought smiles to the congregation, which faded as John continued. "They call us Separatists. They put us in jail. They pass new laws every day making it harder and harder just to live!"

There was some quiet for a moment and then William asked, "The congregation at Gainsborough went to Holland. Is that something you think we should do? Leave England? Go to a foreign land?" William sat down at the end of the table. He leaned on his elbows and scanned the group looking for a reply. It wasn't long in coming.

"Yes." Elder Miller crossed his arms and looked down at his boots. "But we probably couldn't get away. When Bishop Bennett found out that the Gainsborough group had escaped, he changed the law. Now it is unlawful for a person to leave England without a licence and Bennett will see to it that there'll be no licences for Scrooby!"

"No licences for any Separatists!" Joe Miller, the Elder's son, piped up. "You need to find a sea captain who will take you without papers." He lowered his head, "Otherwise there's no way out."

Richard Smith stood up. "I have news of the congregation that gathered at Great Grimsby in hopes of boarding a ship for Amsterdam."

The elders nodded for him to proceed.

"The ship's captain had accepted a bribe and preparations were well under way when the captain had a change of heart; he betrayed his passengers to the authorities."

"What happened to them?"

"They were locked up until Bishop Bennett could arrive with warrants for their arrest. He sentenced them to a month in jail."

"And the children?"

"They went to jail, too."

Another member of the congregation stood up. "I'm just back from Lincolnshire, tonight. A group was captured at Boston after their captain informed on them. Bennett put them in jail, the children too."

Elder Brewster rose and signalled that he would lead the congregation in prayer. He raised his voice over the bowed heads, asking for God's blessing on the immediate task of helping their brethren who had been put in jail. He especially pleaded that God protect the children from the evils of the English jail system. The Scrooby congregation would act as quickly as it could, but in the meantime, they would rely upon God to protect the children from harm.

"Amen." The congregation filed out swiftly to leave the elders to their task.

When they were alone, William expressed concern for the health of the children who would be spending at least a month in jail. He discussed the problem with the ministers and the other elders.

"It appears that I must dare the wrath of Bishop Bennett at least one more time," said William. "My friends at Court cannot help me with this but the ratepayers of towns like Grimsby and Boston might want to give us some aid."

William rubbed his chin, putting his goatee into wild disarray. "Think of it. The cost of each family in jail is charged against the tax rate and it is the landowners, as taxpayers, who must pay and pay. Perhaps the taxpayers would rather we looked after the Separatists at Scrooby Manor; it would be far less costly to them."

The elders chuckled at the thought and sent William off on his rescue mission.

William presented his clever argument before the ratepayers of each of the towns where the Separatists were in jail. Very quickly, the local authorities co-operated in the release of the families.[3] As a result, large groups travelled safely to Holland.

* * *

Several years passed. While the Separatists won the occasional skirmish, like the ones at Boston and Grimsby, the hordes of sheriffs, bailiffs, and priests let loose amongst them by Bishop Bennett were defeating them by the sanctions, fines, and imprisonment against which they had little recourse. To be a Separatist was to endure daily injustice and intolerance.

At Scrooby Manor, the Brewsters were providing refuge (entertaining, as William liked to describe it) for families displaced by the Court of High Commission's actions. Mary, working with the wives, managed to serve hearty meals and William provided solace to people who had lost their homes and all of their possessions. Despite the losses, the members of the congregation maintained their faith; they believed their ministers and elders would, with God's help, lead them to a better life either here on earth or in Heaven.

William Brewster, however, could see the end of their resistance fast approaching. He spoke often of the necessity of leaving England because soon there would be no haven like Scrooby Manor because there would be no money. There would be no friends left outside the congregation to speak up for them. The law was against them and Thomas Bennett encouraged his minions to enforce every jot and tittle. There would be a bitter end to the Separatist dream of religious freedom.

The decision was finally made. The Scrooby congregation would leave England for Amsterdam as soon as they could. They spoke of themselves not as Separatists any more, but as Pilgrims. They would search for their new homeland where they could worship God without the interference of governments and kings. At the word of their Senior Elder, they would begin their pilgrimage to such a place. Perhaps it was Amsterdam where they could live a Christian life and worship God in their own fashion. William Brewster would tell them.

*   *   *

The Pilgrims met at Scrooby Manor. All of the members knew that it was time to leave England but they waited, expectantly, for their Senior Elder to appear.

William came into the room and stepped up to the pulpit. He didn't hesitate, but began speaking immediately.

"We have discussed our options and have agreed that we will go to Amsterdam, where there is already a large Separatist population and we can expect some assistance." He looked around the room into the faces of his followers. "We will leave England."

There was an audible intake of breath. It still came as a shock to hear William say it! They were really going to leave England!

"In future years it will be remembered that we did not bend to persecution and tyranny. It will be said of us," and at this point William began to read from some notes, "we entered into a covenant to walk with God and one with another, in the enjoyment of the Ordinances of God, according to the Word of God." Now William looked from face to face of the people in front of him. He spoke slowly and with great deliberation.

"But finding we could not peaceably enjoy our liberty in our Native Country, without making offence to our persecutors, we left to seek a happier land." He looked at Mary, who was crying, and said, "It is difficult to do this but we must begin our search for a homeland."

And the congregation replied, "Amen."

## Endnotes

[1] John Masefield, in his introduction to *The Chronicles of the Pilgrim Fathers* (edited by Ernst Rhys and first published in 1910) quoted one of the leaders as first expressing this sentiment. My attribution to William Brewster better serves the purposes of the novel.

[2] Brewster's group (the Puritans) believed (contrary to the official position of the Church of England) that the priesthood was not a distinct order. The Puritans believed that priests should be selected by the congregation.

[3] Local authorities were glad to get rid of the financial burden. The prisoners were soon released and the authorities connived to help them leave the country.

*Prologue*

*1618*
*Leyden*
*Holland*

"Several of the Van Kleek children played ball with our boys today. Love and Wrasling got along very well with them," Mary said in a conversational tone. "They seemed to enjoy each other's company." She looked over at her husband to see his reaction as she added, "They were speaking Dutch."

William sighed. He said nothing. Covered with filth from the Van Kleek stables, he was getting cleaned up for supper. He stood there, leaning over the bucket, cold water streaming from his hair onto his arms and shoulders, and said nothing. He thought about the year they had spent in Amsterdam.

*After escaping from England, his congregation, the Pilgrims, had settled in and around Amsterdam. Most of the men were able to get employment at the textile mills where the work was hard and dirty with not much pay, but they believed times would get better. At least they had religious freedom; religious freedom was more important than comfort and possessions. However, their children were growing up and that posed a serious problem for the elders of the English community.*

*In a big city like Amsterdam, it was impossible to stop the English children from having almost daily contact with the Dutch population. Very quickly, their children were picking up Dutch mannerisms and language, totally unacceptable to a religious community that considered itself as being the best of the Church of England.*

*Despite the suffering that another move would bring, and now calling themselves Pilgrims, they uprooted in 1617 and moved to the small village of Leyden. In Leyden the Pilgrims believed they would be able to control or reduce Dutch contact with their children.*

Shaking his head, William took the cloth that Mary handed him and wiped himself dry. He sat on a three-legged stool and looked around the small house that Van Kleek rented to them for more than half of William's wages as a farm worker.

"Did Frau Van Kleek bring the used clothing for the children?"

Mary nodded her head. "She also brought eggs and greens, but no meal for bread. And she had barely enough milk for her own use so we didn't get any."

William bowed his head and Mary thought, *perhaps he is going to pray.* Instead, with his head lowered, he said, "Our children were speaking Dutch. It's not their fault. They hear and see things Dutch all the day long. We even dress them in Dutch clothing. They can't help but feel more Dutch than English." He looked up. "Dutch ways are not our ways. We must get our children out of Holland."

Mary nodded her head but remained silent; she knew her William wasn't through speaking.

"At Prayer Meeting it was suggested that I could earn more money by teaching Latin and English instead of working in the fields. There are merchants who will pay good money for my services." He got up and took Mary's hands in his. "If I do that, I will have to go to Amsterdam. Times would be difficult for you, Mary. We wouldn't be allowed to stay here on Van Kleek's land; he would need the house for his next farmhand. You and the children would have to live with our friends, but we would have more money for food."

Mary smiled a sad smile as she said, "At least Brewster children could stop dressing like poor Dutch."

William Brewster left for Amsterdam as soon as his family was resettled amongst friends.

\* \* \*

Since the summer of 1616, William had been writing pamphlets for the Puritan causes, and they were distributed by hand in Amsterdam. With his arrival in Amsterdam, he arranged for Renolds, a master printer, to turn out hundreds of copies, far more than could be used locally. In a port city as large as Amsterdam it was not difficult to find ships' captains to smuggle the pamphlets into England, where they were very well received because, in England, the Anglican bishops controlled the printing presses and censored the contents of newsletters and pamphlets. Consequently, the general populace was hungry for information other than Church dogma. Demand for the pamphlets increased so rapidly Renolds hired a twenty-two-year-old assistant, Edward Winslow. At a farthing for each pamphlet, money poured into the hands of the congregation. Life for the Pilgrims became better and better.

Mary, her two sons Love and Wrasling, and her two daughters Honour and Fear, now had the comfort of a good home and plenty of food and clothing. Not only were the pamphlets a success, but William was being paid handsomely as a language teacher; he was teaching English to the children of affluent Dutch businessmen.

As with everything he did, William had approached teaching English in a structured way. He made language rules for his students to follow. He called it "teaching English in the Latin manner." Even his slowest pupils were soon able to read and write English very well, to the amazement and pleasure of the wealthy clients. Holland was being good to Elder William Brewster and his flock.

* * *

At the print shop, Edward Winslow was cleaning the press and putting away unused sheets of paper after the most recent run of pamphlets

"Why do you write the pamphlets as 'Anonymous' instead of using your name? I would think the readers would want to know who was writing for them." Edward put a stack of pamphlets on the table and began bundling them, getting them ready for shipment.

As usual, William considered his reply carefully. "Since it is against English law to distribute papers, the bishops have every bailiff and sheriff searching high and low for us. Not knowing who they are looking for makes it more difficult for them." William smiled at the thought. "They have probably searched every hen house in Nottinghamshire by now."

"But we are in Holland! The sheriffs can't reach us here!"

"If the bishops knew it was I, they would have King James' spies in the Secretary of State search us out. They would try to stop us."

Edward laughed at that. "Well, we do a lot of good for the Puritan cause. Maybe someday the Anglican Church will change because of something you write."

"I write with little hope of changing the Church of England. King James will not allow change. No, I write for people who want to follow their conscience and the Word of God. These people know there is more to religion than a priest mouthing dry, dusty words and posturing in front of graven images on elaborate altars."

Edward smiled and said, "I wonder if God listens when he hears them saying the same things, time after time."

William looked at Edward and said, sternly, "We can't presume to know what God does. You must not try to put yourself in God's place." Then, relenting, he put his hand on Edward's shoulder. "Puritans know that using routine phrases, word by word, can't reflect the love of God in our hearts which changes, day by day, getting stronger as we understand more from His Word."

William walked toward the door. "I must get along to my classes." He turned with his hand on the latch. "I have almost as many students as I can handle. You're a bright lad. Maybe I can find something for you to do in language training." William went out the door and down the street.

Later, William and Mary had just finished their prayers at the supper table when Edward Winslow arrived at the house, breathless and with very bad news.

"The Dutch have issued a warrant for your arrest! They broke into the shop and seized the presses. Renolds has been taken. I managed to get away to warn you."

Getting up quickly, William went into the bedroom, with Edward and Mary following. He reached under the bed. Taking out an old travel bag, he began to throw clothes into it. "Tell me what happened," he said as he bent over the travel bag.

Mary gently pushed her husband away and removed the rumpled clothes from the bag. "I'll do this, my dear," she folded the first piece of clothing and stowed it carefully in the bag, "while you find out what's going on."

William took Edward by the elbow and led him to the window where they could watch the street. When he had satisfied himself that there were no strangers lurking in the courtyard, he repeated his question, "What happened?"

Trying to catch his breath, Edward explained that a man had come into the print shop asking for copies of the latest pamphlet. "When I said we didn't have any copies left, he asked who was the author."

"What did you say?"

"I told him that it was the work of our Senior Elder. He asked if the Senior Elder was William Brewster."

"Then what happened?"

"He started to go into the back room. He seemed to be searching for something but I told him he couldn't go there. He got real mad and tried to push his way past me." Edward smiled. "Imagine, a little man like him thinking he could push me around!" Edward reached out his hand. "I grabbed him by the arm, like this. He pulled back and I saw there was something wrong with his hand! It was like a claw!"

"Bishop Bennett!" William exhaled a long breath. "They had to read the warrant out loud. Did you hear any part of it?"

"Yes, I did," said the still breathless Edward.

"Tell me what you can."

"I remember that he said 'Upon complaint from the Ambassador from the Court of King James' and then, 'seize the premises, presses and stores and such person or persons found therein shall be taken into custody.' That's when I started out the back door. They were demanding to know the whereabouts of 'one William Brewster' when I got clear of the building."

"Well, we could expect that once they found us, Bennett would go to any lengths to shut us down."

Mary gestured to the two men that she needed help closing the bag. Edward pushed down on the bag while William secured the fasteners. William hefted the bag and then placed it on the floor. He put his hand on Edward's shoulder. "I won't need your help teaching languages, not for a while at least. Now, get off home and make sure that you throw away all of your printing clothes. Keep washing your hands and arms and stay indoors until you get it off."

Edward moved to leave. "Are we going to jail?"

William gave the young man a reassuring smile. "Don't worry too much, Edward. We have broken no Dutch laws. We have incensed the Anglican bishops and they have complained to the king. Sir Dudley Carleton, the British Ambassador, must have been ordered to put pressure on the Dutch authorities and the Dutch have closed the print shop. No one, other than the bishops, will have much stomach for pursuing this matter . . . and the bishops are in England."

Edward seemed relieved. "You think this will all blow over."

"Yes, but I don't think we'll be printing any more pamphlets." Waving his hand at the young man he said, "Go with God and do as I told you." Without a pause, William turned to Mary. "I must go to England. Robert Cushman is there inquiring about a land patent so that we might settle in Virginia. I must tell him to act quickly because Thomas Bennett has found us. Bennett will continue to cause trouble."

Mary put her arms around her husband. "Will you be safe in England?"

"Yes. The Bishops won't be looking for me there." William stroked her hair. "I will send word as soon as I can, Mary."

Nestled against the strong form of her husband, Mary gave a muffled reply. "I will wait to hear from you, dearest William."

*Prologue*

*1620*
*Atlantic Ocean*

"Why must we go back to Dartmouth?" Mary asked her husband. They had been eight days at sea in the ship *Mayflower* and this time the one hundred and twenty immigrants had prayed that they might continue on to Virginia, but the other ship, *Speedwell,* carrying about half of the party, had turned back and *Mayflower* had followed.

William thought for a moment before answering. "The *Speedwell* is a smaller craft of about 60 tons compared to our 180 tons. She doesn't take kindly to these heavy seas. She sprung a leak the last time we set out for Virginia and we turned back. Her captain must have a good reason for turning back again." William held onto Mary and braced himself as the ship lurched. "We must return with her or we lose half of our party and a third of our supplies." The ship rolled heavily to one side. William stepped protectively in front of his wife and sleeping children, as some of the luggage came loose and crashed past them to the other bulkhead. When it had wedged itself against the animal pens, William patted the shoulder of a wakeful child, and turned and continued speaking to Mary. "There is the problem that we have already paid the *Speedwell* captain. He is probably not as committed to completing the voyage now as he was before we paid him."

Mary clung to her husband as the ship was pitched and tossed by the heavy seas. "How long before we can have some fresh air?"

William didn't respond. He held Mary close as they waited in the dark space under the spardeck of the old freighter *Mayflower.*

* * *

Almost a week later the Pilgrims were finally allowed to come on deck to face a grey, blustery September morning. Gulls were wheeling overhead and the crew were busily opening hatches and warping the ship to the pier.

"This isn't the same pier that we sailed from," William observed. He examined the harbour for something familiar as one of the crew said, "We are in Plymouth, sir. The other ship took the first port she could get into."

"They must have had a bad time," said the Second Mate as he casually lashed the neck of the crewman with the end of a knotted rope. "Get on with it or I'll have your backside ruined!"

The sailor jumped quickly to the spardeck out of sight of the officer. The mate admonished the Brewsters, "No talking with the crew," and struck at the exposed flesh of another sailor with his rope before descending to the main deck. "And keep your whelps from underfoot."

William was displeased but said nothing. He waited until they were alone again before he led his little group to the rail. They looked across at the *Speedwell* at the next pier. She looked so small and had certainly taken a battering from two weeks of heavy seas.

"Those poor souls. What a terrible time it must have been," said Mary, thinking of the other wives and their children who were just now being allowed on deck. She waved to them but no one responded.

William squeezed Mary's hand, saying, "I must go ashore to meet with the elders. Stay on deck, Mary, in the fresh air. I will bring something to eat when I return." He almost ran down the gangway onto the pier and into the crowd, heading to the *Speedwell.*

\* \* \*

Late in the afternoon, Mary and William huddled in the lee of some deck cargo as they ate some bread and fish. William held a tankard of ale he and Mary shared.

"*Speedwell*'s captain has declared his ship too much battered to keep the seas. I feel the man is lying in order to escape from the fulfillment of his charter, but the elders accepted his word."

"What will happen now?"

"Well, *Speedwell* will be abandoned and we have bidden the Pilgrims on her to come aboard the *Mayflower*. Some of the *Mayflower* passengers are quitting and *Speedwell* people will take their space. There are quite a number who have been discouraged by the hardship and seasickness."

Mary thought, *he's bowed his head. He has something to say that really disturbs him. I must wait for him to say it.* She sat there through the moments of silence.

"Robert Cushman is leaving the expedition here, at Plymouth," William finally said.

After a few moments Mary carried on for him. "Robert Cushman. What a loss! He helped you to negotiate the terms of the land patent with the Virginia Company."

"Robert did most of the work," William said, firmly. "When the company wouldn't let dissidents like us into Virginia, he convinced them that we would not be rebellious or dangerous colonists."

"He served us well," Mary quietly said.

"Few of us realize that he staved off Bishop Bennett's efforts to stop us." Scratching his goatee, William looked up at the gulls. "Bishop Thomas Bennett told the Virginia Company that we intended to make a free popular state. The company was unhappy with the thought. Bennett was able to delay the patent for two years with stories just as fanciful."

"Why does Bishop Bennett keep after us?" Mary looked up at her William. *There is so much grey in his beard, now,* she thought. *He is still a handsome man. He would be so embarrassed if I ever said so.*

"Well, he's trying to punish me because of something I said to him, years ago, in front of Lord Walsingham. I was young and should have held my tongue. As for the congregation, he can't bring himself to let us go. We are like a counterfeit coin in his purse."

"What do you mean?"

"We were in his purse when he was given charge of a set number of souls. Like a bad penny, he can't use us, or spend us, or even get a credit for us, but he can't throw us away either, because by doing so he thinks he diminishes his net worth. We are in his purse and we keep turning up," William grinned, "like, as they say, a bad penny."

"And he almost stopped us from going to Virginia?"

"Yes, but Robert Cushman didn't give up."

Mary glanced over at the *Speedwell*. "It must have been dreadful on the *Speedwell* to make a man like Robert Cushman give up on his dream."

William continued almost as if he hadn't heard his wife. "Robert convinced the elders that they must sign a document saying that we Pilgrims would assent to the doctrines of the Church of England and acknowledge the king's authority. Robert said there wasn't much to discuss; we either gave the company that sort of assurance or we didn't get the patent. Without the patent, we would not be allowed to sail and Bishop Bennett would have won, after all." William shook his head. "We must have Robert with us. I must speak to him one more time."

On Wednesday, 16th of September 1620, the *Mayflower*, with one hundred and fifty souls, sailed west to Virginia. Robert Cushman was not with them.[1]

### The Third Attempt
### At Sea

The Pilgrims had been allowed on deck for the first time in almost two months. They stood in small, silent groups and looked out over the wide expanse of dark, green, hostile water. The ship was only a hundred feet long, and narrow at the beam; consequently, the haggard, white-faced passengers took much of the deck space. The crew, ruddy and robust looking, jostled and pushed their way through as they went about their assignments.

One of the Pilgrims had been left below in the filth and stench of between decks. He was too sick to move and would probably die without seeing the sky again.

Another of the Pilgrims was heavily pregnant and she had asked to be left with her misery. Mary had wanted to remain and minister to their needs, but William took her arm and firmly led her topside to the fresh air. Mary was grateful for her husband's persistence; the area between decks—where the Pilgrims lived—was a hellhole at the best of times.

On its previous voyage, the *Mayflower* had transported barrels of wine from Bordeaux to London. Now, loaded with enough beds, tables and chairs to furnish nineteen cottages, plus family pets, goats and poultry, and a generous supply of dried ox tongues, spices, turnips and oatmeal, there was little room for passengers. Brewster's Christian patience and understanding had been sorely tried when William Mullins, perhaps the richest Pilgrim, had insisted on including 126 pairs of shoes and 13 pairs of boots in his personal baggage; Brewster had prayed for forgiveness for his unkind thoughts about Mullins.

Under the spardeck, where the one hundred and four Pilgrims were stowed, half that number would have found it miserably cramped. They lived, ate, slept, and were seasick in that low, narrow space. There could be no privacy, packed as they were among all their belongings and stores. The woman would bear her child there; the man would die there. Most of the time, the hatches and gun ports were battened down and there was no natural light. If the seas were rough, water would come across the deck and leak through the deckhead's caulking, putting out the feeble light from the lanterns. If the weather were bad enough, accumulated water would slosh from bulkhead to bulkhead, carrying pots and blankets with it as the ship pitched and rolled. In the stink and misery, they could do nothing but lie there, seeking God's grace through prayer.

\* \* \*

The Second Mate was the first to see the squall line approaching, heralding a storm. He struck out with his rope at the nearest sailor. "You should have seen that 'fore now. Get the passengers below and be quick about it!"

The Pilgrims were herded below. They were not settled into their spaces when the ship heeled well over to starboard as the first of the storm struck the sails—before they could be set for the change in the weather. They heard the desperate cries of the crew as the ship heeled further and further to starboard. Flailing bodies were thrown across the deck, adding to the weight on the down side of the ship.

"She's going over!"

"Crawl up the high side," Miles Standish ordered, and he began to push people up the incline to the far side of the ship; Miles had been a soldier and he reacted to situations faster than most. "Must get more weight on the high side to bring her down. We have to help the ship right herself."

Slowly, the ship began to come back down from her dangerous angle. Between decks, the Pilgrims moved to the high side of the ship as, topside, the crew struggled to reduce canvas. The *Mayflower* seemed to be sailing much better, when there was a wrenching, tearing sound from the bowels of the ship. The captain must have heard it as well because, very soon, the hatch popped open and a sailor, dripping wet, scurried down to the keel in the bowels of the ship.

William could tell there was something terribly wrong by the look on the sailor's face when he returned. The sailor went straight topside and didn't bother to close the hatch. He returned with the captain and the mate and the three of them went below to see the damage. Everyone knew there was damage because now there was a continuous grinding, screeching noise, as if the *Mayflower* were in great pain. The ship's officers soon returned.

The captain paused under the open hatch and spoke to the elders who had gathered there.

"The main beam's gone; broke clean through. She won't last long."

"There's nothing we can do?" asked Standish.

"I suppose a prayer or two, but God can't fix a main beam," replied the Captain.

One of the passengers, standing just behind the elders, stepped forward and asked, "How do you fix a main beam?"

The mate laughed, but the captain answered, describing the large beam that goes down the centre of the ship. Using his hands, he showed how the beam had broken and was now pulling away from the hull. Soon the hull would rupture and the ship would sink, quickly. "I suppose if you were strong enough, you could push it back into place and then hold it there for the rest of the voyage."

The Pilgrim, a carpenter by trade, said, "I think we can do that." He turned to his neighbour, "Get our jackscrew.[2] We can put a lot of pressure against that beam by pushing against the ceiling. Maybe she'll go back in place. At least we should be able to stop any further movement."

Miles Standish looked over the captain's head and said, "You'd better get that hatch closed or we will have so much water down here that we won't have to worry about the beam."

The captain pushed the mate ahead of him up the ladder. "You look after the beam. We will sail the ship. Let me know when you've done what you can."

"We have to get the jackscrew from 'tween decks and into the bilge," the carpenter cried. Just then the deck hatch slammed shut and the men were in almost total darkness. William managed to strike a light and a lamp was lit. They could hear the seas thundering across the spardeck just over their heads.

The sailor, who had been left to help, jumped down into the bilge. He took the end of the jackscrew and pulled it into the hatchway. It slipped, but he managed to hold it. "Christ! It's heavy."

The Pilgrims sprang to his aid. William, gritting his teeth as he took most of the weight on his back, lifted the screw up so that it would fit down the hatch. "I-trust-you-were-praying-and-not-blaspheming." The jackscrew slipped easily into the bilge. "Ha! You were praying."

The rest of the men jumped down into the bilge. They found the break in the main beam by following the noise to its source. William and Miles each had a lamp. They lighted the area for the two carpenters and the sailor as they worked to put the jackscrew in place. Knee-deep water rushed from one side of the ship to the other as the *Mayflower* rolled and pitched. Each time the ship bore the weight of the seas on her deck, the break in the main beam would open and the planks of the hull would shift and more seawater would come in.

"We must be quick," the sailor cried above the noise. They almost had the jackscrew in place when William was knocked down by something in the rushing water. He surfaced several feet away.

"I've lost the lamp," he spluttered. Then he threw himself at the screw, as another wave was about to dislodge it from the beam. In the darkness, the four men worked the screw until there were still some creaks coming from the broken main beam but the horrible wrenching sound was gone.

The carpenter sat up on the beam. He wore a huge grin as he told the sailor, "Tell the captain that our prayers worked and I'm sitting on the break to hold it for the rest of the trip."

Exhausted, the sailor started the climb to the main deck. Standish saw a head peering over the lip of the bilge's hatch. It was young John Howland.

"John! Get up to the main deck and find the captain." Miles hollered. "Tell him the main beam will hold."

The boy waved that he understood and disappeared heading for the hatch to the spardeck.

The sailor shook his head. "You shouldn't have sent him topside. He'll be gone. The sea always gets the green hands." The sailor clambered up the ladder. "I'll try to catch him. Maybe he can't get the hatch open."

Miles slumped down. He had sent the boy to his death. "I'm a soldier, not a sailor. I didn't know . . ."

William put his hand on Miles' shoulder. "Our faith is strong. John is a strong boy. The sea won't get him. But, either way, he's in God's hands."

\* \* \*

Two days later, in calmer seas, the *Mayflower* came onto land.

Bleary-eyed, the passengers were on deck and looked in wonder at the new world. With tears of joy and relief, they hugged each other and chattered that the terrible voyage was ending.

Elder William Brewster suggested a song of gratitude. From the old freighter soared the words of Psalm 100. "Make a joyful noise unto the Lord, all ye lands. Serve the Lord with gladness: come before his presence with singing. Know ye that the Lord he is God."

John Howland had a group around him as he showed where he had been carried overboard by a huge wave. Grabbing a line hanging over the side of the ship, he had held on until he was fished out with a boathook.

As the excitement died down, Christopher Jones, the captain, broke the bad news. Landfall was on the strange, curving hook of Cape Cod. It was 19 November 1620 and they were a long, long way north of Virginia. Winter was almost here and they could not go down the coast to Virginia.

*The New World*

Captain Jones would proceed no further and he made it very clear: the Pilgrims were going to disembark somewhere near Cape Cod. They had better send men ashore to search for a safe haven, was the advice the Captain gave his passengers.[3]

In other circumstances, William Brewster would have acted promptly to comply with the captain's suggestions, but first he had to defuse an insurrection that threatened to destroy all he had worked for, because not everyone in the expedition was in quest of religious freedom. Some of the younger men—like the carpenter who saved the ship from sinking—had joined the expedition in search of economic opportunity, while others were hired servants. Since they were landing at the wrong place, a number of them planned to go off on their own. They claimed that they were no longer bound by the Virginia land patent and would accept no further orders from anyone. Burly and aggressive men, they did not hesitate to suggest that if anyone tried to stop them, blood might spill.

William realized that it would take almost a day for the *Mayflower* to reach the harbour on the tip of Cape Cod so, during that time, the leaders debated how to deal with the crisis. They were aware that a split in the group would be disastrous; every able-bodied man was needed to get shelter up before the winter snows.

The ex-soldier, Miles Standish, growled that he was ready to use force to quell the rebellion, but William Brewster would have nothing to do with violence. Instead, he would use the authority of his position, his personality and, above all, his experience in political situations, acquired while he worked at the Secretary of State, to bring the wayward sheep back into the fold. He called a meeting and the rebels were surprised when the Senior Elder quickly agreed that the land patent for Virginia was not valid. Once William was sure he had them off balance, he presented them with a Compact: an agreement on how their community would be governed. It called for spiritual support in the name of God. It stated that they would combine themselves together into a "civil Body Politick" that would enact, by majority vote, just and equal laws to which everyone pledged "due submission and obedience."

It took precious time for William to get it all down on paper and, by the time William had written the Compact, the *Mayflower* was entering the harbour. If he were to be successful, he must act quickly. William assembled the members of the group below decks and read the provisions of the Compact. He wanted every man to be signed up before the ship anchored. He invited the men he could rely on the most to sign first.

Twelve older men, well off enough to have servants and entitled to be called 'Master,' affixed their signatures, one after the other; Master Stephen Hopkins, a ringleader of the insurrection, lined up with his peers, signing without comment.

Next came the 'Goodmen,' the social rank below Master. All twenty-seven signed.

Finally, four servants, including the most unruly, signed on stern orders from their masters. William omitted nine other servants and workers from the ceremony because they were ill.

After carefully gathering the pages of the Compact and placing them in a strong box, William led the group in prayer, asking God to bless the rededication to their enterprise. The "Amen" was overtaken by the rattle, clatter, booming, and bumping of the anchor being dropped in the harbour. Everyone hustled topside to see the sights.

The *Mayflower* was anchored about a mile offshore. The passengers roamed from larboard to starboard, stem to stern, studying the land before them. On the one side, they gazed out on sand hills that reminded them of Holland. On the other side of the harbour, bristling forests ran right down to the water's edge. The longer they looked, the less enthusiastic they became.

Sensing the disappointment and rising fears of his flock as they studied the wild and savage seacoast, William suggested to John Carver, the newly elected Governor of the Colony, that he order the Pilgrims to get to work. Since Captain Jones had suggested that the Pilgrims put men ashore to search for the site of their new home, Governor Carver decided they should get on with it.

A small boat, a shallop, was taken out of the hold of the *Mayflower* and re-assembled on the aft deck. It was launched without fanfare. Sixteen well-armed men boarded her and sailed away to find a convenient, safe harbour.

William watched them leave. He was fretting. As far as he was concerned, Cape Cod was a good place to seek shelter. He liked what he could see. The waters at Cape Cod lived up to the name; there were plenty of fish, and they had sighted great whales of the right kind for oil. He accepted that an exploring party had to be sent out; perhaps the soil, while rich, might be too heavy for the Pilgrims to work; they had neither ploughs nor beasts to plough. Perhaps the natives were hostile. Given all that, he was still impatient to get his congregation ashore

"Sixteen, well-armed men boarded her and sailed away..."

because much had to be done before the onset of winter and, in his heart of hearts, he knew that God had brought them to this place. Somehow, everything would be all right. Cape Cod was going to be their home, not Virginia.

When the shallop returned, the news was not good. The exploration party had not found a suitable site but they had found many signs of native settlement. Several well-trodden paths led from one cleared field to another and, finally, to a storage cellar filled with corn. The Pilgrim party had brought baskets of corn back with them to supplement the ship's scanty stores. The elders, particularly William, were not pleased with this action, which they felt could be regarded as stealing. William permitted the use of the corn; the rightful owners of the corn would be compensated as soon as they could be found.

Foul weather delayed the departure of the shallop on another voyage of discovery. It wasn't until the 6th of December that a landing party sailed along the shores of the deep bay of Cape Cod. This late in the season, the salt ocean spray froze on the Pilgrims' coats. Watching them, William was dazzled by the sunlight reflecting from the backs of the party; it was if they were sugar glazed.

Notwithstanding the cold, the party reached the far end of the bay. When they drew near to the shore, they sighted some ten or twelve Indians. Miles Standish ordered the shallop's crew to put directly in to shore so that the party might accost the Indians, but there were shoals between the boat and the beach. It took over an hour, because of the shoals, before the party could come ashore. By that time, the Indians were gone. There were signs that the Indians had been cutting up some fish but, otherwise, they left no sign or trail.

Miles was not concerned by the size of the Indian party but, just in case they were in contact with a larger group, he had his men build a barricado of driftwood and logs. He posted a guard of three men on two-hour shifts while the other sixteen men slept.

\* \* \*

At five o'clock the next morning, following prayers to seek the guidance and protection of God, the men were enjoying some food by the fire. Several had carried their muskets, wrapped in their coats to keep out the dampness, to the beach, where they loaded them into the boat. It was a quiet time before the hard work of the day.

Richard Warren, walking back from the shore, thought he saw some movement in the trees. He asked Edward Tilly to look toward the trees.

"I don't see anything," Edward said.

"Maybe I was wrong, but we should tell Miles." Richard ran over to where Miles was seated by the fire. Miles took a good look, but nothing could be seen in the darkness and all was quiet along the shore.

Men were in the boat and scattered on the shore. Most of them were unarmed since their weapons were on the boat or in the barricado. The dawn of the day was just starting when a great, strange cry jerked the Pilgrims alert.

The man nearest the trees, John Tilly, cried, "Indians! Indians!" at the moment arrows came flying among them. John, his pants not quite pulled up, ran tripping and falling to the barricado, where he threw himself, head-first, over the logs into the comparative safety of the little fort.

Stephen Hopkins discharged his musket at the racing Indians but missed. Another musket discharged by his ear. His head ringing and with tears in his eyes, Stephen tried to charge his musket for a second shot.

Edward Tilly, all the while laughing at the other Tilly's efforts to cover himself, aimed at the nearest attacker but his weapon was damp and misfired. The Indian, having seen Edward raise his weapon, hid behind a log.

"Don't shoot unless you have a clear target," Miles ordered. They now had two muskets loaded and waited for the enemy to present themselves. Arrows continued to fall amongst them but, so far, no one had been hurt; John Tilly's face was bleeding but that was from his jump into the barricado.

The men, without their weapons, made a run for the shallop. Indians wheeled around the fort to cut them off and there was hand-to-hand fighting; all the while, the Indians were making that dreadful cry. Unable to shoot for fear of hitting their own men, most of the Pilgrims in the barricado could only watch the combat from the shelter of the logs. Two of the men from the fort wore coats of mail and they went out to fight the Indians in close combat. They were armed with cuttle-axes and were able to drive the Indians back from the shallop.

The men at the shallop had regained their muskets. They fired at the retreating Indians but none of them faltered so the shots were more noise and smoke than anything else. It seemed to be over.

An arrow embedded itself into the log by John Tilly's arm.

"Stay under cover," Miles commanded. "One Indian is still shooting at us from behind that grey tree." He raised his musket. Another arrow hit the log near John's head. Miles fired but to no effect.

"Can't we stop him, Captain Standish? I'm as close to this beach as I can get," complained John.

Edward Winslow carefully aimed at the Indian, who was about half a musket shot away. He missed, too. The Indian shot another arrow but it went over the fort and didn't hit anything.

Miles had charged his musket. He quickly sighted and fired as the Indian stepped from behind the tree to release another arrow. The bark and splinters from the old tree exploded around the Indian, who then took off into the woods.

The landing party charged out of the fort and chased the Indians for about a quarter of a mile, but there was no catching them.

The men from the landing party returned to the barricado by ones and twos. There was relief that they had survived the attack without serious harm. Nervously they joked about fighting the Indians on the beach while John Tilly had been fighting the beach and, by the looks of John's nose, the beach had won. John was good-natured about the teasing.[4]

After the exertion of the early morning, the day seemed even colder than it was. For the first time they realized how bitter the winter might be, and that was a sobering thought. What would they do if all of the Indians were as hostile as the group they had just met? There was little choice since it was far too late to sail to Virginia even if the *Mayflower*'s captain would agree to do it. Cape Cod would have to do. They reboarded the shallop and sailed on. They found nothing suitable that day or the next day.

\* \* \*

Suddenly, it was there! The site for New Plymouth! Upon their return to the *Mayflower*, John Carver and Captain Standish described what they had found.

"We found a nice little harbour. We sounded her and she'll take boats of any size that we'll be using," said John Carver. John, as Governor of the Colony, felt that he should have the first say as they told the elders about their new home. "There are running brooks . . ."

"If the Indians give us trouble," interrupted Miles, "we will have a good water supply that is easily defended. We marched into the land for several miles, where we found many cornfields. Natives lived here, not too long ago, but they are gone. Fresh graves in a sort of hollow and more storage cellars make it seem fairly certain that there had been a large Indian population. There's plenty of tall trees so we can build our defences . . ."

John Carver stepped forward, saying, " . . . and build our homes. As Governor of New Plymouth, I say that we move along the coast, tomorrow, to our new home."

William Brewster pursed his lips, as he was wont to do when he was in favour of something but at odds with the person or the person's manner. He was finding this new governor to be aggressive in decision-making, while the elders were more used to discussion and compromise. Glancing at the others, he said, "The elders will support your decision, John."

John knew that William had been the first person suggested for governor but William had declined, saying that the spiritual needs of the congregation were far more important than putting order and discipline into the Pilgrims' everyday lives. Subsequently, when John was elected governor, he remembered the remark and felt that he, as governor, was a poor second best to the Senior Elder. John had admitted to the elders that he was guilty of a sense of pride; he begged them to help him develop a better sense of humility. William liked the man and was careful to show support for John every way he could.

"Yes, John, the sooner the better," William said with a smile. "We agree with you that we should build shelters before forts, since we don't have time for both before the winter really comes. It won't be long coming, now. There's little warmth left to the sun, even at midday."

*　*　*

The next morning the shallop and the *Mayflower* moved down the coast to what was to become Plymouth Harbour. After anchoring, the Pilgrims began hauling their furniture, tools, and other belongings by boat to the shore, a mile and a half away, and constructing a makeshift shelter for storage. Since the following day was the Sabbath, which would be observed by prayer and Bible discussions, they moved quickly throughout the long day and into the darkness to get as much work done as possible before the Sabbath commenced.

Miles Standish still argued that a defensive system should be constructed, first thing, at the top of the hill overlooking the harbour. "We must fell trees and square the timber. We will need to use a block and tackle to get the timber up there. The gun ports should be shoulder high and we will have to arrange for storage of water. The fort should be imposing so that the Indians will not think of attacking us." Miles could see that the Governor could hardly wait to speak so he added, "We need protection if the Indians should come."

"Every bit of timber will be used for the cottages that must be built before winter comes," Governor Carver argued, his face slightly red. "Gun ports can be built into the walls of the cottages and stout doors should keep the Indians out."

John Tilly thought that winter was almost here. Maybe they would all have to live on the *Mayflower* if it kept getting colder and colder. Everyone shuddered at the thought.

The carpenter said he had looked at the winter shelters that the Indians left behind. "They are made with saplings tied together to form a frame that is rounded at the top. There is a door at one end and a place for a fire at the other. The frame can be covered with bark, thatch and wattles daubed with beach mud. I don't think we have the time to build cabins with horizontal logs before the ground is frozen and, once the ground freezes, it will be hard to build anything. If we build a proper hearth and chimney with clay, beach stones, and logs in each shelter, we could be quite comfortable no matter what the weather."

Standish suggested that the wigwams be built close together so that the men could come to each other's aid if the Indians should appear.

And so it was agreed. The men quickly mapped out building lots, measuring 8 feet by 49 feet. On the 25th of December 1620, the Pilgrims of New Plymouth began the construction of their first house.

## Endnotes

[1] Not to mislead the reader, Robert Cushman finally did come to the New World. According to the *Chronicles of 1620*, "About the ninth of November came in a small ship to them unexpected, in which came Mr. Robert Cushman . . . and there came with him in that ship thirty-five persons, to remain, and live in the plantation, which did not a little rejoice the first planters." The ship, bringing the extra souls, brought no extra supplies – probably a contributing cause to the famine that occurred shortly after.

[2] In one of the storms during the passage, the Mayflower broke her mainbeam. ". . . by a screw said beam was brought into his place again; which being done, and well secured by the carpenter . . ." *Chronicles* of 1620.

[3] The Pilgrims were supposed to settle in Virginia but Virginia was far to the south, too far and too late in the season for the journey to be attempted. They did not consider Cape Cod a suitable place to winter; there were no European settlements and the coastline being so bleak and barren. Instead,

they wanted to sail down the coast to the Hudson River near the Dutch settlement where they might expect some support. The ship's captain refused to sail any further in the treacherous November seas, down a dangerous coast to an uncertain welcome. He was blunt in his advice. Send men ashore to find a haven before winter sets in.

[4] Both John and Edward Tilly died during that first winter. *Chronicles* of 1621.

*Prologue*

*1621*
*New Plymouth*

It was a hard, hard winter for the Pilgrims. The Atlantic crossing had weakened them and the hardship of building an entire village in strenuous circumstances took its toll. Everyone looked forward to spring.

Spring did come and so did the Indians. At least there was one Indian who walked up the front street of New Plymouth. He was in among the Pilgrims saying, "Welcome, Englishmen," before they could think to get their muskets. He stood there, smiling and waving his arms, speaking broken English he said he had learned from coastal traders. The Pilgrims stood around him, not knowing quite what to do. Governor Carver sent for William Brewster, who came down the street and invited the Indian to spend the night. During the evening, they learned much.

His name was Samoset of the Wampanoag Indian Nation. He was native to Patuxet, which was where the Pilgrims had built Plymouth. Samoset was the sole survivor of the plague that had killed all of the people living near Cape Cod.

William said, "Thanks be to God that we found the caches of corn and beans. Our ship's supplies would not have been enough to get through the winter. The winter was so terribly cold and long."

Samoset thought it very odd that the Englishmen found the winter so severe. "Warm winter . . . cold spring, yes, but warm winter."

"Then we would not have survived, any of us, if it had been a normal season. As it is, we lost half of our congregation. There are only four of our wives left. Half of the seamen died as well. It was a hard, hard winter for us." William then led the group in a short prayer of thanksgiving for their survival and for the gift of the Indian food.

Samoset watched with great interest as the Pilgrims spoke, in everyday words, to their God. After prayers, Samoset told stories about his people and assured the Pilgrims that there were no Indians who would want to claim the lands they were on since the Indians were all dead. He, Samoset, would bring his great chief, Massasoit, to them and they could sign the big paper, in the white man's way. Then the Pilgrims could pay the chief for use of the land.

"What about the Indians who attacked us at the beach?" Miles Standish was sitting there casually cradling a musket and he leaned forward with a second question, "Why did they try to kill my men?"

"Narragansett tribe . . . more warlike than Wampanoag . . . but . . . they obey Massasoit. When paper signed . . . give no more fighting." Samoset looked at William and asked, "Is time . . . speak again to God?"

William led the group in prayer. They sat about the fire until it was time to sleep. Samoset was almost childlike in his pleasure when he was given a white man's pallet to sleep on.

In the morning, Samoset declined a meal and left, saying that he would return with his chief.

That day, Governor John Carver went to bed with the fever. He was the last of the Pilgrims to have the winter sickness. In his little home that overlooked Plymouth Harbour, John drifted in and out of sleep on his rope bed. The elders had voted to give him the best location in the village and he had been very, very pleased to get the special treatment. He was thinking about that as he lay there, barely a part of this world.

*Governor John Carver. I liked the sound of that. My wife had been so proud. Poor soul, she's waiting in one of the empty houses for the spring thaw. Perhaps I will still be alive when it's time to bury her. If it is the will of God that I be taken, we can be buried together.*

*It seemed no colder here than England, but I am so-o-o cold. When someone comes again, I will ask for another blanket. There are lots of blankets, now. So many have died. More than one third of the colony. What a shock when William Mullins died. That man had been my main supporter for governor. I had thought Mullins was indestructible and he had considerable outward estate. If it had been the will of God that he survived, he might have proved a useful instrument in this place.*

*This place. Should we have stayed in England? No! Holland was no better. King James could still reach us there. The Bishops with their prattle and posturing and their power.*

I am Governor . . .

"John. John, it's William." Brewster looked closely into the sick man's face but there was no response.

*William? I thought you were dead. They had told me you were dead. I'm sure you died. Am I dead, William?*

"I'm sorry that I was gone so long. There are only six or seven of us left who are sound enough to help the sick." William Brewster touched John's head. "You seem to have less fever. I'll get you something to drink." He turned to get a cup. "My dear Mary continues well, thank God. She is tending the women. Two more died this morning. The long journey and the scurvy were hard on our women."

He reached into the bucket and broke the skim of ice with the cup. He held the cup in his hands to try to take some of the chill off the water. "The sun is much warmer now." William returned to the bedside. He lifted John to give him the water. John didn't respond when he pressed the cup to his lips. William poured some water into the slack mouth. John swallowed, once or twice. The rest of the water spilled down the front of his shirt onto the bed.

"Soon the sun will shine and the waters will glisten with fish. We'll be warm again, John." William spoke with soft measured tones.

> *Soon be warm? I must explain to him how much I need his help to be governor again next term. Bradford wants to be governor. He hasn't said anything, but I know he wants to be governor. With Mullins' help, I will win again . . .*

> *Oh, my God! My . . . God.*

"It will be like England. You will have a lovely garden and all of our friends will come to admire it." William stopped talking and listened carefully for some sound of breathing. "John?"

But Governor John Carver was dead.

* * *

True to his word, Samoset reappeared with Massasoit, Sachem of the Wampanoag and all of the lesser tribes such as the Narragansett. He was met by the new governor, William Bradford.

With as much pomp and ceremony as they could muster, the Pilgrims led Massasoit to a green carpet that had been spread on the ground. When all participants were nicely seated on the carpet, Massasoit made it very clear that he wanted to sign the white man's paper.

Hastily, the Pilgrims put quill to paper and drew up a list of points that, hopefully, would serve as the basis of peaceful relations between the Indian tribes and Plymouth. William Brewster read them aloud. Samoset turned the English phrases into the flowing Indian language.[1]

"That neither he [Massasoit] nor any of his, should injure or do hurt to any of their people.
That if any of his did do hurt to any of theirs, then he should send the offender that they might punish him.
That if any thing were taken away from any of theirs, he

should cause it to be restored, and they should do the like
to his.
That if any did unjustly war against him, they would aid
him; and if any did war against them, he should aid us.
That he should send to his neighbour confederates to
inform them of this, that they might not wrong them, but
be likewise comprised in these conditions of peace.
That when his men came to them upon any occasion, they
should leave their arms behind them.
Lastly. That so doing, their sovereign Lord, King James,
would esteem him as his friend and ally." [2]

William, looking right into Massasoit's eyes, asked,
"Samsoset, does he understand what is on this paper?"

Samoset spoke to his chief. The Sachem of Pawcawnawkit,
chief of all of the tribes, even of many lands extending to the
west, spoke slowly and deliberately. Samsoset, sounding very
much like the chief, and using the same gestures, translated for
the Pilgrims.

"I am Massasoit, chief of many tribes. All you have read I
like well. I am content to be a friend and ally of your Sachem."
Massasoit stood and opened his arms as he spoke. "I will sign
the white man's paper."

Bradford placed the scroll of paper on the top of a barrel.
He handed the quill to Massasoit.

Massasoit signed the declaration. The governor signed
and so did Brewster.

Samoset asked if it was time for Brewster to speak to God.

The Pilgrims bowed their heads and William Brewster,
Senior Elder of the Plymouth Colony, led the group in prayer.
The two Indians bowed their heads, too.

Later, other Pilgrims, and nine of the lesser chiefs selected
by Massasoit, put their marks or signatures on the historic
document.

* * *

Captain Jones had been forced to winter at Cape Cod because
over half of the *Mayflower* crew was sick and he dared not put
to sea until they were better. As soon as the weather moder-

ated, he made plans for his ship's departure. Of course, he would take with him news of the colony for those Separatists still in Holland; it would not be a happy report. Not only did the Pilgrims lose about half of the colony to the rigours of the Atlantic crossing and the terrible winter, but also the colony expected a return of the pestilence that killed the Indians when the summer heat came upon them. Jones departed with great haste as soon as the weather improved.

It was a good summer; there was no sickness.

The Pilgrims had the benefit of the fields that had already been cleared by the Indians so they had been able to plant crops early. The English peas and wheat seeds that they had brought with them did not grow well. Mistress Mary Brewster thought it was because of the effects of the new world's hot sunshine.

Not meaning to disagree with Elder Brewster's wife, Goodwife Eleanor Billington suggested that perhaps, during the voyage, salt water had spoiled the seed.[3]

Miles Standish, when he overheard the women discussing the matter, bluntly informed them, "They sold us bad seed in England. It wouldn't grow properly no matter what we did with it."

However, everyone agreed that Squanto, the Indian brave that Massasoit had loaned the colony, was a special instrument sent of God for their good, and beyond expectation.

Governor Bradford, speaking more softly than usual, added his thoughts. "Praise be to God that we made peace with the great chief Massasoit. Massasoit's nation controls many tribes and, with his pledge of peace, Plymouth can feel safe. Praise be to God."

The Pilgrims replied, in unison, "Praise be to God."

"It has been a time of plenty." William Brewster stroked his belly, contentedly. "We should have a day of thanksgiving," he said.

Governor Bradford stood up. "What we deserve is a good old English-style Harvest Home Celebration!" Speaking to Samuel Fuller, he said, "Go out and tell everyone that we must prepare for a feast."

The men stood up to leave. Samuel said, with enthusiasm, "We can hunt some wild fowl! Invite our Indian friends to join us!"

Miles Standish said he would take the remaining men to launch the shallop. "We shall catch some fish and perhaps an eel or two."

Nearly everyone was gone on some errand or other. That left Governor Bradford with the four married women of the Colony: Good Wife Billington, Mistress Brewster, Mistress Hopkins and Mistress Winslow. "I will rely upon you to use your cooking skills to make this Harvest Home Feast one that will be remembered for years to come."

With all of the decisions made, the Governor stepped out of the cottage into the sunlight and watched the activity.

\* \* \*

Soon there was indeed much activity. The clay oven was being prepared for baking. Dough was being kneaded for the bread. Someone had to bring buckets of water from the brook. Baskets of herbs and vegetables were delivered to the women's household, where most of the cooking would be done. Wrasling Brewster carried more wood for the fires than he thought had ever grown in all of the forests of the new world. At the Brewster house there was a huge kettle of tasty soup, enough to feed fifty. Mary added the final ingredients and put the lid on for the soup to simmer. It would be ready soon.

The men, back from hunting and fishing, rolled out barrels to hold wide plank boards so there would be plenty of table space. These were covered with fine English linen cloths the Pilgrims had brought from England.

Everyone stopped their work and looked up when the children ran down the street shouting, "The Indians are coming!"

The Indians strolled down the street, Massasoit smiling broadly as he led four score Indians to the front of the Brewster cottage.

"We shall have to add more vegetables to the pots," Mary whispered to her ladies, "and bake more bread."

The Indians hunkered down at the side of the street and smoked their pipes as the Pilgrims continued the preparations for the feast. Cooking and baking smells filled the crisp autumn air. Pilgrims and Indians alike gathered near the tables.

Vessels of ale were already on the tables. Now bowls and trenchers filled with turkey, puddings in the belly, venison, stuffed cod, goose pudding, fruit tarts, corn pasties, soup trifle, boiled pumpkin and greens were placed beside them.[4]

The Governor raised his hands in prayer. "Lord God Jehovah, we ask Thy blessings on this day of peace and plenty. We have welcomed our friends to share the bounty that you have provided. We give thanks for their presence and ask that You continue to watch over us and give us guidance. Amen."

There was a moment of silence and then the eating began. At first some of the Indians were hesitant to try the strange dishes, but soon broad smiles followed each bite. The food began to disappear. Servants and Pilgrim children reloaded the tables from the pots they carried brimful from the busy kitchens. There was a time for singing and games, competitions and displays, but the eating went for three full days.

The people of Plymouth danced, frolicked, and ate until they could celebrate no more.

\* \* \*

In the quiet before the end of the feast, William Brewster, with his arm about his wife Mary, called to his children to gather 'round. When they had, they made a handsome group: the father and mother with grey hair but standing erect and strong; the children blue-eyed, with hair so blond that it was almost white. Obviously each cared for the others as they stood close to their father and looked to him for what he had to say.

William began by speaking about his love for them and he thanked God for their every moment of family life. He spoke of the hazards they had faced, the hard work that they had been called upon to do in Plymouth. "This world, and everything in it, is good and was made of God, for the benefit of all creatures."

There was quiet, now, and all were listening to this man who had led them from persecution, through hardship and the real threat of torture and death, to this wonderful day of feasting and fellowship.

Squanto began translating for his Chief and all of the Indians were listening, as well.

"In our new homeland we have found friends who have been faithful and true. We embrace them. Our new homeland seemed cruel and demanding. Our friends helped us and now, today, we all share in the bounty."

William took a few steps forward so that he could see everyone. He had a clear view of the harbour and out to the sea. "This feeling of family and fellowship that we share today will be remembered, perhaps long after we are gone, as a day of thanksgiving. All we see, all we have, all we enjoy from God's grace, will be savoured year after year as we gather our friends and family about us on Thanksgiving Day."

## *Endnotes*

[1] There was another Indian with better English than Samoset, named Squanto, who was loaned to the plantation sometime after this meeting.

[2] Taken word for word from the *Chronicles.*

[3] Mistress Billington's husband, John, was the first planter to be executed. "Oct. 1630. The first execution in Plymouth colony; which is a matter of great sadness to us, is of one John Billington, for waylaying and shooting John Newcomen, a young man, in the shoulder, whereof he died." *Chronicles.*

[4] The menu of the meal was taken from a newspaper article about The First Thanksgiving Meal.

*Addendum*

**Elder William Brewster and Mistress Mary Brewster** lived at Plymouth many more years before finding their final resting place on Plymouth's Burial Hill.

That should have been the end of the story: the Pilgrims founded their New City of God in the Wilderness and lived happily, ever after. It was not to be.

Later arrivals of Puritans brought with them a rigidity and intolerance to any ideas other than their own and harshly imposed a type of religious uniformity that surpassed anything the Pilgrims might have suffered under King James in Merrie Olde England. Recalling Elder William's reaction in the seventeenth century, "Religious persecution that endeavours to drive a flock along a path is successful, as a rule, only with the sheep. It makes the goats unruly," it is not surprising that his descendants became unruly in the eighteenth century.

The second William of the Brewster line, son of Samuel, refusing to accept the Puritan imposition of religious uniformity upon his family, left Plymouth and took up land further west. With hard work and God's grace, they prospered.

By the days of the third William, son of Jonathan, grandson of Benjamin, the Brewster family was well established in Lebanon, Connecticut. They were wealthy and should have been the picture of contentment. Perhaps, finally, they might have been at ease, but the Church of England was becoming more of a force in the daily lives of the colonists, always seeking ways to bring "the word" to the unenlightened. The religious community had a name for the people like the Brewsters who refused to conform, refused to accept the dogma set down by the established churches; they were disdainfully called Dissenters.

The third William Brewster's eldest son, Samuel, struggled against the power of the established churches by seeking to set up his own Dissenter congregation. He met with mixed success since the Church of England ran the schools and built imposing church buildings, which gave them an overwhelming presence in the community.

Samuel became aware that the Colonial Government of Nova Scotia had deprived the Acadians of their lands and was planning to resettle politically more dependable New Englanders in their place. Governor Lawrence's Proclamation dated 12 October 1758 offered many inducements for New Englanders to settle on these vacated lands. The one condition that caught Samuel Brewster's eye was: "Full liberty of conscience is guaranteed, Papists excepted."

Just like Elder William Brewster, Preacher Samuel Brewster uprooted his small family and set sail for an unknown shore where he hoped to found a New City of God in the Wilderness.

*Chapter One*


*May 1761*
*Minas*
*Nova Scotia*


Agnes Brewster stepped over the muddy ruts that served as the trail from Boudreau's Bank to Cornwallis Township, choosing to walk on the wet grass. Her husband, Samuel Brewster, perhaps not as nimble, stumbled into one of the ruts and took on a load of soupy clay in his fine leather shoes while splattering his hose as far up as the gold buttons on the knees of his breeches. Agnes extended her arm to steady her man but he refused the assistance. She stood on the grass, waiting for his anger to subside, knowing that he was struggling to control his temper.

A portly man, wearing a checked shirt, barefoot with trousers rolled to the knees, ran to give aid to the newly arrived Planter from New England, but Brewster waved him off as well. The man in the checked shirt introduced himself.

"Silas Woodworth, at your service, and I know you to be Preacher Brewster from Lebanon, Connecticut."[1]

Samuel Brewster, mired as he was in the mud, was still tall enough to meet the other man's gaze, eye to eye. "The Woodworths of Lebanon are Church of England."

Woodworth stepped down into the mud. "Lift your left foot, slowly, and I will rescue your shoe. You don't want to get more dirt on your fine clothes." He placed one hand on Samuel's calf, sliding it down as though he were raising a horse's hoof while reaching into the mud with his free hand.

"You were a Congregationalist preacher in Lebanon."

Silas looked up, "Please lift your foot, Preacher." While he waited for Brewster to comply, the crouching man added, "You have the home site across the road from mine; we will be neighbours."

Samuel lifted his foot. "We are Dissidents and not formally affiliated with the established churches." He looked down; he had lost his second shoe in the mud.

"Aha! I have it!" Woodworth handed the muddy object to the preacher. "Step out onto the grass and I will get the other one."

"I appreciate your help, Mister Woodworth."

Silas retrieved the second shoe. "Since we are neighbours, I hope you will call me Silas . . . despite our differences."

Now standing on the grass in his filthy, stocking feet, Samuel accepted the second shoe. He gave the other man a small nod. Indicating his wife he made the introductions; "My wife, Agnes Brewster, Mister Silas Woodworth."

"It is a pleasure to meet you, Missus Brewster."

Agnes gave him a curtsy but, bearing in mind that the man's hands were dripping mud, did not extend her gloved hand. "You arrived last year?" she asked with a smile.

"Yes, on *HMS Wolfe*." He bent down and wiped his hands in the grass, finishing the job on the front of his shirt. "When we arrived, we were faced with broken dykes, heavy rains, marauding Indians, and Acadians, but we persevered and . . ."[2]

"Oh dear!" Agnes put her hand to her mouth. "I thought they were all gone!"

"Didn't actually see Indians, probably because we had a detachment of redcoats stay with us most of the season." Silas pointed at the muddy shoes. "There's a brook on your property where we can wash those down some. I'll show you where it is."

Samuel noticed the omission. "But there are Acadians lurking about?"

Silas led the way up the hill. "Just ahead is the Parade. On the other side, where you see those little markers, that's where the school and church will be." They walked along in silence after Silas added, "Church of England church and Church of England school."

Samuel Brewster seemed to take a while to digest the new information. Finally, with a note of suspicion in his voice, Samuel asked, "I suppose Dissidents were pushed off to one side? Far from the Parade?"

"That copse of fruit trees by the brook, that's where your townlot is. You can see it's not far from the centre of things. When the first Planters landed at Boudreau's Bank back in '60, they elected lot-layers who divided up the forestland, farmland, dykeland, and townlots, and they were drawn for . . . all fair and square. Your dykeland happens to be with mine. I kept a careful eye on the Acadians and redcoats as they worked on our dyke last fall. Our dykeland is dry, now."

"Then we have the Acadians in custody?"

Silas shook his head, negatively. "Not in custody."

"Why not? They're dangerous, aren't they?" Samuel stopped fussing with his shoes, alert to whatever Silas might have to say about the dreaded Acadians. "I heard they were making raids, murdering Colonists in their beds."[3]

"No. A few were left behind . . ."

Agnes Brewster stamped her foot. "It's not fair!" Tears filled her eyes. "They were supposed to be gone!" She turned around and it was apparent to the men that she was going to walk down the hill to Boudreau's Bank, get back on the ship, and probably head right back to Lebanon.

Samuel hastened to his wife's side and took her arm, turning her around. "The Acadians are not a threat!" Over his wife's shoulder he cast an appealing glance at Silas, seeking reassurance. "Isn't that right, Silas?"

"That's right, Missus Brewster."

Agnes allowed the two men to reassure her.

"I know the story of one of the Acadians, a fellow named Richard Bourgeois." Silas paused to see if the woman would listen, then he hurried on. "At the time of the Acadian deportations, Bourgeois escaped from an English transport ship anchored in Minas Basin. Using a chisel he had hidden on his body, he broke loose, leading a dozen men over the side of the ship. They swam to shore and spent the next five years hiding out in the woods."

"A likely story," Agnes said with a tremor in her voice. "He probably spent the time murdering and . . ."

Silas shook his head, holding up his hand to slow the woman down. "There were no colonists here; just redcoats on the lookout for any Acadians who were missed or who might have slunk back."

Samuel was not interested in the plight of the stranded Acadians but he noted that Agnes was distracted by the story, so he asked, "How did they survive without being caught?"[4]

"Not very well, because they weren't able to farm or keep animals for fear of being caught by the patrols."

Samuel, holding his wife's hand and stroking her arm, mused, "I was told the militia burned everything so there wouldn't be anything left for Acadian renegades to use."

"Not everything could be destroyed. Bourgeois and his men found caches of food and supplies, but the pickin's must have been mighty thin. By the time the first Planters arrived, there were only three of them left."

"The rest died?"

"They died."

Agnes freed her hand. She adjusted the angle of her little bonnet, neatly tucking the fancy ribbon off to one side. "When will they be . . . taken away?"

"Well, right now we need 'em because they're the only people who know how to repair the dykes. So we use 'em. When everything is fixed, the governor will probably have them gathered up and shipped out as before." Silas could see the anxiety rising in Agnes' eyes, so he pressed on: "Meanwhile, we built a stockade on the rise, just over there, for our protection." He nodded his head at the other man. "You and I can get our families there in jig time . . . if there's any trouble."

"And there won't be any trouble, will there, Silas?"

"Naw. The three of them do poorly. They are so weak from their years in the wilderness they couldn't harm a fly. Elizabeth—that's my wife—makes 'em a broth from time to time and they do chores in return."

Agnes shivered. "I don't want them around."

Silas allowed his voice to assume a reassuring tone. "They don't live down here, with us. They have a camp in the uplands, on the scrubland. You won't hardly see them, Missus Brewster."

Samuel bent down to clean up his shoes in the sparkling water. "Must be hard on them."

"The Acadians?"

"Yes. We confiscated their possessions . . ."

"Naw, we let 'em take their personal things when they were deported."

"What happened to their livestock and implements?"

"Destroyed. Just over by those trees we found piles of animal bones and ruined wagons and carts. They must have belonged to the Acadians."

Samuel paused a moment as he pictured the New England Militia herding the farm animals to slaughter. "And then the governor of Nova Scotia invites New Englanders to come take over their lands . . . giving the land away, free. Must be hard to live in the bush and see strangers take over your old farm."

"Maybe so, but the land is good, well drained. We would have had a fine yield last season but for the drought and the vermin . . . but all the Acadian trees bore fruit." Silas pulled at some vines that were creeping over what looked like a pear tree. "These are grape vines . . . pretty good, too. The Acadian must have planted them near his house. See! There's where he had his house."

"There's no cellar."

"The Acadians didn't make cellars." Silas Woodworth stopped talking and listened. "That's my wife ringing the bell; I'm wanted at the house." He turned to go. "You can stay with us until you get some shelter up."

"Thank you, Mister Woodworth. I have two strong boys and an indentured servant. We will manage. It was nice of you to offer. I thank you kindly."

\* \* \*

*Later that evening*

Judging by the noises coming from the tent, Agnes and Samuel knew that their boys were already asleep. Samuel picked up the lantern and pulled down the tent flap. Holding high the light, he guided Agnes to the front of their own tent.

Some movement beyond the light from the small fire gave Agnes a start. Samuel patted her arm. "It's all right, my dear," he reassured her, believing that it was their servant dropping another load of dry wood that he was collecting from the remnants of the Acadian farmhouse. Nevertheless, Samuel grasped the handle of an axe and shielded his eyes, staring into the darkness, waiting for the servant's approach.

"That's the last of it, sir." Tom Pinch stood just inside the circle of light, cap in hand, waiting for a word from his master.

"Fine, Tom. Good work. Let's go see to the animals."

"Beggin' your pardon, sir. I done that before it got dark. The cow is good but the horse is poorly."

"No improvement?"

"None I could see, sir."

"So be it." Samuel dismissed the man with a wave of his hand. "Have a fire going at first light. We will have much to do."

"Your pardon, sir . . ."

"What is it, Pinch?"

"I was wanting to clean up at the brook. Will you tell the missus that I will be over that way?"

"No. You won't. You will be further down the hill near the beach."

"Yessir. Good night, sir."

Agnes watched as the servant disappeared into the darkness. "I wouldn't have gone over that way tonight, Samuel."

"We start him off on the right foot, knowing his place."

"Where will he sleep?"

"With the animals." Samuel forestalled further discussion by adding; "He has some canvas and, being with the animals, he'll be warmer than we are. Now, we must review our day, my dear."

They both sat on a rock ledge which the Acadians had probably used as their front step. Samuel lifted the lantern shield and blew out the candle. He placed the lantern up against a metal rod that must have been used by the Acadians as a boot scraper. "There! We won't step on it in the dark." He took his wife's hand in his. They both bowed their heads. After a moment of silent prayer, Samuel said, "We dressed in our Sunday best for our first moments on this land. It would appear that He considered that a pretentious act and directed my steps into the mud."

"It would appear so," agreed the preacher's wife. She hesitated but when her husband didn't speak, she added, "You denied my help. Was that so a member of the official church could rescue you? And if that were the case, why would He put us in that position? Was it a sign that we are to associate with the Church of England priesthood?"

A pair of heads poked out of the other tent.

Samuel Brewster pointed at his two boys, his finger and thumb cocked like a gun. "Alexander! Junior! You should be asleep. It will be a long day tomorrow. There will be much to accomplish."

The older boy, Samuel Junior, did as he was told. The five-year-old crawled out a bit further into the firelight. He waited for his father to address him.

"Did you not hear me, Alexander?"

"Father. I heard you say they are here already. Will we have to move?"

*Ah, the dilemma*, Samuel thought. *Young minds are quick to take the family stories and fit them to what they perceive. How much should they be told and at what age?* Samuel beckoned to the boy. "Have Junior come out too."

When the boys reappeared, the flickering light from the small fire turned their blond hair almost white, accenting their ruddy complexion, and casting glints from the deep blue of their large eyes. Alexander crawled onto his father's lap while Junior snuggled into his mother's embrace.

Caressing Alexander's hair, Samuel cleared his throat, which was the usual signal to his flock that he was going to speak. His family fell silent, waiting for the word.

"In England, the Brewsters became Pilgrims when the king's churchmen began to persecute them for the way they lived by God's teachings."

Junior pulled his head far enough out of his mother's embrace to affirm, "William Brewster led his people to the New World . . ."

Not to be outdone, Alexander piped up, "Where he started a new church . . ."

Samuel hugged his little boy, squeezing him tightly, "No, no, Alexander! William did not found a church. He led his flock to Plymouth, where he hoped they would be free to live a godly life . . . a life of their own choosing."

"But the Puritans came!"

"Yes. The Puritans came bringing their ideas of what was a godly life and they punished those who didn't agree with them."

"And we moved!"

"Our family moved away, yes, that's right. We kept moving further away from the Puritans—and the king's men— with all their rules and their punishments."

Almost in unison the boys asked, "But the English church is already here! Why did we come here?"

"The king's man in Nova Scotia, Governor Lawrence, promised us freedom of religion if we came here. Even though the English Church is here, we have been promised that we do not have to follow the English Church tenets and we do not have to tithe."[5]

Alexander squirmed around so he could watch his father's reaction as he asked, "What's a Church Tent like, Father?"

*I never know whether this little fellow is being funny or serious.* Samuel looked down at his son. *Serious, I think.* "Not tent, Alexander. I meant that we would not be expected to follow the Church of England rules." He gave the boy a little squeeze, "Tenets are a little bit like rules." He kissed the top of the boy's head. "You understand what a tithe is?"[6]

"Yes, Father. It's what we give to the Church."

"That's right. The English Governor made these promises in writing. Nova Scotia will be a good place for us; it will be a better place."

"If it is going to be better here, why didn't Grandpa Brewster come with us?"

Samuel sighed. *So many questions.* "He was too old to move again. He said his heart would be with us always, even though his body is in Lebanon." Samuel hugged his little boy and reached over to pat Junior's head. "Don't worry about the English Church. This time they will leave us alone . . . and it's time you both went off to bed." He spanked their bums as they went by. "Say a prayer for your Grandpa who misses you so," he advised them.

"Will you lead us in prayer, Father?"

"No, Junior." The father fixed his boys with his deep blue eyes, first one boy and then the other. "Use the words that are in your hearts, boys."

\* \* \*

*Later in the month*

There were no chairs in the shell of a house being built by Samuel Starr, but Silas Woodworth had perched on a keg and Samuel Brewster sat on an upturned wooden box; they were sitting chatting, as they waited for the meeting to begin.

Silas had a straw sticking out of his mouth. He moved it off to one side as he said, "I told Bourgeois he could keep the meat as long as he skinned the horse and properly tanned the hide for you."

"Thank you, Silas." Samuel gazed out the window at the cold, drizzling rain. "My servant is so simple-minded. I would have had to pay strangers a pence or two . . ."

"Or three . . . the meat's no good and they would have to bury it."

"Maybe so. Did you tell Bourgeois that we don't know what the horse died of?"

"Naw. He'd use it all anyway. He needs everything he can get."

Letting his eyes wander about the big room, Samuel remarked casually, "I was surprised we could hold a meeting in here."

"Couldn't meet in the rain, now could we?"

"With nine rooms, it's probably the largest structure in Cornwallis."

"Lieutenant Starr was lucky! The Acadians left a pine grove here; Starr cut it down and used it to build his home."

"He's a lieutenant now?"

"Yes. He's now Lieutenant Samuel Starr of the Cornwallis Volunteers. Being a man with a strong military background, he's much in favour with the bigwigs at Halifax."

Samuel's mouth dropped open.

Silas grinned. "What's the matter, Samuel? Swallow a fly?"

Brewster closed his mouth. "Sam Starr is my cousin. I can assure you that he is not in the least militarily inclined."[7]

"Doesn't mean he can't be an officer." Silas leaned forward so that he might speak to his companion without being overheard. "It's said that Richard Bulkeley—you might not know, but Bulkeley's the Provincial First Secretary—well, Bulkeley told Morris—uh, Morris is the Chief Surveyor for the Province of Nova Scotia—well, Bulkeley told Morris to grant Lieutenant Starr a prominent property in the community."

"Here, near Boudreau's Bank?"

"It's not going to be called Boudreau's Bank any more. It's been renamed Starr's Point."

There was motion in the room. Someone pointed out one of the other windows. "Here he comes!"

Both men looked up. Through the window they could see a solitary figure marching through the rain, seemingly untouched by the weather.

"Starr has title to all this land?"

"No. He'll have a neighbour."

Another shout from the front of the room, "Here comes Mister Burbidge!"

"Who else gets land near the ferry?"

Samuel Starr opened the front door. Holding the door open, he gave instructions over his shoulder. "Boys! Stand up for John Burbidge, member of Nova Scotia's first House of Assembly, soon to be Major of Militia! Hurrah!"

Silas began clapping his hands as he said in Samuel's ear, "Him."[8]

An austere man with short, clipped hair, his broad smile displaying a row of nicotine-stained teeth under a black moustache, allowed himself to be ushered into the middle of the throng of men. "Tut, tut, Sam," he said as he preened his moustache and then stroked his beard. "Mustn't add to the rumours that are flying about . . . although I am glad that my Halifax friends finally got it right; I hear that your appointment as Lieutenant of Volunteers came through. Congratulations!" Not allowing the cheers to die, John Burbidge stepped over to the hearthstone and raised his arms. "We don't have time to waste, boys. We didn't gather here just to come in out of the rain, now did we?"

There was general agreement and some laughter. Burbidge waited until he had everyone's attention. Then he began the business of the meeting.

"I called you together because I have good news. Halifax informs me there will be fourteen additional Acadian prisoners available to Cornwallis Township this season."[9]

Some men clapped, others called out, "Hear, hear!"

Burbidge raised his hands to quell the noise. "I suggest we carefully assess the skills of these extra prisoners. While it is vital that we continue the restoration of the dykes, I am told that we had enough dyke workers last year and were able to spare a couple of the stronger Acadians to work on the roads." He looked into the faces of the men and, when he saw general agreement, he proceeded. "It is my intention to construct a modest cottage near the ferry wharf and I would ask you. . . ." He paused and then restarted. "Understand that I make no complaint about the rough and untidy nature of the ferry landing area . . ."

Sam Starr stepped closer to the hearth. "I think that I can speak for the boys . . ."

The men around Starr made positive sounds in the backs of their throats.

". . . we can assign two or three of these extra Acadians to clean up the ferry landing . . . that's if you can handle the supervision and security of the prisoners, Major."

There was an audible intake of breath as the men waited to see if Starr's sally at humour would be well taken. To everyone's relief, Burbidge smiled, nodding his head. "Much appreciated," he said. "Now, I understand that the next point we must discuss are dyke duties. I believe they have all been assigned except for . . ." Burbidge pulled a folded paper out of his vest pocket; he was fiddling with his glasses from another pocket when a tall, imposing man raised his hand. When the Major nodded his head, the man spoke.

"They've all been chose but for the Driver and Sizer on Union Dyke, yer honour."

"And you are . . .?"

"Deacon John Newcombe, yer honour. I mean to recommend my son, Eddy, just arrived this past week, as the Union Dyke Driver."

Spreading his hands, Mister Burbidge bowed his head in the deacon's direction. "You have me, sir. Being an untutored Assemblyman from Halifax, newly arrived myself, I hardly know what a Driver is."

The deacon smiled in return. "No harm admittin' what you don't know if'n it's not your place or duty to know it. A Driver, yer honour, a Driver takes care of the animals what are turned on the dyke to graze. My son, Eddy Newcombe, would be a good Driver."

With his eyes, Burbidge passed the problem to Sam Starr. "Are there any other recommendations?" Starr asked.

Deacon Newcombe raised his hand. "Yes. I would like to recommend my other son, Jonathon, as Sizer." The deacon smiled at Burbidge as he explained, "A Sizer, yer honour, walks the dyke before the animals is turned on and he figgers out the amount of feed out there tellin' each owner how many animals he can put on the dyke for his share. My Jonathon can tell a crop yield almost to the bushel."

Starr swept the room with his eyes. "I will take their names under consideration and let you know after Sunday meeting, Deacon." Sam Starr looked around at the circle of faces. "Any other business?" Not expecting a reply he went on, "I want our Major to know how much we appreciate his good news about the additional prisoners. We can make good use of . . ."

A voice from the rear called out, "What about the Acadian who's living up in the bush . . . that Bourgeois fellow?" When there was no immediate answer, the voice went on, "I saw him skinning a horse on the Dissenter's property . . . and there were two or three of them, not just the skinny one we've seen up to now."

The room was quiet. Someone cleared his throat, as if to speak, but changed his mind, and the silence continued.

Samuel Brewster held himself as erect as if he were speaking to a congregation in a large barn, trying to ensure that the furthest worshiper would have him in view. He raised his voice, speaking in a slow, measured manner. "The Dissenter's name is Samuel Brewster and, if you have anything to say about what happens on his property, he would appreciate you speaking to him about it and not make it a subject of a township meeting."

The same man stepped forward where he could be seen. "Well, my name is Benjamin Belcher and what Acadians do around here is everyone's business." Belcher turned away from Brewster as if dismissing him from the conversation. "Lieutenant Starr, sir, we could have a nest of Acadians sheltering right here in the Minas uplands. This Bourgeois fellow is the only one we have seen up to now but today there were three vipers—that I could see—when I came down the hill." Belcher stuck his thumbs in the armholes of his vest. "Mark my words! If we leave Acadian snakes free to come and go in Cornwallis, someone will get bit!"

Silas Woodworth raised his hand to speak but Belcher ignored him.

"Bourgeois must be caught and taken to Fort Edward and put in with the other prisoners." Belcher shook his finger at the assembled men. "While this Acadian's loose, he's a threat to our wives and our children."

Silas bristled, his face getting red, "When I came down the hill, I saw Bourgeois and two small boys . . . one of them belonging to Preacher Brewster."

Scorn dripping from his voice, Belcher stared down Silas, making the poor man step back. "We don't have a preacher. The nearest we have to a preacher is Deacon Newcombe." Hands on hips Belcher turned, "Deacon, have you been passing yourself off as a preacher?"

"You know better than that, Benjamin."

"Did his lordship from the Board of Trade and Plantations—or even the Society for the Propagation of the Gospel—drop a preacher in amongst us, unannounced?"

"No, sir."

Belcher turned back to Woodworth. "Then, Mister Woodworth, we don't have a preacher in Cornwallis."

The men in the room grew silent, waiting for whatever was going to happen next.

Burbidge signalled to Samuel Starr. Both men, putting their arms around the Planters nearest to them, began a move toward the door.

"I think we've covered everything we can, today."

"Time's a-wastin', as we used to say in Connecticut."

\* \* \*

Silas and Samuel didn't have much to say as they walked up the hill together. The drizzle had stopped, the sun was trying to come through the clouds, and the tidal bore had passed by so that the replenished waters of Minas Basin sparkled in the scattered shafts of sunlight. The men paused to watch the ferry leave Starr's Point for the far shore, the oars glistening and the squawk of the oarlocks carrying across the water. It was so beautiful that Samuel felt like doing something, so he waved at the ferry passengers. By chance, one of them waved back. Samuel grunted with satisfaction. They turned and continued up the hill.

When they were within sight of their townlots, Silas said, "Your house is coming along right some good, Samuel."

"My servant is skilled at woodworking and I transported enough materials from New England, even windows and sashes."

"Sam Starr has a mill going. If you run short . . ."

"I brought enough so I wouldn't have to deal with local gougers."

"You'll have to deal with Sam Starr for a horse."

"Oh?" Brewster turned in surprise to face his companion. "I was told there were plenty of Acadian horses available."

"Maybe so, but they're so small they're not much good for nothin'."[10]

In the distance, they could see Bourgeois on his hands and knees, working on the horsehide.

"Then I'll have to deal with Sam Starr."

"You'll find he's honest and fair . . ."

Samuel Brewster raised his hand. "Who is the other boy?" He quickened his step because he could see a dark-haired boy, larger than Alexander, raise his arm, getting set to throw something. "Stop!" He shouted again, "Stop, I say!" Samuel groaned with relief when the boy lowered his arm, turning to face the distraught man. "Drop it!" When the boy didn't move, Samuel Brewster held his hand out for the object.

"Looks like a ball," Silas said as he reached over and fingered the object now in Samuel's hands. "Bourgeois made them a soft ball out of horsehide."

Brewster smiled at the child, motioning that he would throw the ball to him. The boy cupped his hands. The preacher was careful to toss the ball into the waiting hands. "What is the boy's name, Alexander?"

"His name is Joseph, Father. He belongs to that man," said Alexander, pointing at the Acadian.

The Planters nodded to the Acadian. Silas, fingering the hides, said, "C'est bonne, m'sieu."

"Merci, m'sieu." Bourgeois bent to his task.

Silas tugged at Samuel's arm, drawing him away from the area. "Did you notice?"

"What, Silas?"

"Did you notice that the carcass is gone? All of it." He

kept tugging on Samuel's arm. "Don't look back because I can assure you, the horse meat is gone."

"How . . .?"

"He couldn't have done it alone." They stood in front of the Brewsters' cottage where the construction noises were drowning out the birds, but neither of the men was thinking about the progress being made on the house. They both realized that there might be more Acadians than they had thought.

Brewster took off his hat and wiped the sweatband. "Belcher was right; there could be a nest of them."

"Three Acadians were supposed to have survived but there could be more than that."

Samuel turned so he could watch Bourgeois out of the corner of his eye. "Did you know there was a boy?"

"No. I didn't."

"The boy was born here . . . must have been." Samuel Brewster felt His guidance as he came to a decision. "Look at the boys playing together. There's no harm in that. We'll let things be."

"Not tell them at the town meeting?"

Samuel Brewster shook his head in agreement. "Not tell them," he said.

\* \* \*

*Late summer*

Agnes Brewster was homesick for Connecticut. *It's so different here.* She pulled her bonnet further down over her forehead to shield her eyes from the sun. *At low tide the Cornwallis River is barely a trickle but, twice a day, the salt water comes back and raises the river's level over forty feet!*[11] She sighed and a look of anxiety flitted across her face. *When it's my time, what will I do? There's a competent midwife across the river, in Horton, but how will she get to help my new baby and me if the water is gone? There's so much mud! Silas says there's a crossing on the river about a mile upstream. He says when the water's out she would be able to make it across—but only when the tide is all the way out—and only if she has a proper horse—not one of those little French animals.* Again, Agnes sighed. *She patted her belly. This one's a girl and, if she's anything like my family, she'll be contrary, that I know. She will cause no end of fuss if she finds out about that river.* Agnes turned away from the view and looked back at her house and barn. *I won't think of it again.*

Two boys ran out of the half-finished barn, one carrying a saw, the other brandishing a hammer like a tomahawk.

Agnes smiled. *On the one hand, Samuel Junior acts like a grownup craftsman when Tom Pinch or the Acadian lets him handle a tool. Junior's even made some cuts; under strict supervision I made certain . . . but those two . . . those two are two little Indians!* With a start she realized that she had not thought of the threat posed by Indians or Acadians since Bourgeois had begun to work on the barn at the beginning of the summer. *He's so very patient with the young mischief-makers.* She listened as the boys ran away from the barn door, chattering in French and English. Inside the barn, an adult voice was raised in mock anger. Yes, it's a happy time, she thought.

Tom Pinch bolted through the door; head swivelling as he searched for the thieves. "Come back, you devils!" He stopped short, lowering his eyes and then his head. "Your pardon, Missus. I didn't mean harm."

"We should not mention the Prince of Darkness for fear he might heed us."

"Yes, Missus. I will be more respectful."

Agnes smiled. *Despite his station, Pinch is a nice enough man. If he seeks God's grace, he might be permitted to prosper . . . but . . .* she pursed her lips . . . *not if he calls out to the Fallen Angel.* "Do carry on, Tom," she said, because she had found that Tom Pinch would hold his place until he was dismissed. "Yes, do recover your tools from those little rascals."

Tom Pinch bobbed his head a couple of times and went in search of the boys.

Agnes didn't continue to watch as the servant departed. Instead, she studied the lines of her new house. *It is such a light and airy house: two windows centred on either side of the front door . . . or they would have been centred if I hadn't insisted on an extra room on the main floor.* "It's our borning room, my dear," she said, as she stroked the child in her belly. "That's where we will go when it's time, you and I, together." She walked to the front of the house and opened the door. She stepped into the little foyer. Pointing at the steep stairs that wound around the central chimney, she explained, "Upstairs there are two bedrooms for the boys. When you are old enough, you will have a bedroom on the second floor—you and your sisters—when they come." *Oh yes! I hope we have sisters, my dear. Three men are enough, what with their airs and their posturing . . .*

"Forgive me, Lord. I meant no disrespect to my husband." Agnes bowed her head. *It was a thought that came unbidden, Lord. If it is unsaid, must I review it with Samuel after prayers tonight? I will practise good thoughts until sleep time and perhaps You can guide me, please.* She waited, head bowed. After a respectful interval she thought, *meanwhile, I will tell my child the good things of the life You have led us to, Lord.*

"God has allowed us to prosper, my dear." *I will name you Alice.* "To the right, Alice, in the east end of the house, we have a large kitchen where you will learn to cook. I have iron pots of several sizes, pewter bowls that your Grandma Sweatland gave me," Agnes walked over to the huge fireplace where she swung the crane forward so she could reach the teakettle, "and you will love my teakettle. Your Daddy made a little whistle for it; yes, if we get it hot enough, it will whistle for us. Not a tune, mind you, just a whistle." *I will have to teach her not to burn her fingers on the crane.* "At night, Daddy will sit in the grandchair and, by the light of the fire, he'll read you stories from the Bible." Agnes laughed. "You will have to lie on a blanket on the floor; we only have the one chair. I sit on the pine box with the boys. When you get older, we might have another box for you to sit on." She pointed at the fireplace. "That's a bake oven, and on the other side of the bake oven is another fireplace." She skipped along, past the door and the staircase into the parlour. "See! This one's even larger than the kitchen fireplace."

Agnes Brewster gazed at her front parlour as if she were seeing it for the first time, drinking it all in for her baby to enjoy. "Two people can sleep on the trundle bed. You will be surprised how it pulls out to make a bigger bed . . . and we have a mirror! Not everyone has a mirror, dear Alice, but we Brewsters do." Very softly Agnes said, "It's a sign of God's grace, you know." She moved to the doorway of the borning room. "This case of drawers will be used for your pretty things, Alice, and look! You have three windows to watch the sun set over the river."

Through the window, Agnes could see that her husband was returning along the ridge that overlooked the Cornwallis River. Since most of the ridge belonged to Belcher she thought, *Samuel must have gone to see that man,* but then she remembered*, no, Samuel told me he had to go talk with the three Dissenter families. It is hard to be a preacher with no church and very little congregation.* Agnes sighed. *Samuel will do whatever is best for his flock.* She patted her belly. "I have to go look after my husband, Alice."

Agnes met her man at the front door.

He kissed her cheek, closing the big door behind him. Careful not to track dirt across the pine floorboards, Samuel wiped his feet off before entering the kitchen. "If our evening meal is ready, we should call the boys in."

"I'll ring the bell."

\* \* \*

After the children had gone to bed, Samuel beckoned for his wife to join him in the grandchair. With their arms entwined, and sitting side by side, they watched the fire. When it was time for their prayers, Samuel took much longer than usual. When he finished, he was a long, long time before he began the review of the day with his wife.

"I was having a good, Christian day until I met with the other families at Wiggin's."

"My dear, what happened?"

"They do not wish to continue—separately—as we have in the past."

"What do they want to do?"

"They mean to worship with the Congregationalists." Samuel excused himself from his wife and stood. He went to the fireplace and stared into the fire. With his back to his wife he said, "When I realized that I would have no congregation, I would have no church, I would not be a preacher . . . I felt that the light of God's love had left me."

Agnes gasped, but otherwise remained silent.

"But I know the fault is mine; I had acquired pride in my station as Preacher Brewster. The Lord has brought me down."

"What will you do, Samuel?"

"I will live my faith even if I cannot teach it. I will tend the souls around me the best I can. God will continue to watch over us." Slowly, he walked over to the pine table and picked up the sermon he had been working on. He held it in both hands as he went back to the fire.

In almost a whisper, Agnes said, "Please don't, Samuel."

His eyes brimming with tears, Samuel faced his wife. "With God's help, Agnes, I will be a better husband. I will be a better father. I will be a better neighbour."

Agnes bowed her head.

Samuel Brewster threw his sermon into the fire. "Perhaps God will see my renewed commitment to a godly life and permit us to prosper."

\* \* \*

*Early winter*

His breath coming in short, white puffs in the still, bitter cold of a December morning, Samuel set the log upright on its end. Twice it fell over. The third time he slammed it down hard enough to make its own place in the hard packed snow. He hefted his axe, carefully taking bead on the top of the log. Swinging hard, he jumped back a pace or two as the axe blade glanced off the wood and dug into the snow near his foot.

Wearily (he had been swinging at this particular log for some time), he went to the woodpile and selected two more logs. He placed these, one on either side of the target piece, and stepped back. It was then he saw Richard Bourgeois standing in the lee of the barn, watching him.

"I didn't see you there." Then he quickly added, "Bonjour, Richard."

"Bonjour."

Bourgeois walked past him to the woodpile and selected a thick piece of stump that he manoeuvred to where Samuel had been working. He placed the stubborn log on the stump and, with an easy swing, sank the axe blade about three inches into the wood. Then he lifted the axe, log and all, turned it over and let it drop onto the stump. The log split by its own weight on the blade.

"Mercy!"

"De rien, M'sieu."

"You made that look so easy, Richard."

"L'essayez," Richard said as he handed the Planter the axe. "Try it."

With Richard's example to follow, Samuel quickly split an armload or two of wood. Richard Bourgeois helped carry the wood to the shed.

"Come inside," Samuel said, gesturing for the other man to enter the house. "You look cold."

"Merci."

Knocking the snow off their boots, the men entered by the door from the shed. Bourgeois nodded to the mistress of the house and smiled at the two boys as he entered the kitchen. "Bonjour, mes beaux gars!"

Junior smiled and gave a little wave but did not leave his place by the fire.

Alexander ran to the Acadian and hugged his leg. In almost a whisper he said, "You must speak English so my mother will understand."

Taking the Acadian's outer clothing, Samuel picked up on Alexander's comment. "You speak English, Bourgeois?"

His weathered face turning even a darker shade, Bourgeois mumbled, "Not very good, M'sieu."

"I didn't know you people spoke our language."

Agnes lifted a cover off a tureen sitting on a little pine table. "Alexander, you tell Mister Bourgeois that we have some potato soup but not much else."

"He will speak English for you, Mama."

Samuel persisted, "I didn't know Acadians learned English."

Agnes, not having heard Alexander's original loud whisper, expressed surprise. "Eh? He knows English? Why didn't he speak it before now? It's been such a bother using Alexander to translate for us."

Samuel gave the Acadian a wary look. "Why keep it a secret? Missus Brewster is right; it has been difficult speaking through the boy."

For several minutes, the only movement in the kitchen was the shadows cast by the flickering flames in the fireplace. Finally, Agnes motioned to her boys. "Pull the box over to the table." She nodded at the Acadian as she began to ladle the thin soup out of the tureen. "Please sit down and get something hot into you. It's all we have—some potatoes that Mister Brewster managed to harvest after the early winter killed everything else."

Bourgeois sat down. The boys joined him, one on either side. Samuel lifted the grandchair, pulling it under him as he took his position at the head of the table. Agnes ladled the steaming soup into the pewter bowls, handing them to each person in turn, beginning with Samuel. "We have no bread," she said.

Samuel Brewster indicated that they should join hands for the benediction. Never one to mince words, Samuel Brewster came right to the point in his talk with his God. "Help us, Lord, to live through these difficult times. Make the government officials in Halifax understand our dire need and answer our pleas for food. In the meantime, we continue to live by Your laws, sharing what little we have with our visitor . . ."

Samuel lifted his head and stared right at the Acadian. "I tell you Lord, that Richard Bourgeois has been a help this day," then Samuel's face turned crimson as he met his wife's surprised look across the table. Samuel averted his eyes as he finished with the invocation, "Bless this food that we take to our bodies, Amen."

"Amen."

Alexander's blue eyes pleaded for permission to speak.

"Yes, Alex. You have something troubling you?"

"Father, where is Tom? I haven't seen him the whole day."

"I sent him to Horton to pick up a horse."

"We are going to have another horse?"

"Yes. I bought him from Lieutenant Starr this morning."

The other son, squirming as if he had ants in his pants, asked, "Father, may I also speak?"

"Yes, Junior."

"Did you buy a horse, unseen?"

"No, son, certainly not." Samuel supped his soup. "That would be like buying a pig in a poke." He smiled broadly at his older boy. "I would do neither."

"Then . . ."

"Starr's friend brought the horse from Horton for me to see. He had to get back home to Horton and he rode the horse home. Tom will ride her back." Samuel Brewster looked out the front windows at the darkened sky. "Looks like he will have to wait for the tide."

"Oh," both boys said, and busily ate their soup.

"You ask me . . . why I not speak English. Joseph Bourgeois de Grand Prè . . . speak English . . . go to Halifax . . . for . . . la justice."

The clatter around the table stopped as the Brewsters waited for whatever the Acadian had to say next.

"When Joseph Bourgeois speak to the English . . . the word, en français, is corriger . . ." Bourgeois looked to Alex for help.

"Go ahead, son," Samuel encouraged the boy.

Alex watched Bourgeois as he made slapping motions with his hands. "Something like spank, Father."

"Perhaps he means correct?" Samuel glanced at the Acadian for comment. "Perhaps they corrected his English?"

Richard Bourgeois crossed his wrist and then held his arms over his head. "Corriger!" he said with vehemence. "Corriger!"

"Whipped. . . . Punished?"

"Oui, punitif." Bourgeois nodded his head as he lowered his arms. "Punished. . . . Deport to France." He wore a wane smile as he said, "Acadian leaders speak English. . . . When Bourgeois speak English at Halifax . . . deport to France . . . never see family, ever."

Agnes shook her head. "That seems hard to believe."

Richard continued as if he had not heard her, or perhaps he hadn't understood her. "I not speak English. I want to stay with my son. I do not want to be French man. I want to live here with my son."

"You will be fine here." Samuel smiled at the little Acadian. "No one will take you away from your boy."

The meal was quickly over. Agnes collected the bowls as the men rose from the table.

"Tomorrow, I will . . . you . . . get meat, Mister Brewster."

"I don't know anything about hunting, Bourgeois." He regarded the Acadian with suspicion. "You aren't supposed to have a gun."

"No gun. I teach . . . le lacet . . . uh . . . snare." He put on his coat and hat and went to the door. "Early, I come for you. We get meat."

## Endnotes

[1] *The Port Remembers (The History of Port Williams and Its Century Homes)* was produced by the Port Williams Women's Institute. Interspersed among fine descriptions of early homes are interesting details about daily life in Cornwallis Township. Silas Woodworth was born in Lebanon, Connecticut. His wife Sarah (English) gave birth to Elizabeth Seaborn Woodworth during the voyage. They arrived at the township in 1760.

[2] The storm of November 1759 was every bit as destructive as the guerrilla warfare that was being carried on against the English up until about

1760. However, this storm was the worst gale in Atlantic history and caused enough damage to the dykes that English settlement was delayed until a survey could be completed to determine the extent of the damage. Just imagine the high tides of the Bay of Fundy (the highest tides in the world) and then raise them another ten feet! As a consequence, the main movement of English settlers did not begin until 1761.

[3] The new settlers were terrified by the continued presence of even a few Acadians. Certainly, there was the fear that the guerrilla warfare of 1755 – 1760 might be resumed; the Planters would feel much more secure in the quiet enjoyment of their properties if the erstwhile owners were no longer around. The Planter's hostility and fear of the Acadians was real and there was general support for an Acadian roundup.

[4] There is a tradition in the Valley that a few Acadians escaped deportation and the Planters found them in 1760, hiding in the woods.

[5] "Before the Revolutionary War many New England families—including some from Chatham, Mass—emigrated to Nova Scotia. In an effort to consolidate their hold on Nova Scotia, the British government in 1755 and 1756 deprived the French Acadians of their lands and established measures to resettle politically more dependable New Englanders in their place. By proclamation dated 12 October, 1758, Governor Lawrence of Nova Scotia offered many inducements for New Englanders to settle on these vacated lands as well as in virgin areas . . . each settler would be allowed 100 acres of wild woodland, with an additional 50 acres going to each member of the family. Full liberty of conscience was guaranteed, papists excepted." Article held in the Massachusetts Archives titled "Nova Scotia Settlers from Chatham, Massachusetts, 1759–1760."

[6] Dissenters were excused from paying tithes to the Church of England.

[7] Eric Brewster of Kentville, Nova Scotia, provided a copy of an October 2, 1928 article from the *Yarmouth Herald* titled "New Englanders in Nova Scotia." Major Samuel Starr's great-grandfather married Hannah Brewster, granddaughter of Elder Brewster. We can see that Preacher Brewster is making a slight exaggeration to impress Silas when he casually passes off the relationship as "my cousin."

[8] An interesting item from *The Port Remembers*: 150 Planter families were meant to share the Cornwallis Township lands. Only 128 originally settled. Several men with considerable influence in Halifax acquired larger properties.

[9] Acadians were used as gang labour on the dykes and opening up rough roads.

[10] The Acadian horses were small and only used for riding.

[11] A tidal bore is a wall of water formed as the incoming tide enters the shallow rivers of the Bay of Fundy. The wall of water gets higher as it meets the resistance of the river current and the constricting pressures of the shores on either side.

## Chapter Two
## Acadian Roundup

*May 1762*
*Cornwallis Township*
*Nova Scotia*

"This is the last of the supplies from Halifax, Richard." Samuel Brewster, in open-necked shirt and breeches and barefoot, lifted the last of the bales out of the barn. "What do you need, in particular, for your people?"

"Only what you can spare, M'sieu."

Samuel began dividing the supplies. He held up a bag of flour. "Can you make bread at your camp?"

"Oui."

Samuel continued putting the foodstuffs into two equal piles. He uttered an oath of disgust when he found mouse dirt and then a nest in the bottom of one of the wooden containers. "Shades of evil!" Using his fingers, he extracted the refuse, trying to salvage as much of the food as he could. "Drat! It's not as if the fine burghers of Halifax sent us a surplus amount!"

"And they gave you only enough for your family, M'sieu. That you share with us is wonderful . . ."

A young voice called from the front of the property. "Look what we caught!"

Both men put down what they were doing and walked out into the farmyard where they could see the two boys, Alex and Joseph, holding a stringer of fish between them.

"Perch," Samuel said.

"Oui, perche," Richard agreed.

"They'll have to be gutted."

"I will show . . . les pêcheurs . . . how it is done."

"Fishermen," Samuel said, helpfully.

"Fishermen," Richard repeated.

Samuel went back to his work while the boys followed Richard to the brook behind the barn. Samuel placed the

97

foodstuffs into two sacks and carried them to the house, where he put one sack down on the step and carried the other inside.

Agnes didn't look up from her baking. "The boys caught some fish?"

"Not much eatin'. Just some perch."

"That's all right. I'll make some batter."

"I just brought in the last of the flour."

"You shared what was left with the Acadian?"

"Yes." Samuel regarded his wife but she hadn't looked up from her work. "He feeds more people than we do," he said, somewhat apologetically.

Agnes sighed but kept on with what she was doing. "The boy—Joseph—is . . . handy around my kitchen. I don't mind giving to the boy." She shook her head and fell silent, continuing to work. After few moments, she cocked her head, listening. "Go pick up the girl before she cries. I don't like it when she feels she has to cry."

"I didn't hear anything."

The mother picked up a cloth and began to wipe her hands. "She's awake."

"Never mind. I'll go." Somewhat testily Samuel said, "I suppose she will need changing."

Suppressing a smile, Agnes agreed, "I suppose so. You'll find clean nappies under the . . ."

"I know. I know."

She could hear him grumbling about how men shouldn't have to do women's work. "You be gentle with our Alice, Samuel," she admonished. Agnes raised her voice so she could be heard all the way out to the borning room. "The Lord knows you are a good man, Samuel Brewster."

A small, reedy voice gave warning in the front yard. "They come! Father, they come!"

Recognizing Alex's voice, Agnes rushed to the front door. Samuel met her there, holding the baby Alice to his chest as he looked to see what was happening.

Alex was running to the house. "Mister Belcher comes! He comes with his toy soldiers!"

Samuel grimaced, *that boy of mine doesn't miss a thing.* "Don't call them toy soldiers, Alex."

"That's what you called them, Father."

Agnes took the baby from her husband and went back to the borning room.

"You heard me, son." He stepped down to the front yard. Shielding his eyes from the sun, he watched the soldiers approach; they were coming on the double. When they were within earshot, he waved. "What brings you here, Lieutenant Belcher?"

Belcher halted his squad of six men. He said something to his corporal, something that Samuel didn't hear. As Lieutenant Belcher turned to speak to Samuel, the soldiers fanned out, covering all the exits of the house, their muskets at the ready.

"Well, Brewster! I understand you have visitors today."

"Yes, Lieutenant; thank you for coming by. May I get you and your men a drink? Must be thirsty work, running uphill like that."

The lieutenant bristled. "You know well enough what I mean, Brewster. That Acadian was here today." Belcher then smiled, touched his forefinger to his cap and said, "Good day, Missus Brewster. I see you and your baby are doing well."

"Yes, thank you, Lieutenant."

"I was just about to ask your husband if he has seen the renegade Acadian."

It was Samuel's turn to bristle. "Why do you think you have to bother yourself with him? We see him, now and again. He does some work for me. He is no threat to the community, I can assure you."

"Your pardon, Brewster, but your assurances mean very little. Major Starr has ordered that all Acadians must have supervision as they present a real threat to the women and children of the township."

"I can give supervision . . ."

Belcher interrupted, "*Military* supervision can only be given when they are attached to properly constituted work parties."

"I need his help. I have always been a preacher and not schooled in the ways of hunting or farming. If it weren't for . . ." Samuel was going to argue further but instead he ended up, lamely, "I need his help."

"Well, you can't have it."

"Burbidge has Acadians working around his place."

"*Colonel* Burbidge, Mister Brewster, and you're not Colonel Burbidge." Lieutenant Belcher pointed a finger at the Brewster house. "I want to know if the Acadian is here."

Samuel was startled when Agnes volunteered, "He's by the brook, down behind the barn." She turned around and went back into the house.

The soldiers spread out, carefully making their way around the barn, taking advantage of every piece of cover as they sought out their quarry.

Samuel didn't stay to watch the soldiers' manoeuvrings. He went into the house, following his wife into the kitchen. In a low, angry voice he demanded, "Why help them? If it weren't for Richard, we might not have survived the winter."

"He's an *Acadian!*"

"He's proved himself a friend!"

"He's no friend! He only helps you because you gave him half the foodstuffs we received from Halifax!"

"Richard helped us when we only had potato soup, before the foodstuffs came from Halifax."

They could hear that the soldiers had returned to the front of the house. Both Brewsters returned to the doorway. Samuel was relieved; the soldiers did not have Richard in custody. He smiled to himself when he noticed the disappointment written large on Lieutenant Belcher's face.

Belcher did not speak to Samuel.

"Thank you for the help, Missus Brewster. It looks like he run off."

"If he were ever here," Samuel said sotto voce.

If the lieutenant heard, he gave no sign.

"Again, thank you, Missus Brewster. If he comes back, be sure to let us know."

Agnes Brewster nodded her head but she remained silent, going back into the house.

Samuel watched as the soldiers marched down the hill. When they were out of sight he motioned for Alex to come closer. He whispered in his son's ear, "Run along to Richard. Tell him not to come back here until I send word to him."

Alex ran off but came back right away. "Does that mean Joseph can't come down to see me any more?"

The father gave it some thought. "No, son. Your mother doesn't count Joseph as an Acadian." He waved his arm. "Now, run along."

*July 1762*
*Cornwallis Township*

Samuel Brewster leaned on his hoe, gawking across his potato field at the pathetic figures being herded toward the township stockade by a squad of Cornwallis Volunteers. Each of the four captives had a rope around his neck, looping over the shoulder of the next and then the next, until it came back to the neck of the first prisoner. Hands shackled behind their backs, the men were unable to make any adjustments in the set of the rope; it was particularly hard on the smallest of the four where the loop was chafing against his bleeding nose.

*It was inevitable,* he thought as he ran across the planted rows to the aid of Joseph Bourgeois. *Sooner or later they would be caught . . .. but this is barbaric!* He waved his arms as he ran. "Stop! In the name of God, be more merciful!" Samuel tripped. Pushing himself up he shouted, "He's a mere boy!"

The soldiers made no adjustment to the ropes or the shackles, prodding the prisoners with the muzzles of their muskets, driving them through the gate of the stockade where they disappeared from Samuel's sight. He could hear the cheering that greeted the capture of the elusive Acadians. Samuel stopped running. Dusting himself off, he went home, where he explained to Agnes what he had witnessed.

He finished the sad tale with the statement, "I mean to call for a township meeting." He went into the front room where he opened up his case of drawers and selected his best clothing. He dressed, slowly and carefully. "Did you see the way they were being treated?"

"The Acadians?"

"Yes. Did you see it?"

"No, I didn't."

"Herded like animals. I am going to do something about it." When his wife failed to respond, Samuel asked, "You agree with me on this?"

"No, husband."

Before slipping on his shirt, Samuel hefted the pitcher, then poured water into the drysink bowl. He splashed his face and shoulders and carefully cleaned his hands, getting the dirt from under his nails as best he could.

Wordlessly, Agnes handed him a towel. She returned to the kitchen, leaving her husband to his dressing.

When he came out of the front room, she was standing at the door holding his hat. "Remember who they are, husband. Remember who you are." She stood on tiptoe and gave him a kiss on the cheek. She turned away and did not watch as her man departed.

All the way down the hill, Samuel rehearsed what he was going to say to Burbidge. *Colonel Burbidge*, he corrected himself. *No sense alienating the man right off.* As he approached the cottage, he could see several men standing in the shade of the solitary tree in the front yard. *Starr, Burbidge, Belcher and that new man, Best, they are all here. Ah, well, in for a penny, in for a pound.*

He touched his forefinger to the brim of his hat. "Good day, gentlemen. I come to ask . . ."

"We were just going inside were it might be cooler," said the new man. "It would be a kindness if you could join us." He extended his hand. "We haven't met. I am William Best, newly come from Halifax."

"Pleased to meet you, Mister Best. I . . ."

"Your pardon, sir, but are you of descent from William Brewster?"

"Yes. You have the advantage, Mister Best."

"I know of your family, the William Brewsters. Fine family. Always stand for the highest principles." Best made a circular motion with his hand. "I believe, gentlemen, that we should include the preacher in our discussion." Without waiting for an answer, Best began speaking as he led the way into the Burbidge cottage. "I brought important papers from Halifax. Similar papers were delivered to Horton, across the river, this morning. Not handled very well in Horton, I am very sorry to say. Word is that fifty-seven families have voted to leave."[1]

Samuel was wondering if he should explain that he no longer had a congregation, that he was no longer a preacher, but the size of the number brought him up short—fifty-seven families wanting to leave? There were always families who spoke of going back home, but fifty-seven? He was aghast. "What happened?"

Colonel Burbidge lowered his voice. "Word reached Halifax at the beginning of July that a squadron of French ships swooped down on St. John's, capturing the inhabited areas of that island."

"And we're next!" Sam Starr slammed his fist into the palm of his hand. "When the French attack Nova Scotia, the Indians and renegade Acadians will rise up and catch us in our beds."

Belcher, not to be left out, raised his voice. "Any French attack will be preceded by a bloody revolt by the Acadians and a massacre by the Indians."[2]

The other men immediately shushed him.

William Best looked to the colonel for permission before he proceeded. Best leaned forward, indicating that what he was going to say was highly confidential.

The other men formed a tight circle, their heads virtually touching in the centre.

His voice lowered almost to a whisper, Best explained, "The Assembly at Halifax has ordered the militia to act; to immediately gather up the Acadians. Unfortunately, in Horton, the information about the French capture of St. John's was made available at a township meeting before the militia took the Acadians into custody. The result was panic. The Planters at Horton are boarding themselves up—others are taking ship—abandoning their holdings . . ."

"Fifty-seven families, gone," Major Starr intoned.

Samuel Brewster drew back from the circle. He stood upright. "I must say that I only came to you when I saw the way the militia . . ."

Burbidge placed his hand on Samuel's arm. "My dear fellow. You are so insightful! You saw our militia taking action and you knew . . . you discerned the truth of the situation. You could recognize that the leaders of this community were taking pre-emptive actions against an appalling threat."

Samuel persisted, "But . . . Lieutenant Belcher has been trying for . . . for months to capture the last of the free Acadians!"

"And he was right!" Colonel Burbidge pumped Belcher's arm. "Old Ben here was right! And now, the Assembly of Nova Scotia has ordered us to arrest all of the Acadians and put them under lock and key."

William Best ran his finger along the lines of the parchment he held out for all to see. "Here! Here it says," he squinted but managed to read by holding the paper a bit further away, "it says, these people, seeing the English in possession and enjoyment of the Acadian Lands forfeited, and formerly occupied by them, will forever regret their loss; and consequently will lay hold of favourable opportunity for regaining them, at any, even the most hazardous risk."[3]

Samuel nodded his head. "I often wondered how the Acadians could abide seeing us, day after day, occupying and using their lands."

"Well, they couldn't stand it!" Major Starr shook the paper as he said, "They are in league with the French, and you can bet your life on it!"

It was Colonel Burbidge, again, laying hands on Belcher's arm and Samuel's shoulder, drawing the two men closer together, who summed up the situation. "We must follow the orders from Halifax and we must do it before the next tide, when the usual contacts with Horton will resume. So, this afternoon, I will call a township meeting. After I announce the French attacks and the expected Acadian and Indian acts of terror, I will expect Mister Best to explain how elements of the Royal Navy will prevent French naval forces from entering the Fundy."

"Especially as far up the Fundy as Minas Basin," Mister Best interjected.

Burbidge nodded in agreement and continued, "Major Starr will then proclaim the arrest of all Acadians in the area." Burbidge dropped his hand from Belcher's arm and moved closer to Samuel Brewster. "At this juncture, I will open the meeting for discussion. Our citizens will expect reasoned, opposing arguments from our most famous Dissident . . . a well-spoken man of the William Brewster line."

"The Brewsters have always taken the high road." Major Starr gave Samuel a lavish smile and reached across to take Samuel's hand. "I know only too well since my grandfather married one of them.[4] We need you to take the high road again, for the benefit of your friends and neighbours in Cornwallis Township."

"What would you expect me to say?"

There was some hesitation. It was Belcher who filled the void. "Just say that your wife will rest better knowing that the Acadians have been placed where they will not be able to do any harm."

Recalling his wife's lasting anxieties about the Acadians, Samuel readily agreed. "I could say that."

Colonel Burbidge took Samuel's hand and shook it heartily, keeping hold of the hand as he moved toward the door. "It would be a great help," he said.

Samuel Brewster resisted the motion.

Burbidge released the other man's hand. "Yes?"

"I would want to know that our Acadians would be treated well."

"Yes of course," Burbidge said, agreeably, as he again began moving toward the door.

Still Samuel resisted. "And they would be fed, regularly."

"Of course."

Samuel allowed himself to be led to the door. He placed his hat on his head and stepped outside. He turned and examined the faces of each of the men, seemingly waiting for something.

"You have our word on it," Colonel Burbidge said, solemnly. Without waiting any further, Burbidge began giving orders to the other men. "Major, pass the word for a township meeting. Lieutenant, you go to the stockade and ensure the proper treatment of the prisoners . . ."

Samuel Brewster spoke up. "The gentle treatment of the Acadians."

"Certainly." Lieutenant Belcher almost clicked his heels.

Samuel Brewster could hear the continuing stream of orders as he walked back up the hill to his farm.

When Colonel Burbidge estimated that Brewster had walked far enough away that he would no longer be able to hear them, he hushed the other men with his hand. "That went well."

The others agreed.

"Who arranged for him to come down here?"

Sam Starr shrugged his shoulders. "I think he just came on his own."

"Couldn't have worked better if we had planned it."

William Best pointed at the parchment from Halifax. "We are to expect a ship to take the Cornwallis prisoners to Halifax for disposal."

"Good. Let's arrange it so the little preacher man is part of the escort," Belcher suggested.

"Good thinking," the colonel agreed. "If it looks like the Dissenter is on the side of the government, then we won't have trouble with the other bleeding hearts in the township."

* * *

During the two weeks that the Acadians had been locked up, the Planters of Cornwallis Township came to realize how much the success of their daily living depended on the hard work of the Acadian prisoners. In particular, Samuel Brewster learned that his elder son Junior was a laggard, his indentured servant Tom Pinch suffered from bad lungs that prevented any form of heavy work, and he, Samuel Brewster the out-of-work preacher, wasn't much good for anything without the hands-on guidance of the Acadian Richard Bourgeois.

"It's soul-destroying. I am so helpless without Richard. I need him here so much that I raised the subject at the township meeting," Samuel grumbled to his wife. "I went to the meeting and begged that the Acadians be released to resume their work."

"And you weren't listened to?"

Agnes was helping her husband dress for his trip to Halifax. She would miss him, terribly, but the honour of being the wife of one of the escorting officers acting on behalf of the Assembly of Nova Scotia in the elimination of the "Acadian Problem" gave her an elevated position in the eyes of her neighbours that she enjoyed thoroughly.

"It wasn't as if I was alone in speaking out against the continued incarceration of our labourers." Samuel stopped his dressing and enumerated his supporters on his fingers. "There was Woodworth, the Deacon, Terry, Bishop . . . even Major Starr himself; we all requested relief from the imprisonment order but the colonel wouldn't hear of it. Even when the township members voted to allow strictly controlled day passes for selected labourers, the colonel over-ruled the vote, citing the need for military security over democracy during these dangerous times."

He looked at himself, once more, in the family mirror. "There. That seems to do it. How do I look, Agnes?"

"Vain, husband."

Crestfallen, Samuel looked away from his image. "You are most probably right. I will review my shortcomings with the Lord tonight, and praise your worthiness and essential goodness."

Junior knocked on the door. "Father, the prisoners are coming out of the stockade. Your horse is ready at the front of the house."

Agnes watched as her husband left the room. She said to his back, "I appreciate your good opinion and value your prayers, Samuel." When he only raised his hand in acknowledgement, she meekly added, "I shall miss you terribly."

If Agnes could have seen his face, she would have witnessed a fleeting moment of annoyance; however, he did return to his wife and took her hands in his. "I must go now, my sweet." He kissed her on the cheek. Patting her hands as he released them he said, "I must go about my assigned duties, for the good of the township, my dear." He stepped out through the door and quickly mounted his horse. The animal shied away from Alex, who was steadying the mount, making a dozen or so tiny steps, allowing the rider to make a show of flashy horsemanship for anyone who might have been watching. With a small wave, Samuel Brewster rode off to head the procession to Starr's Point where the English ship was moored.

The prisoners, the Acadians, were in no hurry to leave. Perhaps they thought they might delay the loading of the ship long enough to miss the tide. Perhaps they just didn't want to willingly participate in the final solution of the 'Acadian Problem'. Whatever it was, they were a long, long time coming down the hill, exasperating the Cornwallis Volunteers who were responsible for their delivery to the English ship. The Volunteers began to harass the prisoners, prodding and goading to make them move along faster. Acadians fell. The Volunteers pushed at them with the butts of their muskets to make them get up and resume the march. Blood flowed.

More and more Planters and their families came to watch the spectacle. Where, at first, the spectators were noisy and active, with children running up and down the parade, as the beating progressed, they grew silent. With each blow, spectators' voices were raised, protesting the brutality.

"My God! Look what they did to André!" Silas Woodworth shouted as he pushed his way into the middle of the procession. He reached down and pulled a middle-aged man to his feet. "Are you all right, Andy?" One of the Volunteers shouldered Silas off to one side and the procession reached the ship, where the impatient sailors began to handle the cargo roughly.[5]

A woman's voice could be heard above the din of human misery. "Not the boy!"

Samuel Brewster was handing the reins of his horse to Junior, who would take the animal back to the barn after the ship departed. He didn't hear her the first time Agnes shouted at the soldiers and sailors. He heard her the second time.

Agnes Brewster shouted, "Not the boy!"

A ship's officer, probably the first mate, motioned to the sailors to ignore the woman and continue loading the cargo.

Missus Samuel Brewster was not to be ignored. She stood on the gangplank, preventing the loading of any more prisoners. With both arms outstretched she said, "Joseph! Come to me."

Joseph Bourgeois clung to his father.

Samuel appeared alongside his wife. He could see the terror in the boy's eyes. He knew that his wife was not going to back down. He did the only thing that he believed he could do. He faced the ship's officer. "I order you to release the boy to this woman's custody."

The naval officer turned his back on the problem and busied himself with another aspect of the ship's operations.

Samuel drew himself up to his tallest. "I am the senior escorting officer and order the release of the boy." He gestured to the father. "Tell your boy to take Missus Brewster's hand, Richard." When Richard Bourgeois hesitated, Samuel coaxed him, "We will look after him. He will be well."

Richard leaned over his son, telling him something.

The boy shook his head.

The father stood up. His eyes brimming with tears, he gave the boy an order in English. "Go to the woman. Stay with her until I return."

Joseph Bourgeois had survived through numerous terrible circumstances by always obeying his elders. When his father released his hand, the boy ran down the gangplank into Missus Brewster's arms. She carried the boy to the end of the pier. They stood, unmoving, while the prisoners were loaded. They watched as the lines were singled up and the ship was warped to the end of the pier so the bow of the vessel would catch the outgoing tide. At this point, Richard Bourgeois was so close to his son they could have touched; but they didn't. Agnes might have made a small wave to her husband, but, then again, maybe she didn't; several onlookers commented that she and the boy seemed to be as still as the fancy figures in the English Church.

The ship moved swiftly into the stream carrying the last of the Acadians to Halifax and an uncertain future.

## *Endnotes*

[1] Rumours were everywhere. The Council of War at Halifax was acting on the rumour that 70 persons had already fled Horton.

[2] Wholesale panic swept Halifax when intelligence was received that a French naval squadron had captured Saint John's. Halifax believed they would be next; the Indians and the Acadians would rise up and massacre everyone.

[3] This is a quote from the minutes of the Halifax Assembly demonstrating they believed that the Acadians would seize the very first opportunity to take back their lands.

[4] Of course, we know that Starr is exaggerating the closeness of the familial relationship.

[5] Concerning the day of the resolution of the Acadian Problem at Cornwallis, for the purposes of this novel, I assume that it would not be unusual for the military to be impatient with the prisoners, who could be reluctant to leave the only place they know. Given the presence of muskets, force could have been used, onlookers could have been shocked by the brutality, and it would have been natural for a Christian woman to rescue a nice little boy from the roundup. My story, however, shows Agnes Brewster retrieving Joseph because of her sense of social position and proprietorship.

## Chapter Three
## The Return

*June 1763*
*Carleton House*
*Halifax*

*He doesn't look much like a preacher man.* John, major-domo of Carleton House, sniffed as he took the visitor's hat and cane. *Fancy hat, silver knobbed cane, well-tended shoes; he must have at least one servant.*

John closed the door. Bowing his head, he said, "The master is in the front room taking the sun. He is expecting you, sir." John recalled that, in his letter of introduction, Colonel Burbidge identified this fellow as a "person of ability." *Wish I could have seen more of the letter; it's not often a first-time visitor to Carleton House has enough wealth or influence to earn the sobriquet "person of ability."*[1]

John smiled his broadest and, backing away a few paces, said, "Please accompany me, sir." *A person of ability might even have more than one servant, he thought. I wonder how grand his house is? Burbidge's letter said Preacher Brewster planned to travel all the way from Cornwallis to Halifax, if Master Richard would agree to meet with him. Well, he's here. Hmmm. If I get the chance, I must listen.*

John led the way across the vestibule to an imposing double door. He tapped lightly and, not waiting for an answer, swung the doors wide so that the guest could make a proper entrance. John was disappointed when the preacher spoiled the effect, sidling in, off to one side, stopping just inside the room so John wasn't able to close one of the doors.

Richard Bulkeley, First Secretary of Nova Scotia, was sitting in the sunlight, making notes on a small pad. Bulkeley rose to meet the visitor, extending his hand, and after a brief shake, indicated that Samuel should take the other chair in the small alcove of the large room.

John, now free to complete his duties, paused with his hands on both door handles. "You would prefer tea, sir?"

"Port, John, thank you." Bulkeley inclined his head. "Our teas are not very good, certainly nothing like we could have in England, where there is more selection." Bulkeley shook his head. "Dear me, I forget that there are families like yours whose roots in the colonies are much deeper than mine, families who have never experienced the mother country."

"Tea would be fine, and I want to thank you for seeing me. I was told that you wouldn't be in the offices today and my ship leaves . . ."

"No trouble at all. Colonel Burbidge spoke highly of you; praised you as a stout fellow who freely gave of his support last year."

"I tried to do the right thing."

"And it would have all worked out fine except for that interfering lout in Massachusetts, Governor Pownall."

"I presumed he was concerned for their safety."

"Not at all! He just didn't want his New Englanders bothered with the resettlement of a few Acadians throughout his much wider domain."

"Not at all, Mister Bulkeley. I am informed that Governor Pownall believed that common humanity would have required that the Acadians not be driven from port to port at the approach of the storm season. It was my understanding that the governor . . ."

Somewhat archly, Bulkeley interrupted, "Your understanding! Where do you get your understanding?"

"I have family in New England. It was reported to me that they believed the Acadians quite blameless in the whole St. John's affair; didn't even know about the French attack until we locked them up and then shipped them out."

"Well, they came back, thanks to people like Pownall."

"Given half a chance, the Acadians will take the oath and become good British subjects."

"What hogwash! Who would believe such a thing?"

"My family tell me that Governor Pownall believes it."

Richard Bulkeley waved his hand in dismissal. He gazed out the window as he asked, "What is it that brings you to Halifax?"

"Well, we gathered up all the Acadians from Cornwallis and vicinity and brought them here last August. They were quartered in a barracks with about one thousand other Acadians from all over the province."

"Yes, yes. I know. What is your quest?"

"Many of the Cornwallis Acadians have returned. Some of them died, I am told, but some of them are . . . missing."

"And that raises a problem?"

"No one can tell me what happened to Richard Bourgeois."

"You are on first-name terms with an Acadian?"

"Well, no . . . not really. Well, yes, we are. We want to know . . ."

"We? There are other Planters involved with this Acadian?"

"Yes, I mean, no. My wife and I want to know if he lived, if he came back to Nova Scotia."

"I remember the policy discussions and there was no plan to return the Acadians to where they had been picked up. In fact, after the Pownall fiasco, our governor wanted them spread in small groups to distant parts of the province. That way they would pose a lesser threat to our communities."

John quietly entered the room and set the tray on the small table between the two chairs. He moved just as quietly out of the room when his master waved him away.

"Your Acadian friend might have died, might have come back and been resettled elsewhere, or he could have been put into one of the work parties that were assigned to projects in different areas of the province." Bulkeley held his glass of port up to the light. He seemed to be examining the colour of the Madeira, but he was really watching for the Planter's reaction to his next question. "Why would you have an interest in an Acadian? You are sympathetic to their cause?"

Samuel put his teacup down with a clatter. "No! I mean, we have his son with us."

"You are harbouring an Acadian?"

"Yes. No! He's just a boy, a baby really. My wife wants what is best for the boy and doesn't mind being his . . . I mean, we would want to return him to his father, if his father could be found."

"Let me understand this. You are in direct communication with friends of Governor Pownall who are sympathetic to . . ."

"No. Not really. They are cousins, really, distant cousins who believe . . ."

"Who believe the Governor of Nova Scotia mistreated the Acadians?"

"No, not at all. You can understand how we would want to do the right thing by the boy." Samuel's voice faltered when he recognized the rising repugnance in Richard Bulkeley's face. Samuel stood up. "We would want to return the boy to his father, at the first opportunity," he hastily added.

"Acadians will never make good citizens," the man of power declared. "They can never be trusted."

"Yes, of course. I shouldn't have troubled you with a matter of such little import but I was here and you were so accommodating . . . I can't thank you enough for having received me at your home."

Richard Bulkeley remained seated. He watched, unmoving, as the supplicant backed out of the room.

Samuel Brewster felt behind him for the handles to the doors, but was bumped forward into the room as John tried to open them both with his usual flourish.

"Excuse me," Samuel said to the servant and to the master. He turned and hurried out into the vestibule where another manservant was waiting with his hat. When Samuel stepped outside, with the front door finally closed behind him, he found that he was sweating.

"Lord!" he said in a prayerful voice. He looked left and then right, afraid someone might overhear him. Not satisfied he was entirely alone, what with all the windows overlooking the driveway, he hurried away from Carleton House.

"Lord, protect us from the wrath of that man." He took his hat off and wiped the sweatband. He looked behind to see if he were being followed. He put the hat back on his head, feeling the sweat immediately beginning to gather. *Richard Bourgeois is dead or gone—it doesn't matter which—he won't be back. And even if he does come back, men like Bulkeley will . . .*

"Good day to you, sir." A man in green livery paused long enough to touch his hat and bend slightly at the waist before hurrying on toward Carleton House. Samuel inclined his head ever so slightly but did not slow his descent to the harbour. Looking ahead, he could picture the hustle and bustle on the pier. *It won't take long to get home. The ship will sail on the tide and the day after tomorrow I will have my little family around me. And Joseph.* He could picture the little fellow sitting astride Agnes' knees, getting his fair share of lovin'. He smiled but his mind resumed an earlier thought: *and even if Bourgeois does come back, men like Bulkeley will . . . will what?* He answered his own question: *will continue to harass the Acadians, to use them, to abuse them, to deny them citizenship . . . and what of Joseph? Joseph is Acadian; no amount of lovin' can change that.* He raised his eyes to the heavens and, in a prayerful voice, begged, "Lord help us! Don't let Agnes take Joseph to her bosom!" In a stronger voice, as if he wanted to reach across the miles, he pleaded, "Agnes, don't take the boy to your bosom. Men like Richard Bulkeley won't hesitate to tear him from you."

## Endnotes

[1] Nova Scotia officials used the phrase "persons of ability" to identify men of substance.

## Chapter Four
## The Woodworths' Kitchen

### Spring 1765

"Silas! Do you see her comin' yet?"

Silas Woodworth got up from his chair and ambled over to the window that gave a view of the Brewsters' house.

Without turning around, Betty Woodworth, slopping water as she hurried with her scouring and washing of a large skillet, impatiently demanded, "Well! Are you going to look or do I have to stop and do it for myself?"

"I'm here, darlin', and I'm looking for you . . ."

"Well! Is she comin' or not? I can't bear the thought of Agnes Brewster finding me in a mess, and this skillet is the most trouble it's ever been."

"I can see clear to her front door . . ."

Exasperated, Betty pivoted and marched to the window. Shouldering her husband aside, she leaned on the sill, almost pressing her little nose against the glass. She felt her husband's hands slip around her waist and then move up to cup her breasts. She pushed his hands down, even more exasperated now that she realized his intentions. "You stop that right now, Silas Woodworth!"

He turned her around and kissed the lock of hair that had escaped the confines of her wimple. "Now, hush, Betty. The children won't be back until they hear the dinner bell . . . Agnes Brewster never stirs this early and . . ."

"And it's daylight. You know how I don't like doing it in the daylight."

"You could close your eyes."

"No!" Betty relented a trifle. She stood on tiptoe and kissed Silas, lightly, on the cheek but when he again reached for her breasts, she moved quickly across the kitchen to the sink. "I want to get this place cleaned up. Agnes is going to show me how to make vinegar out of honey and she'll be into every nook and cranny."

117

Silas decided to try a less direct approach. He pulled out his tobacco pouch. "Mind if I have a pipe . . . inside?"

"You can have your pipe on the way to the fields." When Silas made no move to get his hat and boots, she added, "Weren't you going to put the cows out today?"

"I planned to do that . . . but first . . . I thought I would spend a little time with you, Betty."

There was no hesitation in Betty's reply, "Well, you can't."

Silas got up. Sighing, he put his pouch away and cinched his belt tighter. He pulled his knife from its sheath and checked the edge. "I might have to sharpen my blade." Without waiting for a reply, he took a leather bag from its peg and went to the little table near the window. He sat down on the window box and began to fiddle with the drawstrings on the bag.

"Then you can keep watch for Agnes while I get some things done."

For the next few minutes there was little sound other than the stropping of the blade and the occasional grunt as Betty reached with a damp cloth into some corner of a shelf or cupboard,making it ready for the onset of Agnes Brewster.

Silas resumed the conversation. "She be bringing the new one?"

"I suppose so. She's still breast feedin'."

"Let's see. There's Samuel Junior, Alex, Joseph, Alice,and Sarah. What's this one called?"

"Lydia. Joseph isn't one of hers."

"I know that! But everyone's taken to calling him Joseph Brewster."

"Well, he isn't a Brewster."

Silas knew when to let something be, especially if he wanted amenable access to his wife's sweeter parts.

"You're right, Betty. Joseph will never be a rightful Brewster."

"It's not that Agnes loves him any less than her natural born."

"No. She loves them all."

"But she does coddle the boy."

"Joseph?"

"Of course I mean Joseph!" She slammed shut the last of the kitchen drawers. Silas winced. He had built well, but was not sure that he had built the drawer strong enough for an exasperated Betty Woodworth.

"Who else would I be talking about? Sometimes I believe you have your mind set on only the one thing!" Immediately regretting that she had raised 'that subject' again, Betty softened her voice as she hurried on, "What is Samuel going to do about the new church?"

"I dunno."

"Was he consulted by the Colonel?"

"I don't know what you mean, Bette."

"Please don't call me Bette."

Despite the objection, Silas noted a distinct softening in his wife's tone of voice. He felt somewhat encouraged, and continued, "Before Colonel Burbidge and Mister Best built the church, they talked to Samuel, if that's what you mean."

"Do you know what was said?"

"No, I don't." Silas sucked on his teeth a couple of times and then added, "Samuel told me the congregation would depend for church services upon"—here Silas did a very good imitation of Samuel Brewster's speaking voice—"the occasional ministrations of the Reverend Doctor Breynton of Saint Paul's Anglican Church, Halifax." He could hear his wife giggle softly. He waited to see which way the conversation would go; a giggle was a very good sign.

"They're not going to use Samuel as a preacher?"

Silas tried not to let his disappointment show in his voice. "No," he said. "Samuel's not Church of England. Couldn't let Samuel preach because then the Colonel would have a fight on his hands with the Society for the Propagation of the Gospel. No sir. The Colonel's not going to have a Dissenter preachin' in his English Church."

"I feel sorry for Samuel, him bein' a preacher and such a good man . . ."

"And him and his wife takin' that little boy in and treatin' him as if he were their own."

Betty had finished in the kitchen. She made some small adjustments to her hair. "I wish we had a mirror like the Brewsters.'" She reached for the polished brass plate so she could see her reflection.

Silas covered her outstretched hand with his. She let go of the brass plate and allowed Silas to lift her hand to his lips.

"I don't think she's comin' this mornin'."

"It doesn't seem so."

He drew her to him. "Remember the last time?" He enfolded her in his arms, "You thanked me, after."

"Yes, I did." Betty nuzzled his neck. "I remember. Yes."

## Chapter Five
## The Garrison

*Summer 1770*
*Cornwallis Township*

Decidedly out of breath, Samuel Brewster slowed to a walk the last dozen or so paces before he arrived at the stockade. He called out, "What's the emergency?" Taking out a handkerchief, he was mopping his brow as he entered the little fort. A large number of men were gathered around someone who was speaking in a loud voice. Samuel leaned against the doorpost to regain his wind as he listened. He soon recognized the speaker as an agitated William Best.

"With the sack over my head, they bound my arms and shoved me into the house where my wife, Annie, and my boy, Richard, were already lying on the floor, bound and gagged."

"Had they hurt your missus?"

*That's the Deacon,* Samuel thought but, before any answer could be made, a second, more authoritative voice silenced the crowd.

"Do you know who they were, William?"

*That's the colonel.*

"No. They got my head in the sack the minute I came out of the barn. I didn't see who they were. They took my cash box and everything of value and of easy carriage."

"How many were there?"

"I don't know. They left us on the floor, tied and sacked. This morning, my man came up to the house to see where I was; he'd been waiting for me to come to the barn. He said he didn't see anyone."

"You think they're gone; not skulking around the township?"

"We didn't see anyone when we come to ring the alarm."

"All right, men! Get your weapons and gather at Bests' as quick as you can. Major Starr, break out some horses for the

121

boys." Burbidge pointed at Samuel Brewster. "Get your mount, Samuel." He was turning away when Samuel said, "I can't come with you."

Everyone still within earshot stopped to see why the Dissenter wouldn't join the men of the township in the hunt for brigands.

Samuel knew he was the centre of attention. With a sweeping motion of his hands, he indicated his best clothes. "I am dressed for a funeral. At the sound of the bell, we left the body, unattended, at the cemetery. I sent my wife and children to take refuge in the church while I responded to the summons. I must go back."

"If you must."

Samuel gave the colonel a hard look to see what he meant by that.

Colonel Burbidge was quick to recover. "Of course you must. The dead must be attended to and the family's safety assured."

"Thank you, Colonel," Samuel replied, rather archly. "I will make myself available as soon as the ceremony is over."

"Yes, of course, Samuel."

As Samuel trudged across Belcher's land to the little church, he considered who the raiders might be. *French? Yes, there were French privateers and they wouldn't hesitate to raid a rich-looking farmhouse if the pickings on the Fundy were scarce.* "And William Best's home certainly looks prosperous from the Bay."

As usual, whenever he began speaking to himself, he looked around to ensure he wasn't being overheard—even though he was walking the cleared path that led across the top of the Belcher lands to the little church on the hill. "Sure wouldn't want people to think that I was my only audience." He laughed as he resumed his ruminations.

*They could be pirates; rogues from New England who find it easier to prey on scattered Planters than risk running afoul a Royal Navy warship.* "Yes, they could have been New Englanders," *but no! We all have New England relatives. They wouldn't come up here to give kinfolk some hurt.*

*That leaves the Acadians! It could well be Acadians.* He thought about Richard Bourgeois. *But we gathered them up. They're either dead or in work parties where we feed 'em military provisions, keep 'em busy all day, and store 'em in barracks at night. Besides, there can't be enough of 'em loose in the country-side to make up a raiding party. No, it couldn't be Acadians.*

Samuel had been trudging along, his head down, his thoughts keeping him busy. He stepped through the break in the spruce hedge into the rougher end of the cemetery. He looked ahead. His family must have caught sight of him; they were coming out of the church, walking through that part of the cemetery reserved for members of the Church of England.[1] He waved, indicating that they should join him near the pine box at the edge of an open grave.

When they were reassembled at the side of the grave, Agnes asked in a subdued voice, "Was there trouble?"

"No, not really." When she gave him a quizzical look, he said, "Nothing to trouble us."

"What was it, then?"

"The Best farm was robbed."

"Oh, my!"

Preacher Samuel Brewster stepped up on a little mound of dirt and raised his hands in supplication to the Lord. "Lord, we are gathered here today to mourn the passing of Thomas Pinch."

Agnes and the children lowered their heads and closed their eyes.

"We have known Thomas as a good man who honoured six years of his seven-year contract before you called him away, Lord. He never raised his voice in anger . . ."

Agnes placed a hand on Samuel's sleeve and squeezed his arm.

Samuel looked down, questioningly, at his wife. He thought a moment and then, nodding his head in agreement to some unspoken reminder, resumed his eulogy to the late Tom Pinch. "He didn't want to come to Cornwallis, Lord, and made some heartfelt objections before he realized that his con-tract obligations were paramount over his wishes."

Agnes released her husband's arm.

"Otherwise, he never raised his voice in anger and always worked to the limits of his talents." Samuel lowered his arms. "Make place for Thomas Pinch, Lord, as best you can." He stepped down from his perch. Almost immediately he stepped back up again. "He was a good man, Lord, and, as far as I know, he lived by Christian principles as best he could given his station." He stepped down again. "Amen," he said.

The family said amen.

Samuel held out his arms behind his family, herding them away from the gravesite.

Alex wanted to look back but his father caught him up in his herding and directed him along the path to the hole in the spruce hedge.

"But we can't just leave Thomas on the edge of the grave like that." Alex moved around his father's arms and ran back to the box.

Samuel beckoned to his boy. "Come along! The Acadian work party will lower the box into the ground after we are gone from here."

"Oh."

Still Alex hesitated at the side of the pine box. "Why is Tom 'way down here so far from all the other graves?" The boy flinched as he became the object of his father's stern looks and was quick to try to make amends. "I'm sorry, sir. May I speak about Tom?"

"You are tall for your age, Alex, but you must remember your place. Just because we are far from our relatives doesn't mean you can forget your manners, son. If Grandpa had heard you, he would believe you hadn't been properly raised." Satisfied by the boy's demeanour that he regretted his brashness, Samuel relented. "What is it you want to know, Alex?"

Alex pointed up the hill to the door of the church. "The path goes right to the church. There are graves near the door—some on either side—but all of them up close to the church." He made a forlorn little gesture at Tom's rough grave. "Why is Tom here, down here by the hedge, all by himself?"

The rest of the family had gone through the spruce hedge. When they realized that the father and son had remained at the gravesite, they came back.

Agnes knew better than to question her husband when he was admonishing one of the boys, but not so Junior; Junior Brewster, at sixteen years of age, considered himself one of the men of the Brewster clan.

"What has Alex done now, Father?"

Samuel waited until the last of his family had come through the opening before he answered.

"Alex has asked why Tom Pinch is to be buried here, far removed from the church."

Junior gave a suppressed laugh, which was cut short by his father's next comment.

"It is a good question and goes to the heart of our status in Cornwallis Township." He pointed up the hill. "The top half of this cemetery is for church members. The lower half is where slaves, indentured servants—and Dissenters—are buried." He raised his arms as if in the middle of a sermon. "We choose to be separate from them in life and they choose to keep our bodies separate from them in death." He dropped his arms to his sides. "And we believe the Lord God Almighty will continue to keep us separate from them in the life hereafter."

Junior's mouth sagged open as he considered his father's remarks.

Alex pointed at a small wooden grave marker that, up to now, he had failed to notice. He walked over and pulled the huckleberry branches away from the letters so he could read it.

"Cloe," he read out loud. "No date. No last name. Just Cloe."

Agnes held out her hand to Alex. "Come here, dear." When the boy ran to his mother's embrace she reached up to stroke his blond hair. "Cloe was one of Mister Belcher's girls."

"A slave?" Junior asked.

"A slave," Agnes confirmed. "She died in the winter and her body was kept in Mister Belcher's barn until the ground could be dug."

There was an audible sound when Junior snapped his mouth shut. He turned to face his father. "Sir, if I have permission to speak?"

"Yes, of course, Junior."

"We do not belong here."

When his father didn't respond right away, Samuel Brewster Junior repeated his statement. "We do not belong here," and made his first life decision, "and I plan to return home." In case there might be any doubt as to his meaning he added, "Home to Connecticut."

Samuel shook his head as if getting rid of the thought, forever. His lips compressed into a thin line, the father said, "This is not the time, Junior. I have duties to perform and must return to the house. Junior, when we get home—when we get to the house—I want you to saddle the horse while I change. I must join in the hunt for the brigands who raided our township and stole William Best's possessions, possibly violating his wife." When he saw the alarm in eyes of the ladies of his family, he hastened to say, "Violated her peace of mind and the sanctity of her home and hearth." He waved his family to move along. "We must hurry! I want to be seen to be of help in the capture and punishment of these brigands."

The family hurried down the hill, only Alex looking back to see if anyone were actually going to take care of Tom. Two men Alex knew to be Acadians came down the hill from the church. An armed Cornwallis Volunteer escorted them. Satisfied, Alex raced along to catch up with the men of his family but eventually gave up the pursuit. He shouted to them, "Tom is being looked after, Pa."

If the men heard him, they gave no notice.

By the time the females, Alex, and Joseph arrived at the house, Samuel was mounted and Junior was handing him the family's only weapon, an old-style musket. Reining sharply, Samuel turned the beast in the direction of Starr's Point and goaded her, sharply, into a fast trot. He called back over his shoulder, "Go in the house and bar the doors. Do not open them until you hear my voice."

Alex thought he could still hear the sound of the horse's hooves when he dropped the bar on the door, but probably not, since his father was drawing up in the Bests' front yard at that moment.

*There must be a dozen horses,* Samuel thought without counting them. *Major Starr certainly put on a grand effort for his friend, William Best. I wonder if they found anything?* He knocked on the door but, gauging that he had not been heard over the general din of people talking in the main room, he entered.

"Ah! The late Mister Brewster!" someone joked.

"Such humour is not appreciated," Mister Belcher chided the unseen wit. "Samuel's just come from a funeral."

"I'm sorry." The man stood up, revealing it had been Stephen Chase. "I didn't hear of your loss."

"I didn't lose anyone. My man died."

"That's a shame. It'll make things harder for you."

"Yes, it will. Was there any sign of the brigands?"

Major Starr must have overheard the question because he spoke up at this point, explaining to all the men the nature of the assault on the Best farmhouse.

"From signs on the beach at the Point, they came ashore in at least five ship's boats, making about thirty or forty raiders. A half-dozen or so seemed to have stayed with the boats as a defensive force while the rest waylaid the Bests. They carried away anything of value . . ."

"To the tune of a thousand pounds, I'm unhappy to say." William Best spoke louder to be heard over the hubbub raised by his comments. "I want to tell you, men, that I appreciate your efforts and I also want to tell you . . ." There was too much noise so William Best stopped speaking.

"Quiet down, boys." It was the colonel giving the order and the room hushed. "William and I have discussed this. He has something important to say."

"Two brigantines came up the Bay and into Minas Basin in daylight hours yesterday. We know that much because we saw them and assumed they would approach the landing on

128 *The Planters*

the morrow. They anchored in the basin, peaceable like, but dropped the pretence of being honest traders after dark, coming ashore when they liked and staying ashore for as long as they liked."

Stephen Chase raised an angry fist. "Halifax knows we need protection! There should be naval forces stationed in the Fundy!"

"That's right," William Best seconded. "Those pirates feel free to help themselves to anything they want because there is no Royal Navy presence in the Fundy."

"Boys, boys." The room went still for the colonel as he spoke. "The Fundy is a big, big place and the patrol ships can't be everywhere. If I were a pirate, I would know where the warships were and avoid them." Colonel Burbidge seized the moment. "We need a fort here, at Cornwallis!"

"With regulars garrisoned here for our protection," Major Starr enthused.

William Best stepped forward and raised his arms, waiting for the shouting and grumbling to stop before he spoke. He lowered his arms. "I know from my sources that Halifax has approval to build a fort on the Oromocto River. It's going to be named Fort Hughes and should be erected by this time next year."

"What good is a fort way up there? What will it do for us?" Major Starr had spoken up without thinking. He shrugged his shoulders in apology while he muttered, "It's a question that would have been asked, anyway."

William gave the major an understanding smile. "Fort Hughes will give the Bay of Fundy some protection from renegades and Indians who might have chosen to come at us from the north and west. What I am going to suggest at Halifax . . . Nay, with the colonel's support, we should be able to *demand* that a military facility be built here at Cornwallis. Even if it were only a barracks, regular soldiers could be billeted here and we would have no more raids."

There was general applause.

"The colonel and I will write, presenting our case . . ."

"We'll do more than write," the colonel loudly exclaimed. "I will travel to Halifax and make our situation known to the authorities, demanding immediate action."

"And I would be pleased to accompany you, Colonel, and exercise whatever minor influence I might have in the capital."

Colonel Burbidge stepped over to put his arm around William Best's shoulders. "Yes! We'll make it a team effort! Together, we will raise some dust in those musty halls! You can count on that!"

Huzzas, loud and boisterous, filled the room until, finally, Burbidge quietened the crowd by shouting, "Go home, now! Tell your families that their men will make Cornwallis Township a safer place."[2]

Samuel Brewster waited until he saw Silas and then joined him on the trek up the hill.

"What do you think, Silas? Do you think Halifax will do anything for us?"

Silas grunted but didn't say anything.

"You don't have an opinion, my friend?"

"We shall see what we shall see," Silas grunted again, "although we shall probably see more since it was William Best who lost his possessions and not a Woodworth or a Brewster."

"Certainly not a Brewster," was Samuel's reply.

## Endnotes

[1] Tradition says that the cemetery was divided into sections—a corner for Roman Catholics, a corner for Church of England, a corner for Dissenters and a corner for Negroes. (Many families had slaves or bond servants.)

[2] Despite this, one hundred and fifty families left in the intervening years because of raids and threats of raids.

## Chapter Six
## The New Schoolhouse


### 1773
### Cornwallis Township

Samuel Brewster waited outside until what appeared to be the last of the students had departed. He entered, planning to confront the teacher, but no one was there. "Hello," he ventured, quite softly. When there was no reply, he walked to the front of the classroom, examining everything as he went. *New desks*, he thought, *some of them quite elegant, with glass inkwells and contoured seats.* "Quite elegant," he said.

"Yes, that desk belongs to one of my students, Richard Best." A tall man had come in from the back carrying a bucket of water, which slopped some when he came to a stop. "Obviously, his father provided the . . . best." The man smiled, a trifle smugly Samuel thought, obviously pleased with his own humour.

"You must be the teacher."

The man put the bucket down, slopping more water. "Yes. I'm Cornelius Fox, the teacher. And you are?"

"Samuel Brewster, and I want to get right to the point; you sent my girls home. You said there wasn't a place for them here."

"Lydia, Abigail, and Betty."

"My three youngest."

"You will need to provide desks." When the teacher saw the surprise on Brewster's face, he hurried on. "They don't have to be as elaborate as this one." He quickly moved to the second row of desks, placing his hand on the writing surface. "This type is perfectly serviceable, although the children have to be careful with their ink; there is no recessed inkwell." Brewster still made no comment so Cornelius Fox added, "Two Smith children share this desk for the time being; their father has ordered another desk from a craftsman at Fort Edward."

"I don't mean to be rude, but how was I supposed to know about buying desks for my children?"

"It is the ruling of the Society for the Propagation of the Gospel; SPG, we like to say for short. The SPG ruled that the families . . ."

Samuel Brewster interrupted, "I know about the Society. I know you are their employee, but how was I supposed to know about the desks if you didn't tell me? My children were excited about coming to school and . . . and . . . you sent them home!"

"I was informed that our school's requirements were announced in church." Again, with that smug little smile, the teacher said, "It was announced three weeks in a row. You must have been sick for a long time."

"I wasn't sick!"

"Away, then?"

"You know full well . . ."

"I am newly arrived from Cape Breton, just in time for the school year. I must be excused for not knowing the local"—the teacher searched for a word—"situation."

"We Brewsters are Dissenters. We do not conform."

"Oh. Well. Then you know the Bishop of the diocese is responsible for the school."

"Church of England."

"Yes, Church of England."

Samuel Brewster drew himself up tall, measuring himself against the teacher as if girding for a battle. "You would teach my children to read."

"Yes, I certainly would, but first you have to provide a desk."

"You would teach my children to read so they could be catechized and later confirmed in the Anglican Church."

*This isn't about the desk,* the teacher realized. "You are not concerned about furniture."

"I am concerned about the souls of my children."

"Yes, well, the Anglican Church knows that even Dissenters will risk doctrinal infection of their children when there is no other source of learning but the Anglican School."

Samuel started to say something but the teacher waved him silent.

Cornelius Fox leaned down and picked up the water bucket. Careful not to make another spill, he placed it in the middle of his desk. He gestured at the bucket, "In any school and for many, many reasons, half the children do not complete their learning. Those who stay in the system, who are not spilled out of the bucket," at this moment he lifted the bucket and poured its contents into the large tub sitting on the top of the pot-bellied stove, "are invariably absorbed into the body of the church." He gave the parent what could pass for an apologetic smile. "I'm heating water to wash down my chair and desk." Then, flashing a look of distaste, he commented, "I will have to wash them down everyday until I train the students to keep their grubby hands off my things."

The teacher bent over to check the draft on the stove. "I have seen it before; the church assimilates any student who remains in school long enough to learn how to read." Straightening up, Cornelius rubbed any possible soot from his fingers. "But I believe you were aware of that, weren't you."

Samuel chose not to respond.

Gesturing toward the door, the teacher suggested, "It's so warm with the fire going, why don't we step outside?"

They didn't speak until they were looking out over the sparkling waters of the river and Minas Basin.

Samuel pulled his hat firmly down over his forehead to shade his eyes from the brilliant sun. "My eldest son learned to read and do sums in Connecticut. Since coming here, we have tried to teach the others, but Junior is still the only one who reads."

"And you want them all to read."

"Yes. Now that we finally have a school, I want them all to read." Samuel hesitated before saying, "It might be too late for Alex and Joseph; they are more interested in hunting and fishing."

"Joseph? He's the Acadian orphan."

Samuel greeted the teacher's observation with a long, slow smile. "You do know something about the local . . . situation, don't you?"

"When I saw them together, one son so fair, the other so dark, I had to ask."

Waving the subject aside, Samuel persisted, "I need help. I don't want to add to the Anglican Church bucket—half full or not."

Cornelius Fox gave it a moment's thought. "Indolence is the enemy of learning," he said.

"My girls are anything but indolent."

"Then there's the expense. I receive £10 from the SPG. Your girls could come to my home at Fox Hill if . . ."

"It's called Fox Hill?"

"Some might deem it an affectation but, if that's all I am guilty of, the Lord might forgive me."

"I could pay you a fee."

"£10."

Without hesitation, Samuel Brewster responded, "£3."

"Done!" Cornelius stuck out his hand. "But only three times a week; I must have time for my other interests in the community."

*Outfoxed*, Samuel thought, but held his tongue, not wishing to involve himself in the lowest form of wit. "I understand and I do thank you, sir."

* * *

By the time Samuel was on the path that led across Belcher's cleared land, he was having second thoughts about his agreement with the schoolteacher. His main concern was the reaction he would have from his wife.

*Perhaps Agnes won't really mind. Perhaps she will believe the money to be well spent when she realizes the girls will learn to read without receiving any religious training from those people. But three pounds! Agnes will want to know where we will get the hard money.*

Samuel trudged along for some minutes.

*Perhaps I can have the boys do a little hunting and trade off a regular supply of fresh meat for some of that three pounds.*

He became aware of construction noises from over near the Parade Square.

*Now there's a waste of money! The plans call for a barracks with space for fifty-six soldiers, a good fireplace, tables, chairs, and musket rack—all to the tune of seventy pounds—and they can't get it half done for that price!* "What we needed was a fort, not a fancy barracks with fancy furniture!" After ensuring that he was still alone, he concluded, "I wish I had a piece of that contract." *Then I wouldn't have to worry about any part of the three pounds, since Halifax pays in hard cash.*

When almost within sight of his home, Samuel noticed a young couple walking, side by side, through the little Acadian orchard. Immediately, he recognized the woman. *The woman? That's my little Alice! She's much too young to have a beau! And what in heaven's name is she doing wearing her good dress on a weekday?* "This is too much!" He lengthened his pace so he could catch them up the quicker but they entered the house while he was still coming abreast of Silas Woodworth's place. During the interval, as he hurried along, he rehearsed his objections about this Stephen Hall fellow being seen as a consort to Alice Brewster. "I'll not have it," he concluded.

He scraped his boots off at the front step. The door, being thrust open, startled him, and he was even more at a loss for words when the same Stephen Hall grandly announced, "Sir, my father has arranged it all!"

The entire Brewster family was gathered at the door as if they had been waiting for his arrival. Samuel Brewster looked from face to face and, finding nothing to guide him, resigned himself to wait for the next pronouncement. It wasn't long in coming.

"My father has arranged for Junior to take ship right here at Cornwallis! In a matter of weeks, Junior will be in Connecticut!"

Stepping through the door, Samuel slipped his coat off and handed it to Joseph to put on the peg. "That's very kind of your father, Stephen. I'm sure that when my dear wife and I have had the opportunity to discuss the matter of Samuel Junior visiting Connecticut . . ."

"Please, Father." Junior pulled the great chair closer and helped his father to sit. "I want to return home. Grandpa isn't well and he needs someone from the family to look after things for him." Junior shook his head. "We can't leave Grandpa in the care of cousins. I'm sure they might look after Grandpa well enough but they wouldn't have our best interests at heart. Matters concerning our money and our family business should be handled by one of us, not by relatives."

Now realizing that there had been family discussions that he had not been a party to, Samuel began to feel that he might be the victim of an ambush. When Alex introduced another subject, he knew he was being subjected to a well-organized campaign.

"Father, Joseph and I want to go to Yarmouth. Captain Turner has several ships sailing out of Yarmouth and . . ."

Samuel's riposte was quick and unerring. "You have no seafaring experience! No sane captain would give you a berth." Instantly regretting his harshness, Samuel sought to soften his position but, before he could speak, Agnes launched a counter-attack.

"The Turners agreed to sign them on." Never meaning to misrepresent the situation to her husband under the eyes of God, she hastened to correct herself. "Actually, Captain Turner was at sea when last we wrote, but his son-in-law, Captain Ring, said he would be pleased to make places for two Brewster cousins."

Without thinking, Samuel countered, "There are not two Brewster cousins!" *What a dumb thing to say!* He cast a quick look at Joseph, checking for the hurt he knew he had caused.

Then Alice took a turn, speaking so quietly and politely that she captured Samuel's attention right away. "Father, we want to give you warning that Stephen's father means to speak to you of an alliance between our families."

"An alliance? If you mean marriage . . ."

"We do, Father, and while Stephen is of age, I might have to wait before . . ."

"You certainly shall wait! No daughter of mine, who isn't even thirteen years old . . ." Samuel faltered in his arguments, waiting for his wife to support him, but when his wife picked up the argument on behalf of the young couple, he realized that his life's partner, knowing how he hated change, had sold him out.

"Alice has matured early, my dear. There can be little reason to keep them apart and advantageous to have her settled with a good man of her choice." Agnes came forward and leaned down so she could speak, softly, into her husband's ear. "We can expect a man of his age to wait for such a proper wife but not for very long."

Samuel Brewster held up both hands. "That's enough!" He stood and faced his wife. "I would like a hot meal, wife." He faced the rest of the family, "You have my permission to go on about your concerns. Please do so."

Agnes signalled with her eyes that the young people should leave the elders alone. When she had placed a bowl of hot stew in front of her man and he had resumed his seat, she drew one of the boxes over to the table and sat down before him.

"I know you will give these requests every consideration."

"Requests?" Samuel Brewster hesitated, considering further argument, but then let it all go with a deep, deep sigh. "That I will, Agnes. In the meantime, you can anticipate that your girls will attend Mister Fox at his home three times a week for their schooling. There is a cost: three pounds."

"I am very pleased, husband."

"I had carefully planned that the boys might provide fresh meat for the teacher as an offset to finding that much hard cash. You, on the other hand . . ."

"I have some money my father gave me." When she saw the look of surprise on her husband's face she added, "It was for an emergency, like going back home to Connecticut if we had to." By her husband's reaction she realized that she might have pushed too far so she let it hang there, waiting for his reaction.

Samuel didn't have anything to say to his wife's revelation.

Emboldened, she pressed home her advantage. "We can pay the teacher his fee and use the rest of the money for Junior's passage home." She waited, but Samuel still didn't comment, so she continued, "There would be enough to get the boys to Yarmouth, where they can learn seamanship from Captain Ring."

Samuel continued eating his stew. He asked for some bread and Agnes got some for him.

"Mister Hall's arrangements are for this Thursday; the boys would have to leave on Thursday."

"Is there some butter?"

"Yes. I'll get you some."

Agnes placed the butter on the table. "It's a little runny," she said. She waited until Samuel had finished buttering his bread before she continued. "Hall's captain friend sometimes makes a stop at Yarmouth to check for unassigned freight. This trip he will enter Yarmouth harbour to let the boys off."

"Why would Hall go to all that trouble?"

"I think Mister Hall is doing this because he expects you to say yes to Alice and Stephen's betrothal."

"He's Church of England, Agnes."

"To tell a Brewster, even a young female Brewster, what church to get married in would be a mistake."

"I know, Agnes." He sighed and then ran his fingers through his hair. "I know, I know."

"I believe it's a compliment that the Hall family consider our Alice a good match for their son given that we are practising Dissenters."

"Best, Belcher, Burbidge, and Starr believe that I am a person of ability." For the first time since he had returned home, he grinned. "Yes, the Cornwallis Clique has come to accept my Dissenter status. You know, my dear, what we have here in Cornwallis is a better social position than the Brewsters were able to achieve during three generations in Connecticut."

Agnes picked up the empty bowl. "Would you like some more, dear?"

"No, thank you."

She wiped the contents of the bowl into the slop bucket. "Did I get the chance to tell you that Joseph Starr is going back to Connecticut on the same ship? Our boys would travel in the company of the major's only son."

"You don't say!" Samuel was searching his pockets for his pipe and pouch.

Agnes found them in his coat and handed them to him. "He's older than our boys by a few years." She went to the fire and selected a taper. Lighting it, she shielded it with her hand as she gave it to Samuel. "He's being sent home for more schooling. The major wants him to know more than just his letters and his sums."

Sucking contentedly on his pipe, Samuel Brewster mused, "Thursday, you say?"

Agnes smiled encouragingly at the cluster of family faces peeking in from the kitchen window. "Yes. We should let Mister Hall know in the morning."

"You are willing to let the boys go?"

"I don't feel we have much choice. Junior is old enough to return home without our blessing."

"I know that. I meant Alex and Joseph."

Agnes' voice choked when she said, "Yes."

"And Alice?"

"We should agree to the union when she is fifteen."

"And tell the Halls that, now?"

"The Halls have already agreed that their Stephen would wait." Agnes tensed and bit her lip but visibly relaxed when she heard her husband's response.

"So be it."

*Three weeks later*

"Why do you want to go this way, Samuel? I don't mean to be bossy but I would much rather go in the other direction, the way we usually go." Dressed as they were in their very best,

Samuel, Agnes, Betty, Abigail, and Lydia made a brave display on a fine Sunday afternoon. "It's not that I am a creature of habit, now mind, but it gets so dusty down High Street. This time of year in particular, Samuel, it's very dusty."

"Well, there's something I want you to see."

"What would that be?"

"From what I just heard, we will most probably find Deacon John Newcombe working on a Sunday."

"My goodness, no!"

"It's the truth! Silas saw him drive his wagon down to his wood lot—Newcombe's little wood lot—the one down behind his barn. Big as life, Silas said. Big as life the man drove his wagon out the front gate and down to the wood lot in full view of the whole community."

Interested now, Agnes walked faster and actually twirled her parasol in anticipation of seeing such an outrageous act on a Sabbath. "I can't believe he would do such a thing! He's a deacon! Of course, he's merely a deacon in the English Church, but even Anglicans have standards of behaviour."

At the Newcombe house, there were several families craning their necks trying to see around the corner of the barn without actually going onto the Newcombe property. Apparently, if a person walked right to the edge of the road and leaned across the rail of the Newcombe fence, a person could see what was going on behind the barn. There was a knot of people doing just that.

As they approached, Agnes and Samuel could hear the general comments being made by the spectators.

"He's working, all right!"

"Saw him myself! He's been unloading that wagon for the last ten minutes. Drove straight in and began taking the wood off the wagon and throwing it to the ground right beside his chopping block."

"Workin' like a Trojan, he is. On a Sunday, too!"

"Shame!"

"Yes. Shame on him!"

Silas broke away from the knot of people and approached the Brewsters. He was smiling.

"What's so amusing, Silas? Seems to me the old deacon is doing himself a lot of harm this day."

"Undoing it would be more the truth."

"What do you mean?"

"Early this morning, Deacon John loaded some wood and drove it up to the house. Took him about an hour to unload and stack it near his shed. When he went into the house, Martha suggested it was time he put on some decent clothes, it being Sunday and all. It was only then Deacon John realized that he had worked on a Sunday. Now he's undoing the work he did on a Sunday."[1]

"I hope someone makes it clear what happened. The way those people are talking, they are angry enough to string him up."

"Yes. I'm doing that. I thought I would start with . . ." Silas got a hangdog look about him as he tried to figure out how to complete the sentence without hurting his friend's feelings.

Smiling, Samuel interrupted, "You thought you would start with the Dissenter family."

"Well, I am Church of England, you know."

"And he's your deacon."

"That's right, Samuel. He's my deacon and he's trying to fix his mistake."

"I wish him well." Samuel touched his hat. "Good day to you, Silas." Samuel took his wife's arm. "Let us proceed now, my dear. Which way did you say you wanted to go?"

"Along High Street would be nice, thank you, dear husband. It's a fine day and, with such an auspicious beginning, I plan to enjoy every moment of our walk. I hope we encounter dozens and dozens of people, English Church people."

"You are being uncharitable, Agnes."

"Be careful not to judge, Samuel."

"You are right, Mistress Brewster. God may judge and he serves up recompense, good or bad."

Agnes Brewster gave a little wave of acknowledgement to a young couple coming toward them. "The Lowdens; they're Anglicans, aren't they?"

"Yes. They considered joining my congregation but . . ."

Agnes was smiling but through compressed lips she whispered, "All the better." She waved again.

Mister Lowden touched the brim of his hat. "I trust you are well?"

"Very well, thank you," Agnes and Samuel said in unison.

"You aren't missing your boys too much?" Missus Lowden touched her nose with a small kerchief. "My! It is always so dusty along here."

"Yes," Agnes replied and then laughed. "I mean, yes, I miss my boys and yes it is always very dusty when it hasn't rained for a bit." Agnes took out her handkerchief, which was larger by half than the one displayed by Missus Lowden and more artistically embroidered. She dabbed at her cheek as she said, "We were just watching Deacon Newcombe load some wood."

Samuel coughed and then said, "He was unloading wood, my dear."

Mister Lowden, instantly alert to the significance of what was being said, allowed his mouth to drop in surprise. His wife, however, carried on in polite conversation, enquiring why watching Deacon John would be of such interest. "Was it a very large amount of wood?" she finally asked.

Obviously uncomfortable, Mister Lowden growled, "The Brewsters are saying the deacon is working on the Sabbath."

"Oh dear me, no!" Agnes put her hand out to touch the other woman's wrist as a gesture of understanding. "It was explained to us that he had already worked earlier this morning and now he was working to undo his work." Twirling her parasol, Agnes fluttered her eyes as she looked up at her husband for support. "At least, that is what we were told as we passed by. We can't say anything for sure since we weren't able to see the deacon loading . . ."

"Unloading," Samuel corrected.

"Unloading or loading, we weren't able to see what he was doing from the road and we certainly didn't mean to intrude on the man it being a Sunday."

"Good day, sir, Missus Brewster." This time Mister Lowden lifted his hat and gave a stiff inclination of the head to the other couple.

Samuel returned the salute while Agnes continued speaking to Missus Lowden. "Usually, my husband would have helped Deacon John with such a large load, but it being a Sunday . . ." She didn't stop until the Lowden's were out of earshot.

Samuel, in an exasperated tone of voice, cautioned his wife, "If we meet anyone else, I don't want you to do that again."

"Oh? Why not? I didn't exaggerate, or tell any falsehood." Her husband's dark looks led her to change the subject. "Isn't that an imposing building? That must be the new barracks. Really, we come this way so seldom. There is certainly a lot of development going on and it's just around the corner from us." Her husband still silent, she continued, "I count seven windows in the front. Are there soldiers in there, right now?"

Samuel grunted.

Agnes put her hand on her husband's wrist in the same sort of gesture she had tried on the Lowden woman. "You aren't mad at me, not in front of the children." She squeezed his arm and whispered, "They shouldn't hear you ignore my question. Besides," she continued more loudly, "the girls would like to know when the soldiers are coming." She smiled at the family. "Wouldn't you, ladies?"

On the way back to the house, Samuel explained that completion of the building had been delayed because the contractor had to seek approval for more funds from Halifax. "That always takes a long time."

"Why is that, Father?" Abigail was an inquisitive young lady and easily impressed with the flash of the uniforms of the regulars.

"Pettifoggery! Anyway, it will be a while before we will have soldiers billeted here . . . at least at the rate they are going."

Lydia pointed ahead toward the house. "Look!"

The mother corrected her daughter. "It is never polite to point, Lydia."

"There is someone sitting in the shade of our tree."

It was true. A person had been sitting with his head resting in his arms. He had raised his head and, when he saw the approaching family, he stood up. He looked frail and leaned on a cane. He waved.

Samuel couldn't believe his eyes. "Richard Bourgeois!" he exclaimed.

"Dear Lord, no!" Agnes prayed. "Let it not be, Lord. Please, let it not be."

## Endnotes

[1] One morning Obadiah Newcombe harnessed his team and brought a load of wood to his house. When he realized his mistake—he had worked on a Sunday—he reloaded the wood and hauled it back to the woods. *The Port Remembers.* I told the story under the proper family name (as I have tried to do with all of the stories) but, in this case, I changed the generations placing the story in the time of John Newcombe.

*Chapter Seven*

*1774*
*New London*
*Connecticut*

"It looks like porridge." Joseph Bourgeois stuck his finger in the cold, grey mash at the bottom of the tin cup and then, tentatively, licked what stuck. "Doesn't taste like anything in particular."

"At least it's better than the rotten fish we've been getting."

Joseph handed the cup to Alex. "You eat it, then. I'm going to wait for the rotten fish."

Alex Brewster made a swipe at the contents with three fingers. Scrunching up his eyes as he inserted his fingers into his mouth, he sucked and then swallowed very quickly. Shrugging, he wiped the cup clean and picked up the second cup. He offered it to Joseph. "Sure you don't want any? It's bad . . . but better than nothin'."

Joseph pushed the cup away.

Keys rattled in the prison's door. Nineteen prisoners turned to face the entrance. After some delay, the door finally opened, making a squeeling sound as it swung on its rusty hinges. An officer of the Revolutionary Militia entered, closely attended by two soldiers holding their muskets and bayonets at the ready.

"Stand back!"

The prisoners, some of them sailors from the impounded ship *Shirley Anne*, out of Yarmouth, Nova Scotia, did as they were told, all except one man, Captain Ring. He stepped forward.

"We are neutral in your quarrel with the king. You have no legal right to hold my ship and cargo."

The American officer pointed. "And who might you be?"

"Captain George Ring. You have taken my ship and hold my men in unlawful custody. I demand . . ."

"Your ship has another officer?"

A big man with a swollen face moved to stand beside his captain. "I'm mate."

"I see you've already caused some trouble." The officer motioned to the armed guards. "Take them both away."

Both Ring and the mate made motions as if to resist but several stiff thrusts of lowered bayonets forced them to obey. The soldiers herded the two Nova Scotians out the door, which was then slammed shut. Ever hopeful, Joseph went over and gave the door a tug. It held firm.

Alex ate the rest of the grey stuff from the second cup. "What was that all about?" he asked as soon as he had finished. He tossed both cups into the pile of eating utensils in the corner of the big room. "Why'd they take away our captain?"

"Separate the goats from the sheep and the sheep'll be easy t'handle." The man known as Cookie saw the questioning look on Alex's face so he put it in other words. "They takes away our leaders. The Yanks are goin' t'get us to do somethin'. Maybe they'll want us to join the rebel navy, eh?"

Joseph sat down, his back against the wall. "I just want to go home," he sulked. "I'm not interested in their bloody fight." He looked around for agreement.

Cookie was going to say something but Alex spoke up first.

"The captain's right! We're neutral; besides, nobody can stand up to the Brits for very long." Alex allowed his back to slide down the wall until he was sitting alongside the friend he had come to think of as his brother. "And, when we go home, I won't fight against Connecticut." Alex looked around at the faces of the other men. "My grandfather and brother live in Connecticut." He grinned. "I can just imagine what they'd say if I took up arms against them."

Cookie joined the boys on the floor. He pulled out some chew tobacco and cut himself off a piece. He handed the knife and the tobacco plug to Alex. "Want some? I got more in me boot."

"No, thanks, Cookie." He handed the plug back to the ship's cook. "Me and Joseph don't use it. They didn't take your knife?"

The keys rattled in the lock.

"Someone's comin'!"

Cookie hid the tobacco and the knife.

The prisoners formed a semi-circle, all facing the entrance. They remained silent while they waited. Whoever was handling the keys made several tries before he got it right and the door squawked open. This time it was a naval officer followed by a half-dozen sailors carrying blankets.

"I present the apologies of the United States, gentlemen. I gathered up blankets as soon as I heard that friends were being kept under lock and key. Tomorrow, I assure you, we'll have better food for you." The officer waited while the blankets were handed out, one to each prisoner. "Tonight, I want to offer you the chance to get out of this old barn."

"Just give us back our ship." It was Cookie. "We was deliverin' corn to the docks of New London accordin' to contracts signed . . ."

"The United States is at war with the tyrant King George. Contracts don't mean a thing when you fly the English flag and you enter an American port."

"We didn't know a war was on! You didn't give no warning."

The officer smiled. "English ships are fair game."

"We're from Nova Scotia. We're not English! Some of us were born here, in Connecticut."

"That's what I want to hear!" The naval officer signalled to a soldier on the outside who entered with a small table and a bench. "The sergeant will take your names and add them to the rolls. Just sign your name or make your mark and you can leave this musty old building. There's hot food, a good bed, and a bounty of three dollars for any patriot who is willing to step up to defend Connecticut against the tyranny of the English king."

There was a buzz in the room as little groups of men discussed the offer. Joseph, however, didn't need to talk it over with anyone. "I thank you for the blanket, sir, and I bid you good night." He wrapped the blanket around his shoulders and sauntered off to the corner of the barn. Balling up his hat and jacket, he settled down next to the wall. "You coming, Alex?"

"You bet!"

Pointing his finger at Alex's back as he walked away, the officer raised his voice. "For those gentlemen who do not take advantage of our offer, please understand that we will certainly attempt to arrange a prisoner exchange." A look of smugness flitted across his face as Alex turned to face him. "Yes, we'll be doing that as soon as we can . . . but it might be years and years before we come to discuss terms with the English. In the meantime . . ." The officer paused, taking the time to make eye contact with as many of the prisoners who would meet his glance. "In the meantime, you will be locked up and fed whatever we can spare."

Alex lifted his chin as he claimed, "We are neutral." Then, raising his voice and using the same authoritative tone the officer had used, he flatly stated, "You want to fight a revolution; we want no part of it. We have family here and family with the English. We aren't going to fight against family— neither one side nor the other."

The officer's face turned red, but he persisted with his arguments. "We fight a war of independence! We fight to make our country free!"

It was Alex's turn to pull the blanket around his shoulders and settle down by the wall. "You fight the British Empire. Good luck!" He squirmed around until he faced the wall. He stayed facing the wall until he heard the keys jangling on a soldier's belt as they marched away. It was only then that Alex looked around to see if anyone had accepted the American offer. No one had.

Joseph, puffing up his ball of clothes into a better pillow, asked, "Do you think he will keep his promise?"

"About arranging a trade with the English?" Alex sat up and took his jacket off. He rolled it into a ball and put it down where his head would be.

"No. About getting us some hot food tomorrow."

"He didn't say hot food."

"Yes, he did."

"No, he said better food, didn't he, Cookie?"

Cookie sighed. "They's goin' to keep us here 'til we signs the muster roll."

Joseph, burying his head in his pillow, kept his eyes open long enough to say, "I'd even settle for some of that grey mash. I wish you hadn't eaten my share, Alex." He closed his eyes and, shutting out the prisoners' nattering, promptly went to sleep.

### *Three days later*

Eleven prisoners formed a semi-circle as the keys rattled in the lock. Cookie moved to the front.

"I'm gonna ask 'em for some t'baccie. Long time since I had a chaw."

Joseph scratched at his crotch. "I'm going to ask to go down to the river and get cleaned." He looked around at his fellow prisoners. "I think you guys need a good wash more than I do, and I need one bad." He grinned when he received a couple of solid pokes in the side and back.

It was Alex who warned them that they were falling into the trap the Americans had set. "When they find out what you want, they will offer it to you for your signature. Tell them nothing, eh? Ask for nothing."

The door opened and a tall man, arms tied behind his back, was pushed into the barn before the points of several bayonets. As soon as the newcomer felt the pressure of the bayonets removed from his back, he turned and gave the Americans a small bow. "I can't say how much I have appreciated your company, gentlemen. Now, if you would be so kind, remove my bindings."

The prison door slammed shut.

Pivoting, the man faced the semi-circle of scruffy faces. "I see their hospitality is no better in here." He wiggled his arms. "Someone please have a go at these knots."

Cookie took his knife from his boot and made quick work of the ropes.

The new man grasped Cookie's wrist. "You have a knife, eh?"

Cookie was very quick to respond, "You have t'baccie?"

"My name is Joseph Starr." He reached into the breast pocket of his shirt and pulled out a plug of tobacco. He held it up where Cookie could examine it but didn't let go of Cookie's knife hand.

"Right," was all Cookie had to say as he reached for the tobacco.

Joseph Starr let go of the plug of tobacco and grasped the blade, giving it a little toss so that he had the knife by the handle. "A sailor's knife. Are any of you sailors?"

Cookie, his mouth full of tobacco answered, "Seven of us are from the *Shirley Anne*, outa Yarmouth. Them four are from a coastal cutter that was in the harbour when we was."

"Are there any other prisoners?"

"Our captain and mate was taken the first day. Six others gave up and signed muster papers."

"How long have you been here?"

"Four or five days, I dunno for sure."

"Is that your ship at the pier?"

"Brigantine? Flyin' the Jack?"

"She's flying the revolutionary flag now."

"That'd be our ship."

Joseph Starr motioned for all of the men to join him in a huddle as far away from the prison door as they could go. He whispered, "They mean to keep us here until we sign up or rot."

"Damn!"

Starr looked at the speaker. "I know you. You shipped out with me last year."

"Alex Brewster and this here's Joseph."

"I thought I recognized you. Your father is the Dissident preacher at Cornwallis. I'm the son of Major Starr." Joseph Starr did not acknowledge the Acadian.

Alex didn't notice the slight. Nodding his head he said, "Yeah, your Pa sent you to Connecticut for some fancy learning. What brought you here?"

"When the Americans held the draft for the militia, my name came up because I was born in Connecticut. I told them I was a Nova Scotian and refused to serve." Starr moved his hands wide in a gesture of helplessness. "What happened to you fellows?" For the first time Starr included Bourgeois in the conversation.

"Me and Joseph took ship out of Yarmouth. One of our ports of call was New London. The Americans met us at the pier with guns. We didn't have a chance to get away."

Joseph, used to the incivility of a number of the Planter families in Cornwallis, accepted the inclusion as a sort of apology. "They were nice to us for a while and then dumped us in here." Joseph smiled at Starr. "It's nice to see someone from home."

The three of them shook hands.

Cookie, a trifle impatiently, complained, "Now you got that outa the way, why are we standin' here in the corner? What do you have in mind, eh?"

"Escape. I do not propose to remain here long. Have you checked the barn to see if there is a way out of here?"

Most of the men shook their heads negatively. Cookie said, "Just a quick look. Nothin' that I could see."

"While it's still light, I suggest that we push and kick at every board and examine every crack in this barn to see if we can find a way out of here."

"Then what?" Cookie asked.

"Then we'll see." Starr pointed at Joseph Bourgeois. "You look agile. Climb up onto those beams. Start your search right at the peak of the roof."

With a saucy flip of his wrist in a mock salute, Joseph said, "Aye, captain!" and off he went, shinnying up the nearest beam.

Cookie put his hands on his hips. Assuming a belligerent stance he challenged Starr, "An' who made you captain?"

"I did." Starr pushed past Cookie and addressed the rest of the men. "Anybody have a problem with that? Somebody else want the job?" He turned around and stared at Cookie. "I will find a way to get out and get you out also, if you will help me."

The men were quick to respond.

"I've had enough of this place."

"Get me out of here? The sooner the better."

"You're the captain, mister."

"Count me in."

Starr waited until the men had settled down. He lifted his head up and watched Joseph Bourgeois as he walked a cross beam near the roof of the barn, teetering as he went. "Don't miss anything, Brewster."

Joseph didn't look down but he replied in a confident voice, "If there's a loose board up here, I'll find it, Captain."

"Good man!" Starr pointed at Cookie. "You take half the men and examine that side of the barn. Alex, you and your team do the other." When it seemed that Cookie still wasn't going to take orders, Starr gave him a stern look. "Hop to it!" Then Starr smiled. "Please."

"Let's get on with it, eh," Cookie said. "Let's do what the captain says."

Starr walked back toward the door. "I'll check the entrance because you just never know about a barn door." While each man went silently about his work, Starr poked and prodded at the prison door. He was the first to report. "Barn doors are meant to keep the weather and wild animals out and domestic animals in, so it should have been easy for us to get past it, but that's not the original barn door. The Americans have replaced the whole structure to make it stronger—except for the hinges, which seem to have been borrowed from the old barn door." He looked around the group. "Any luck?"

"Not a thing," Cookie replied.

"Then we have to dig the bolt out of the wood."

"The hinge bolts?" Cookie asked. "That's three sets of bolts and, even if we could, the Yanks would find out the first time they opened the door. Damn thing would fall on 'em."

Starr shook his head. "No, I had the lock bolt in mind. We dig the wood away from where the lock bolt is. Once we remove the wood, the door will open without the keys."

Cookie nodded his head in agreement. "Maybe we could do it in one night."

"No, not at night. The guards would hear us. It must be done in the day while we make normal noises to hide our work."

Cookie had the idea. "Yeah. We could sing and argue, eh?" He stopped as he thought of something. "But they would see what we was doin'; the gouges in the wood would show up, plain as day."

The men were silent until Joseph spoke. "We can save the wood chips and make a paste of the grey stuff they feed us— that's if Alex doesn't eat it all first."

"Fill in the hole with the paste so the guards won't see our work."

Starr smiled a satisfied smile when he heard the enthusiasm in his companions' voices.

"We can do it!" He lowered his voice. "It's pretty dark now, so tonight we'll have our first singsong. The guards will probably check us out because it's the first time we sing. Tomorrow we start."

*Two days later*

Alex cut away the last of the wood encasing the bolt in the locked position.

Starr pulled on the door to open it but Cookie stopped him. "The hinges! The guards will hear those friggin' hinges from a mile away."

"What'll we do?"

"We need something wet to put on them."

"What about holding jackets over the hinges to deaden the noise?"

Joseph whispered, "Piss. Piss in the cups and pour it over the hinges as we pull the door open."

"Will it work?"

"Got a better idea?"

Several of the men turned away as they filled some cups.

"Here's a cupful. Give it a try. Real slow now, mind."

The door was moved as three men poured liquid over the hinges.

"It's working!"

"That's far enough. We can get out."

"Be quiet!

Alex was the last man to slink past the half-opened door, only to find that the prisoners were bunched up not more than a couple of feet outside. "What the hell!"

"Sh-h-h-h."

Alex stepped to one side to see what the hold-up was. In the moonlight, the plain plank wall seemed impossibly high. "It's a prison yard," he breathed. "I knew there was a wall, but . . ."

"It's so high."

"Twelve feet, I do believe," Starr said in a business-like voice. He walked away from the group, scanning the yard for something or other.

"Spikes all along the top of the bloody thing."

Cookie sighed, "Sharp spikes."

Joseph motioned for the men to follow him. "The captain wants us," he whispered.

Captain Starr had found a rain barrel. "Where's that knife?"

Cookie brandished the knife.

"Careful with that thing," Starr cautioned. He pointed at the bottom of the barrel. "Dig a hole in the side of the barrel to let the water out."

"Aye, Captain."

Alex came out of the darkness dragging a couple of poles.

"Clothes-line poles!" Starr gave Alex a pat on the back. "We, gentlemen, are going to get out of here."

The barrel had been relieved of enough water so the men could tip it on its side and roll it over to the wall where they pulled it upright again. The two wooden poles were stuck into the barrel, their tops achieving the same height as the spikes on the wall.

Joseph was the first to hop onto the barrel but Starr motioned him to come down. "I lead, you follow," he said in a manner that brooked no argument. Joseph obeyed. Starr, using his purchase on the sides of the two poles, climbed to the top and then disappeared from view.

Joseph quickly scrambled up the poles. Reaching the top, he gingerly levered his body over the spikes and lowered himself over the other side. He couldn't see much below him but he heard the captain's whisper. "Feel for the timber I have leaned against the wall. Use it to support yourself before you let go and jump down."

Before Joseph let go, Alex's head appeared before him. "There's a timber below," Joseph explained. "I've got my feet on it—makes it easier—pass it on."

While the rest of the men were scaling the wall, Joseph and the captain made a quick run in the direction of the harbour. As soon as they saw the brigantine, Starr sent Joseph back to lead the men to the wharf. By the time all the men were reassembled, Starr had returned from the ship. "There's no guard 'cause everything's been stripped off her. There's nothing left."

"They wouldn't carry the stuff very far." Alex pointed at the warehouse. "Perhaps we'll find it in there."
Joseph appeared out of the dark with something in his hand. "Found it near *Shirley Anne's* entry port." He held it up for all to see; it was a marlin-spike. Not waiting for any sort of permission or instruction, he used the iron tool to force open the warehouse door. Inside they found *Shirley Anne's* cargo as well as her sails, ropes, halyards, sheets, pulleys, and the like.

Starr gave a grunt of satisfaction. "Everyone carry out the ship's equipment and spread it on the deck. You six men of *Shirley Anne's* crew rig your ship; start with the mainmast fore-and-afters. Leave the square-rig sails for now; we won't have time for them. The rest of you, as soon as the ship's equipment is on board, stack the corn, three bales high, at the bow and at the stern."

Sweat pouring, the escapees worked in the dark of the stuffy warehouse. Only occasionally was there a spoken word.

"What about the anchors?"

"Leave 'em."

"Water casks?"

"No. No way to fill 'em."

"It's getting light outside."

"Move faster."

"I heard somebody whistling, up the lane."

"Leave everything! Get on board the ship."

Before he jumped on board, Starr surveyed his ship. The fore-and-aft sail had been rigged. "That will have to do," he said to himself. "Raise the sail," he whispered. It was obvious that the sailors had not heard him. He grabbed the nearest sailor who was manhandling a bale of corn down the wharf. "Leave it," he ordered. "Board ship and tell them to raise the sail." Starr heard the whistler getting closer, coming down the lane. He ran to the ship and closed the entry port. Turning, he pushed two men forward. "Release all forward lines. Maybe the river current will move our bow away from the wharf."

He leaned over the bulwark and studied the movement of the water. *It might work.* He ran to the other side of the deck and looked at the space between the ship and the pier. *Yes! The bow is moving away from the pier.* He looked skyward. *Gonna be a bright day. Now, if the wind would only freshen.* Almost as an answer to his thought, the morning breeze fanned across his cheek, partially filling the sail.

A boyish voice shouted, "What are you doing? Alarm! Alarm!"

"Release all lines!" Starr watched as a man in a nightshirt ran down the wharf with a musket in his hands.

"Stop! I'll shoot!" he said.

"Take cover!" When Starr realized that several of his sailors wouldn't be able to seek shelter because they were working the ship, he stood tall and waved his arms. "Long live King

George!" he shouted. "Down with the revolution!" He didn't have time for another harangue before he had to duck behind the bulwark to avoid being shot. The musket ball passed through the sail canvas in a burst of cursing from the man in the nightshirt, who realized he had been duped.

Gradually the stern of the ship swung round, the stacked corn bales providing shelter for the sailors working the ship. There were now a dozen or so Americans on the wharf; a constant spatter of musket balls into the bales and through the ship's rigging served to remind the escapees that they could still be stopped by the rebels. Indeed, soldiers could be seen running along Water Street intent on reaching the next wharf that jutted further out into the stream, where their musket fire would be more effective.

Starr could see that the soldiers would reach the end of the next wharf in plenty of time to cause some real hurt. "Sailors stand fast! All other hands, move bales to the port side!"

The first of the soldiers had already raised their muskets, sighting on the ship. They fired.

One of the sailors cursed with pain, but Starr couldn't tell which one it was who had been hurt since none of the men stopped moving. A second burst of musket balls battered the ship and ship's rigging but, by now, the bales were providing good protection and *Shirley Anne* was nobly moving down the Thames River. Very soon she would be in Long Island Sound.

Starr noticed activity on the waterfront of West Mystic, the village opposite New London. There were ships there; would they come out in pursuit? He saw the glint of the sun off eyeglasses, several sets of eyeglasses. Any one of those ships, even the smallest, would be able to catch them up because *Shirley Anne* had been able to raise so little canvas.

"Find a rebel flag!"

The escapees regarded their leader as if he had lost his marbles, not a one of them making a move to obey.

"I need a rebel flag, so they think we are still one of theirs."

The men scurried around the ship, searching for an American flag.

"Keep searching!"

Starr studied the shores of the Thames, watching for signs of naval pursuit until Long Island Point cut off the river from his view.

Cookie reported to the captain, giving Starr a proper Royal Navy salute. "There's nothin' on this ship we can use fer a flag, Captain. Joseph took a ball in the chest but I dug it out."

"How is he?"

"Barrin' he don't go septic, and I've seed lesser wounds go bad, he'll be all right."

"Good."

Cookie turned to go but apparently thought better of it and faced his captain. "Sir, you said you would get out and take us out with you."

"Yes?"

"Well, sir, I'm fer tellin' you that I never really doubted you would."

"How about at the bottom of the twelve-foot wall, Cookie?"

Cookie smiled. "Well, maybe, at the foot of the wall, I had me doubts."

Starr smiled at the man. "Did the boys locate any maps, a compass, anything we can use to find our way home?"

"We has only what we brought on board ourselves, Captain. Nothin' else. And we took a real good look, fer sure."

*And we have no water*, Starr thought. "All right then, I'll take the helm."

"Are we gonna make it home, sir?'

"I'm headin' her east by the sun to get us away from American waters. Then we head for home."

Alex came by at that moment. "God helps them that helps themselves, Captain."

"Right you are, Alex. So see if you can liberate some canvas from somewhere because we need to make a water container.

When God sends us some rain, I want to be able to catch it in something wider than Cookie's mouth."

There was general laughter on the *Shirley Anne* as the Captain's humour was repeated.

Starr set his course. *I'm not a ship's captain and there's no one who can serve as mate. Fine pickle!*

Starr steadied the wheel. "Course set!" he shouted for all to hear. *But they are good men. If they can work this ship, we'll find our way home.* "Cookie!"

From forward came the immediate response, "Aye, Captain?"

"How many ways can you prepare corn?"

Again there was the laughter.

*They're tough. We'll make it.*[1]

*September 1774*<br>*Cornwallis Township*

Alice Brewster stood at the window of the borning room anxiously watching for Stephen to come down the road for his evening visit. *If he doesn't come soon it will be too late for us to steal a few moments alone.* She could hear her mother bustling around in the kitchen preparing the tray for Mister Bourgeois. Any time now, Agnes Brewster would call out and expect her daughter to fetch the tray and take it across the yard where Bourgeois was using Tom Pinch's old quarters in the barn as a sickroom.

*He certainly is a sick old man,* she thought. She had heard the story, a number of times, as the old man had filled in his days by telling anyone who would listen how the English had mistreated him. *According to Bourgeois, he had been assigned to a barracks in Liverpool where he had been . . .*

"Al-ice!"

"Yes, mother." She stole a last look out the window; *no Stephen.* "Yes, Mother, I'm coming." She had heard her mother say that Bourgeois was younger than her father. *That can't be; my father is so hale and hearty, while Bourgeois looks like death warmed over.*

"Please, Alice! I go to all the trouble to make up this tray, I would like him to have it while it is still slightly warm."

Alice entered the kitchen. "I'm right here, Mother."

Agnes smiled at her daughter, a sly knowing smile. "No Stephen tonight?" Before the girl could say anything, the mother gave her instructions. "Take a dishtowel and spread it over the top of the tray."

"I know, Mother. It's not the first time I've taken a tray to Richard."

"It's the first time you haven't had Stephen to carry it for you. There must be great goings-on in the Hall household for him not to show up to help his sweet little Alice." Seeing a pout beginning to form, Agnes hurried on, changing the subject. "And you shouldn't call him Richard; he's not really a friend and certainly not a member of this family."

"He's Joseph's father."

At the mention of dear, dear Joseph of whom no one had heard anything since the beginning of the American Revolution, it was Agnes' turn to pout. "Oh, those boys! They will break their mother's heart if they don't let us know where they are soon."

Now it was Alice's turn to change the subject. "I'll get the towel, Mother." She opened the chest and picked out a hand towel. "This one is larger and will cover the entire tray."

"That's fine, dear."

Adjusting the towel over the tray, Alice asked, "Mother, is Mister Bourgeois younger than Father?"

"I believe he is. Why do you ask?"

"He looks so old."

"He's had some hard times. He's Acadian and should have gone with his people in '55 but he hid out in the woods. Richard Bourgeois would have had an easier life if he had gone when he was supposed to."

"There's a lot of them coming back to Nova Scotia."

"Where they go and what they do is not our concern."

Alice heard the hardening in her mother's voice. Agnes Brewster had always considered the Acadians to be only slightly less of a threat than smallpox or the Micmac—and Alice had heard it all before.

"I'll take the tray now, Mother." She lifted the tray and waited for her mother to open the door for her.

"Thank you, Mother."

"Bring back any dirty dishes you find," Agnes said as she closed the door.

Alice almost dropped the tray when Stephen stepped out from behind the corner of the house. "Lordie! You almost gave me the death, sweetheart! Where have you been?"

Stephen took the tray and kissed his fiancée lightly on the lips after making sure they couldn't be seen from the kitchen window. "Sorry I was late. We have a houseguest, a Captain Hall. I'm not supposed to tell anyone that he's with us."

"Why the secrecy?"

They had reached the door to the barn. Alice grasped the rope handle but didn't pull on it while she asked more questions.

"You must know something about why he was here."

"Well, yes. I overheard some things."

Alice waited but Stephen seemed to be hesitating even more. "You tell me, Stephen Hall, or we won't have any more cuddles, no we won't!"

He smiled down at his sweetheart. "You would miss them more than I would."

"Just try me, Mister Hall." Her words were firm but her voice was filled with entreaty.

Stephen Hall wasn't stupid. In a conspiratorial tone of voice he said, "Captain Hall is a cousin from Maine. His schooner is hidden in one of the little harbours along the Fundy shore. He left his ship and crew while he came over the mountain to see where the Minas sympathies lie."

"What kind of sympathies?"

Before Stephen could answer, a voice from inside the barn made a plaintive appeal. "If someone is there with my meal, would you please bring it in? I'm hungry."

Alice pulled down on the rope handle. The door opened and the two of them entered.

"It's just me and Stephen, Richard. We have your meal."

"Thank you, thank you. I was afraid that I had been forgotten." Richard Bourgeois was sitting on a straw pallet, his back and head propped up with blankets and a pillow. "Even when I worked hard on the roads all day they sometimes forgot to feed me. There was water in the pail but the mice always got whatever bread I had hidden from the night before. Sometimes I had just a drink of water for supper. It was a terrible time. I think the English forgot me on purpose."

"Mother made you some potato soup," Alice moved the spoon around in the bowl, trying to show him the liquid's thickness, "and fresh bread, and some milk, and a couple of apples. We didn't have butter but Mother had some cooking fat. Do you want me to spread it on the bread for you?"

"I took the English oath of allegiance, you know. That's why I'm allowed to come back to Les Mines."

Alice gave Stephen a despairing look. "You told me all that before, Richard."

"Yes, yes, I'm sorry. My English is good, is it not?"

"You have good English, Richard."

"I spoke some English before Mister Brewster took me to Halifax." Richard had picked up a piece of bread but now he put it down as he said, in a small voice, "They put hundreds of us in boats and took us to Boston." He picked up the bread again and held it in front of his mouth. "At least I was told it was Boston but they wouldn't let us go there. We came back to Halifax.[2] Then the English made me walk to Liverpool."

"You should eat your supper now." Alice patted the sick man's hand. "We have to go back to the house. I will come back tomorrow for the dishes."

"Yes. I understand."

Alice knew the answer but she asked the question anyway. "You still have some candle left? Do you want me to start another one?"

"No. I can eat in the dark. Mustn't waste candles. We didn't have candles at Liverpool."

Alice motioned for Stephen to leave. She herself backed out of the room, saying, "I know, Mister Bourgeois. I know."

Once outside, with the barn door closed, Alice was quick to question Stephen. "What did this man from Maine want?"

"Who, Captain Hall?" When he saw that Alice had nodded her head he said, "He wanted to know if the people of Cornwallis Township would support the American Revolution."

"No! What did your father say?"

"The Halls are Tories, I heard my father say."

"Maybe so—all except this Captain Hall from Maine."

Stephen lifted the latch on the kitchen door. "I think my father's sorry he drew a map for the American."

"A map? What in heaven's name for?"

They paused at the door, their conversation not finished.

"Captain Hall told Father he needed a map so that he could find his way back; he promised he would come for other visits."

"Did your father draw a map?"

"Yes. I didn't like the captain's smile when Father told him that the township didn't have any regular soldiers stationed here because the barracks wasn't finished yet."

Alice was cautioning Stephen, "You mustn't tell all this to anyone," when her mother opened the door.

"The door wasn't barred, my dears." Agnes looked sharply at the two of them. "What is it you can't tell anyone, Stephen?"

Alice patted her fiancée's hand. "He's not to tell that I wasn't particularly nice to old Bourgeois when we talked about candles."

"Hmpf!" Agnes waved her hand at the thought, turning away to go back to the fireplace. "Come in, come in, you're letting all the millers in." Over her shoulder Agnes Brewster light-heartedly added, "You have permission to keep family secrets to yourself, Mister Stephen Hall."

## *Endnotes*

[1] Joseph Starr's escape is found in *The Port Remembers* produced by the Port Williams Women's Institute. It makes good reading what with the lock bolt, twelve-foot plank wall, clothes-line poles, marlin-spike, corn bales, irate guards—in fact, everything I needed to make what I hope is an interesting story.

[2] This was not the first time the Massachusetts Legislature had objected to having Acadians dumped in their colony but the first time they wouldn't cooperate with the Nova Scotia officials. The Acadians returned to Halifax at the end of summer.

# Chapter Eight
## Starr's Point

### Spring 1775
### Cornwallis Township

"Let me help you, Joseph."

A very weak Joseph Bourgeois allowed his two companions to lift him from the rower's thwart on the little ferry. He looked up at the pier, the top of which was still some six or seven feet above his head, the tide not yet having reached the flood. "How will I manage that? I can't nearly walk and I won't be able to climb because my chest still hurts."

The ferryman, Samuel Lowden, jangled the coppers the shabby strangers had given him. "It was a hard row, gentlemen. We should have waited for the flood tide when I have a better and quicker crossin'. As it is, I earned my fee bringin' you over before dark as you wanted."

Joseph, discouraged, sat down again. "I can't climb."

Alex Brewster heaved on his brother's arm. "We're almost home, Joseph. Get up!"

The ferryman looked more closely at the bearded faces. He stared into the hollow eyes of the two standing men. "You're not from around here, are you?"

Starr grabbed their stricken friend by the other arm, heaving him to his feet. When the ferryman made no move to help them, Starr growled, "We've killed ten men to come this far."

Alex made as if to draw a weapon from under his jacket. "You want me to do this one, Captain?"

"Get him to give you all his money first. I hate going through the pockets of dead men."

"Aye, Captain!"

"Wait!" Instinctively, Sam Lowden clamped his hand against his hip, protecting his coins. "Please wait!"

Pointing at the ferryman's jacket pocket, Alex snarled, "I know where he keeps it, Captain. I don't much mind lookin' through one pocket."

"No-o-o . . ." Sam hastily grabbed up a coil of rope. "I can rig a seat for the gentleman! We can hoist him up, no trouble at all!" Sam Lowden quickly fashioned a sling around Joseph. "There's a block and tackle in the shed. I can go up and . . ."

Still using his threatening tone of voice, Alex leaned over and whispered in the frightened man's ear, "*We* will go up, Mister—you and me, and I'll go first. We can't have you gettin' excited and tryin' to run away, can we?"

"No, most certainly not. I'm pleased to be able to help you gentlemen."

It only took a few moments and Joseph had been winched up to the pier and the ferryman was rowing hard, back to the Horton shore.

Joseph Starr watched the little boat as it skipped along over the waves. "I'm surprised Sam didn't recognize me. I've spent a lot of money in his Horton grog shop near the ferry wharf."

"Now that you mention it, Captain, you look the worse for wear," Alex said. "I'm not sure our mothers would know us after all this time we've been on the road." Alex put his arm around the other Joseph's shoulder. "And you didn't think we could bring you through, brother."

Slowly they walked up the incline toward Major Starr's house. As they were passing the little cape cod house that Colonel Burbidge had built, Bourgeois staggered, only being saved from a fall by his companions' support.

In a weary voice, Joseph pleaded, "Couldn't we go in here, get some help from Burbidge?"

Alex gave Starr a knowing look while saying, "Colonel Burbidge would be the last person we could ask for help; he knows I'm a Dissenter and he thinks you're an Acadian."

Brewster and Starr felt the strength come back to Joseph's legs as he stood taller and took a broader step.

"I *am* Acadian. I can do this." He kept on walking.

When they reached the edge of the Starr property, the brothers stopped. Joseph Starr turned around. "What are you waiting for? Come on. My family will be glad to see my friends."

"We're going to rest here on this stump and listen to the sounds of celebration for return of the prodigal son." Alex waved Starr on. "Go ahead. They're going to be too excited to bother with the likes of us."

Joseph Starr didn't argue. He staggered to the front door and knocked. In the semi-darkness, the brothers watched. It looked as if Major Starr himself had opened the front door and had, just as quickly, closed it.

Joseph Starr stood there, staring at the closed door. When he came back down to the stump, Alex got up to make a place for him but Starr motioned that Alex should remain seated.

"The old bugger told me to take myself to the servants' door where he was sure someone would look after me." Joseph Starr shook his head. "I guess I don't look prosperous enough."

Alex rose. "Do you want us to go with you?"

"No." Through their leader's beard and dirt the brothers could see the mischievous grin. "I've always done what my father told me. No sense stopping now." He patted both young men on the shoulders and went around to the side door of the house. Alex and Joseph could hear the knock and the quiet voice of Joseph Starr begging for something to eat and a night's lodging.

Joseph Starr knew the old Negro slave woman; she had been his nurse when he was a boy. He made his plea for food and shelter but the woman seemed to hesitate, taking a long time to make the reply.

Starr put his hand out to the door frame to steady himself. "Your Master said I would be looked after if I came to the side door. Please, may I come in?"

The old woman backed into the kitchen and sat down near the chimney while another slave got some food and drink for the disreputable-looking white man. The nurse watched him, not saying anything, but not taking her eyes off him. When Joseph Starr smiled at the serving girl, the old woman jumped up and ran into the parlour.

"Massa Joe," she cried. "It's Massa Joe! I know 'cause I seen him smile!"[1]

The brothers listened for a while to the celebrations. They could hear the story being told: how they had brought the *Shirley Anne* back to Yarmouth where they were treated like heroes, how they had walked as far as Annapolis where Joseph's wound had turned septic, forcing them to stop and seek work to pay for shelter over the winter, and how, in the spring, as soon as Joseph was well enough to travel, they had set out on the Old Military Road for home.

The boys knew how the story would end so they resumed the trek up the hill, past the Woodworths' farm to the Brewsters' door. It was here the boys separated, each standing alone, deep in his own thoughts, preparing himself for when the door would open to their pasts.

A dog barked and the door was thrown open. Standing in the light of the doorway, Joseph swayed and held his hand out toward the person framed in the portal.

Perhaps Agnes Brewster didn't see the second figure in the darkness. Perhaps she only had eyes for Joseph, the little boy she had saved from the English that day at Starr's Point. She certainly didn't think of the possible consequences as she flew into Joseph Bourgeois's arms, closing her eyes tight against the world that had inflicted such obvious injury and pain on his young body.

Several heartbeats later, Samuel Brewster came to the door and saw the dejected figure standing off to one side, arms hanging uselessly at his side. "Welcome home, son," he said, extending his hand in salutation. "Welcome home," he repeated when the boy failed to acknowledge his father's presence but continued staring at Joseph and his mother.

The father turned around and shouted to the family inside the house, "Alex is home! Joseph is here!" A flurry of females cascaded out the door, filling the farmyard with the chattering and excitement of a happy reunion.

Joseph Bourgeois's body stiffened when he heard the shaky voice from the barn.

"Son! Is that you?"

Joseph pulled Agnes' arms from around his neck. "Father? You're here?"

"Yes. I am in Tom's old room!"

Joseph disappeared into the barn.

The Brewsters stood in a group around the golden light from the open door, listening to the sounds of sobbing coming from the barn. Occasionally they could hear the familiar words, "They made me walk to Liverpool . . . sometimes they didn't feed me . . . I worked hard all day on the roads . . ."

When Richard Bourgeois came to the part where he had taken the English oath and the Bourgeois would now live anywhere they wanted, Agnes Brewster stalked into the house, slamming the bedroom door behind her.

Samuel and the girls brought Alex into the kitchen, where they tended to his sores and wounds, cleaned him up, and made sure that he was well fed before he went to bed for the night.

Joseph Bourgeois stayed in the barn with his father. For the remainder of his time at Cornwallis Township, he did not enter the farmhouse, taking his meals at the barn and only mingling with the family in the yard or in the fields.

*Summer 1775*
*Cornwallis Township*

Alexander Brewster sat on the front step, whittling a peg out of a piece of maple wood.

His sister Abigail had been sitting with him, reading from the Bible, showing him how much she had learned with Mister Fox as her teacher. She had been pestering Alex, asking him why he wasn't going with his sisters to the Fox house three times a week, so he could learn to read and do his sums. She had been nagging at the young man for so long that Agnes had finally gotten up from her sickbed and come to the door, shooing the girl away to give Alex some peace.

Alex walked to the barn, where he tried the peg in the sea chest he was making. He checked his measurements and decided it was time to give the peg a turn or two on the foot-driven lathe. He was searching for a half-inch chisel, when he thought he might have heard something in Tom's old room.

He peeked in; pigeons were fluttering around some crusts of bread the old man had tucked out of sight near the window. As he shooed the birds away, he spoke in falsetto, "Why don't you go to Mister Fox's house; learn how to read and do sums?" With the edge of one hand he wiped the crusts and crumbs into the palm of the other and carried the mess outside, where he dumped it on the ground. It was then he noticed the Bourgeois father and son coming up the hill as fast as they could move. *Didn't think the old bugger could walk that fast. Joseph's been doing a good job nursing Richard back to health. I wonder what's wrong, though. They seem to be quite agitated. They're shouting something . . .*

"They're all gone!"

"Who's all gone?" When they didn't answer, Alex thought, *they must be winded from their running. Can't be anything too important or Joseph would have come on ahead.* Alex took the time to place the peg on the barn's workbench before going down the hill to meet them. He happened to look back at the house over his shoulder; *there's someone in the window. Mother!* Somewhat bitterly, Alex corrected himself. *Agnes. The woman known as Agnes Brewster is checking to see if there is anything wrong with her most favoured son.* He turned away. *Dear God, I can't help myself. I have shared much with Joseph but I am so jealous of the favour he has found with my mother.*

Joseph seated his father on the edge of the horse trough and then ran on up the hill. "I followed the trail, Alex! The cattle have been driven off. Probably over to the other side of the mountain."

"Slow down a little, Joseph. Who . . .?"

"I don't know but, by the tracks, they are a great party of men. They also broke into Stephen Chase's storehouse and plundered it of anything worthwhile."

"What about our cattle on the dyke?"

"Gone. There's nothing left on the dyke. The pirates took 'em all. Drove 'em to the other side of the mountain."

The assembly bell rang at the stockade. Samuel Brewster came out of the house, tucking his shirt into his trousers as he hurried along. "Come on, boys. Must be some sort of emergency!"

"What about Richard?" Alex pointed down the hill at the tired old man sitting on the edge of the trough. "We can't leave him there."

"The women will see to him. We must hurry."

On the way to the little fort, Joseph told Samuel about the stolen cattle, about the ransacked storehouse, and about the tracks leading over North Mountain. At the stockade, men were still arriving, all of them incensed by what seemed to be a random act of piracy. The excited and angry buzz of the crowd quietened to nervous shuffling when Colonel Burbidge walked over to the foot of the flagstaff. Even that noise was stilled when he raised his arms for attention.

"I have news from Halifax." The Colonel lowered his arms. "The governor means to introduce a Militia Act calling for the raising of one thousand volunteers to defend our fair province against the blag'ards and hooligans of the so-called revolutionary states."

Silas Woodworth, who had lost cattle off the same dyke as Samuel Brewster, interrupted what might have become a speech. "Where would this militia levy be located?"

"The men would be assembled at Halifax and be used in defence of our capital."

Some unidentified farmer at the back of the throng muttered, loud enough to be heard at the front, "Fat lot of good that will do—our sons at Halifax and the pirate bastards here, stealin' us blind."

Samuel stepped forward. "Last night thieves took all my cattle. Why isn't the local militia out chasing them down?"

Colonel Burbidge had a ready answer. "They appear to be a superior military force. I have intelligence they posses an armed schooner and several whaleboats. If we send our militia in pursuit, they could appear behind us, pillaging our homes, ravaging our families. I do believe that they will not attempt to winter in the Fundy but retreat to wherever they came from. Bearing in mind that the barracks may be finished next season, we could soon expect to have a company of regulars right here in Cornwallis Township."

It seemed the appropriate moment for Major Starr to support his commander. "The regulars know how to defend their post. The thieves won't soon return to Cornwallis Township."

There was no rebuttal from the men.

The question of some stolen cows having been settled, the colonel went about doing his service to his king.

"Meanwhile," he said with a grandiose swing of both arms, "we must turn our province into a bastion of the British Empire. Once the Military Act is passed, recruiters will travel to each of the townships seeking volunteers for the levy."

"To be used against our cousins, our brothers?" It was that same disgruntled-sounding voice from the back. "Our New England relatives might have an argument with King George but it is nothin' to do with us, eh, fellas?"

Silas Woodworth nodded his head in support but it was Samuel Brewster, the Dissenter, who spoke next. "Almost all of us were born in New England. We have brothers, fathers, and sisters in that country. We bear a natural affection to our nearest relations and we also mean to continue to bear allegiance to our king. The only way in which our wives and children can be in any tolerable degree safe is for us to remain neutral."

"Neutral!" Scorn dripping from his voice the colonel repeated, "Neutral! I have never heard such balderdash. We must fulfil our duty to King and Country."

Silas Woodworth looked around him for support before speaking. "We mean neither disaffection to King George nor aid and friendship to the Americans. We mean to remain neutral during this fratricidal dispute. It's the safest way to protect what is ours."

"Ten days ago the Americans invaded this country, capturing and burning Fort Fredrick at the mouth of the Saint John. We're next."

"I don't believe it." Silas Woodworth voice shook with anger as he challenged the colonel. "You just made that up."

"No, Silas." Captain Belcher put his hand on Silas' shoulder. "You know I wouldn't mislead you, neighbour. The Americans are on the move. They mean to come here. They will pillory anyone who doesn't give them support."

Colonel Burbidge added in a very solemn voice, "And the king will search out those who are not loyal to the Crown, brand them as traitors, and banish them from this realm forever." He lifted his chin and surveyed the crowd, forcing some to look away when subjected to his direct stare. "On that I can promise you."

"Captain Belcher said the Americans are coming here." Not the least bit cowed, Samuel met Colonel Burbidge's eyes without flinching. "Why would he say that?"

"It is widely touted by the Americans that they plan to come here, to the heart of Nova Scotia, and capture Fort Edward. Once they have put all Tories to the sword, they expect to have the support of the remaining populace and march on to the destruction of Halifax."

"And you said *we* are speaking balderdash!" Samuel turned on his heel and marched out of the stockade, but not before saying, "New Englanders will not come here to do us harm. They will recognize our neutrality and so must the king."

More than half of the men of the township followed Samuel out of the stockade.

Samuel, Joseph, and Alex walked in silence along the track. Looking ahead, they could see that Richard Bourgeois had not been taken care of by the women. They hurried along to the old man and helped him to his feet.

"What was the meeting about, Samuel?" Richard was standing but he was obviously unsteady on his feet. Samuel slipped his arm around Richard's waist. "Let me help you," he paused but then continued, "old friend."

"Tell me what the meeting was about, Samuel. Was it about the cattle?"

"The colonel isn't going to do anything about our cattle. The colonel expects us to take up arms against New England."

"Are you going to?"

"No. We told him that we would not fight against our fellow New Englanders nor would we ever take up arms against the king. We intend to remain neutral."

Richard Bourgeois stopped walking. "You told the king's man that you would remain neutral?"

"Yes." Samuel tried to get Richard to move along but Bourgeois resisted, wanting to clarify what was meant by "neutral." "As I understand you, you do not want to fight against the intruders but, at the same time, you prefer not to serve your king." Before Samuel could say anything, Richard Bourgeois laughed himself into a coughing fit.

Samuel waited for Richard to catch his breath.

Despite his rasping breath, Richard declared, "We tried to do that and look what happened to us."

"Us?" Samuel didn't quite understand what Bourgeois was saying. "Who do you mean by us?"

"I mean the Acadians. We said we were the Neutral French but the French King's man ordered us to fight against the New Englanders. Just like you, we said that we preferred to remain neutral. Then the English King's man ordered us to pledge allegiance to him. We said we would be loyal but that we wouldn't fight against our own kind; we refused to bear arms against the French."

"It isn't the same."

"Tell me what is different." When Brewster didn't respond, Richard continued, "You believe being neutral is the only way to protect your possessions and families. It won't. You must not remain neutral when the fighting is going on around you, or you will end up like the Acadians. Like us, you will be no more."

*November 1775*
*North Mountain*

"Ah, there you are. You left early this morning, Joseph. I had to follow your trail to find you."

Joseph had watched Alexander Brewster come up the track behind him, but now he turned his head and looked out over the valley below. "It's a wonderful view from here." Idly swinging his legs back and forth over the edge of the ledge, Joseph picked up a reddish brown maple leaf and tossed it into the breeze, watching it flutter down, down toward the floor of the valley.

"It might reach all the way to the bottom," Alex said as he sat down, dropping his legs over the side of the cliff as well. "No, it's going to get caught up in those pines."

"Yes, there it goes."

The leaf sat for a moment, like a bright bird on the branch, but then it fell from view.

"Gone."

"Yep."

There didn't seem to be much more to say, the young men silently enjoying the warm sunshine that was beating against the southern face of North Mountain.

After a while, Joseph broke the silence between them. "Your mother still down?"

"She hadn't come out of the bedroom when I was leaving, though I heard her coughing." Alex pulled a linen out of his jacket and opened it up. "I took some sweet breads out of the kitchen. They're not as good as Mother used to make." Alex gave Joseph a half-embarrassed smile of apology. "Alice made them. She tries to make them just like Mother used to, but . . ."

Joseph selected a couple of pieces. "I appreciate that." It was his turn to half-smile, "In the barn, my father always squirrels away whatever is left from the evening meal." He shrugged his shoulders. "I couldn't find so much as a crumb this morning."

"You could have come into the kitchen."

"I didn't know if there was anyone awake."

"We wouldn't have heard you, but you never come into the house any more."

There it was, out in the open, the rift between them.

"I don't mean to come between you and your mother."

"You're already there."

"I don't mean to cause any further trouble."

Alex picked up another leaf and tossed it over the side. The leaf blew back into his face. "The wind has changed," he said. Alex pressed his lips together and then blurted out, "She's sick and getting sicker. It would do her some good if you would come into the house to see her—to encourage her so that she might get better."

The changing wind brought fresh sounds from the cleft that provided access from the floor of the valley to the brow of the mountain.

"Men and cattle," they both said, almost simultaneously.

"Maybe it's the Chase brothers." Alex pointed behind them. "The Stephen Chase grant is over near the long beach."

"Listen!"

The brothers could make out the individual voices of the drovers.

After listening for a while, Joseph asked, "How many men in the Chase family?"

"Three; I mean, Stephen has three sons. There could be four men if that's the Chases."

"I make it a dozen."

"Or more."

They both got up.

"What'll we do?"

Joseph, always the one for adventure and devilment, pounded his brother's arm in excitement. "We go see!"

Alex placed a restraining hand on Joseph's shoulder. "Better that we wait until they pass us by. Then we can track them. They won't see us behind the cattle, in the dust."

"Good thinking." Joseph resumed his place on the ledge. He held his hand out to Alex. "Any more sweet bread?"

Alex sat down. "No. That was it."

They sat there enjoying the November sun, the view, and perhaps each other's company, but they didn't have much to say because everything important had been said. When it was time, they followed the trail across the flat of the mountain down into a tiny harbour at the base of a rapidly flowing stream.

"They are Americans." Alex pointed at the schooner; she was flying a rebel flag. "The bastards have built a little pier. Look! They're loading the cattle right onto the ship."

"They must have been operating out of here all summer."

"Might be Cornwallis cattle."

"Or Horton."

"Well, we will never know."

"They seem to be in a great hurry to leave."

"Yes, they're trying to catch the ebb tide."

The two young men watched the activity for a while. When it seemed that the schooner was ready to cast off, Alex suggested they leave so they could get home before dark.

At the top of the hill, just before they crossed the flat top of the mountain, they took one last look at the American schooner as it left the little harbour and entered the Bay of Fundy.

Joseph noticed some other movement on the bay. He stopped and shielded his eyes against the western sun. "It looks like there's a ship near the far shore."

"The Americans haven't seen her yet; they're still heading out into the Bay."

"I bet she's an English patrol ship. I can make out the top-gallants. Might be as big as a frigate. With any luck at all, the Americans will run into her and that will be the end of them."

"Maybe we'll see a battle!"

"No! Look! The Americans are scuttling back. They mean to hide in the harbour."

"If the American captain takes her far enough into the harbour so that she's against the shore, the English won't see the schooner's masts." They watched as the Americans attempted to make the masts disappear into the background of the pine forest by stripping their masts and rigging of as much as possible, leaving the bare wood.

"The tide's falling."

"That means if we want to catch these bastards, we have about twelve hours to get back here with the militia." Alex jumped up. "Let's get going."

"Right."

They had both found their second wind by the time they were running downhill through the mountain cleft; there was no doubt in their minds that they were going to bring the militia back in time to teach the Americans a lesson.

*Two days later*

"I asked my cousin if there could be an American raider in the Bay of Fundy." Stephen Hall took the opportunity to try to steal a little kiss from his Alice.

Alice Brewster pushed her fiancée back. "You didn't tell me that Captain Hall had returned to the Minas!"

"I didn't know myself until he dropped in for supper last night. He said his men were doing some hunting on the north slopes of the mountain; getting in some supplies before heading back to Maine. The snowstorm caught them unprepared for winter. You remember, Alice, that we never had snow this early in Maine."

"I don't remember anything about Maine, Stephen, because I was born here."

"Oh, my, yes." Stephen took his finger and traced the line of Alice's lips as he said, "I don't much remember what it's like in Maine, but it's what my father told me." Casually, he allowed his finger to rest under her chin and applied some pressure to hold her mouth steady while he drew near for another attempt.

"Don't, Stephen. We're in front of one of the windows."

Stephen put his arm around Alice and drew her back a pace or two. "Well, anyway, Captain Hall has been delayed and, he says, it will take them several days to dress the meat and be on their way."

"Did your cousin know about the American raider?"

"Says he hasn't been out on the Bay for at least a month. Prior to that, he'd seen nary a soul."

This time, when Stephen puckered up, Alice let him steal a quick kiss. He was savouring the sweetness of her lips and thinking about trying a little squeeze or two when he saw a figure at the window.

"I think that was your brother at the window."

"Alex doesn't really matter, Stephen, but you had better take the tray." Alice gathered up her skirts and waited for Stephen to open the door for her. He wasn't able to balance the tray and pull up on the latch, so Alice did the honours. "Let's go inside," she said so her mother and father, if they were listening, would hear. "It's too cold to stand around outside." Once inside, she got a knowing look from her brother, but otherwise there was no comment about how long it took them to deliver food to the barn and pick up the soiled dishes.

Father and son were having a discussion about the American raider and the possibility that it might still be there.

Alex was of the opinion that the schooner must have left. The storm that brought the snow would have driven the English warship off station, clearing the way for an easy escape for the Americans.

"Not so," countered Samuel. "The same storm that you believe would have forced the warship off station would have kept the Americans in their safe haven." He shook his head. "They are still there, safe and snug in their little harbour, and Major Starr is correct to wait for more volunteers before mounting an attack."

Alex moved so his sister could join him on one of the pine boxes. He glanced up. "Have you volunteered to come with us, Stephen?"

"Yes. I'm looking forward to it. This will be my first military experience." Stephen placed Alice's coat on one of the wall pegs but he made no move to take off his own winter apparel. "There are some chores I must do for my parents before we leave for the mountain." He bowed to Mister Brewster. "I hope you will excuse me if I rush away, sir." He gave a polite nod to Alex. "Is Joseph coming?"

"I'm afraid I won't know that until we form up at the stockade, Stephen." Alex sadly shook his head. "Joseph doesn't tell me much any more."

"Well, I hope he comes. He's a jolly companion."

Stephen opened the door and stepped out into the cold night air. He was having difficulty pulling the door closed over some ice that had formed on the threshold.

Alex hurried over to give him a hand. "See you in the morning," he said, as the door was finally closed.

Samuel Brewster shivered as the blast of frigid air swirled into the kitchen. "You can be sure it's going to be a cold trek to the Fundy shore."

\* \* \*

Alex was finding it desperately cold as he slogged along the rocky shore near the entrance to the small, unnamed harbour. The winds and tides had piled ice cakes crazily from well out into the water all the way up to the tree line, where many trees had been flattened from the weight of the huge pieces of ice. Twice he had fallen into crevices but the men in his party had been able to pull him out. Any forward movement was a nightmare. Alex was beginning to believe that the Americans would never be able to escape along the shore, but the major had said two parties of volunteers were to enter the harbour, one on each side. So be it. He and six men were doing as they were told even if he should become a cripple from his next fall.

Finally, they were at the entrance to the harbour, where there was no sign of the party that was supposed to appear on the opposite headland. Alex was feeling so bruised, cold, and miserable that he didn't worry about the military implications. He waved his men forward, encouraging them to climb up on the huge rocks from where they would have a commanding view of the little harbour.

Standing on the slippery black rocks, he and his men could see the schooner. It had been pulled up the beach, well above the high tide mark, where it could safely spend the winter. Other than the schooner, two small cabins, two dozen exhausted Cornwallis Volunteers, and finally, the errant headland party, there was nothing. There were no Americans, no provisions, no munitions, no whaleboats, and no tracks in the snow leading anywhere but to a well-used latrine.

Major Starr's face was mottled with fury. "They were warned!"

*They loaded everything into their whaleboats and skedaddled while we were trying to surround the place,* Alex thought. He suddenly felt very, very tired. It had been a long, cold, trek through deep snow. The march along the shoreline had been terrible. The Volunteers would destroy the schooner but the Americans could be anywhere, even as Colonel Burbidge had said; they might appear behind them, in Cornwallis, where they could rape and pillage.

The same thought must have occurred to the major. "Burn everything," he said. "Move quickly, men. We have to return to the township as quickly as we can."[2]

Stephen Hall appeared at the doorway to the larger cabin, a piece of paper fluttering in his hand. The desolate look on his face told the story that he had found something truly devastating. He hesitated but finally called out in a faltering voice, "Major Starr!"

Several men looked his way but the major was trying to get his men turned around and started for home. He did not respond.

"Major Starr, sir!" Stephen shouted in a much more vigorous manner, as he became more convinced that he had no choice. He must reveal what he had found.

"What is it, Hall?"

"It was Captain John Hall who has been making the raids."

"John Hall from . . ."

"Yes, sir. He's our cousin. He's been visiting us, off and on, for months now." Utterly dejected at this stage, Stephen held out the paper. "Father drew a map for him . . ."

"What the hell!"

"This is the same map. I found it with other papers and some chewing tobacco that got left behind." *I'm going to get lynched,* he thought.

"Well, son, I can say this much for you . . . you sure have balls to 'fess up right away." He took the map from Stephen. "John Hall was a bloody fine skipper and now he's loose behind us with a gang of thugs and a couple of whaleboats," he said as he dug out his spectacles. In a moment, he crumpled the map and shoved it and his spectacles into his pocket. "The map was a good one; showed John how to get around without runnin' into anyone." Cupping his hands around his mouth, Major Starr shouted to get the attention of his men.

"Listen up!" He didn't wait, but kept right on with what he had to say. "The man leading the Americans is Captain John Hall. He's got a couple of boats and a crew of thugs intent on causing harm in our country. Now, let's burn everything and get back to Cornwallis."

The schooner and the cabins burned well, giving some comfort to the Volunteers for a short while. When they were ordered to move out, there were many gripers and even some laggards among the men who did not have wives or sweethearts to worry about but, finally, Major Starr got the Volunteers moving back the way they had come.

Alex was neither a griper nor a laggard. He did as he was told but he was careful to keep his thoughts to himself. *Deep snow, steep hill, and it's so bloody cold out. Maybe Father is right; we should remain neutral in this fracas and let rebels like John Hall fight it out with Tories like Starr and Burbidge. Maybe Father is right.*

## Endnotes

[1] I first heard this story (the recognition of a young master after years of absence) when I was doing research about Maryland for a later book. "The young massa! It's the young massa. I knowed his smile!" I hadn't planned to use it because the story seemed contrived. This incident that is mentioned in *The Port Remembers* is more plausible and adds to the plot, don't you think?

[2] In actual fact, the Planters did trek over the mountain, surrounded the little harbour but the New Englanders had escaped. The Planters burned everything and returned home.

*Chapter Nine*
*Township Stockade*


*Early Spring 1776*

Major Starr stepped forward so that he was standing on the little raised area at the foot of the flagstaff. "I asked the colonel to call this meeting because . . ."

Silas Woodworth, Samuel Brewster, and John Whidden gave each other a knowing glance and then separated themselves from the listeners and began to thread their way through the crowd to the gate.

"Now wait, men!" Major Starr raised his finger, pointing at Samuel. "Why do you always have to disagree with everyone?"

"Not everyone, Sam, and not all the time. I have heard what you're going to say and I do continue to disagree with you. We chased Captain Hall out of the country last November. He's not here any more!" He's not a threat and why you keep bringing him up, I'll never know!"

Sam Starr was so exasperated that he was almost doing a dance as he prepared to make his point for perhaps the tenth time at township meetings such as this one. It was becoming the comic story of the season: crafty Captain John Hall had hoodwinked dull Major Sam Starr and Starr couldn't stand the thought of it. According to the comic line, come hell or high water, there was going to be a rematch even if it only happened in Sam Starr's imagination.

"I keep bringing it up because I know this man Hall! Because I know he isn't finished with us! Because he will be back!" Starr raised his voice, shouting. "He will be back when the spring tides float your ship, John Whidden!"[1]

John Whidden had been almost out the gate but he turned around and sighed, "One more time, Sam." Slowly, as though explaining something to a child, Whidden went over the situation, point by point. "You know I've been fittin' my ship for sea. My captain says he will crew her in the next few days. Then, with the first of the spring tides . . ."

Starr interrupted, "With the rains, that should be in the next couple of days."

"Yes, I suppose you're right. In the next couple of days, when the higher tides come in, she'll float off and she'll be moved to the pier and take on her cargo."

"Put a strong guard on her. I believe she could be floated tonight and Hall will make a try for her."

"Sam, if you will pardon me, I think that's all nonsense. We haven't seen hide nor hair of Hall since we burned his ship and his camp. He's left the country, Sam. I can't see myself sittin' out in the rain, babysittin' a ship . . ." John Whidden looked around to see where sympathies lay and was encouraged by what he saw. "I don't expect to see John Hall on the beach . . ."

"Why not!"

"Because he can't be in two places at once. He can't be on the beach stealin' my ship and in your imagination pesterin' you to distraction." Whidden joined the flow of men out the stockade's gate. "You can sit on the beach if you have a mind, Sam; just don't shoot yourself. That would sure upset your wife."

In short order, Major Starr was alone in the stockade. Actually, he was not quite alone because his son Joseph had stayed behind.

Sam finally noticed his son. "Do you believe me, Joseph?"

"Father, the man has gone back to Maine. He wouldn't stay here over the winter. What would he live on?"

"Maybe so, maybe not." Major Samuel Starr seemed to take his son's comments under consideration but, suddenly, he clenched his fist and raised it against his unseen foe. "John Hall came to Nova Scotia with a ship, and he means to go home with one." Starr lowered his arm. "I know it! I just know it!"

"Father . . ."

Starr turned on his heel and stormed out of the stockade. "He'll not have that ship! I'm going to guard her myself."

\* \* \*

The rain had finally found its way through Alex's clothing, trickling down the middle of his back. He shivered. "Oh! It's bloody cold!"

Joseph Starr gave a soft laugh. "Buck up, me hearty! 'Tis better sittin' here in pleasant company than walkin' me plank! Har!"

Starr didn't make a very convincing pirate but Bourgeois went along with the humour. "Aye, Cap'n, but I'd be just as wet." Bourgeois was going to say something else but a flash of lightning and the almost immediate crash of thunder made him duck his head. "Mother of God!" He cringed as another lightning strike seemed to light up the whole sky and everything beneath.

Joseph Starr took the opportunity to check the area. He could see Whidden's boat, *Emily*, safe in her cradle, the incoming tide lapping at the supports. "Maybe tonight's the night, boys!"

"You think Hall will come?"

When Major Samuel Starr's son didn't answer, Alex poked him with his elbow. "What did you mean, tonight's the night?"

After some more hesitation, Starr replied, "My father was right; tonight's one of the nights when Whidden's ship could be floated off."

Bourgeois, sounding a bit annoyed, confronted his leader. "You don't believe your father! You don't think Hall is coming tonight, or any other night."

Alex wiped the rainwater from his eyes as he moved over so he was nose to nose with Starr. "You suckered us into coming out here in the rain!"

Starr put his finger to his lips, cautioning Alex to be quiet.

In a very forceful whisper Alex said, "You said we had to provide backup for your Pa and that he shouldn't have to face the Americans all by himself."

In the flash of lightning, the boys could see that Starr was nodding his head.

Joseph didn't wait for Starr to reply. "Even your pigheaded father didn't come out in this rain! We're going home."

Alex and Joseph got up but Starr reached over, touching each man's arm in pathetic entreaty. "What if Father is right?" When the two men didn't respond, Starr grabbed each of their jackets. He jerked hard, bringing them down; Alex lost his balance and fell to one knee in the muck.

"Damnation!"

"If Hall is ever going to come, he will be here in the next hour." Starr extended his arm to give Alex a lift up out of the mud. "Sorry about that," he said.

"My knees were the only dry spots." Alex took advantage of another lightning flash to check the look on Bourgeois's face. What he saw there encouraged him to say, "We'll stay, eh, Joseph?"

Bourgeois sat down again on the chunk of cordwood he had been using as a stool. "If your father comes," he began but thought better of it, so he started again. "When your father comes, where will he position himself?"

"Methinks he will take cover behind the largest stack of wood; the one down front. That way he would have a clear view of anyone coming along the river shore. I picked this pile because we would be able to give him cover if he had to move back to the next stack."

The three men sat in the rain for the better part of an hour. The line of thunderstorms came and went, the rain let up and then began again, and the cold wind became more or less constant, blowing in their faces. Of the three men, only Joseph Bourgeois wasn't shivering because his father had given him a couple of heated rocks, wrapped in muslinet, to hold under his armpits. Probably because he was a little more comfortable than his companions, Joseph felt quite talkative.

"Now that my father is better, we have to think about what we must do."

"Who's 'we,' Joseph?" This time there was no lightning to show Alex his brother's face, which remained dark and deeply shadowed.

"We received a message that members of the Bourgeois

family have settled in the Miramichi. They sent word that we should join them."

"Sent word?" Starr shared his father's military interest in the activities of all possible adversaries, particularly the Micmac and the Acadians. "How would *you* get word?"

Before Joseph could reply, Alex blurted out, "You wouldn't leave Minas, would you?"

"We have been living off Brewster generosity for long enough. It's time we Bourgeois find space where we can live our own lives."

Starr persisted, "How would you get word here, at Cornwallis?"

Bourgeois was not about to answer Starr. Instead he said, "I'm sorry, Alex. We grew up like family and I . . ."

Alex pointed off into the dark. "There's a person over at the large stack of wood, just where you said your father might come to hide."

The three men stared off into the dark but they couldn't confirm who was now skulking behind the woodpile. They waited. There were lightning flashes in the distance but not close enough to help the men see better.

"Listen! That's a squeaking oarlock."

Sure enough, they all heard a rhythmic chirp, or least they thought they did, before a sudden downpour masked any sounds from the river. A flash of lightning revealed Major Starr standing behind the cordwood, his musket steadied on the top of the pile, an oilskin shielding it from the rain. The major was studying the river, obviously searching for the source of the squeak.

Alex whispered, "I hear muffled oars."

Joseph Starr signalled that he didn't want any more talking, which didn't stop Joseph Bourgeois from observing, "Somebody is talking out there; I can hear low voices."

Starr chastised the Acadian, "If we can hear them, they can probably hear us! Now, shut up!"

The keel of a boat grated on the sandstone bed of the river. Heavy footsteps could be heard on the shale. One of the intruders must have stumbled in the dark because there was a curse and then some splashing.

"Do we go over and help the old man?" It was Joseph Bourgeois. When Starr didn't answer, Bourgeois stood up. "I think we should go over there!"

A flash of lightning showed Captain John Hall in the fore of his raiding party, directly in line with the levelled musket of Major Samuel Starr.

"John Hall! I knew you would come!" was what the major hollered before he discharged his weapon.

In the darkness, a fearful voice sang out, "My God, let's get out of here!"

The second flash of lightning showed Captain John Hall, hatless, running for his life.

Major Starr stepped out from behind the woodpile, shaking his fist at the fleeing Americans. "And you had better not show yourself on the Cornwallis River, ever again!"

It was then the major saw the three younger men walking toward him. "Out for some night air, men? Couldn't sleep knowing that the old major was down here, all by himself?" Ashamed of his boorish behaviour, Starr apologized, "I'm sorry. I want you to know that I'm proud you men believed in me and came to my support."[2]

Starr spotted something at the edge of the water. He strolled down to see what it was. "Yes, men, I'm right some proud you came to my aid." He scooped up a soggy hat, and examining it, he laughed. Sticking his finger through the bullet hole in the crown of the hat he boasted, "I knew I was a pretty good shot! This tells the tale; I didn't miss."

"At least, not by much," Bourgeois joked. A sour look from both Starrs, father and son, prompted a very quick "sir."

"Too bad Captain Hall has such a low forehead," Alex suggested, trying to make light of Bourgeois's gaffe.

The scowl left the major's face. "There's some hot cider for you men if you would like to join me at the house."

Brewster and Bourgeois declined the offer.

"No thank you, sir."

A flash of lightning
showed Captain John Hall in the fore
of his raiding party ...

"Not tonight, thanks." Alex added, "There's enough darkness left to rescue a few hours of sleep."

The men walked up to the hill, the Starrs breaking off at their house, the brothers continuing together until they reached the Brewster barn.

Joseph said his "good night" but Alex grabbed his sleeve.

"Are we going to talk about this?" Alex asked.

"About what?"

"About you leaving. About you going to the Miramichi."

There was a touch of twilight on the clearing horizon. Joseph Bourgeois looked past his friend to the place where the sun would rise. "My father wants to return to the arms of his family. I go with him."

"Then you will come back?"

"Someday . . ."

Alex smiled, "Good!"

"Someday Acadians will again live here, in Les Mines." He looked into his brother's eyes. "But for you and me, we will say our goodbyes."

*June*
*Brewsters' farm*

Lydia Brewster twirled around and around, enjoying the feel of her best dress against her legs. A little dizzy, she stopped to look at her shoes, hand-me-downs from Alice to Sarah, but now they were her very own shoes to be worn only on Sundays. Lydia was sure this wasn't a Sunday but she wasn't complaining; Lydia Brewster just loved dressing up.

Seeing her reflection in the kitchen window she whispered, "You're so beautiful. Someday you will marry a prince." She bent over to wipe some dust off the toe of her shoe and then began to twist and twirl. Suddenly, she stopped. "They're comin' out of the barn, Pa," she screamed, running so fast into the house that she almost fell when the folds of her dress caught her between her knees. "They're comin' out," she said, more sedately, because, once inside the door, she was confronted by Samuel, Agnes, Alex, Alice, and Sarah, all formally attired, all standing around in the kitchen.

Samuel peeked through the kitchen window. He saw Richard and Joseph Bourgeois coming out of the barn, blinking their eyes as they adjusted to the bright sunlight.

"Now would be an appropriate time to join them in the yard." He spread his arms, ushering his family out of the kitchen.

Agnes hesitated at the door but the children were right behind her and she was eased into the yard.

"Richard, Joseph," Samuel said, rather formally.

The rest of the family were quiet, their eyes down.

Alex went right over to Richard and took the travel sack off the older man's shoulder. "I'll carry this for a ways, Richard."

"Thank you, Alex."

Nothing much else was said as they trooped down the hill to the ferry.

Once at the ferry landing, Alex handed the sack to Richard and shook hands with him.

"I want to thank you for saving our lives," Richard mumbled. He cleared his throat, and in a firmer voice added, "We will never forget your kindnesses." He boarded the ferry, taking a seat on the stern thwart.

It looked as though Joseph Bourgeois might say something but, instead, he gave the family a little wave and joined his father.

Sam Lowden untied the painter and tossed it into the boat. Pushing off, he took his position on the middle thwart, fussing with the oars, splashing a bit when he thrust the oars into the oarlocks. He began rowing for the other shore.

There was just time for a couple of goodbyes and then the boat was too far away.

The girls crowded the edge of the pier, intending to watch the boat cross the river, but their mother was already striding back up the hill, back the way she had come.

Chattering, the children ran to try to catch up to their mother.

Agnes didn't take the usual cut-off path for her house but continued up the hill until she was at the bald patch on Belcher's path, from where she would have a fine view of the river and the Horton shoreline. Agnes shielded her eyes from the sun and watched as the ferry blended into the background of the opposite shore. She stood that way until a cloud blocked out the sun; she lowered her arm. She continued to stare at the opposite shore.

After a while, Samuel took the children home. Later, he rejoined Agnes on the hill, not saying anything, just standing by her side.

When the tide had receded enough that there could be no more ferry crossings, Agnes dropped her eyes. She took her husband's hand and allowed herself to be led home.

Just before she entered the house Agnes said, "I thought he might come back."

## Endnotes

[1] The story that is told relates that Sam Starr made a pest of himself that winter. He was convinced that Captain Hall could not go back to New England unless he acquired another ship. Starr brought the subject up time after time until it was considered to be something of a joke.

[2] In the story told in *The Port Remembers*, Joseph Starr, along with a couple of friends, follows Sam Starr to the beach where they stay out of sight but are close enough to provide back-up if needed. For the purposes of the novel's story, I selected Alex Brewster and Joseph Bourgeois to be Joseph Starr's friends.

## Chapter Ten
### Death Is Retribution

*Spring 1777*
*Cornwallis Township*

Agnes Brewster could hear a noise from somewhere in the bedroom. With effort, she opened her eyes, but it seemed to be taking a long while to bring her eyes into focus, so she spoke.

"Is that you, Samuel?"

"Yes, my dear."

"What are you doing?"

"I was waiting for you to wake up. Betty Woodworth left a fine broth. Would you like some?" When his wife didn't answer, Samuel called out, "Alice, please bring some of that hot broth for your mother."

"Yes, Father," was the reply from the kitchen.

Samuel studied his wife's drawn features. She was lying there, still as death, and then he noticed that there was no evidence of breathing. Concerned, he grasped her hand, giving Agnes quite a start.

"My Lord, Samuel. What are you doing?"

"I just wanted to make sure you were still with us."

"I'm going to die?"

"We all die, Agnes, but if we get some of that broth into you, I'm sure it will make you better."

Alice came through the door with a steaming bowl and a big spoon. "Here you are, Ma. It looks like a fine soup."

Petulantly, Agnes corrected her daughter. "You never were a good cook, Alice; it's a broth, not a soup."

"I thought broth and soup were the same." Alice raised her eyebrows with a questioning look at her father.

He shook his head in a 'never mind' gesture.

"Well, they're not! And that's how much you know about the kitchen. And I don't want any. Take it away."

Alice did as she was told and left the room.

The petulance was still in Agnes' voice when she spoke again. "You said that the Lord always gives recompense for our actions." Before Samuel could reply, Agnes kept right on, "and recompense can be good or bad, can't it?"

"We live a good life, Agnes, so I expect any recompense to be good."

"I haven't been good."

"Of course you have. I know that . . ."

Agnes raised a weary hand signalling that she wanted her husband to stop. She lay there, her eyes open but otherwise not moving as she slowly dropped her hand until it was flat on the counterpane.

Samuel waited. When Alice came back to the doorway, he waved her away and continued to wait to hear what his wife had to say.

"I took pride in our possessions, husband."

"As you should, Agnes. We practised our faith and we were rewarded with success in a worldly way. It was evidence of our . . ."

Agnes raised her hand, silencing the ex-preacher. He waited.

"I took pleasure in other people's troubles, in other people's mistakes. I was prideful in the position we had achieved here." From somewhere she gathered the strength, speaking in a firm voice. "I felt so secure in our new status that I rescued little Joseph from what I believed to be a voyage of the damned. He belonged to me. He belonged in my kitchen. I saved Joseph and lifted him to our status; all I had to do was raise my hand and it became so." She smiled. "I was proud."

"It was a good thing you did for the Bourgeois."

"No!" Agnes expelled her breath, the coverlet receding and receding until Samuel was convinced that his wife would never breathe again. Finally, the coverlet began to rise. "Not Bourgeois. Brewster." Then in a very weak voice she said, "But the father came back."

"Richard?"

Agnes nodded her head a trifle. "But I continued to believe that we had been specially favoured. I had faith that Alex and Joseph would come back to me from the sea, I believed the girls would learn to read," she paused to take a better breath, "that Alice would be betrothed to an English Church family who would convert." Agnes gave her husband a wan smile. "I wanted to win back your congregation, Samuel."

"You are a wonderful, loving creature, Agnes. You did nothing wrong . . ."

"I gloried in the notoriety of Deacon John Newcombe's mistake of working on a Sunday."

"We prayed together that night. We prayed to be forgiven our foibles."

"I continued to work against the interests of the English Church by repeating the Newcombe story at every opportunity. Despite our prayers and my promises to the Lord, I was deceitful; even in our prayers I was not truthful in what I was doing."

"Oh!"

"I turned my back on my children in a effort to win Joseph over from his own kind. When he chose the wilderness with the Acadians rather than . . ."

Samuel interrupted, "He merely honoured the wishes of his father. It was admirable that he gave up this life to follow his father."

If Agnes heard her husband she gave no sign. "I knew that I was being punished. That last day, I waited on Belcher's path for Joseph to return to me and when he didn't, I knew the wrath of the Lord." Her voice filled with finality she sighed. "It is the Lord's recompense that I lie here."

"No, Agnes! It's because you haven't eaten a fair meal since Joseph's departure."

Agnes closed her eyes and turned her face to the wall.

*Summer 1777*
*Township Cemetery*

Samuel Brewster stepped up on a little mound of dirt and raised his hands in supplication to the Lord. "Lord, we are gathered here today to mourn the passing of Agnes Brewster." He paused as he tallied the circle of mourners: the Woodworths (all of them, Betty sniffling into her handkerchief), Sam and Ida Lowden, the Halls (Alice holding tightly to the arm of her fiancée), the three erstwhile Dissenter families, and, surprisingly, Deacon Newcombe. *But none of the Cornwallis Clique. I have been fooling myself thinking that I had been accepted as a man of ability, as one of the boys!*

Samuel cleared his throat and began speaking.

"We have known Agnes as a fine woman who honoured her vows, kept a good house, and helped her husband bring up their children in your light, Lord. She accepted another woman's child as her own, taking the boy to her bosom, giving unstintingly of her love . . ." He stopped.

"Whatever faults she might have had, it was more than compensated for by her love for her family." Samuel stopped again.

"All of those who knew her, loved and appreciated the woman who was Agnes Brewster." He raised both hands over the mourners. "Please find a place for her, Lord. Keep her safe by your side until I am able to be with her again. Amen."

Samuel lowered his arms to his side. He closed his eyes and said a small prayer of his own. When he reopened his eyes, the mourners had moved off a few yards, allowing him a moment of privacy at the graveside. When they saw he was ready, most of them rejoined him by the casket, all except Alex; he was on the other side of the path that ran up the middle of the graveyard from the spruce hedge to the church.

Samuel could see that Alex was scratching around in the scrub bushes, obviously looking for something. *I can't be concerned about what that boy is doing; I have other duties to perform. Now, where are those boys Belcher said I could borrow for the afternoon?*

Silas tugged at Samuel's coat sleeve. "Were you able to find someone to . . ." Silas hesitated, trying to find the right word. "Somebody to . . ."

Samuel grimaced. "No, I wasn't able to find anyone who was willing to do Acadian work."

"Want me to get some shovels?"

"That won't be necessary. Although Captain Belcher wasn't able to come to the funeral, he was good enough to loan me a couple of his boys. I just don't see them anywhere." Samuel shielded his eyes from the sun and scanned the graveyard.

At that moment, two figures detached themselves from the shadows at the base of the spruce hedge.

"Ah! There they are." Samuel waved his arm to attract their attention.

"Must have been sitting out of the sun, waitin' all this time."

Samuel, his hand impatiently tapping the side of his leg, replied, "Must be like an afternoon off for them—sitting around like that." *Look how they amble along! Not a care or worry in the world!* "I must remember to thank Captain Belcher for the use of his slaves."

"Me and some boys would have done it if you'd had a mind, Samuel. It would have been nothin' to stash some shovels up here this mornin'."

"I know, Silas, but this way, we can all go down to the house together, for some refreshments. Anyhow, it was hard to turn down the captain's offer."

"Nice of him, I must say."

"I thought I might give the boys a copper or two but then I thought better of it; what possible use would slaves have for money?" He nodded at the Negroes and turned his back on them to rejoin the other mourners who were making ready to leave the graveyard.

Alex came over to his father, intent on saying something to him privately.

"What is it, Alex?"

"Tom's marker is down," he whispered. We should put it back up."

"I suppose we could do that." But then Samuel had another idea. "Explain to Belcher's boys what has to be done. They'll do it."

"Yes, father."

His son still didn't move along, so Samuel thought Alex must have some other problem.

"You have something troubling you?"

"There used to be another grave marker, not far from Tom's. It's not there any more."

"Do you remember which family?'

"Captain Belcher's."

"Not likely. Not down here."

"There was no last name but you said she was a Belcher slave."

"Ah!" Samuel took his son's elbow and steered him toward the path. "The gleaners probably took it for firewood." When he saw the questioning look on his son's face, Samuel went on to explain.

"In late winter, when supplies of firewood are low and dry wood is at a premium, any wood found lying around would be picked up and burned. The grave marker was probably sticking through the snow."

"But to take a grave marker!"

"You could always scratch the name on a stone, if you feel strongly about it."

They had reached the path and walked along, single file, through the gap in the spruce hedge.

"Do you remember the name?"

Alex shook his head negatively. "I could ask at the Belchers."

"I wouldn't do that, Alex. It would draw attention to the fact that we were paying notice to their affairs."

The path widened once they were through the hedge.

Samuel gestured in the direction of a tall young woman who was walking alone. "Why don't you lend your arm to

Miss Woodworth? I do believe she's a shy thing, so make sure she joins us at the house for refreshments; we have so few mourners present."

Alex made a mental note to do something about the grave markers as he waited until Elizabeth Woodworth caught them up; then he offered his arm to the eldest of the Woodworth clan. "May I walk with you, Elizabeth?"

"I would like that, Alexander." She placed her hand in the crook of Alex's arm, "You never paid any attention to me before; what made you want to walk with me?"

Alex, a little bit flustered, gave answer before he had thought it through. "My father told me to."

"Oh, la, sir! The man is still a boy at heart!" She squeezed his arm to demonstrate that she was just teasing, "I often wondered why we didn't get along."

"We got along just fine, Elizabeth, except we've been doin' it separately."

Elizabeth gave a throaty laugh. "We've been doing it separately! That's clever, my handsome Alexander!"

Now, Alex had been told he was handsome, once or twice, by his mother, but to have this tall, attractive woman call him handsome was an entirely different kettle of fish. Suddenly, he didn't know what to say. He stuttered, "I . . . er . . . we should . . ."

Elizabeth, concerned that she might have embarrassed Alex, was quick to reach across with her other hand and touch Alex's wrist.

"Were you close to your mother?"

Titillated at the feel of her warm flesh next to his, Alex swallowed several times before he managed to say, "I loved her, if that's what you mean."

"I heard my parents talking; they said Joseph took up a lot of room in your mother's heart."

Alex nodded his head but didn't say anything for several minutes as they walked along. "I will miss them both. I loved them both. Now they're gone. . . . Life can't be the same with them gone."

Elizabeth could hear the hurt and anguish in the young man's voice. She stopped and turned him around to face her. "You are never alone, Alexander Brewster. Your mother will watch over you and, in God's time, you will see Joseph again."

Alex shook his head, refusing to believe what she was saying.

Cupping his face in both her hands, Elizabeth stared into Alex's eyes. "You must have faith, Alex," she said. "When you have your faith, everything is possible!"

They made a pretty picture, standing at the high point of Belcher's path, dressed in their Sunday best, their lips almost touching. Then Elizabeth leaned forward, the tiniest little bit, touching her lips to his. They kissed. Elizabeth drew back, letting her hands fall and then, changing her mind, slid them around Alex's waist. She bowed her head and snuggled into the hollow of his neck.

"You nose is cold," he said, flustered.

"I think I have found a place to warm it, Alex." She snuggled closer. "You can put your arms around me, if you like."

When Alex had done as he was told, he was surprised when she said, "I could always see that your heart was full with the love of your mother and your friend. I thought that now, maybe, there might just be a little spot for me." She looked up at her man; she had decided that he was her man. "We should hurry along to the reception now, Alex. We wouldn't want to give old Newcombe reason to lecture us about how our generation lacks all sense of propriety."

Laughing that throaty laugh, she took his arm and began skipping down the hill, forcing Alex to skip along with her.

\* \* \*

By September of 1777, the Planters of Cornwallis and Horton were smug in their sense of well-being—quite a change from the way they had felt just a few months earlier. During the closing months of 1776, the Minas Planters had been given a real fright when a significant number of New Englanders and Acadians living on the Isthmus of Chignecto helped an invading Americans force capture Shepody Point and Partridge Island. The Planters' anxiety was heightened with reports that Fort Cumberland was besieged and likely to fall to the invaders. It seemed like the long-feared nightmare of the Acadians and the Micmac descending on their scattered and defenceless homes was about to become true!

Fortunately, Cumberland was successfully defended and the American attackers forced to retreat to the other side of the St. Croix River, where they were less of a threat to the Cornwallis Planters. Even the turncoat New England settlers and Acadians of Chignecto faded back into the Nova Scotian countryside, where they busily demonstrated their loyalty to the British Crown as much as necessary to avoid charges of treason. It was true that there were rumours and counter-rumours of American privateers making raids along the shores of the Bay of Fundy but nothing much came of it—as far as the Minas Planters were concerned.

When the military barracks at Cornwallis Township was finally completed and occupied by British regulars, it was believed that 1777 would see the beginning of the good times. The people of Cornwallis became accustomed to the beat of the drum, the raising and lowering of the flag, the reality that finally Cornwallis was an integral part of the British Empire. They also became accustomed to seeing, on a Sunday after-noon, the handsome young couple walking along High Street, taking the air, in this the most tranquil of townships.

"Why is it that everyone we meet grins at us?" Alex's face was crimson with embarrassment. "It's not as if this is the first time we have been seen together, walking out." He cast a quick look back over his shoulder and caught a smiling Missus Wiggins looking back at him. "And the infernal giggling!"

"They just mean to be nice." Elizabeth then said it again, imitating her mother: "They just mean to be nice, girl, and encourage you to bring that Dissenter boy into the Church!"

Alex made a playful move to wrench his arm from Elizabeth but, of course, with the smallest of pressures, she 'managed' to hold on to him.

"Well, I've had enough of the giggles and knowing smiles." He gestured down the hill. "Why don't we get away from High Street, take a stroll toward the pier? Nobody would be walking down that way, this being a Sunday."

Elizabeth allowed herself to be led away from the heavily trafficked High Street down the trail to the bottom of Belcher's path, where they had a good view of the river and the basin.

"Oh, look!" Elizabeth pointed. "There's a little sailboat coming up the river!"

The seaman in Alexander Brewster made him critical. "There's far too many men in that boat to be safe." The wind having dropped off as the shallop passed under the lee of the two ships tied to the pier, the crew of the small boat broke out two sets of oars and began to pull heartily.

"That man on the bow is wearing a sword!" Elizabeth shielded her eyes from glare of the sun off the water. "Yes, oh yes, Alex! He's wearing a sword!"

"What the devil!" Alex began to run toward the pier. Over his shoulder he called back to Elizabeth, "It looks like they're going to board the schooner! Run up to High Street! Get some help!"

Elizabeth stood as if her feet were rooted to the ground. "Alexander Brewster, you come back here this minute. What do you think you are going to do? Those men have guns!"

The marauders—at least that's what Alex now believed they were—disappeared aboard the schooner, where loud swearing and some scuffling announced that something was amiss. Alex slowed to a walk but he continued his approach to the moored boat. By the time he had reached the end of the pier, a huge man appeared at the starboard bulwark holding a man's body over his head like a sack of potatoes. The body was casually tossed into the water, where it lay motionless. Almost immediately another man came running across the deck performing a flying dive over the bulwark into the water. Even before the diver could surface, the big man reappeared holding a struggling, screaming sailor by the hair. The sailor was thrown by the scruff of his neck over the side, missing the gasping diver by inches.

Alex had decided what he was going to do. "I'm going to help that first man! Run to High Street, Elizabeth! Get some soldiers down here!" He made sure Elizabeth was on her way before he got any closer to the schooner. He could see the pirates cutting lines and working the ship. *They mean to steal the schooner—on a Sunday, and in broad daylight! God is going to get you heathens.*

One of the pirates saw Alex coming. He stopped what he was doing and picked up a musket he had left leaning against the bulwark. He raised the weapon and sighted on Alex's chest. "I wouldn't come along any further, laddie!"

"I need a rope to help the man in the water."

"You won't be able to help anybody in a second or two." The pirate broke into an evil smile as he tightened his finger on the trigger. "Say your prayers, Tory!"

"I am not a Tory," Alex protested but the pirate continued to apply pressure to the trigger. Alex dove over the side of the pier. If the pirate fired the shot, Alex didn't hear as he plunged deep into the water. In the red murk of the tidal-bore-churned water, the cold clutched at his heart, causing a moment of panic. It was so, so cold, numbing his senses, stealing away the strength he needed to get back to shore. *Which way is up? Just relax.*

Alex allowed himself to float to the surface, where he could see four men in the water, three of them struggling to drag the fourth to the riverbank while keeping his head out of the water. The fourth man was retching, which was a good sign. Alex turned over on his back to see what was happening to the schooner. Mooring lines had been cut. A sail had been set. If the redcoats didn't come soon . . . he began to swim to the shore. There was no evidence of any activity in the township. *Maybe something had happened to Elizabeth! Maybe this wasn't the only raiding party! Please Lord! Don't let my Elizabeth be hurt!*

The stockade alarm bell began to ring at the same time as the muster drum sounded at the barracks.

Shivering, Alex slipped several times in the mud before he found enough footing to walk upright. Slicking the mud and water from his hair with his hands, he pulled out the tail of his shirt and was wiping some of the grit from his eyes when a squad of redcoats, at the double, came around the corner, their dubbing giving off little white clouds as their accoutrements clattered this way and that, their muskets at the port, and bayonets glistening in the sunlight. One of the soldiers in the first file lost his headdress but he didn't falter; the wayward piece of equipment was trampled several times by the rest of the squad. The headpiece was in danger of being further crushed when Captain Belcher led twenty-seven of his Cornwallis Volunteers down the same path, but they all managed to avoid stepping on it.

By this time the schooner was midstream, its bow turning, turning with the river's current, the sails hardening, and the pirate helmsman getting good steerage. The schooner's new crew cheered when American colours unfurled on the flag halyard. The revolutionary war had come to Cornwallis Township.

The sergeant of the guard marched his squad to the end of the pier, where he lined them up in firing order. "Make ready!" he ordered.

The soldiers stood in two rows; the first row knelt while the second row took a half step to the right.

"Aim!"

The men raised their weapons and sighted at the ship that was rapidly moving out into the basin.

"Fire!"

"What utter nonsense!" Captain Belcher shouted at the top of his lungs even before the musket smoke had dissipated. "You can't hit anything from here!" He stood there, watching with scorn as the redcoats reloaded and then re-formed ranks.

The sergeant marched to stand in front of the militia officer. He performed a butt salute, holding it until Belcher informally acknowledged it.

"My officers are in Horton, sir. Do you have orders for me?"

Belcher didn't answer immediately. Instead he shouted at the men on the pier, "Anybody know what the schooner's cargo is?"

One of the wet sailors trotted over, answering on the way, "She's the *Gladys* laden with hay bound for Saint John." He grinned at Belcher. "They won't get far. I heard my cap'n say it war a hazardous course out of the Minas Basin. They'll get hung up, fer sure."

"How many crew?"

"There's the four of us but the Cap'n wus over to Horton for the soirée he calls it. He's not back yet."

Belcher put his hands on his hips while he thought it through. *They wanted the ship, most likely, because the cargo is not important. Came in here bold as brass . . . they knew about the social event at Horton last night!* It dawned on him. *They got help from one of these goddamn neutral Planters!*

"Is there crew on the other ship?" Belcher pointed at the sloop that was now alone at the pier.

Several heads popped up, here and there on the sloop. "Is the shootin' over?" the nearest one asked.

"Where is your captain?"

"He's over at Horton. I'm mate. John Mackenzie's the name."

"Prepare your ship for departure."

"We don't have a full crew!"

Belcher gestured at the four wet seamen standing on the pier. "Use them." When the mate began to protest, Belcher signalled his Volunteers to board the sloop. "See that the sailors follow my orders, boys."

The regular army sergeant, still standing ramrod straight, reminded Belcher, "Beggin' yer pardon, sir, I await yer orders."

"Get your men on board that sloop."

"You mean to leave and take us with you?"

"Yes, I do mean to teach those brigands a lesson."

"I'm sorry, sir, but my orders are to protect Cornwallis, not to chase pirates."

"Ready to cast off, Captain Belcher!"

"Cast off, then!" Belcher strode the short distance to the sloop and vaulted the bulwark. He looked back at the pier. Sighting Alex he smiled. "They tried to kill you, son. Up for some excitement?" Not waiting for the answer, Belcher gave his orders to the regular army sergeant. "Continue with your duties, Sergeant."

"Yes, sir!" Giving a butt salute, the sergeant did a proper about turn and marched back to his squad, where he began to harangue the unfortunate soldier who had lost his headdress. "You horrible little man! You're naked! You are on report!"

"Coming, Brewster?" Belcher raised his voice to be heard above the sergeant's shouting. "Or are you going to stay with the ladies?"

The sergeant had tired of berating the soldier. "Shoulder arms!" he ordered. "Right turn!" Taking his position alongside his squad, he marched his men away in the direction of the barracks.

Alex could see open water between the ship and pier. He took several steps toward the sloop but stopped when he heard a sharp intake of breath behind him. It was Elizabeth. She saw him hesitate but she waved him on.

"I'll be all right, Alex. You do what you have to do for the king."

He waved back and jumped to the top of the bulwark, where he teetered for a moment before he was able to step down to the deck.

The onlookers cheered as he turned to salute his sweetheart.

"Oh, Alex! Do be very careful!" she shouted as the sloop moved more quickly into the stream.

"Take her to port," the mate ordered.

When the helmsman complied, the ship turned, the expanse of hardened canvas blocking Alex's view of his loved one. He turned to face the captain.

"What do you propose, Captain Belcher?"

"I mean to catch the buggers and put them to the sword." He beckoned to the mate.

"Aye sir," the mate responded.

"For now, you're the captain of this ship, but understand, I am captain of these soldiers."

"Aye."

"Now, how do we catch the other ship up?"

"We don't, sir, I mean Captain. She bigger than we are and faster."

"All right, she's bigger and faster." Belcher looked around. "What do we have going for us?"

"We are an armed sloop; we are more manoeuvrable, take less draught . . ."

"Take less draught?"

"Y'see, sir, that schooner has more sail so she needs more keel to sorta balance her." When he saw the questioning look on the soldier's face, he explained. "The schooner needs more water under her."

"What does that mean?"

"She'll have to stick to the middle of the channel until she clears Cape Split." The mate stepped over to the bulwark, pointing at the schooner in the distance. "See how she's gone 'way over there? She's 'way over there because that's where the channel is."

In a hopeful voice Belcher asked, "And we don't have to stay in the channel? We could sail in a straight line and cut them off?"

"We would be placing this ship at considerable risk if we leave the channel. The tide is on the ebb and I don't have any idea where the shoals are and we could run aground and . . ."

"Is there another way to catch them?"

"Only if they touch bottom, er, only if they make a mistake and run aground."

"Then cut them off!" Belcher turned on his heel and called for his sergeant, Sergeant Thomas Bell. When Bell appeared, Belcher told him to check the ship's armaments. "Find out if there's anything we can use against them bastards."

"Yes sir."

After a short interval, the sergeant reported back that he had found a swivel gun and two cannon.

Belcher checked the relative position of the enemy ship, which had sailed to starboard again, following the channel. He joined the new skipper at the helm. "How many more jogs will they have to make?"

"There's one more and then they have the tricky bit of passing Cape Split."

"What's so tricky about the Cape?"

"The tides are particularly strong there. A captain must be careful to maintain way . . ."

Belcher interrupted, "I know you mean well, but speak English."

"The tidal water leavin' the basin makes a terrible current," he pointed, "just over there. If the current is movin' past the ship faster than the sails are movin' the ship, the helmsman can't steer. They'll go where the tide takes them—maybe right over under Cape Split—beach them there." The mate shrugged his shoulders, "Or up against the rocks, over there. It's happened before; it'll happen again."

"How would you avoid being cast ashore?"

"I would tack across the tide, er, I would cut across the current; I would not run with the current." It seemed like Belcher didn't understand so the man went on, "They might not know how fast that water is movin'." Skipper Mackenzie stroked his chin. "Yes, they might not know about the waters around Cape Split."

"Good! Get us as close to them as you can." Belcher shouted to his men, "I want that swivel put into action! Start shooting as soon as you can bring the weapon to bear."

Sergeant Bell eyeballed the distance between the ships. "Sir, I couldn't put a large enough powder charge to reach 'em."

"They don't know that, Tom. Don't load ball. I want plenty of smoke and noise but, if there's no ball, they'll believe they missed the fall of shot in the choppy water."

"I gets yer, sir. You wants to scare the pants off 'em."

"Good man!" Captain Belcher stuck his fingers in his mouth and gave a loud whistle. "Gather 'round, men."

The soldiers formed a semi-circle around their leader as the swivel gun was fired for the first time. A shroud of smoke passed over them but was quickly dissipated by the wind.

"Listen up!" Belcher pointed forward as the swivel gun discharged again. He spoke through the smoke. "I want to rattle those Americans. I want to get them to make a mistake. Our skipper tells me the tidal flow is so strong goin' past the Cape, that an unwary skipper might get in the grip of it and be carried ashore. We want the Americans to believe that they are in range of our gun so they will make a beeline past the Cape. If they go beeline, our skipper believes they will be beached."

The swivel fired again. From forward came the call, "Loading with ball, Captain. I think I can reach them now."

Belcher cupped his hands to his mouth. "Carry on, Sergeant! Good hunting!" He ducked down so he could see past the sails. Most of the men moved over to the lee rail where they could watch where the shot fell.

No one said anything while they waited. Finally, the gun fired. They waited and waited, but then there was a white splash one hundred feet or so to the left of the schooner. The men cheered.

The sloop's captain called out, "They're goin' straight through!"

Belcher clapped his hands. "Beeline," he chortled. He motioned for his men to gather around again. "Now, if our skipper's correct, they might be dragged by the current onto the shoals beyond the Cape."

The sloop heeled sharply as she moved onto another tack.

"Hell, sir!" one of the soldiers complained, "We're goin' the wrong way. We're movin' away from the schooner!"

Remembering what Mackenzie had told him about crossing the current, Belcher said, "Not for long, soldier. Not for long." Suddenly all business, he ordered, "Check your personal weapons." He reached over, taking a musket from the nearest man. "Go below and draw another musket from the armoury." Belcher handed the weapon to Alex. "Make certain of its prime, Brewster."

Alex didn't take the musket. "I don't need a gun, Captain."

"You came along just for the ride?"

"I don't know why I came along."

"You came because they made you jump into the river."

"Maybe so, but I will not join in any fight between New Englanders."

"This is a fight between them," Belcher jerked his thumb in the direction of the other ship, "and us." Belcher took a couple of steps forward and thrust the musket against Alex's chest. "Take the gun, Brewster." He held the gun against Alex's chest until Alex accepted the weapon. "Check the prime," Belcher growled as he turned away. Cutting off Alex's protests, Belcher called out, "Skipper! Where's the enemy?"

"Off to port, Captain Belcher."

When Belcher looked the wrong way, John Mackenzie pointed to the schooner. Even a landlubber like Belcher could see that the schooner was in distress: sails flapping, deck canted, rudder out of the water, and the big American shouting at the top of his lungs trying to get his men to do something about their predicament. The schooner had run onto a sand bar.

"What do we do now, skipper?"

"We have to run down on them as quickly as we can. If there are any real sailors over there, it won't take them long to use the swift current and the wind to work themselves off the sand bar."

"What do you mean by run down on them?"

Instead of answering, the captain shouted, "Ready to come about."

Members of the crew moved swiftly, like cats.

"Port your helm! Man the sheets!" In a matter of a few seconds the sloop was moving directly toward the schooner. Mackenzie leaned over to speak to Belcher. "I can bring us down to within a hundred yards of the other ship. With this wind, I think I can hold my ship against the current."

"What does that mean?"

"In relation to the other ship, we'll look like we aren't moving at all."

"Isn't it dangerous to go in that close?"

"Yes. We could be trapped by the current just like they were. But the difference is, we are going against the current and will have good steerage. They were going with the current and lost all control."

"Sergeant Bell! Fire a shot across their front!" He corrected himself when he saw the skipper's grin. "Fire across their bow, Sergeant!"

"Yes, sir." Almost immediately the swivel gun roared and a spout of water rose about ten feet in front of the schooner. The schooner's crew, easily visible, raised their hands in surrender.

"Let's get some boats in the water," Belcher shouted to the skipper.

Mackenzie shook his head. "The captain took our long-boat to Horton so we only have a dinghy. It will only hold—maybe four men." He regarded the swiftly moving water. "Three might be safer; I suggest two strong rowers and only one passenger. And I can't spare any of my crew."

"Get the boat ready."

"Boat's crew! Make ready to launch the boat!"

Belcher had a problem—his men were farmers, not sailors. What was he going to do? *I know one man who knows how to handle a boat.*

Alex could see it coming, so he volunteered. "I'll be one of the oarsmen."

Belcher sighed. "I'll be the other." He pointed at the sergeant. "You're the best marksman, Sergeant. You come and keep them honest."

"Yes, sir."

The three men began to clamber over the side.

Mackenzie waved for them to stop. "I will take my ship upstream before I let you off. If you start from here, you will never reach them because you will be swept too far down the shore before you get across the current."

The sloop began to move upstream relative to the stranded schooner. When she was two hundred yards closer to Cape Split, the captain gave the nod for them to get into the little boat. "Be sure to have your strongest oarsman man the starboard oar. That's because he will have to hold the bow against the current."

Alex pointed down at the little craft. "That means I sit on the right, Captain."

"Whatever you say, Brewster." Belcher took the musket from Alex and handed it to Sergeant Bell. "You hold all the muskets, Sergeant. Don't get 'em wet. Let's go."

One at a time, the three men jumped down into the boat. When the sailor released the painter, the dinghy almost capsized but Alex rowed hard to save them. Then it was a terrible struggle to keep the boat moving in the right direction and not be swept away. When they had reached the side of the schooner where the water eddied around the hull of the ship, Alex chose to row to the stern, where they were able to tie on to the rudder.

"You go up first, Sergeant. Don't take any nonsense. Shoot anyone out of line!"

The sergeant disappeared over the stern.

Then it was Belcher's turn.

It seemed to Alex, waiting below for his turn, that Belcher got on board without a hitch. Alex considered leaving his musket behind, which would make it easier for him to clamber up the stern but, at the last moment, he decided to carry the weapon with him anyway.

Once on the deck, Alex knew right away that they were in serious trouble. Thirty men, some of them still armed, formed a semi-circle around the small boarding party. The big American was encouraging his men to take some action.

"We can move our ship off this here sand bar. No trouble. We only have these three farmers in our way! I say take 'em! I say take 'em now while the sloop is out of position. We can outrun her once we get movin'.'"

The big man had a big knife that he brandished, making cutting motions against the nearest intruder—Alex Brewster.

"Come on! There's thirty of us! This one is dead meat, right now!" With that, the big man threw himself against Alex, the knife held close to his body, his huge frame bearing Alex down.

Alex just had time to raise the muzzle of his musket enough so that it discharged into the pirate's gut. Both bodies fell to the deck, the big man on top, squirming and screaming. Blood spread everywhere.

\* \* \*

It seemed like a very long time before the big pirate became still, even longer before someone moved the body off Alex Brewster.

Alex raised himself on his elbows. "Did we win?" he asked no one in particular. He looked around. Obviously it had been the sergeant who had pulled the pirate's body away because he was the only other person on the deck. "Where did everyone go?"

"You sure enough took the fight out of 'em when you killed the big one. Seein' him down like that, spoutin' blood, screamin', the rest of 'em jumped overboard and swam to shore." He inclined his head toward the bay. "Captain Belcher is on the sloop tryin' to round up enough bodies to sail the *Gladys* back home. Mackenzie tells us that we can't leave her here alone; he thinks she'll float off of her own accord the next high tide." He extended his hand to help Alex to his feet. "You look a mess."

For the first time Alex saw how much blood was on the deck. He ran his hands over his chest and belly looking for any slits or cuts where he might have added to the lake of blood. After a moment or two of checking, he was starting to feel better because everything seemed to be in its right place and in its proper proportions.

"He had that big knife! I was sure I was going to die."

"Doesn't look like you did," the sergeant said with a large smile. He clapped his hand on Alex's shoulder. "When we get back to Cornwallis and the story is told, everyone will know you're a true soldier of the king. That's somethin' to be proud of."

Alexander Brewster experienced a definite sinking feeling as he thought, *I'm not so sure. Wait 'till my father finds out I killed a man.*

\* \* \*

The next morning, the make-up crew of the *Gladys* followed the sloop home, Skipper Mackenzie trying as best he could to remember the deeper channels so as not to lead the schooner into waters too shallow for her. The sloop warped into the pier first, while the *Gladys* made a slower approach, giving the first ship time to get moored. Thus, by the time *Gladys* was moored and the crew could come ashore, Cornwallis Township was aware of the heroics of the Cornwallis Volunteers under the able leadership of Captain Belcher and, particularly, the spectacular exploits of Alexander Brewster.

"Who'd of thought it," said Silas Woodworth to his wife, expressing the feelings of most of the Planters who were at the landing to welcome back the heroes. "Imagine! A son of Samuel Brewster saving the day like that!" Silas shook his head in disbelief. "It's hard to imagine!"

Betty Woodworth caught a quick glimpse of Samuel at the edge of the throng. "I don't think it will sit very well with our Samuel."

"Probably not."

There were rousing cheers as the men from the second ship came ashore, Alex in some borrowed clothes. Alex, acknowledging the accolades in a very self-conscious manner, moved as quickly as he could to his father's side.

"I'm glad you're safe, Alexander," Samuel said in a voice completely lacking in enthusiasm. "The men on the first ship weren't sure that you were whole."

"I am whole, Father."

"That is good." The father shuffled his feet, wanting to ask more but hesitating. Finally he said, "They said there was a lot of blood."

"Yes, there was." Alex looked away for a moment and then added, "It wasn't mine."

"Whose blood was it then?"

*I might just as well get right down to it. He's going to keep prodding until he hears me say it.* "The blood came from the man I killed."

Samuel Brewster sucked in his breath sharply. He half turned away. "Your woman is just over there. I suggest you go see her."

"My woman? You mean Elizabeth, Father, don't you?"

"I suppose so. The people are watching. You should go to her. She says she is very proud of you."

Alex pushed through the crowd, accepting congratulations and good wishes until he was by Elizabeth's side.

"I was so worried about you, Alex, but they all say that you handled yourself well. You make me so proud."

Her parents shook his hand, her mother giving Alex a kiss on the cheek.

Alex saw the look of disapproval on his father's face as the older man turned and slowly, tiredly, began the climb up the hill to the Brewster farm.

Making his swift apologies to the Woodworths, Alex took Elizabeth's hand and pulled her after him as he rushed to catch up with his father. "Wait for me, Father!"

There was a slight hesitation in the elder Brewster pace but he resumed his plodding way with no further acknowledgement.

Alex and Elizabeth caught up and then matched their pace with the old man who walked along in silence. Any cheerfulness the young couple might have been feeling was leached away by the time they reached the side door of the Brewster house. Samuel faced his son.

"Ask Elizabeth to excuse us, Alexander."

Without any comment, Elizabeth backed away and wandered over by the horse trough.

Satisfied that no outsider would overhear what he had to say, Samuel announced, "I have something to tell you."

"Yes, Father."

"You should marry the Church of England woman and have Anglican children by her."

"What . . .?"

"You killed a man in the name of King George. You took sides in this fratricidal war between cousins." For the first time since he began speaking, Samuel looked his son right in the eyes. "How do you know that the man you killed wasn't kin?"

"I couldn't help it . . ."

"And I can't help you since you have chosen a different path than that taken by all your Brewster forebears."

Alex didn't know what to say. His mouth open, he was conscious of his own heavy breathing. In a daze he watched as his father stepped up and opened the door to the house.

"Marry your woman. You have chosen to be Tory. Go live with them. Let me know where you will be staying and my daughters will drop off your possesssions." He entered and closed the door.

Alex looked up at the house. A face appeared at the window. *Probably Alice,* he thought. *The old man had told my sisters to stay away from their brother's homecoming. My father had known that he was going to disown me before he came to the pier!* He heard his father's voice.

"Come away from that window! We have nothing to say to him. Not now, not ever!"

Alex stood there until Elizabeth came over and took his hand, leading him away.

## Chapter Eleven
### Belcher Street

*Summer 1780*

Normally Alexander would have considered the saltbox house they were renting to be large enough for his family. but not today. Today his two sons, Silas and Joseph, both cranky with the croup, were in full, discordant voice and Alexander had retreated to the kitchen to get away from the noise. Even that was not far enough.

Irritably, he picked up the note that had been delivered to the house, not twenty minutes ago. To have his brother-in-law, Stephen Hall, drop off a note with Samuel Brewster's fancy wax seal on it had been unnerving since, in the years since he had been cast out, Alexander and his father had exchanged exactly two "good mornings" and one "good day."

Alexander had been quick to break the seal but when he found that it contained nothing but writing, he had gone to the front room to get help from his wife. The antics of the two sick children had made conversation impossible so he had retreated to the kitchen. He reopened it and stared at the words, willing himself to make some sense of them but, of course, he couldn't; Alex couldn't read.

The house, one of Benjamin Belcher's rental properties, was situated on the south side of Belcher Street where there was a pleasant view of the river and the dykes. The young couple had often sat on the step while they planned their future and the future of their children. Alex, his mind in turmoil, his ears under brutal assault from the caterwauling, went there now. The light breeze, the beautiful reflections off the water, and the constant greens of the foliage over Greenwich way were no comfort to the troubled Alexander Brewster.

*I should have made a better effort to explain that I hadn't meant to kill that man. I wasn't the big hero they all said. I was just . . .* he lifted his head; the babies seemed to be settling down a bit. He tapped the paper against his wrist, willing Elizabeth to come through the door and read the note *and put me out of misery*, he thought. But the crying quickly resumed.

*I should have told my father that I'm no more Tory than he is. I didn't make a decision to take up arms against my brethren. I boarded that cursed ship because I wanted to show off to Elizabeth who was watching me. I got to row the dinghy because no one else could have held her against the ebb tide. I shot that American because I had no choice. Damn! If I had only told him all that!*

One child had stopped crying. He thought of Elizabeth, all sweaty, coddling the two howling infants. *I could never do woman's work.* He gave a long sigh of self-pity but then shook his head. "Cryin' over spilt milk! That's what I'm doin', cryin' over spilt milk." He shoved the note into the breast pocket of his shirt. He stood up. "I've got things to do. I can ask Elizabeth to read the damn thing later tonight."

Elizabeth came through the doorway holding the younger son in her arms. "Joseph just won't go to sleep, Alex." She held the child out for the father to take. "If you want me to read something for you, you'll have to hold your son."

Alex handed her the note and gingerly took the child in his arms. He sat down. When the baby began to fuss, he looked to his wife for help.

"Go back into the kitchen. Take a clean washrag and dip it in the honey pot. He will suck on that for a while; he might even go to sleep." Alex seemed to be hesitating so she told him, "I'll start to read this note." She put her head down but quickly looked up. "It's from your father." Then she began to read again.

Alex went into the kitchen. By the time he returned with a more contented baby, Elizabeth had finished with the note and was waiting for him.

"You remember when you told me you had gone past the house and there didn't seem to be anyone there? Well, your father took the girls over to Windsor and then went to Connecticut."

"He couldn't have told anybody. Even your parents didn't know anything about where they were."

"You know your father. He wouldn't tell anyone about his personal business."

Alex nodded his head in agreement. "He's a stubborn, independent cuss."

Elizabeth pointed at the note. "It says here your grandfather died last July." She squeezed Alex's arm, "I'm sorry, darling."

"That's all right, Elizabeth. I hardly remember him; we left Lebanon so long ago. Mother used to read his letters to us." A tear came to his eye. "Those were the happy days with Tom Pinch and Joseph and my brother . . . and Richard." Filling with self-pity again, he sighed, "Those were the happy days before . . ."

Elizabeth briskly interrupted her husband. "We are to go see him, tonight, after supper."

"He wants me to go to the house?"

"He says he wants me to be there as well."

"You being there might make it easier. I thought he always liked you."

Business-like, Elizabeth agreed, "He favoured me until he came to believe that I was part of the Tory conspiracy to trap the Dissenter—lure him and his family into the king's church."

"I don't know why he felt so threatened. There are more Congregationalists and Dissenters in Minas than Church of England."

"You must remember that he had already put his girls into the hands of the Church's teacher. His congregation was subverted, one by one, to the other churches. Then his son, against his strongest feelings, took up fighting for the English King, killing a New Englander in the name of that king." She gave her husband a rueful smile. "I can understand your father's anxiety." She extended her arms for the baby. "Give me Joseph. I think he can sleep now." She cuddled the baby and then gave her husband a peck on the cheek. "We will have something to eat, get dressed in our Sunday best, and then go see what your father wants."

* * *

Samuel Brewster must have seen them coming up the road because his voice could be heard telling someone to invite them in.

A strange woman came to the doorway. "Samuel would like you to come in, please."

"Thank you, ma'am," Alex said and stepped back to let his wife enter.

Samuel was seated in the grandchair. Two other chairs had been drawn up facing his. "Please take a seat," he said.

Alex looked around to see where the other woman would sit, but his father gestured for him to sit. Alex sat.

By way of introduction, Samuel nodded at the couple. "Anne, this is Alexander and she is Elizabeth."

The woman gave a small curtsy. "Pleased to make your acquaintance." She faced Samuel. "Shall I serve tea?"

Elizabeth sat forward in her chair. "Alexander and I would rather know why you invited us this evening."

*My darling wife always gets to the point.* "Yes, please. I understand from your note that Grandfather died."

The little woman bobbed her head. "Then you won't be wanting any tea?"

Elizabeth felt sorry for the strange woman. *She's just trying to be nice.* "Thank you, but we have just finished supper."

"We call it dinner, where I come from."

"Do you, now? And where do you come from?"

The woman smoothed her jet-black hair. She didn't respond but instead said, "I think you had better explain, Samuel."

Samuel took a deep breath. He spread his hands as a magician might at the end of his trick. "When my father died, he made special provisions for Samuel Junior."

Elizabeth interrupted, "And why would there be special provisions for one of the grandsons?"

"Junior was there for his grandfather. He saw the old man through his sickness. My father made special provisions for Junior. Otherwise, my brother and I had equal shares of his considerable estate." At this point, Samuel Brewster caught Alexander's eyes and locked onto them. "I wish to assure you that the fact that I remarried will have no effect on your inheritance when the time comes." He reached out to the little dark-haired woman who took his hand and kissed it.

Anne Brewster continued to hold the hand, somewhat possessively, while she said, "Samuel and I were married in Lebanon two days before we began the journey to come back here. I have the honour to be his wife."[1]

There was silence in the house. Elizabeth was the first to speak.

"Of course we congratulate you on your marriage," she nudged her husband, "don't we, Alexander?"

"Yes."

"And of course, if there is anything that we can do to make your stay in Cornwallis more pleasant, Missus Brewster, you only have to let us know." Again she nudged her husband, "Isn't that right Alexander?"

"Yes."

Elizabeth rose, dragging Alex upright with her. "We left the children with the neighbour and must return. The boys haven't been well." She moved to the door but had to go back and take Alex by the hand; he seemed rooted to the floor. "Come, dear," she said.

Alex finally seemed to have found his senses. He regarded the woman who was his stepmother, staring at her as if to memorize her every feature. "I wish you the very best of luck," he said. He hesitated and then said to his father, "It must have been a happy time for you, being married in the midst of your old congregation."

Samuel Brewster took his wife's arm. "We were married in a Congregational Church. My old group was assimilated by the Congregational Church."

Alexander nodded his head, hoping his father would

understand he knew how much that must have hurt the ex-preacher.

Samuel Brewster looked away and then down.

*I should tell him now,* the son thought. *Tell him I'm not a Tory. Explain that it was all a mistake . . . it all just . . . happened.* Alexander sought his father's eyes but the second Missus Samuel Brewster, oblivious to Alexander's plight, bubbled with the details of the wedding until Samuel finally looked up and gently reminded her that the young parents would have to return to their children, who weren't well.

Anne Brewster chatted about the wedding day, the food, and the weather right up until the goodbyes, which were said with no mention of further family get-togethers.

## Endnotes

[1] Samuel Brewster might have married a second time; the records of the marriages of his daughters, Alice and Sarah, give Anne Brewster as the mother.

## Chapter Twelve
## Cruel Death

### 1784
### Belcher Street

"What took you so long?" Elizabeth lifted the sleeping Joseph from his father's arms.

Alex put his finger to his lips. "Sh-h-h! You'll wake him. I went as far as Starr's Point," Alex explained in a stage whisper.

Elizabeth gave her son a little kiss, whispering down at him, "No wonder you are a tired little man. Your Pa must have walked the feet right off you."

"Carried him most of the way. On the other hand, Silas did pretty well until we started for home." Alex hoisted the older boy off his shoulders and swooped him, like a hawk, to the floor.

Silas chortled with pleasure. "More!" he shouted.

Giving a despairing look at her noisy husband, Elizabeth hugged her sleeping son to her breast and hurried out of the room.

Silas wanted more playtime but Alex was shaking his finger at the boy. "No, little feller. It's time you put your head down."

Silas made a dash for the open door, almost getting away from his father, but he was caught and soon tucked in bed. Then the parents tiptoed out the door to the step, where they could enjoy the view and the soft caress of the early spring air.

"Did the boys mind the heat while you were out walking in the sun like that?"

"Not a bit. We ran into some strangers. The boys played with their children. If they settle in the area, they could be new friends for the boys."

"Strangers?"

"Yankees, actually, name of Taylor. They came to Nova Scotia because they picked the side that lost. They were Tories; call themselves Loyalists now."

"When things settle down a little, will they be going back to New England?"

"No. They can't go back. The revolutionaries took their land, took their property, and almost took their lives, according to these folk. They have nothing. They hope the Crown will help them."

"Land grants?"

"I suppose so. The family I met said there were hundreds of Loyalists over Windsor way." Alex changed the subject. "Anything happen here while we were gone?"

"Samuel and Anne came by for their usual little visit." Elizabeth put her hand on Alex's sleeve. "Anne Brewster is a very understanding woman." Elizabeth grinned. "She certainly has her Samuel toeing the line. I can just imagine her saying, no more of this nonsense, Samuel. He's your son . . .'"

"More likely she said, they're our grand-children."

They both laughed, softly.

\* \* \*

Several days later, as Samuel and Anne came around the corner of the saltbox house for their little visit, they knew something was wrong. Anne stopped in her tracks and listened to the sounds of shallow breathing and ragged coughs. "Oh dear God! It sounds like . . ." Anne Brewster ran into the house, fearing the worst.

She took in the scene at a glance, Alex holding Silas, trying to get him to drink some water. Anne could see the boy spit up whatever was put in his mouth and then cry, a pitiful little cry followed by a bout of weak coughing. Elizabeth came out of the front room holding the other boy, who was having a terrible time getting his breath.

"How long have they been like this?" Anne asked the nearest parent.

"Since yesterday. We thought it was croup again, but they keep getting sicker."

Anne was all business. Pointing at Samuel, she ordered, "Samuel, you get on your horse and ride like the wind. We need some oil of vitriolis."

"Oil of vitriolis," Samuel repeated. "Where will I find it?"

"An alchemist would have some for sure." Suddenly Anne's face was overtaken by a troubled look. "There is an alchemist somewhere in the Minas, surely."

Samuel shook his head. "I know there's one in Halifax but . . ."

"Why do we need that oil of-whatever-it-is?" Elizabeth kissed the wet forehead of her darling baby. "He's burning up. We have to do something for him! What would the oil do?"

Before trying to explain the terrible situation the family faced, Anne Brewster helped Elizabeth over to the bench near the fireplace. Keeping her panic down, Anne said, "I heard that the strangers living in the other rental house on Church Street have sick children. The foul parasites must be in the air. Our boys must have inhaled them."

Elizabeth shot an accusatory look at her husband. "You let our boys play with Yankee children!"

Anne put some pressure on her daughter-in-law's shoulder, getting her to sit down. She then turned to face her husband. "Samuel, get on your horse. Go to the houses of the more wealthy, especially the ones who have large numbers of animals. Ask for oil of vitriolis."

Alex handed Silas to his mother-in-law and joined his father at the door. "I'll go with you to the house, Pa; I'll help you get saddled." He grasped his father's arm. "I think we should try the Colonel's, then Best's. Belcher might have some of the oil." The two men went running down the hill.

"What's the oil normally used for, Mother Anne?"

"Full strength, it's used to etch metal, but I'll put just a couple of drops in a tumbler of water. The boys must have breathed in the parasites, which are now attacking their throats, making it hard for them to breathe or swallow. One dose and the parasites will be dead and the boys will get better. Diphtheria doesn't stand a chance against a dose of vitriolis."

With a quaver in her voice, Elizabeth repeated the dreaded word, "Diphtheria."

\* \* \*

The two women cuddled the boys, alternately singing and praying as they waited for the return of Samuel Brewster with the life-saving oil.

Toward dawn, Alex came back saying that Samuel had gone to Horton; there had been no oil found at any of the more well-to-do homes in Cornwallis.

As the sun rose, Joseph breathed his last.

Silas lived until his grandfather returned. Even if Samuel had found some of the oil, it would have been too late for the boy; he hadn't been able to swallow anything for hours.

* * *

The new, full-time Anglican preacher, Reverend John Wiswell, performed the burial service for the Brewster boys in the little church at the top of the cemetery. The boys were interred with the Anglicans, far removed from the likes of Agnes Brewster, Tom Pinch, and the nameless slave girl down near the spruce hedge.

* * *

The week following the funeral, Samuel Brewster came by the saltbox house. He passed a few pleasant moments with Alex and his wife and then suggested that the men go outside for a walk and a smoke.

"It's quite all right to smoke in here, Father," Elizabeth said. "It still gets mighty chilly once the sun sets so I'll get a wrap and you can settle down, all comfy, by the fireplace." She went to the blanket box to get a cover for the old man.

Alex knew his father. Samuel, never a man to choose a walk on a buggy evening over the creature comfort of a pipe by the fire, must have something he wanted to say. "Thanks, dear, but I'd appreciate a bit of air, too."

Elizabeth shrugged her shoulders and put the blanket back. "I'll see you later, then," she said as the men left.

Once outside, Samuel didn't stop to light his pipe. He led the way to the bottom of Belcher Street, where he stopped, apparently to admire the view. "Freedom of conscience! That's what we were promised! I brought my family to Nova Scotia because of the promise of religious freedom."

Alex tried to interrupt, "Pa . . ."

"Hear me out!"

The son pulled out his pipe and began to stoke it.

"I was called to a meeting at the Colonel's house this morning." Samuel held his hand up to stay any questions that his son might wish to make. "The Cornwallis Clique is going to build a grand, new Anglican Church. The Society for the Propagation of the Gospel has placed funds in the hands of the two Anglican wardens."

"That would be Burbidge and Belcher."

"Yes." Samuel shook his head. "The amount of funds involved is immense: £800 from the King, £200 from the SPG, and £200 from each of the wardens and vestrymen. I was asked to contribute as well."

"Why would they call upon you, the Dissenter?"

"My grandsons were buried Church of England. My son married Church of England, as well as my eldest daughter. They presume that my remaining children will be Church of England."

"I know, I know, Father. The girls are being led into the Church of England by their schooling."

"And, of course, I am paying extra money for the privilege!"

Both men paid attention to their pipes. Alex imagined that even the fine taste of the Virginian tobacco that Samuel Junior had sent as a Christmas gift was probably souring in his father's mouth. Alex finished stoking his pipe first.

"What did you tell them?"

"I said I would consider their request," Samuel looked over at his son with fire in his eyes, "but they can go to the devil for all I care about their precious church!" He was so agitated, his trembling hands knocked some of the fire from his pipe and the men had to quickly stomp the dry grass at their feet to prevent a conflagration. Samuel put the pipe in his pocket. "I mean to leave here, to go somewhere where I can remove my family from the crassness that has become Cornwallis Township. Perhaps I will find a place where I can build my church. Once my church is built, the congregation will come."

"But I thought we would be safe and happy here!"

With some irony in his voice the father responded, "I thought there would be freedom of religion, but the Papists have more freedom of choice than we have as Dissidents." He sighed, "I will take what's left of my family and try to find a place where we can be at peace with ourselves and our God, where we aren't tempted by the pride of social position, or absorbed by the consequences of other persons' personal ambitions. "

"Where would that be?"

"I don't know, but I will find it." Samuel Brewster lifted his chin and stared at the moon as it rose over Minas Basin. "And when I find it, I will go there and build my church."

*Addendum*

Samuel didn't expect to found a New City of God in the Wilderness when he and Anne, along with his three youngest daughters, moved away from Cornwallis Township to Division 15, Lot 7, facing onto Sixty Rod Road (later to be renamed Saxon Street) in Centerville. No, he seemed to be past all that. Instead, he immersed himself in the building of another fine house and barn, cleared his land, and worked his farm while communing with his God. In 1802, Samuel Brewster suffered a stroke and was largely incapacitated.

Alexander and Elizabeth occupied the Cornwallis Township home until 1802, when they went to live with the elder Brewster on Sixty Rod Road. Before arrangements could be made to sell the Cornwallis property, gleaners stripped most of the wood from the buildings during the particularly harsh winter of 1802–03. The property was eventually sold for the land value.

Samuel died in 1808, the same year the fourth William Brewster was born to Alexander and Elizabeth.

Anne Brewster died the following year, sitting by the fire, with the baby, William, nestled in her arms.

*Intermission*
*Long Beach*


*July 1848*
*Saxon Street*
*Centerville*

William Brewster hoisted the grandchair to the top of the wagon. He gave it a little jiggle to make sure that it would stay and then looped a rope around one of its arms, tying it down. He looked around for one of his boys to give him a hand. *They're never here when I need 'em.* He tossed the other end of the rope up and over the pile of furniture and limped around to the other side to see if he could reach it. *I'm only forty-two and the rheumatism's got me, real bad.* He reached for the end of the rope. *Ah! Got it! But I'll still need the boys.*

"Joseph! Charles! Watson! Come here! I need you."

He finished checking the tie-downs on the rest of the furniture. *Those boys are just about as much use as tits on a bull. They're never around when I need 'em and then they're bone lazy."* He continued grousing as he picked up the two pine planks from the wagon's tailgate. Balancing them at his side with one hand, and carrying a shovel in the other, he began the long trek to the far side of the property, keeping an eye peeled for his errant offspring. When he finally reached the Brewster cemetery, he carefully separated the two planks and leaned them, one beside the other, against the little white fence surrounding the graves. *Don't want to scuff the carving, considering how much trouble I had to go to, just to get 'em right.* He had another thought. *Damn Margaret, anyway. What does she know? Schmidt, down at the feed store, said they was done right! What does she know about it—just because she can read! Schmidt told me they was right, so they's right!*

He opened the gate and marched to the head of the two mounded, unmarked graves, giving a nod of his head to the other two graves: the nearest one for Samuel Brewster, died

233

1802, and the other for Anne, wife of Samuel Brewster, died 1803. William worked at loosening the dirt at the head of the first mound and then dug down about a foot and a half. Tossing the shovel out of the way, he walked back to where he had stacked the pine boards and studied them minutely. He hesitated but, finally, chose one and, carrying it back to the freshly made hole, dropped the end of the plank into it. With his foot, he scuffed the dirt back into the hole while holding the plank upright. He decided that, before tamping the soil, he had better see if he had got it right. He stepped back, pulling a piece of paper from his pocket, trying to remember what Schmidt had told him about the names. *That's 'E,' so it's hers*, he thought. He tamped the earth tightly at the base of the plank. He did the same with the second plank at the head of the other grave.

| ELIZABETH | ALEXANDER |
|:---:|:---:|
| wife of | BREWSTER |
| ALEXANDER BREWSTER | 1756 – 1815 |
| died of smallpox | died of a broken hart |
| 1811 | |

"Sorry it took so long, Pa, but I done whatcha tol' me, 'cept Schmidt could only do letters. He didn't do broken hearts. I had him put it in words, though." He scuffed a bit at the ground before going on. "I had to put it up today, Pa. After today, we won't be here no more."

A voice from behind him said, "They can't hear you, hon'. You're just talkin' to yerself."

Without turning around, William answered his wife, "They hear."

"Then tell them why we sold the place and are moving to the God-forsaken other side of the mountain."

"Margaret, I don't know why Grandpa came here. When my sisters was bringin' me up, they never tol' me that, but he musta had his reasons in his day for doin' what he done, same as I have reasons for doin' what I do." He turned on his heel and walked past his wife. "Have you seen the boys?"

"No, and why are we leavin' Centerville?"

"Centerville is no-where's-ville. There's nuttin' here for us 'cept too many people. The fish are goin' from the river, there's nuttin' left to hunt and we're too far from the water to have a boat. It's no-where's-ville."

"Getting good money for the farm had nothing to do with it," Margaret Brewster said, slyly.

William flashed a thin smile at his wife and was about to say something but he changed his mind. "We have to find the boys. Go look down by the barns. I'll go over by the creek."

Before they had gone very far, the boys came running and hollering across the field, holding a stringer of brook trout in the air.

"Look what we caught!"

Margaret Brewster gave her husband a wary look but decided she could comment. "No fish, huh!"

"Those aren't fish! You wait 'til I get a boat! I'll show you what fish are," William growled as he moved as fast as his aching body would let him, motioning for the youngest boy to get on the wagon. "Get on the wagon, Watson. Joseph, you and Charles lead the cow. If we mean to get to our land before dark, we have to get a move on."

Watson, his lip all a quiver, asked, "Where is our land, Pa? Does it have a house as big as our'n?"

"Son, we'll be able to build our own house on a nice road that leads all the way down to the Bay of Fundy."

"What's down there?"

"There's a long, long beach with fancy coloured stones. Some of them stones has little fish froze in them for all time." William pointed at the grandchair. "Now, you get up in that chair and keep an eye out for strangers."

Watson clambered up the stack of furniture laughing and whooping. "I'll watch for the road that leads to the beach where the fish are froze in the rocks," but he was sound asleep by the time the Brewster wagon turned onto the long beach road.

*Intermission*
*The Letter*

*1857*
*Brewster Farm*
*Long Beach Road*

"Who's that comin' down the road?" Margaret Brewster raised herself on her elbows and squinted as she tried to make out the figure in the distance.

William got up from where he was working on the trellis that was meant to give Margaret some shade in the late afternoon. He joined his wife on the veranda, sitting on the edge of her cot, taking her hand in his, and making little stroking motions with his other hand on hers. He sighed, "You know full well who it is, Margaret."

Margaret let her head fall back on her pillow and turned her head away. "If it's that woman, I want you to tell her to go away."

"You know it's Alice Huntley and that she's comin' to lend you a hand around the house."

"I don't need help." Margaret put her hand over her face as she coughed, and coughed and coughed.

William held a towel out for his wife to use, but her eyes were squeezed shut as she coughed. He pushed it against her hand. She grabbed it and pressed it to her mouth, continuing to cough. She retched, hard, and spit something into the towel. She folded it over and held a clean spot against her face. "I . . . want . . . her . . . to leave," she managed to say.

"You know every time you allow yourself to get upset, you get a coughing spell." William stood up and waved to the approaching woman, who was close enough to be spoken to.

"Hello, Miss Huntley. You've come to give my Margaret some help with the house?"

"Yes." She waved her hand in the direction of the veranda. "Isn't that nice, what you've done, Mister Brewster, bringing the Missus' sickbed out here where she can catch the breeze." The young woman curtsied to Margaret Brewster. "I sure hope you're feelin' better, Ma'am."

Margaret lifted a listless hand as a form of acknowledgement but, otherwise, remained still and silent. Her eyes followed the younger woman's every move.

Miss Huntley approached the bed. She removed the soiled towel from the slack hand. Without looking at the contents, she carried the towel into the kitchen while saying, "I'll soak this in some cold water. I should be able to get the blood stains out." She went into the kitchen, closely followed by a seemingly concerned husband.

"Why don't you close your eyes, dear," William called out through the open door as he slid his hands around the young girl's waist and drew her close. He whispered in the girl's ear, "She's not been havin' a good day Alice; she just might go to sleep."

Alice Huntley pushed away from the farmer's embrace but he didn't let her go. He was nibbling on her ear when his wife said, "That wasn't a very smart thing to do, William."

The couple in the kitchen jumped apart, Alice going to the water barrel, William pushing against the bulge in his trousers before he went back to the veranda. "What do you mean?" he asked, trying to keep any concern from his voice. "What are you talking about?"

"Well, aren't you worried, just the least little bit?"

Defensively, William responded, "No! I don't see why . . ."

"You sent that boy all the way to Horton Corner, all by himself, to get a letter that's supposed to be there, that we don't know anything about, that we don't know where it came from or what kind of terrible news it might bring."

William turned his face away so as not to reveal the relief he was feeling.

From the kitchen, Alice Huntley's cheerful voice declared, in firm tones, "You Brewsters have been on the Mountain too long; the place is called Kentville now, not Horton Corner."

Margaret lowered her voice. "He's been gone since the day before yesterday," she hissed at her husband. "Aren't you going to do something, try to find out where he is?"

"Oh, he's all right. There ain't no harm in them valley folk and no Acadians left to bother anybody." He went back into the kitchen. "I mean to help Miss Huntley with whatever chores she thinks needs doin'," he said, over his shoulder.

"That's nice, husband," the sick woman said, somewhat dryly. Margaret's hands fluttered in dismissal, or resignation. She let her head fall back on the pillow and she closed her eyes while trying to shut out the sounds from the kitchen. She lay that way until she heard whistling on the road.

"That's Watson!" She lifted herself onto her elbows the better to see. "That's Watson on the Long Beach Road." With a grin she raised her voice, "He'll be here any minute now!" The scurrying noises from the house gave her some satisfaction. She pretended to look more closely at the entrance to their road. "No, they didn't turn in here. Whoever it was went along toward the beach."

Minutes later, she saw her son coming down the farm road. She remained silent until the boy waved.

She waved back. "Everything all right, Watson?"

"Yes, Ma." He took off his hat and wiped the sweat from his forehead. "Pa inside with Miss Huntley?" He smiled sadly at his mother while he added, "Doin' some chores?"

Margaret nodded her head. "Doin' some chores that needs some doin'."

"Uh."

Mother and son understood each other.

"Did you get the letter?"

"Naw. It was there but I didn't get it."

The father came to the veranda, an expression of anger and annoyance written large. "You didn't get the letter?"

Watson Brewster raised his chin and faced his father, forthrightly. "It wasn't at the Post Office. It was at the Chase warehouse. A ship's captain brought it from the United States. Four pence due."

"You told him we were good for it?"

"If he gave up the letter, he would have to give money to the captain from his own pocket. He said he wasn't about to do that."

William Brewster stormed back into the house, muttering loud enough for mother and son to hear the "spineless whelp" part of the ranting.

The mother patted the side of the cot for her son to sit with her. "What did you eat, son; did your father pack you some eats before you left?"

"Naw." When the boy saw the look of concern on his mother's face, he hastened to add, "It made no never mind." He lowered his voice so he couldn't be heard from the house, "I did some chores for the smithy. Thought I might be able to earn the coppers." He shrugged his shoulders. "When I didn't earn enough, I used what money I earned to get something to eat." He held out his hand, offering the Nova Scotia penny to her.

Mother closed her son's fingers over the coin. "You keep it, Watson." She pushed his cowlick back from his face a couple of times. "Where did you sleep?"

"I slept down by the river. The bugs weren't so bad." Watson grasped his mother's hand, tenderly holding it for a moment. "I'm sorry about the letter. Maybe I can go back again. Maybe Father will give me the money for it."

"Did you learn anything about it?"

"I think it was from a place called, con . . . net . . . ti . . . kit."

Margaret lifted her chin. "William!" she shouted.

An exasperated-sounding William Brewster gave a muffled answer, "What do you want?"

"Do you know somebody in Connecticut?"

"No, I don't!"

"You have relatives there, don't you?"

"Not that I'm going to spend good money on."

Mother and son gave each other a knowing look.

Margaret was still curious as to who might have gone to all the trouble to write a letter and send it from the United States. Knowing that her son was learning to read and figger from the Huntley woman and might have some other information, she lowered her voice as she prompted her son to tell her more. "The warehouseman said he would keep the letter for a while?"

"He said he would give it back to the captain on his next trip."

"What else did he say?"

"I saw where it was supposed to go to W. Brewster at Cornwallis Township. The man said he asked around. Someone told him there was a W. Brewster on the Mountain."

William Brewster returned to the veranda. He picked up his tools and went down to the trellis where he had been working earlier.

"What are we going to do about the letter, Pa?"

"Nothin'. Got more important things to do." He looked around at his wife. "Where are the other two?"

"Joseph and Charles?"

Sarcastically, William answered, "Who else would I mean?"

"Joseph is over at the Wheaton farm helping get the hay in. Charles may be at the Kennedys'."

William pounded on a piece of board. "They're sniffing after Augusta Wheaton and Julia Kennedy! The only thing on their minds these days! They're never any help! They're never here!"

Watson stood up. "I'll be glad to help, Pa."

"Forget it! You're good with boats but you don't know 'bout nothin' else." He looked up from what he was doing. "But at least you bring fish home," he acknowledged. He cursed as he split the wood he had been working on and he threw it aside. "The only thing the other two will ever bring home is the pox!"

Margaret Brewster had enough. "Stop it, William!" She began to cough.

Alice Huntley came through the door with a fresh towel. "Here, now, Missus Brewster. Take this, my dear."

Margaret accepted the towel and pressed it against her mouth. She kept on coughing.

Alice stepped down to where the farmer was working. In a lowered voice she asked, "Don't you have relatives in Connecticut? Somebody could have died and left you money from an estate."

"Maybe so."

"You could borrow our wagon and go in to Kentville and find out."

"Yes, I could," William seemed to be considering the suggestion as he selected another board from the pile, "but I don't want to be beholden to your father."

Alice paused and then took another approach. "You could send the boy again."

"That would mean another three days where the boy doesn't bring a catch home." He picked up a board and examined it. "And it would probably be a waste of four pence."

"It might prove to be a good investment."

"I ain't got no need to hear from Yankees."

Alice persisted, "But you could . . ."

"It's settled in my mind."

"Well, it's not settled in mine!" She sucked in her breath and held it because, by the look on William's face, Alice Huntley knew she had pushed too far.

"Now, I mean for this to be the end of it. I got no need for that letter." He fixed her with his steely blue eyes. "And I got no need for more pesterin', woman."

Alice stepped back up on the veranda. She nodded her head at the boy. "Go inside now, Watson. Tend to your letters and sums while I tend to your Ma." She took the soiled towel from Margaret. "I will get you another fresh one, my dear," she said, sweetly.

Margaret, her voice hoarse from coughing, whispered to the other woman, "What did he decide?"

"He won't have any truck with Yankees. He says it's the end of it."

"In more ways than one," Margaret acknowledged. *That was probably a Brewster reaching out to us.* She closed her eyes. *Now we'll never know.*

*Intermission*
Jane McLeod

*November 1861*
*Off the South Shore*

The sailing ship *Jane McLeod* was full-rigged.[1] Built of spruce and birch at Black River, New Brunswick, and intended for the long ocean passages bringing teas and spices to W.H. Schwartz and Sons at Halifax, she was 225 feet 4 inches in length, 41 feet 1 inch in beam, and 24 feet 3 inches in depth of hold with a double deck. To say she was beautiful, with her studdingsails, royals, and skysails set, was to tend to forget that she was a workhorse of the oceans, transporting large loads while overcoming the perils of vast oceans and capricious weather.

Watson Brewster, swinging gently in his lash-and-stow below decks, was studying his navigation notes, moving his paper from side to side as he followed the apparent movement of the shaft of sunlight that had somehow found its way into his area. After a while, he closed his notebook and took out his leather-bound diary. He flipped through the pages, recalling how his captain, Captain Stewart, had chosen to take a short cut between some islands in the China Sea. He grinned when he remembered the look on the captain's arrogant face when the *Jane McLeod* had shuddered onto some rocks. He turned the pages. On this leg of the journey, the *Jane* had been at sea for eight months carrying a cargo out of the ports of Iloilo and Manilla worth $100,000. Her only port of call had been Delaware Breakwater, where she had been detained for more than a month, undergoing repairs of the damage caused when she had touched bottom in the China Seas. He turned the page to his final entry, made early this morning.

Tomorrow we off-load at the Schwartz pier. This is the captain's last trip on the *Jane* because, after the crew is paid off, the ship will be turned over to representatives of H.D. Troop and Sons of Saint John, who will be the new owners. It will be my last trip, too. Tomorrow, I take my wages and go back to the Fundy. No more China Seas for Watson Brewster!

Somewhere above his head, he heard the companionway door open and then slam shut. Since only the captain was allowed to let anything slam shut on this ship, Watson made an assumption: *the captain is on deck, but that's not my problem—it's the watch officer's problem—so I think I'll get some shut-eye.* Tucking his arm under his head and closing his eyes, he gave it one more thought before drifting off to sleep. *I wonder what the old man's going to find wrong. He always finds something wrong when he first comes on deck.*

"Steer small, damn you," the voice said, petulantly.

*Didn't take him long.* Watson thought of how the shaft of sunlight had found its way to his hammock. *Must be a hatch open because, otherwise, I wouldn't be able to hear what's going on up there.*

"Aye, sir."

*And that's the helmsman. The helmsman should know by now that the captain is a stickler for sailing close.*

Determinedly, Watson shut his eyes and let his mind seek rest. *It's not my watch and I'm getting some shut-eye.*

"Uh, sir."

*Oh, shit! I suppose I'd better go find that open hatch or I'll never get any sleep.*

"What, Peterson!"

"Well, sir, you probably saw it. The wind is changing and has freshened."

*Oh, oh. I know what comes next.* Watson sprang out of his hammock.

"Call Mister Brewster."

Watson lashed his hammock together and stowed it in his locker and then began to dress for going topside. *If the wind is changing, I'll probably need my foul weather gear,* he thought. By the time he had dug his slicks out of the locker, young Haggerson was pulling at his sleeve.

"Captain wants you topside, right away, Mister Brewster."

"Thank you, Joe. Run back now, like a good lad, and tell him I'm on my way."

Haggerson was still talking to the captain when Brewster stepped out on deck. "I'm here, sir."

"The weather is changing."

"Aye sir, it is. The wind's backing and will soon be out of the southwest . . ."

"Bringing heavier seas."

"Aye, sir."

"According to my reckoning, we should come abreast Sambro Light in just under five hours. We might see Devil's Island lighthouse on our starboard beam an hour later, say, a little after four pm. With good visibility and a following wind, we can sail past Cornwallis Island and be anchored at Dartmouth Cove in no time at all." He paused, sucking his teeth.

"What about a harbour pilot?"

"We won't stop to take one on."

"Aye, sir." *These are difficult waters. If I were captain, I'd take on a pilot.*

As if reading his mate's mind, the captain explained, "I know this harbour. I do not need a pilot."

"Aye, Captain. Your orders, sir?"

"Set storm sails. Even with reduced canvas, we should still make my estimate for Sambro Light."

"Aye, aye."

"You have the watch, Mister Brewster. Call me when we sight Sambro."

With that, Captain Stewart went below to his cabin.

\* \* \*

A little after 4 pm, Robert Malloy, the officer of the watch, sent word to the captain that they had sighted Sambro Light to larboard.

"It's going to be a foul night, sir."

This was the first voyage that Malloy had served as a watch officer on any vessel. As a very junior officer, he knew his place but he always tried to make a good impression on the captain; Malloy wanted his own ship one day and he needed his captain to speak well of him to the new owners. "We're going to have rain, what with this wind coming out of the southwest, and we have a heavy southeast sea."

"I can see that!"

"Sir, I recommend that we not make an approach to Halifax in these conditions or, if we do, we ask for a pilot from Chebucto Head."

"Tend to *your* duties, Mister Malloy. Where's the First Mate?"

"I relieved him at four, sir."

With an aggravated tone, Captain Stewart observed, "I didn't ask you that."

"He's below, sir."

"Get him."

"Aye, sir."

Robert Malloy hadn't gone more than a few steps when the captain demanded, "Where are you going?"

"Sir, you told me to get the mate."

"Mister Malloy. You are the officer of the watch. You don't get the mate; you send for him!"

"Aye, sir."

Before the First Mate appeared on the upper deck, the view of Sambro Light was obscured by heavy rain.

"Wear ship, Mister Brewster.[2] We will stand off until morning. Take us to the southeast."

"Aye, aye, Captain."

The captain wiped the water off his face; he hadn't dressed for rain and was thoroughly soaked. "Call me in the morning, Mister Brewster." With that, the captain went below to work his navigation plot so that he would be ready to give orders to the crew in the morning.

In the cabin, Stewart considered the situation as he stripped off his wet clothes. *I know the approaches to Halifax . . . I have done it a number of times. With good visibility and reduced sail, I can take the Jane right into Dartmouth Cove. I will save time; I won't have to wait off Chebucto Head for a pilot to come out. And I will save the fee, too.* He chaffed his arms and legs with a rough cloth, trying to increase his circulation and make himself feel more comfortable. *November is so bitterly cold off Nova Scotia!* He hopped into his bunk. With only a momentary nagging thought about something being left undone, John Stewart fell directly asleep and didn't move until the cabin boy shook him awake in the morning.

Stewart liked the cabin boy, Joseph Haggerson, so he was reasonably polite to him.

"Joseph, have the mate come down and bring the ship's log." Stewart realized he had not done his navigation plot. Before going on deck, he would have to work out his position and figure a course that would take the *Jane* up past Sambro on the left, and they might see Devil's Island further off to the right as they approached Cornwallis Island. After that, he would watch for Pleasant Point buoy and the Ives Knoll. *Not difficult.* He was almost finished dressing when the mate knocked on the cabin door and entered. Brewster handed the captain the ship's log with the record of the courses over the last hours and the approximate speeds. Captain Stewart hurried with his calculations because he could feel that the seas were even heavier than last night. He was a bit anxious about the weather and wanted to be on deck as quickly as possible. With the course for Halifax and the estimated times for Sambro and Cornwallis Island in his head, he joined his officers on deck.

The seas were mountainous and the visibility was almost zero in fog. Fog! More like low clouds being driven by the winds! When he stepped out onto the deck he was almost knocked over by the strength of it! High wind, heavy seas, and low visibility; this would not be a good day, but he and the *Jane* had seen worse and had won through. It would be the same today. He wasn't concerned.

Captain Stewart beckoned his officers to bend in close so they could hear him. "We'll shape our course under easy sail for Halifax Harbour." The men went about their duties.

Several times during the next two hours there were breaks in the fog where the men could see for a few miles. The rain had stopped but it was a frightening sight even for experienced seamen because the wind was tearing off the tops of the waves and driving the chunks of water in salvoes at the rearing, bucking ship while the waves advanced over the ship and poured across the deck, the previous wave hardly finishing with *Jane McLeod* before the next arrived.

Watson Brewster noted that the new officer, the Malloy fellow, was moving his lips, almost continuously, *probably in prayer. Oh shit! The helmsman's praying too!*

Captain Stewart was going to speak to the men, when he heard something over the noises of the storm. It was faint but there was no doubt. Somewhere off to the left was Sambro. "That was the Sambro fog trumpet!"

The men listened. Sure enough, they could hear the foghorn.

"It sounded faint, like she was maybe fifteen miles away." Mister Brewster listened again. "Maybe as much as eighteen miles, since the wind is coming from that general direction."

The captain nodded his head vigorously in assent and clapped Brewster on the shoulder. "We are on course so it would be eighteen miles away." He yelled to all of the men on deck, "We're doing fine. A little wind and rain never bothers our *Jane.*"

Watson leaned closer to the junior officer so he could be heard above the din. "Malloy, it's noon. Go below and get thawed out. Be prepared to relieve me at the end of my watch."

Malloy didn't wait to be told a second time. He gave the captain a quick salute and disappeared below.

Speaking to Brewster and the helmsman, Stewart gave courses and times for the next couple of hours. "Maintain this course for the next hour. Keep an eye peeled to starboard. We might have a glimpse of Devil's Island if the fog lifts a bit." With everything taken care of for the moment, Captain Stewart went below to see if he could find a cup of hot tea.

\* \* \*

Captain Stewart couldn't believe his ears. He could hear a bell buoy and it sounded like it was right under their bows! *That can't be,* he thought. *The Sambro foghorn . . . I heard the foghorn with about the right strength to confirm our position.* He had a moment of doubt but then reassured himself, *I wasn't the only one to hear it! Mister Brewster heard it, too! He estimated the distance to be about eighteen miles. That would be about right.*

He hurried to his navigation table and began checking his charts. *Yes, my plot would show us about fifteen miles.* He was not overly disturbed; perhaps the buoy had broken loose from its moorings and was adrift in the sea-lane. Navigation, after all, was just a series of vectors representing direction, speed, and time. After applying such variables as tides and currents, it was easy to determine an accurate position. The bell buoy had probably broken away and was . . . "My God!"

Sweat broke out on his face. He felt sick. He had failed to apply a vector for the sea currents which in this area . . . ran . . . westward toward . . . Sambro! The bell buoy could be . . . he ran his finger on a line from what he thought was his present position to . . . Black Rock near Inner Sambro Island!

"There is land dead ahead, sir!" It was Mister Brewster. His voice was calm but the message was fatal.

Almost immediately, "There are breakers dead ahead, sir!"

"Put the wheel hard down!" he shouted. He ran to the deck. Visibility had improved. *God! That's land!* His feet were knocked out from under him. They had struck!

The crew of *Jane McLeod* began the fight to save their ship.

The sea, however, never deals kindly with the careless navigator. *Jane McLeod* had chosen to strike Black Rock just abaft her foremast. She was in the grip of a merciless foe and the first mighty wave lifted her up like a feather onto the Rock. She fell back and, with the crew desperately working to take the best advantage of the howling wind, she moved some small distance past the edge of the Rock, but the sea held her tight; the next mountainous wave lifted her back up on Black Rock for the second time, striking on her beam. The gallant lady slid back into the sea and tried to sail on.

Watson was helping the helmsman. "She might make it clear!" he screamed. But, for the third time, the *Jane* was caught up in the sea's mighty grasp and flung against the Rock, striking abaft the mizzenmast. She fell back into the sea, finally clearing the Rock.

"Man the pumps! Sound the hold! Tell me quickly how bad the hull's been breached!" Clutching at the stays and then the railings, Captain Stewart staggered across the crazily canting deck to the wheel. "How is she handling?"

"She's responding, sir, but she's listing to larboard. I fear, with the waves crashing into her stern, she might lose her rudder."

"At least the seas aren't pounding our damaged side. Maintain this course for now . . . but I've got to know how much water is in the hold. Who did you send below?"

"Malloy, sir."

"Send another man."

Conditions were perilous what with the damaged ship carrying as much canvas as she was. Watson had given the order for "all hands to reduce sail." He didn't want to interfere with that vital work so he temporized, "I don't want to send a second man across that open deck, sir. If any man goes by the boards, he would be lost."

Gripping the railing, with rain and ocean water running down their faces, the two officers looked into each other's eyes. What passed between them was unspoken; *maybe they would all be lost, anyway.*

"Very well." Captain Stewart, having given it a second thought, recognized reducing sail must have the priority. He would have to wait for the damage report and there was nothing much that could be done for the moment. He hung his head. "I don't understand it, Brewster. We both heard the Sambro foghorn . . . it sounded like it was at least a dozen miles away. If it had sounded louder, we would have known we were much closer than my navigation plot showed. Then we wouldn't be in this mess!"

"I thought we were at least fifteen miles out, sir."

Neither seaman could have known that the heat engine that drove the Sambro foghorn was properly sending compressed air through the reed horn at forty pounds per square inch just as it was supposed to, but today—with the driving wind and the heavy fog—moisture was being forced into the reeds. Today, the excess wetness was severely reducing the horn's output.

"Yes, but we were in closer than we thought, too close. Where the hell's Malloy?" but Captain Stewart didn't need the soundings to tell him that his ship was settling fast. *How would we launch boats in these seas?*

When the young officer reported there was already eight feet of water in the hold, Stewart knew he must abandon ship.

\* \* \*

The crew managed to get three boats into the water in the lee of the ship, where there was some small shelter from the force of the gale, but it was still a desperate time for the twenty-one men of *Jane McLeod.*

The ship was pitching and rolling and the boats alongside were like apples in a Hallowe'en barrel. Each man had to judge his time and step over into an empty space in the air where he thought the boat would be in the next second. Several men were hurt. The cabin boy, Joe Haggerson, hesitated, falling into the water between the boat and the ship.

Captain Stewart threw himself across the gunwale of his boat and managed to grasp the boy's hair, keeping his head above water, but the sea wanted her victim, ramming the boat against the side of the ship.

Joe put his arm out to hold the boat away so that he wouldn't be crushed; his arm was immediately broken in several places.

Stewart held on to the boy. "No-o-o-o-o!" he hollered and cursed the sea.

Watson, standing above on the *Jane's* pitching deck, could see that the boy was a goner unless something—anything—could keep a small space open between the boat and the ship. He seized a box of rations and dropped it into the suddenly very narrow space. The box held the space open just long enough for the crew to drag the boy into the boat. The ration box splintered and disappeared. Joe fell to the bottom of the boat, reasonably safe for the moment.

Oars were snapped off during the uncoordinated effort to get the first boat away from the ship. Several of the crew had to start bailing for fear of being swamped. Without looking back, Captain Stewart took the tiller and headed north-northeast. It was rougher going in that direction but the captain probably expected they would get help from the pilot station at Chebucto Head. Perhaps he expected the other boats to follow, but the second boat took up the easier course of east-northeast.

Watson dropped into the last boat. By this time the *Jane* had swung into the wind so that the little boat was no longer in the lee; there was no shelter from the awful force of the wind and the waves were dashing the boat against the side of the ship with increasing fury. Using an oar as a pry, Watson tried to lever the small boat away from the side of the ship. He almost fell overboard when a wave jammed the boat against the unyielding side of the ship and the oar was flung upright. Two sailors clambered over the thwarts, grabbed the oar and, using all of their strength and combined weight, kept on trying to pry the boat away from the ship.

"We're doing it!" Watson shouted in encouragement to his crew. "We're going to get away!" As soon as he could, Watson crawled to the stern and grabbed the tiller, steering the boat in the direction the captain had taken, north-northeast. It didn't take him long to realize that, if he persisted heading in that direction, the boat would be swamped. With difficulty he managed to turn the boat and head east-northeast. Suddenly the going was easier and he was able to take stock of the condition of his crew and the status of his boat.

*Two injured. I should put them in the bottom of the boat and give them bailers to handle as best they can. That leaves five men to row . . .* He had a sudden thought. *I wonder what's going on with our ship?* He scanned his horizon, limited as it was by the mountainous waves, sheets of rain, and flying foam, looking for his ship.

*God bless her!* He pointed, shouting, "There she is!" Instantly he had second thoughts about pointing her out to his crew. It wouldn't have a good effect on his shipmates to see their ship, derelict, foundering . . .

"Mister Brewster! Somebody's trying to work the ship!"

*My God, he's right! The sails are being re-rigged for easy handling!* "We'll go back," he shouted. "We'll help save her!"

He turned the boat but almost lost her as the waves came across the gunwales, filling the boat by a third with each wave.

"Bail! Bail, you bastards! Bail!"

The little boat wasn't responding to the tiller; she was sitting too low in the water.

"Portside, backwater . . . now! Two, three, one, two, three . . . Hold! All ahead . . . now! Two, three . . . That's it! We're going to be all right now!" He looked in the bottom of the boat; it was three quarters full of water. He grinned at the two injured men sitting waist-deep in the cold water. "Bail you light-duty bastards! Bail for your lives!" He glanced over his shoulder, looking for the *Jane,* but she was nowhere to be seen. Perhaps she had foundered. He turned his back to the wind. "Row, boys! We'll head for the island." *I don't have any idea which island we'll land on, but the boys don't have to know that.*

### Devil's Island

Thomas Henneberry had finished stoking his pipe. He turned his back to the wind and struck a match. It went out, immediately. He opened the door to the lifeguard station and stepped back inside.

"Dammit, Tom!" It was one of the crew sleeping in the bunk nearest the door. "Did you have to let all that cold air in?" Colin Henneberry, one of Tom's many cousins, pulled his blanket over his head as he muttered, "Either stay in or out. Don't keep coming back and forth, back and forth."

"Sorry, cousin. I just wanted to light my pipe before taking a walk along the breakwater. I couldn't light up in the wind."

Another head popped up in the bunk across the aisle. "You Henneberrys! Talk, talk, and talk! It's not the wind blowing out your pipe, Tom! It's all the hot air and blather." He plumped up his pillow. "Can't you let a man sleep?" He jammed his pillow over his head.

Tom lit his pipe and went out as quickly and quietly as he could manage, given the force of the wind on the door. Someone shouted at him when the door did finally slam shut, and he did toy with the idea of going back in again and asking what they wanted but he managed to restrain himself. *Mother always said my sense of humour would get me into serious trouble,* he thought.

A cinder lifted from his pipe, and the bowl glowed with the draft from the gale. He turned his pipe over so that his fire was sheltered from the storm. He leaned into the wind and headed toward the breakwater where he could be alone with his pipe and his thoughts.

In the midst of the raging storm, Thomas Henneberry felt strangely comforted. *I am truly alone in this world. She wouldn't have me, said her heart belonged to someone else.* "I bet it's Warren Gray! That son of a bitch has to win everything!" He faced the sea, trying to pierce the wind-tossed sea spume, spray, and the dark of night with his feelings of wretchedness so that Hannah Gray, warm and snug at Sambro, would have some sense of his despair.

His pipe was out. He knocked it on the heel of his boot, gave it a little blow to clean out the bowl, and shoved the pipe into a pocket of his slicks. On impulse, he cupped his mouth with his hands and shouted into the wind. "I love you Hannah Gray! I love only you!" He listened to the wailing wind, hoping he would have some message, some sign that she had heard. He smiled at the ridiculous thought. *Even with a good wind, it's the better part of a day's sail from here to Sambro. No one can hear me.*

Tom cocked his head to one side. He lifted the tie-down flaps of his hat so he could hear something, maybe even someone, better. He listened. *Nothing.* He felt sheepish that he had half-expected to hear anything at all above these winds. Still, the hairs on the back of his neck told him that there had been something. He waited for the next turn of the lighthouse lantern. There couldn't be anyone out there, in the middle of all that . . .

"My God!"

A boat was caught in the lighthouse beam, the wet oars glistening with the reflected light. Then it was gone.

When the light swept the area again, he cupped his mouth and shouted, "Go away!" He ran to the edge of the breakwater. "Don't come this way! Go away!" It was then he saw the second boat. *All those men are going to die, unless I do something, right some quick.*

Tom considered rousing the rescue crew but realized that it would take too much time: the lifeboat would have to be pulled from the boat shelter and launched, the crew would have to row around the ell of the breakwater to the open sea where the two boats were, get their attention, and have them understand that they must follow the lifeboat to the calmer waters on the other side of the point. Long before any of that could happen, the two boats and their occupants would be thrust on the black rocks of the island's western shore, the debris and bodies tossed twenty feet in the air, again and again, as the army of monstrous waves encountered their first resistance in hundreds of miles. It was a sad thought but oh so true; in the aftermath of the storm, the beaches of Eastern Passage would be strewn with the remains of the boats and of the people.

*Unless I do something!*

Tom tried to gain their attention, jumping up and down, waving his arms. One of the boats might have seen him, or

A boat was caught in the lighthouse beam ...

just realized their danger, because it was turning and pointing its prow into the storm. They were rowing hard, but they weren't making any progress away from the dreadful rocks. Eventually the rowers would tire but the ocean wouldn't. Those men were going to die.

*I can't stand here and watch.*

"Hold on! I'm coming," he shouted, and began running down the breakwater to the boat shelter.

*Maybe the skiff was in the water behind the ell. Yes! There it is!* He jumped down into the boat. *No oars.* He clambered out again and ran to the boathouse.

The door didn't open with his first turn of the handle. *It's locked! No, it's never locked! My hands must be too wet.* He tore open his slick and wiped his hands on his sweater. He tried the handle. This time it turned. He pushed against the door and it opened. With a sense of relief, he grabbed a set of oars off the rack and ran back to the skiff.

Tossing the painter into the boat, he leaped in and pushed off. Rowing as hard as he could, he turned the end of the ell and was met with the full force of the storm—the skiff tossed in the air like a chip of wood, the oars biting air, and Tom almost falling over backwards. In the troughs he would try to hoist his oar blades clear of the water but the waves just wouldn't let go. It was a nightmare but, with all his struggling, he knew he was making progress. Pretty soon he could look around and see if either of the boats was still there.

*Perhaps they won't understand what I want them to do. Perhaps I'm too late and the boats are lost. Perhaps I'm risking my life for nothing. Maybe, when Hannah hears about what I tried to do, she will feel sorry she had . . .*

The lighthouse light had stopped turning. Someone on shore was using the lantern to light up the rescue area. *Yes, rescue, because that's what I'm going to do! I'm going to rescue those sons of bitches and be a hero and Hannah will be sorry she didn't marry me!* He saw that he was being pushed closer to the rocks than what would be prudent. Tom forced the bow of his little skiff into the swells and rowed like the old devil away from the shore. Looking over his shoulder he caught a glimpse of one of the boats. *I daren't take my hands off the oars. I've got to get closer.* He rowed ever harder to get just a little bit upwind so he could come down on the other boat. *Ah! There's the second boat. There's still two of 'em.*

When he thought he was close enough, Tom shouted, "Follow me!"

One the men sitting in the bottom of the nearest boat waved that he had understood.

Neither of the other crews would know where Tom had come from or where he was going because the high swells and the spray from the crashing breakers continuously hid the ell. Of course, they could assume that, if they followed Tom, they would be led to safety.

Tom made his first moves to head his skiff back to the ell of the breakwater. He was now in a position to watch the progress of the other boats and could see the nearest boat turn its bow just enough to mimic the direction Tom's skiff was headed. The second boat turned too far and was swamped by the first wave to hit it broadside. Two of the sailors continued rowing while the rest used everything, including their bare hands, to fling water back into the sea. The bow had almost come around, heading more into the swell, when another wave passed over the dangerously top-heavy boat. Fortunately, by the next wave, the boat was bow-on to the swell. Now, slowly, laboriously, Tom led his convoy around the end of the breakwater and in behind the ell to calmer waters.

Once ashore, Watson Brewster joined the throng around the hero of the hour. When he had a chance, later in the bunkhouse, he asked Tom how he had known the boats were out there and in trouble.

"I dunno." He shrugged his shoulders. "I guess I heard you before I saw you."

"We weren't making any noise. Most of the men were praying . . ."

"I dunno," was all Tom could think to say. Then he grinned. He clapped his arm over Watson's shoulder. "It just wasn't your time, Mister." Tom motioned toward the other end of the room. "Come on over by the fire. That Atlantic Ocean is so cold, it gets right inside, right into a man's soul, if he lets it."

Watson was reminded of the stories his great-aunts used to tell about an old-time Brewster, a man of some considerable wealth and position, who had defied the King of England and led his religious flock to the New World. That Brewster had survived terrible Atlantic storms in a leaky, old-fashioned freighter, subdued fearsome Indians with nothing more lethal in his hands than an open Bible and, when most of his fellow Pilgrims had died of exposure, disease and starvation, that Brewster had been spared to continue doing God's work.

Watson Brewster experienced a mysterious, warm feeling in the centre of his body where he believed his soul might be. *I have been spared, for what reason I can't fathom.* He looked into the eyes of his saviour, searching for a message, a sign.

Thomas grinned but, sensing something of the other man's personal conflict, put his arm over Watson's shoulder and drew him off to one side. "Don't look at it too close," he whispered. "I've seen it before, in the eyes of the men who came back from the sea."

"What have you seen before?"

"When the sea grabs you, she weighs you, measures you while she's holding you close. During that time, you belong to her—at least your body does." Tom hesitated before going on.

Watson was afraid Tom might stop; Watson really wanted to know what this young man thought. "But?"

"But she knows that your soul belongs to God." He gave a little shrug. "Maybe they talk about it. Maybe the sea and God talk about it and sometimes God asks for the body to be given back." Now totally embarrassed, Thomas glanced around to make sure he was not being overheard by any of the Devil's Island crew. "He needs your body back so your soul can complete its work."

"You believe that?"

"I was told you were out there. You know I couldn't possibly hear you—but I did hear something—and the sea let me come get you." Thomas laughed a nervous laugh and motioned to Watson. "Come on, now. Let's get some more of that coffee." He led the way to the pot on the stove.

There was no human standing close enough to hear, but Watson said it aloud anyway. "I'm not the first Brewster to be spared," he faltered, a quaver in his voice, but then continued, "I might not be the last." Now, firmly, he pronounced, "But I promise I will be a better man for it. I will do good and . . . if you ever give me a sign, I will be sure to carry on in your name."

* * *

Several days later, an account of the rescue was published in the Halifax newspaper.

> Two of the boats from the *Jane McLeod* (see column two, page one for story) sought refuge in the direction of Devil's Island. They rowed and drifted for hours until, finally, they could be seen from Devil's Island.
>
> Thomas Henneberry Junior was the hero of the occasion. He, himself, was credited with saving 12 lives when he rowed, single-handed, through a mass of foam and guided the men to safety.
>
> Devil's Island is a small strip of land, oblong in shape, little more than a deposit formed by the action of the huge breakers that unceasingly hurl themselves on its shores. The people are a hardy race who, of necessity, has been introduced to dangers, which would make landlubbers, and many seafaring men, think twice before risking their lives in braving them. Such deeds of bravery are a part of the existence of these men. Miles away from land they go in pursuit of a living and it is well for the men of the *Jane McLeod* that they fell in with people who never seem to give a thought to their own safety when others are in danger. Among the families are the Henneberrys, the members of which are well known as brave and upright men.

The ship's boats neared the shores of the island and Thomas Henneberry, realizing that the men did not appreciate the danger they were in, without seeking assistance, jumped into a frail skiff and put through the mass of foam. After a desperate struggle, he came near the boats, acted as a guide, and led the men around the head of the breakwater to a safe landing.

Thomas Henneberry Junior is a true hero.[3]

## *Endnotes*

[1] Emma Louisa Gray told the story about her grandfather and father when they tried to rescue a ship off Black Rock. Both men disappeared into the storm and didn't return. I was unable to find a record of a ship that matched the time period of Emma's story so I patterned *Jane McLeod* after the wreck of the *John McLeod* in 1897.

[2] The Brewster family story has Watson Brewster earning his living on sailing ships, not necessarily this one, of course. Family information provided by Helen (Brewster) Fancy.

[3] According to the newspaper account, the real-life Thomas Henneberry was, indeed, a true hero. I had to make him Thomas Henneberry Junior to fit the time frame of my story.

*Intermission*
*Back Home*


*Spring, 1862*
*Brewster Farm*
*Long Beach Road*

"He's just waitin' for her to die." Joseph Brewster picked at the large scab on his hand, not looking up at his brothers, Charles and Watson. "And when Ma is gone, just you watch out! That Huntley witch will . . ."

Watson's face was full of anger as he shouted down his older brother. "I don't want to hear talk like that! Alice Huntley has been nothin' but good for our Ma, feedin' and cleanin' her like she's kin. There's nobody else doin' for Ma the way Alice Huntley is doin'."

Charles grabbed Joseph's hand to stop him from peeling off the scab. In his usual, laid-back style, he chose to disagree with his brothers in an entirely agreeable way. "I don't mean to say that Miss Huntley don't mean to take up with our Pa at some time or other but she's been plenty good to our Ma, Ma bein' so sick and all." He let go of Joseph's hand and watched, showing no sign of the displeasure he must have been feeling, as Joseph resumed digging at his wound. "We oughta give the woman some slack," he continued. He looked back over his shoulder at the veranda. "And we shouldn't talk so loud. Ma might not be asleep."

The boys knew that their mother couldn't be awake or aware because of the laudanum she had been given just before Alice and their father had driven away in the Huntley wagon. Still, they lowered their voices, speaking in conversational tones, which was what Charles had intended.

Joseph gave a grunt of satisfaction as he held the scab up to the light before he popped it into his mouth. "Then why is she over here all the time, if she don't want somethin'?"

Watson didn't have Charles's restraint. He made a face and looked away while he complained, "Hell, Joseph! Don't do that again! Leastways, not with me here!"

"Do what? You little baby!"

"Eat your . . . never mind!" Watson wiped his mouth with the back of his hand, obviously discomfited. "I can't believe we're the same family."

Charles patted his baby brother's arm. "We're brothers. Nothin' ever goin' to change that." He sighed. "Ma's got consumption. Pa's got a girl who seems to love him." He looked at his siblings and then smiled, "We got each other to count on."

Joseph squeezed some blood out of the open wound on his hand. He licked it off. He saw the look on Watson's face and jammed his hand in his pocket, hiding it. "You said we'd have a family meetin' the first time Pa and the Huntley woman went to town for supplies. Well, they gone."

Watson patted the breast pocket of his pea jacket. "I got a letter from Halifax."

"Tell us what it says, Watson."

"It says that Mister Schwartz has been paid by the English insurance company for the loss of his ship." Watson patted the pocket. "It says my money is on deposit at Halifax."

Joseph, who couldn't read, was curious as to what it all meant.

Watson and Charles explained to their big brother that when the *Jane McLeod* was lost off Sambro, the profits that WH Schwartz would have realized from the voyage were lost with her. But, since Mister Schwartz had bought insurance through another company in London, England, there was enough money to pay the crew's wages as if the voyage had been a success.

"You mean you're goin' to get some money?"

Watson squeezed Joseph's arm. "If you can promise me that you won't try eating any more of yourself, the three of us will have money."

Joseph grinned a big wide grin. "I promise." His grin got even wider, if that was possible. "I promise I won't never do it again . . . when you're around." He guffawed.

Charles, ever more practical, asked, "When do we get the money?"

"I told Mister Schwartz to invest the money for us. We have a share in some tea coming from the Far East."

That was not the kind of thing Charles wanted to hear. "You mean, we have bought some tea that is being carried on a ship like the *Jane McLeod*? Your ship didn't make it home again. What about this other ship? What makes it more likely that she will get back safely?" When Watson didn't have an immediate answer, he pressed some more. "Was that a wise thing to do? Is this Schwartz fellow to be trusted?"

Watson, still hesitating a little, nodded his head. "I met Mister Schwartz at the remembrance ceremony for the two ships' pilots who were lost trying to save my ship." He got a faraway look as he recalled catching a glimpse of someone trying to rig the *Jane's* sails that terrible night. "They might have been able to do it if I could have turned around and gone back to help them." His eyes downcast, he said, "They were brave, brave men: Josiah and Warren Gray. Them and men like Thomas Henneberry are the bravest men in the world." He stopped speaking.

The brothers were quiet as they waited for Watson to say something more.

"Anyhow, I met Mister Schwartz. I was so impressed with his fine Christian bearing that I told him about our family troubles. He suggested that I invest my wages until we have a better picture what's going to happen here on Long Beach Road."

"What's goin' to happen here, Watson?" Joseph began picking at his hand but quickly stuffed it back in his pocket. "What's goin' to happen, Watson? Will there be enough money for me to go to Halifax and get a good job on the piers?"

Charles didn't wait for the answer. "Our sister wants to marry one of the Blenkhorns over at Canning."

"If Susan doesn't get married right away, we should be able to dower her. And, as for you Joseph, when our ship comes in, you can go to Halifax."

There was a moment of quiet between the brothers as they considered the changes that would occur with the death of their mother.

"I guess Ma's really going to die, isn't she." Charles didn't say it as a question. "We'll have to do the best we can for her for as long as she can be with us."

"God willing, she will live many, many more years," Watson said.

"God willing," the other two responded.

## *Addendum*

Margaret Brewster, born 1824 at Cornwallis, died during the winter of 1867. Her remains were stored in the Brewster barn until spring, when she was laid to rest in the old cemetery near Terry's Creek.

The widower, William Brewster, married his consort, Alice Huntley, in 1871. They sold the property on Long Beach Road and moved lock, stock, and barrel to Seattle, Washington State, never to return to Nova Scotia.

Watson's "tea money" was put to good use:

*Joseph* married Augusta Wheaton in June 1872 (he didn't leave the Mountain to find that "good job on the Halifax piers").

*Susan Emmeline Brewster* was dowered when she married Joseph Blenkhorn, the proprietor of an axe factory at Canning.

*Charles* married Julia Kennedy (they moved to Scots Bay where the land was less expensive).

*Watson,* using the last of his "tea money," built a house between the fisherman's shed and the lumber mill at Baxters Harbour. He had a grand plan. Watson was going to find a wonderful woman, marry her, and have a large enough family to crew the schooner he was going to build. In his choice of wife, he was most fortunate.

*Chapter Thirteen*
*Sarah Jane*


*June 1877*
*Baxters Harbour*
*Post Office*

Watson watched as his wife opened the clasp on the mail sack. She upended the sack, spilling more than a half-dozen letters onto the counter. Sarah Jane folded the sack and placed it under the counter, not taking her eyes off the letters.

"Land sakes!" she exclaimed. "Never saw so much mail at one time in all my life!" She quickly sorted the letters into little piles. "Those Eatons get a lot, they surely do." She held up a single letter to the light. "Here's one for the Huntleys. Wonder if Hilda's boy is sending her money, regular like, from Boston?" She tapped the envelope on its end. "Could be," she mused, "second letter this year." She considered something for a minute and then made up her mind.

"Watson, you take this along to Hilda. Save her the trip, her legs doin' her poorly like they are."

"But Sarah Jane, I thought I would . . ."

"Well, you don't expect Hilda to get down here on her very own and I can't, in all conscience, have her wait until that no-account son-in-law comes all the way from Greenwich to check on her." Sarah Jane pushed a wisp of hair off her forehead. "Most likely he comes to see if she's died yet. Never stays long enough to do anything for her, certainly none of the chores." With her two fingers she fitted the wayward lock back under the ribbon she wore in her dark brown hair. She looked up and, determining that Watson was not yet ready to comply with her request, she continued, "You can't expect me to take the poor woman her money—although the exercise might do me and the baby some good—but I should be here where Emma May's husband can easily find me—she's due most any time now and I'm the only midwife on the Mountain—besides . . ."

Watson held his hands up in surrender but, by this time, Sarah Jane was filing the other letters in the pigeonholes, most of them being filed under 'E,' and didn't see his signal. Watson noted that, conspicuously, a single letter was left out on the counter.

". . . as postmistress, I wouldn't be permitted to leave until after the Post Office scheduled hours unless, of course, it were Emma May's time and I had to go help her born another one or two." She looked up at her husband to see if he was paying attention; he was, so she continued, "I believe by the size of her, she's goin' to have twins." She sighed, "No such luck for me. Us Parker women have kids one at a time and I expect nothin' different this time. One at a time, for sure."

Sarah Jane picked up the Huntley letter and held it under her husband's nose. "You gonna do it for old Hilda? Remember, she's only Huntley by marriage. You want the Eatons to buy shares in your schooner, you'd best be nice to Hilda, she bein' an Eaton and all."

"Yes." Watson took the letter.

"By the time you come back, I'll have that haddock all done the way you like it." Sarah Jane smiled at her husband as he took the letter from her. "She's cousin to the Baxters, you know, so be extra nice to old Hilda, 'cause you want the Baxters to buy some of your sixty-four schooner shares, too."

She leaned on the counter as she watched her husband saunter up the road in that rolling kind of gait that sailors have their first few days back on land. She murmured to herself, "And you're truly a lovely Christian man, my dear Watson, although you wouldn't have to go to neighbours and strangers to finance your schooner if you had dowered your sister less generously." Sarah Jane shook her head. "But we get another new axe, every visit. Pretty soon, everybody on North Mountain will be the proud owner of a Blenkhorn axe." She felt the baby move, *you be patient, my little darlin',* she thought. She smiled her little smile; *your Aunt Emmeline will bring you your own hatchet if you go full term because your Auntie promises to be here to help us.*

A bell tinkled in the distance.

"Glory be! I didn't see anybody come down the hill," she complained. "Wait up! It'll just take me the minute!" Holding her skirts tight, she squeezed past the end of the Post Office counter and made her way to the other side of the front of the house that served as Baxters Harbour General Store. Coming around the wall of shelves, she could see it was Old Man Eaton. She hesitated a moment and then continued on, forcing a polite smile to her lips.

"Nice to see you, Mister Eaton."

"Good afternoon, Sarah Jane. I thought I might find Watson holding the fort while you were off to the Woods to help the youngest boy's wife . . . what's her name?"

"Emma May, Mister Eaton." She slipped in behind the grocery counter, "It's not her time, yet."

"Harrumph! Yes. I don't much know about those things, woman's things, that is."

"I suppose not, Mister Eaton."

She waited. Mister Eaton never bought anything at her store, having his staples and store-bought goods sent up from Kentville twice a year. She had an idea what would have prompted the man to come at this time but she waited while arranging the candy jars on the counter top, tightening their lids, finally perching herself on the tall stool that stood behind the counter and folding her hands on the bulge of her belly. She waited.

"I take it your man isn't here?"

*He would have seen Watson going over to Hilda's. Yes, he's come about the schooner shares.* "He's gone over to your niece's. Taking a letter to her, he is."

"Well, I can't wait for him. I have business at the Chase farm."

"I'll tell him you were thoughtful enough to come by, Mister Eaton."

"No thank you, Sarah Jane. I would rather you give him the message that I will match the number of shares he is able to purchase."

"The schooner shares?"

"Yes. I will purchase shares in a vessel only when the captain has a significant holding. A captain who owns, say, ten of the shares, will be a more careful navigator than . . ."

A look of pained surprise came over the old man's pallid face when Sarah Jane interrupted him.

"There's no finer seaman on the Fundy than Watson Brewster and you know that!"

In an overly polite tone Eaton stated, "Nevertheless, those are my terms." Mister Eaton swivelled around and, losing his balance, teetered on the edge of the root-cellar stairs. Sarah Jane managed to rush over to steady the old man before any harm was done.

Eaton shook himself free from the woman and stormed out the door. In a moment he returned. Pointing at Sarah Jane he blurted, "The fact that you might have saved me from serious harm will have no effect on my decision." He turned to go and then thought of something else. "And don't you go sending that man of yours to discuss this any further. He covers ten shares or I will put my money elsewhere." He watched the woman for any response or reaction but seemed disappointed by Sarah Jane's calm demeanour. He continued, "I know I had previously indicated to Captain Brewster that Baxter and I would take up ten shares each but . . ." He clamped his mouth shut.

Then Old Man Eaton turned on his heel. "Good day to you, Missus Brewster," he bellowed and was finally gone.

Suddenly overwhelmed by the weight of the baby, Sarah Jane pressed both hands to the middle of her back, just over the buttocks, trying to relieve the discomfort. "Glory be!" she said as she waddled a little coming around the wall of shelves, leaning back, pressing hard with both hands into the small of her back. "Glory be, little one! Don't you be upset, now, because I'm not. Old men like Eaton use their money like a knife and fork, settin' folks up to make a meal of 'em. And don't you worry! Daddy will go back to sea if he must. We will get our ten shares . . ." She patted her belly. "We don't need the likes of Eaton and Baxter." But she knew they did. *Without the support of those two old men, we'll never have a schooner.* "So don't you go bein' upset, little one."

She almost jumped out of her skin when a voice behind her questioned, "Are you talkin' to yerself? Never thought I'd see the day when Sarah Jane Parker would go around mumbling like an old crone!"

Sarah Jane didn't have to turn around to know who it was. "You mind your own business, Wiley Baxter! It's no concern of yours, what I do and what I don't do!"

"You should have married me, sweetheart! Then you wouldn't have to put up with the likes of Old Man Eaton." When Sarah Jane didn't respond, he continued, "You wouldn't be saddled with a spendthrift husband who has to go hat in hand, beggin' for money so's he . . ."

"That's none of your business, Mister Baxter!" She pierced him with her eyes, "And what do you know about our business with Mister Eaton?"

"I was checking your sweet peas under the window while Eaton was doin' the talkin'." He gave her a boyish grin. "Your peas need some waterin'." He allowed his grin to fade. "Besides, I heard my uncle doin' the talkin'; your man needs some money."

"Like I said, Wiley Baxter, you mind your own affairs!" When Baxter pouted and took on a hurt look she relented. "Oh, Wiley! You never, never change!" Sarah Jane touched his arm, lightly, almost with affection. "Now, you do your business and take your handsome face out of here before . . ."

"I saw Watson goin' over the hill. He won't be back for a while. We could at least talk."

"You and Old Man Eaton! Taking the first opportunity to . . ." She stopped as she gazed past the young man to see who was running down the road. Recognizing the boy as one of the Baltzer boys, Sarah Jane took off her apron and, folding it, put it on the counter.

Wiley, misreading Sarah Jane's actions, was encouraged to say, "You know, if there was anything I could do for you— anythin' at all—I would do it at the drop of a hat."

"You can stay here and mind the store and the Post Office until my Watson gets back."

An exasperated Wiley Baxter complained, "But that's not what I had in mind!" He leaned forward, excited by the sweet, fresh smell of the lilac water the young woman used after washing. "I hoped I might be able to do something more real . . ."

"Yes!" Sarah Jane placed the palm of her hand on the man's broad chest and gently pushed him aside. She looked around him toward the front walkway as if checking to see who might be watching them and then, with a mischievous glint in her eyes, she asked, "Anything at all?"

"Anything!"

Billy Baltzer burst into the room, breathing heavily, arms waving, "It's time, Missus! Ma says to come right away!"

Sarah Jane nodded at the boy and returned her attention to the young man who seemed somewhat agitated. "You said anything—anything at all—didn't you, Wiley?" Without waiting for an answer she asked, sweetly, "Then lend me your horse and wagon. I need to go over to West Glenmont. Usually I would ring the bell and Robin Ells would hitch up and come get me. But you're right here—I need someone to mind the place while I'm gone—Watson won't be back for a while—there's a letter in the box for your father—Emma May really needs me—she must be all alone or she wouldn't have sent poor Billy on foot— and you said you would do anything for me, didn't you?"

"Yes."

"Good. Your father's mail is in the slot under 'B.'" She pointed to a basket behind the front door. "Give me a hand out to your wagon with my things, will you please? Billy, you bring my little bag." Sarah Jane Brewster marched out the front door, down the steps, and then waited at the side of the wagon until Wiley came around and helped her up to the seat. Billy jumped up beside her.

As they drove off, Billy said to the woman who would deliver his mother of the babies to be named Maria and Jestina Baltzer, "He sure grits his teeth a lot, don't he?"

Handing the reins to the boy, the midwife of North Mountain rode along in silence for a while, enjoying the breeze off the Bay. "Don't hurry the horses, Billy, it's a long hill."

"Sorry, Ma'am," and by way of apology he explained, "Pa says I will be a fine horseman when I grow up."

Sarah Jane, thinking of Wiley Baxter, smiled down at the boy. "Some boys just never grow up,' she said. When she saw the hurt look on the boy's face she hurried to add, "But you, William Baltzer, are coming along just fine." She gestured toward the horses. "You can hurry them along now, William."

### September 1877

Sarah Jane recognized the scraping sound on the floor overhead. *Oh dear! Watson is dragging out his sea chest.* She tucked the baby, William Francis, into his crib and chose a heavier wool blanket for him, since the air off the Bay had turned decidedly cooler in the last few days. *My man isn't a farmer, he's a sailor, and like all the Brewsters before him, determined to be his own man, which, as far as Watson Brewster is concerned, means that he must have his own vessel.* She heard a sprawling thump.

She looked up at the ceiling and called out, "Do you need some help, Watson?"

"No thanks," came the muffled reply.

She could imagine Watson reaching up into the rafters to unhook his oil slicks, boots, and pea jacket and then missing his step when he sought to get down off the rounded top of the sea chest. *Probably only his pride was hurt,* she concluded from the scurrying sounds on the bare floor. She sighed. *There couldn't have been a greater blow to his pride than when it became widely known on the Mountain that Watson Brewster didn't have the wherewithal to build a schooner.* "Old Man Eaton has as much mouth as he has money," she said to herself.

She walked out into the front yard where she could look out past the harbour to the Bay. Soon, her man would go out on that water to Halifax, where he would take ship for the Far East. She turned her head away from the view and spoke to the open, second-storey window. "Watson! Do the Schwartzes still have tea ships?"

"Tea ships? I do believe, although I think old man Schwartz is dead and gone."

Sarah Jane could see his face in the window. "Did you hurt yourself when you fell?"

"What did you say, my dear?"

"Do you need my help?"

Watson didn't reply right away. *That girl is such a willing helpmate. There isn't anything she can't do or won't try to do. I bet if girl fishermen were allowed on the Fundy, she would be the first on the water!* Then, before he could say anything, she had pointed up the road, said something he didn't hear, and gone back into the building. He stuck his head out and saw that it was the Post Wagon. "Mail delivery time," he said to no one. "That will keep her busy and take her mind off my departure . . . I'll try to get away the day after tomorrow on one of the Chase ships." He continued sorting his sea gear and cleaning out his chest. After the Post Wagon had made its noisy departure, he heard his wife calling him.

"Coming," he answered. He closed the trunk and went down the narrow stairs. *I'll pack tomorrow, get Robin Ells to take me and my stuff over to Halls Harbour, and then work my passage to Halifax on one of Chase's ships.* When he entered the Post Office, he saw that Sarah Jane had already sorted the letters. She had left one tattered-looking letter on the counter. *Uh huh. Looks like I'll be goin' over to Hilda's again.*

With an excited look on her face, Sarah Jane pronounced, "This is the first letter ever to come to the Brewsters. It's addressed to you, Watson." She held it up for him to see. "It has no stamp or post mark. It's from a lawyer's office in Lebanon, Connecticut."

Watson took the letter in his hands and read the address out loud. "W. Brewster, Cornwallis Township, Nova Scotia."

"Well, open it. I can hardly wait to hear what it says."

"Wait! There's a notation in pencil on the back." He held it up to the light. "It says, letter directed to W. Brewster, Centerville on May . . . can't make out the date . . . anyways, May the something, 1857. The rest of the note has been smudged too bad to read." He looked up, an expression of surprise on his face. "I bet this is the letter I saw years ago in Kentville. We didn't get to keep the letter because Pa wouldn't pay the four pence; said he didn't know anyone in the United States who was worth that amount of money." Watson broke the seal. He opened the letter. There were two sheets of paper. He put the smaller piece on the counter while he read the note. When he had finished, he said, with awe in his voice, "a man named Samuel Brewster Junior died and . . ."

"Let me see!"

The letter read:

> The late Samuel Brewster Junior of Lebanon, Connecticut, who died in the ninety-third year of his life, directed that monies be sent to his nephew, William Brewster (other male offspring of his brother, Alexander, having perished), for the purpose of establishing a suitable memorial marking the presence in Nova Scotia of Samuel Brewster, dissenter preacher.
>
> To this end, £200 sterling has been placed on deposit with a reputable Halifax firm to draw interest until the enclosed certificate is presented at which time £200 (plus accrued interest) will be paid to W. Brewster.

With shaking hands, Watson picked up the certificate that directed the Schwartz Company of Halifax, Nova Scotia, to pay £200 (plus accrued interest) upon presentation of the certificate and verification of the bearer as W. Brewster, descendant of Samuel Brewster, dissenter preacher.

"Glory be!" was all Sarah Jane could think to say.

Watson Brewster was speechless as he considered the possibilities. Finally, he picked up the letter, walked over to the stove and, lifting the lid, dropped the letter into the flames. Only then did he say something.

"I am W. Brewster, descendent of Samuel Brewster, the dissenter preacher." His face broke into a broad grin as he stated, "And I am going to Halifax to claim the Brewster money."

*Chapter Fourteen*
*The Decision*


*Spring 1880*
*Baxters Harbour*

Sarah Jane dandled her daughter, first on one knee and then on the other. The child, Lena, gurgled with pleasure but was quick to complain when the mother stopped long enough to shade her eyes to look into the distance at the horse and rider coming down the hill. Hugging her daughter to her breasts, Sarah Jane took young William by the hand, encouraging him to run as best his chubby legs would allow up the hill to meet the rider.

"It's your Daddy, children!" Becoming quite breathless with the exertion of running uphill, and now literally having to support both children in her arms, she stopped. "It's your Daddy and he's bought a horse!" Sarah Jane twirled the children round once and then twice, all the time singing, "We have a horse! The horse has a tail! And if I had to take a guess, I'd say that it's female." She laughed at her silly rhyme as she put the boy down so she could wave to her husband.

"Oh! Watson! Oh, Watson! You got the money!"

Watson waved back, shouting and waving at his little family as he approached, "I did, indeed, Sarah!" Holding the reins, Watson slid to the ground and took his two girls into his arms, planting big kisses on the one and then the other until he became aware of the little fellow squeezing between them, seeking his share of the attention. Watson stepped back, examining the boy in mock seriousness.

"I do declare, Missus Brewster, that my little baby William has disappeared and you now have this fine gentleman in his stead." He scooped up the boy and placed him on the horse, which, of course, scared the daylights out of the boy and he had to be rescued from his lofty perch by his mother.

"He'll make strange now, Watson," which the boy immediately did, hiding behind his mother's skirts. "You shouldn't have been so rough with him," she scolded, mainly for the boy's benefit.

Peeking around his wife's skirts and catching the child's eye, Watson explained, "I'll teach you how to ride, little man."

"Only when he's old enough," the mother corrected.

"Yes, of course, only when you're old enough, young gentleman."

As Watson led the horse into the front yard he began yarning about his trip to Halifax and back.

Sarah Jane held her finger to her lips. "Make up to your boy," she whispered, "there'll be time for us after the children are settled down."

### Later

Watson listened to the creak on the stairs as his wife returned from putting the little one down. When he guessed she was at the last step and would appear at the corner, he assumed an unyielding look and held his finger to his lips. "Sh-h-h-h," he said. He immediately turned the other way and put his hands on his hips, carrying on a conversation with himself.

"What for?" he asked in a falsetto voice with a very quizzical tone. "Isn't it time for some tall tales about the wicked city and the small fortune in gold that . . ."

Watson whipped his head around and answered himself. "Sh-h-h-h!" Sternly he admonished himself, "It is not the time for tall tales about wicked cities."

Again, Watson faced the other way. "Well, what time is it?" again using the falsetto voice. He raised both hands in supplication, "Please, please, oh wise sir, tell me," at this point raking Sarah Jane with hurt and reproachful eyes, "tell me, what should I do?"

Assuming the other character, he paused, as if he were considering his reply. Then he lunged across the room, gathered his startled wife into his arms, and carried her into the front bedroom. "It's time to make up to your wife! There'll be time for stories after you get her settled down." He kicked the door shut behind them.

Sarah Jane giggled. "Take your time, sailor," she managed to say before her mouth was smothered in kisses.

### Later Still

". . . then I met the younger Mister Schwartz. Fredrich was his name; he was much easier to deal with. He took me along to dinner while the company clerks checked through dormant accounts for our file. Told me not to worry." Watson's eyes lit up as he remembered, "We were joined by Warren Gray—a real celebrity—people stopped at our table all the time to speak to him."

"What's he famous for?"

"I don't know and didn't want to ask, Sarah Jane." When he noticed the disappointment on her face he shrugged his shoulders and said, "I must have been introduced to twenty or thirty people. Mister Gray was very, very polite, always making a point of introducing me."

"Did Mister Gray know everyone's name?"

"Probably not." He smiled to himself. "I did notice that, if Mister Gray hesitated on a name, Mister Schwartz either used the name first or introduced himself and me and let the stranger introduce himself in return. Pretty smooth, them two."

"Those two, I think, would be more correct, Watson. We have to be more careful with our English; the children will be learning from us . . ."

Watson wasn't hearing wifely concerns for her children. He continued with his story.

"When we got the documents from . . . from . . . the archives, Mister Schwartz called it, there was a sheet of foolscap called The Brewster Family apparently written by someone in Connecticut."

"Oh, my!"

"I have it in my saddle bag." He moved as if to get up and go out to the shed but Sarah Jane put a restraining hand on her husband's arm.

"Tell me what you remember of it. I can read it for myself in the morning."

With enthusiasm Watson began the telling of the Brewster story.

"There was a William Brewster, the Elder of a congregation of Anglicans, who hoped to reform the English Church and make it more of a church for the common people. This Anglican congregation, and some other congregations just like them, called themselves the Puritans. When the English bishops wouldn't let the Puritans worship God in their own way, some of the Puritans, following the lead of our William Brewster, left England. Now calling themselves Pilgrims, they wandered in search of a place where they could build their own church. They came to New England but the Puritans quickly followed . . . and so did the priests of the English Church. Through the generations, the Brewsters kept moving away from the settled communities, hoping to escape the intolerance of the Puritans and then, later, of the English priests until, in 1762, Samuel Brewster came to Nova Scotia.

"Why would the Brewsters come here? The Church of England was here already, wasn't it?"

"Brewster came because he was guaranteed full liberty of conscience, in writing, by the Governor of Nova Scotia—and not just Brewster—everyone was guaranteed full liberty of conscience."

"And was he allowed to worship as he pleased?"

"I guess so. Mister Schwartz said all the new settlers could worship any way they wanted."

"Then the governor kept his promise." Sarah Jane pulled at her lip, a sure sign that something was still bothering her.

Watson waited.

"But, as I read Samuel Brewster's letter, I had the feeling that there was some sort of persecution—that it wasn't all sweetness and light here in Nova Scotia—maybe there wasn't full liberty of conscience as the governor promised." She smiled her little smile, the one she used when she wasn't sure of what she was saying. "It sounded to me like the man in Connecticut wanted to rub somebody's nose into some dirt—something shameful—I don't know what!" She gave an embarrassed laugh and said, "Anyway, that's what it sounded like to me when he wrote about paying for a monument to Samuel Brewster, the dissenter preacher, so that people would be forced to remember him."

"Yes. I thought so too. The foolscap relates that Samuel Brewster's eldest child, the son named Samuel Junior, returned to Connecticut rather than live here where he was scorned because of the way he worshipped God. The story on the foolscap ends with his death. "

"We never will know."

"Well, I might have gotten an idea of what happened from Mister Schwartz. He spoke about the time his family came to Nova Scotia. He said that all senior government officials were Church of England. The State Church was Church of England. The Anglican bishop was given money to build Anglican churches even where there weren't many Anglicans. The bishop built the church, built the public schools, hired the teachers, and approved what was taught to every child be he Anglican or not."

"Of course! The children learned their catechism as they were taught to read!"

"And naturally went to the same church they were taught about."

"Most natural thing in the world!"

"You bet! Mister Schwartz told me his Lutheran family sent him and his brother to a private school where there was no religion taught in the classroom."

"There might have been a private school in Halifax but there would be none in the valley."

"So we can assume that Samuel Brewster didn't join the Anglican Church."

"The letter said 'dissenter preacher.'"

Watson nodded his head in agreement. "And he wouldn't want his children taught Church of England ways . . ."

"So he moved to Centerville . . ."

"To get away from the Anglican influence on the next generation of Brewsters."

"Just like the Brewsters had been doing for more than a century." Sarah Jane sighed. "Until they came to Baxters Harbour . . ."

Watson gave his wife a rueful smile. "I don't think religion had anything to do with my father, William Brewster, coming here. With him, it would have been the money." Watson pointed in a general way at the Bay of Fundy. "Anyway, even if he did come here for religious reasons, there's no place else to go." He grinned. "We'd get awfully wet, if we did."

Remembering the first letter that brought them news of the money, she asked, "The letter called him a dissenter . . ."

"According to Mister Schwartz, that's what the established churches called anyone who didn't worship as they worshipped."

"Dissenter preacher he was called."

"And Samuel Brewster died a dissenter. He never got to build his church here, even in Nova Scotia, where he had been promised full liberty of conscience. He was a courageous soul to stand apart from the crowd like he did. "

They sat there for a while, listening to the crackle of the fireplace.

Sarah Jane finally said, "That's sad. They beat him."

Watson took his wife's hand in his. "I'd like to take the money and build a church."

"Where?"

"Right here at the harbour. What with the interest over the years, there's plenty of money to build a nice church." He smiled. "Maybe one with a fancy coloured window like the churches in Halifax."

When his wife didn't comment, Watson asked her right out, "Would that be all right with you, Sarah Jane? We take the money to build a church?"

"I'm a Parker and that money is a Brewster legacy."

He hugged her tightly. "You're a Brewster woman now. You have as much say as I do."

"What about the schooner? You always wanted to be your own master—master of your own ship."

"There's enough money to build a small church and still buy ten schooner shares."

"We should do it!" Sarah Jane snuggled against her man and then lifted her face. "When we build his church, it would be like a final win for Samuel."

"Nobody in the world would know what we did or why we did it."

"We would know."

"Yes, and I believe Samuel Brewster would know."

## The Next Morning

His mouth full of fried corn, Watson spoke around the food, "We haf to be careful about the seeling."

"Seals? I haven't seen a seal around here for years."

Watson chewed and swallowed. "We have to be careful what kind of ceiling we put in the church. It has to be high, steep, like this." He cupped his fingers together and steepled his fingers. "The church has to vibrate when we sing. It has to be a beautiful thing when people sing." He gathered up more corn on his fork but paused as he heard footsteps at the front of the house. He put the food down. "Customers already, this early?"

"I'll go, Watson. You finish your food."

Watson continued to eat but he could easily hear them and recognized the voice. It was Wiley Baxter and Wiley was being . . . Watson scowled as he got up from the table and moved to the front of the house. He arrived at the Post Office counter just as Wiley was saying, "I saw the horse and I knew it couldn't be yours." He had not yet seen or heard Watson's approach. "I knew it couldn't be a Brewster horse because . . ."

"Because why, Baxter?"

Astonished to see the sailor husband back home so soon, Wiley backed up a space and then bristled as he realized he had been forced back in front of a woman. He stepped forward again. "I wondered who might be here, botherin' Sarah Jane. I knowed you wouldn't have the money to buy a horse; besides you don't have no barn to keep him in."

"It's my horse and I will build the barn for her."

His face flame red, Wiley blustered somewhat and then blurted, "Everyone knows you don't have two cents . . ."

"Oh?"

"Yeah! You don't even buy one share in that pipedream boat of yers."

"I will buy ten shares in the schooner."

Wiley showed the surprise he felt on his face. "Oh, then . . . you'll be expectin' honest, hardworkin' folk to share in your money-losing schemes, I bet."

"No, I won't need any of your money."

"I just bet you won't! Everyone knows Eaton will only match the shares you buy and Baxter too. By my figgerin' that leaves more than half yer boat to be paid for by the likes of the Huntleys and the Woods and the McCullys and some poorer Baxters, like me." Wiley Baxter was having fun; he was grinning from ear to ear.

"I will undertake to buy a third of the vessel. There will be no need for the support of the likes of you, Wiley Baxter." Watson took two steps closer to the smaller man. "Now, I much appreciate your concern for our financial welfare but I don't like your sniffing around here when you believe I am away."

Wiley lost his grin. "I just mean to be of some help, you bein' away so much and her bein' a woman all alone."

"Well, thank you so very much Wiley Baxter. She won't be needing your attentions any more. I'm going to build my boat here, right here, at the harbour, over next to the sawmill so I'll be close to home."

Wiley sneered at Watson's claim. "Not likely! That's not your land over by the sawmill."

"Don't you worry none about that and, by the time our schooner is built, Young William will be old enough to be the man around here any time I'm away."

Watson took Wiley's elbow and steered him to the door. "Now, I thank you for your concern and would like to bid you a good day."

Wiley resisted the relentless pressure on his elbow but to no avail and soon found himself outside looking in through the closed screen door. He watched as both Brewsters moved to the back room until they were out of sight of the front door and then he turned away, making a great show of nonchalance, whistling, scuffing his boots in the dust, kicking stones ahead of him as he went back the way he had come.

Once in the back room, Watson put his hand out to his wife. He took her outstretched hand and brushed it with his lips in a token of his love for her. "I'm sorry about that, Sarah Jane." He continued to hold her hand. "Perhaps I can buy just the ten shares that we planned . . ."

"No, husband. We have our word in this world and not much else. You told that man that we wouldn't be needing the likes of him when we go to build our schooner. We can't be seen to go back on that."

"I wanted to build that church, not just for . . ."

"I know."

She pulled on his hand, drawing him down so they could sit together in the grandchair.

Running her fingers through his hair, she tried to find the words to console him and to convince herself that they had made the right choice. "Our son will watch our ship grow at the edge of the harbour and, one day, sail on her with his father all over the Fundy."

Watson's countenance brightened with the thought. "We could be shipmates and sail as far out as Boston or St. John's."

What was left unsaid: there would be no church at Baxters Harbour.

Neither of them could know that William Francis would never sail with his father.

## Chapter Fifteen
## The Consequence

*Summer 1887*
*Baxters Harbour*

"Warp her in good and tight, Jack. I want her to sit fair and square on her keel at low water. I got to see what the problem is. I think she's leakin' at the stem."

Jack Eaton shook his head. "Naw! I think she's sprung near the bow where we come in hard on the pier this spring. Some oakum and pitch and she'll be as good as new."

"It's always something goin' wrong."

"Yep. Been a plague of problems ever since we launched her."

"I know, I know, Jack, but *Sarah Jane's* a good vessel." Watson yanked on a hawser and, finding the end of the large rope firmly secured, threw the other coiled end onto the pier. "As soon as she's warped, run up to the shed. I told William Francis to shred some old rope yesterday when he didn't want to come out with us. There should be lots of oakum. You'll find a bar of pitch at the back of the shelf over by the window. The bucket's by the door."

"Right!"

The two men worked in silence as they secured the two-masted schooner to the side of the government pier so that when the tide emptied the harbour, the craft would remain upright, sitting on the bottom of the almost empty harbour. Each of the men had his own thoughts, Jack's being the most unkind.

*He's spoiled that son of his. Shouldn't give the little bugger a choice about whether or not he's comin' sailin'. Naw, the choice should be if he don't get out on the Sarah Jane as a deckhand, he don't get to eat. That's the only choice I'd give'em. I bet he don't shred that old rope. There'll be no oakum waitin' for us in the shed all ready to be used. No sirree. The boy don't know what it's like to do a job proper-like.*

Watson checked the fenders, making sure there was enough slack in the lines for the fenders to keep the ship from wearing on the pier as she settled to the harbour bottom. *I don't see the boy.* He stopped long enough to scan the harbour and the hill toward the house. *The boy should have known we would come in on the tide. Shoulda been here so I don't have to send Jack for the oakum. I'll be right some angry if he's gone to Halls Harbour again.* He walked to the other side of the pier. *Damn! The dory is gone. The boy has gone off somewhere.*

Watson glanced over to the shed where he could see that Jack was coming out empty-handed. *I guess the boy didn't make the oakum like he was supposed to.* Then Watson remembered; during the last low tide, William had been working on the dory, using the bar of pitch to close up a couple of seams in the old boat. Watson spit into the murky water where, some twenty feet down, a bar of pitch was probably resting where a careless boy had left it. Jack confirmed Watson's fears.

"There's no oakum. The pitch bucket's gone and there's no bar of pitch."

"So much for fixin' what troubles our *Sarah Jane.*"

"Leastwise, fixin' her this tide. I can fetch some pitch from our place but we don't have no oakum ready."

"That'll be fine, Jack." Watson took one last look around the pier and at the ship, checking to make sure all was in order. Satisfied with what he saw, he threw his arm over Jack Eaton's shoulder. "We won't sail short-handed again, old friend. Go along home now." He gave his friend a gentle push. "Now, git!"

Jack trotted along the beach and then cut through the bushes along a well-trod path leading to the Eaton cottage.

Watson lowered his head and began the climb to his house, situated as it was on the escarpment leading to the harbour. He didn't look up from his thoughts until he entered the front yard. Sarah Jane was waiting for him, standing in the doorway, rubbing and rubbing her hands with a tea towel.

"William took the dory."

"I gathered that, Sarah Jane."

"He went in the direction of Halls Harbour."

"Captain Chase will send him back. I'll have a talk with the boy. He's got to understand that . . ."

"He took your seabag. His clothes are gone. I sent Lena for Wiley. Wiley came right away. I loaned Wiley our horse to go over to Halls Harbour. Maybe Wiley could catch the boy in time."

"In time? In time for what?"

"Stanley said his brother had run away to sea. Stanley said William knew about a ship loading potatoes at Chase's pier."

"Stanley Wayman Brewster!" Watson didn't often raise his voice at his boys, always remembering how he had felt when his father did so—but he couldn't stop himself— "Stanley!" He stormed over to the stairs, leaning up the staircase, spittle coming from his lips. "You come right down here, Stanley."

A slight, nice-looking lad of six years came to the top of the stairs, a bible in his hands. "I didn't do nuthin' wrong, Pa."

Now somewhat more under control and in a much more subdued voice, father said to his favourite son, "Leave The Book on your bed and come down, real smart like."

"Yes, Pa." The boy disappeared for a moment and then came quickly down the stairs, running to his father's side and placing his little hand in his father's.

"You knew about William Francis?"

"Yes."

"And you didn't tell me?"

"You said I must not tattle. You said we were brothers and there's nothing so close as brothers."

Watson sighed. He took the boy by the hand and led him to the grandchair, where he sat down and lifted the boy onto his lap. "I know that's what I said." He pushed the boy's blond hair back from his forehead. He continued stroking the boy's hair. "You were right to keep your brother's secret."

"Are you angry with William?"

"I'm not as angry with him as I am worried about what might happen to him."

"William isn't worried. He wants to go to sea on a big, big ship and see the world, just like you did when you were a boy."

"But I . . ."

Stanley smiled at his father. "William told me you would say 'but.'"

Watson gave his boy a hug and set him down. He patted his wife's arm as he strode past her to the door. "I will go along to Baxters and see if I can borrow their wagon."

"The ship would have left with the tide, Watson."

"Yes, but perhaps Captain Chase stopped him." When he saw the hope light up his wife's eyes he hastened to add, "But a strange ship's captain will take crew wherever he can find them."

"Even a ten-year-old boy?"

"I was eleven."

"Oh."

They both rushed to the door when they heard the sound of a horse.

It was Wiley Baxter. He was alone.

He slid off the horse, shaking his head as he slipped the reins into the horse ring at the side of the shed. "Thought you was goin' to build a barn, Watson."

"In my own time, Wiley."

"The boy's gone on the brigantine *Elizabeth*. The captain's name was Walsh. Didn't wait for the tide. Load of potatoes for Boston. Next ports of call somewhere's in the Caribbean and then South America. First time she's come this far up the Fundy. Might not come back this way again. Sorry for your worry, Sarah Jane."

Watson was not having any of it, *leastwise not from Wiley Baxter*. "Did Captain Chase see the boy?"

"Guess not."

"Then how do you know my boy was on the ship?"

"The dory was there. Your boy and the ship wasn't."

Relenting on their years of antagonism for a moment, Wiley

explained, "Chase said Captain Walsh run a tight ship and a happy crew. Your boy'll larn."

"Yes, he'll learn a lot . . ."

"And right some quick, too," Wiley said with a flash of a smile.

"I want to thank you for your . . ."

"I done it fer Sarah Jane."

"My thanks, Wiley," she said.

"My thanks, too, Wiley," Watson added.

Wiley turned to go but stopped and looked into Sarah Jane's eyes. "You hear I'm gettin' hitched, Sarah Jane?"

"Yes, I did, Wiley." She took her husband's hands in hers, "We wish you the very best, Wiley."

Watson gestured toward the shed. "Take the horse, Wiley. I can send Lena over to get it later."

"Thanks, Watson." He vaulted the startled horse and, leaning forward, pulled the reins through the ring. "If Lena's still at the house with me Mom, we'll feed 'em both before we sends 'em back."

After the horse and rider had disappeared over the round of the hill, Watson lifted his son into his arms. He nuzzled the boy's neck, causing him to giggle. "You know what is closer than two brothers?" he whispered into the boy's hair.

The laughing, squirming boy said brothers were closest.

"Why do you think brothers are closest?"

"Because my father told me so."

"Your father was wrong, Stanley." He tightened his arms around the boy. "A father and his son are closer."

## Chapter Sixteen
## Happy Days

*April 1907*
Sarah Jane *on the Bay of Fundy*

"That boy oughta be a preacher!"

Watson grinned at his new deckhand, Walter Huntley, who had just spent the last hour with Stanley cleaning up some tangled lines in the top rigging. "You're just sayin' that 'cause it's true!" the proud father laughed back. "His Ma and I taught him all we knew and then he studied the Bible every chance he got—and he went to church every week—walked there and back. Musta done ten miles every Sunday just gettin' to church."

"Yeah, well, I believe it. While we was splicin' in the new bit of rope, he was tellin' Bible stories."

"You don't have to listen to him, Mister Huntley. You can tell him to belt up. Just because he's my son, doesn't give him any right to . . . to . . ." Watson hesitated, trying to pick his words.

"It can't do us no harm givin' some extra thought to the Lord the way things have been goin' fer us."

Watson knew what the sailor was referring to. "Yeah. Too bad we missed that cargo at Halifax."[1]

"Hard choice to make, sir, while we was at Malagash Roads. Cut the anchor loose and git along to Halifax or try'n recover the anchor and take your chances pickin' up a load."

Neither man mentioned the fact that the fouled anchor had been lost anyway.

Stanley slid down the standing rigging, hand over hand, nimbly landing with both feet on the canted deck. He gave a polite nod to his father. "The rope was made wrong, Cap'n. Had a built-in twist." He took the coil of rope from his belt and held it out for his father to check.

Watson fingered the hemp. He handed it back. "Don't put it in the locker. Keep it separate. Next time we go to Halifax,

I'll take it back to Stairs and Sons and show them the shoddy goods we've been getting from the Dartmouth Rope Works."

"Beggin' yer pardon, Cap'n, but I don't think it's a Dartmouth rope," Stanley said. "Wrong colour and, with the twist and all, I think the yardman at Stairs fed in a cheap southern length to make up our order."

"Then we won't be able to prove who supplied it. Cut it up into shorter lengths so it doesn't get put into service again. Stow it in the locker. We'll get some use out of it as oakum."

"Aye, Cap'n."

Captain Brewster gestured at the two men. "Ready the boat, if you please. When we pick up the West Bay pilot, I'm going to want to go ashore and see if there's any messages for us."

"You want two oarsmen, Cap'n?"

"No, Mister Huntley. Mister Brewster will take me ashore. You and the boys tidy up some while we're gone. I want our *Sarah Jane* to look her best 'cause we'll be a couple of days at Windsor."

"Aye, Cap'n," the two men answered and immediately went about the business of preparing to launch the little white boat the crew used to go back and forth when away from their home port. She was called *Pelican* because, no matter how many of the *Sarah Jane's* six man crew were jammed into the craft, she always sat high in the water like a hungry pelican— which made her hard to handle in windy conditions, but her flat bottom made for easy beach landings.

Walter shook loose the boat's tarpaulin cover and pulled it off to one side. He grunted as he bent over to dig the oarlocks from the locker under the middle thwart. "What's he want a pilot fer? I know he's been in and out of the Minas so often he could probably sail it blindfold."

"I dunno." Stanley took one of the oarlocks and fitted it into the slot in the gunnel on the port side while Walter fixed the second oarlock to the upper edge of the other side of the boat. "It's not the first time he's picked up a West Bay pilot . . . probably not the last, neither."

"Set in his ways?"

Stanley waved Walter off. "Here he comes. Swing the davits outboard."

As soon as *Pelican* was clear of the deck and hanging over the water, Stanley ordered, "Lower away." He waited until Captain Brewster had descended and positioned himself on the sternsheet and then Stanley clambered over the side. He released the bow from the davit, knowing that the captain would free up the sternfast. Pushing *Pelican* away from the side of the schooner, Stanley fitted the oars in the oarlocks and pulled strongly for the shore.

When the captain didn't strike up a conversation, Stanley asked the question, "Why take on a pilot to go from Parrsboro Shore to Minas? It's not very far and . . ."

"And I suppose you are going to say that we have done it dozens of times before."

"Well, yes, I was."

"Better be able to apologize for caution than be called upon to lament imprudence."

Stanley rowed, head down, his tousled blond hair shading his eyes. After a moment or two he looked up. "I guess I don't understand, Pa. You know this place like the back of your hand but you go take on a pilot."

"I travel the Minas Basin a dozen times a year." He smiled at his son. "How often do you think the pilot does that?" He didn't wait for the reply. "Probably every day during the season," he answered. Watson could see that his son still wasn't satisfied. "Minas Basin and the Cornwallis River run a hazardous, ever-changing course. The pilots know it better than anyone." He gestured in the direction of Cape Split. "These are not safe waters for a slapdash navigator."

The young man bristled. "A sailor isn't slapdash just 'cause he knows his course."

"That's right." Some movement beyond Stanley's shoulders caught Watson's attention. "The pilot is coming out." Watson waved at the pilot's boat that was just leaving the shore. He cupped his hands around his mouth. "Ahoy! We will be but a moment in West Bay."

The pilot waved an acknowledgement. "Carry on, Captain Brewster. I gets paid the same no matter. Your final destination?"

"Windsor."

"I judge you have plenty of time with the tide but I suggest you not spend it in West Bay."

"Aye, pilot."

Stanley looked back over his shoulder at the approaching boat. "He's some cheeky bastard!" he growled.

"But sound advice, nonetheless, sailor."

Stanley Wayman Brewster recognized authority in the tone of voice. His conversation with his father had been concluded. "Aye, Cap'n," he said.

## Windsor

The last hogshead of rum lifted clear of *Sarah Jane*'s hold, Watson Brewster looked down into the storage area of his ship. What he saw pleased him well enough; aside from the usual packing debris his men were in the process of cleaning up, there were no signs of breakage. He leaned over the edge of the hold and inhaled. "And not much leakage," he said to himself, remembering the time he was unloading at Halifax. On that occasion there had been such a strong smell of rum in the hold that his men had become drunk with the fumes, or so they had claimed as they came topside into the fresh air.

The agent from Schwartz and Sons had scrutinized the men and had told Watson to look for a new bung on one or more of the barrels. "At the very least, those boys have taken a tipple or two."

New bungs were found and two of the sailors were put ashore to find their own way back to their home port. Watson sailed short-handed for quite some time until he was able to sign on men who were neighbours or closely related, like the Huntley brothers and his very own son. "Two Huntleys, two Eatons, and two Brewsters makes for a fine ship." *Now, if we could only shake the bad luck that seems to haunt the Sarah Jane.*

A voice from the pier interrupted his thinking. "What? What did you say, Mister Huntley?"

"I said, we got ourselves our load according to the manufacturer's papers, sir."

"Is it from the furniture factory or the tannery?"

"Says it's furniture, Cap'n."

"No sign of anything from the tannery?"

"No, sir. Just the furniture."

"Begin loading. Adjust the ship's trim. We will spread the tannery merchandise on top." *If it ever gets here.* He waved at Jack Eaton who was below in the hold.

"Aye, Cap'n," the man answered.

"Mister Eaton, go ashore. Rent or borrow a horse. Ride out to the tannery and see what's holding up their shipment."

"How will I know where the tannery is?"

"It's up the river a piece. Right on the shoreline." Watson grinned at his friend. "Just follow your nose, Jack. And don't take long. I need to catch the tide. The pilot is waiting for us."

Jack returned in less than an hour with the bad news that the owner of the tannery had been told the *Sarah Jane* was a hard-luck ship and probably wouldn't return to Windsor this season. "He dumped his stuff on a lighter and had it ferried over to Port Williams." Jack had a hangdog look as he finished up, "It's been done and gone some ten days."

Watson sucked in his breath. He exhaled in a long, slow stream. "Can't say I really blame him," he shook his head, "but we've been later and he's waited." He shouted down to the hold, "Check the ship's trim. Batten the hatches as soon as you're ready." Watson continued to watch the activity in the hold as he spoke to the man beside him. "Make ready to sail, Mister Eaton."

"Aye, Cap'n."

"We might as well have an early departure," Watson commented with a faraway look. "The day is fine and the wind is fair . . ."

"And the pilot gets to go home early."

"It's an ill wind that blows no good."

*Late November*
*Baxters Harbour*

Sarah Jane watched as the Brewster schooner approached the harbour. Right away she knew it wasn't her husband at the helm. No, there was altogether too much sail for it to be her Watson. And, it couldn't be her son; he wouldn't dare such a . . . a flamboyant harbour approach. Mainsail now cascading down, rudder hard over, hawser thrown to catch the end of the pier, foresail being backed to act as a brake to forward momentum, second hawser now in place, *Sarah Jane* swinging at the end of the first hawser in a short circle as she was being snugged into the pier by the second hawser; no, that couldn't be either of her men.

When the foresail dropped, she was able to see who was at the helm. "Lord! It's William Francis!" An excited mother gave a yelp and charged out of the kitchen and down the path to the pier. Her breath soon coming in short bursts, she was forced to a walk and then she stopped, gasping, her arms folded under her breasts, her eyes glued to the woman standing next to the long-absent William Francis Brewster.

The other woman smiled up the pier at the mother. As she did so, she linked her arm through William's and placed her free hand, possessively, over his wrist. Stepping out with long, long strides, she led the way from the ship.

*That woman owns my boy,* she thought. *I do hope William did the right thing by her and married her.* Sarah Jane gave the couple a little wave. *I did so want to see that boy churched.*

Watson, as if reading her mind, shouted, "They were married in Saint John!"

*A tiny woman,* Sarah Jane thought. *She shouldn't be wearing a long skirt like that.*[2]

William Francis surged ahead but the woman didn't let go so she was dragged along, slowing him down. "I brought you things from Cathay, Ma!"

They were close enough for the women to meet, eye to eye. The woman spoke. "He means China, Missus Brewster."

"Welcome to Baxters Harbour, Missus Brewster." Sarah Jane made a great show of wiping her hands in her apron. "I hope you find us to your liking." She reached forward for the surprisingly limp handshake. "Not everyone fits in, here."

"I intend to fit in just fine, Mother." She smiled sweetly. "May I call you Mother?" Before Sarah Jane could answer, her son grabbed his mother and lifted her off the ground, swinging her around and around.

"I missed you, Ma!" He gave her a big, big buss on first one cheek and then the other. "I brought you some jade, and some ivory and some special tea and some silk—you'll just love the silk."

The second Missus Brewster put a restraining hand on her husband's arm. "You go along with your family, my dear. I will go back to the ship and tell one of the men which boxes to bring in first." When William began to protest, she gave him a bright smile as she repeated, "You go along with your family, my dear."

Everyone recognized the voice of authority and were not surprised when William nodded his head in agreement and took his mother's arm as they went to the house.

Sarah Jane recognized the strength of the man who was once her boy. "My! You've grown, William."

"Pa didn't know who I was when I approached him on the waterfront at Halifax. Told me he had a full crew and didn't need another hand."

"He might have been joshing you, son."

Watson gave his wife a sheepish smile. "I truly didn't know the boy; he had put on so much muscle."

"And the beard," the considerate Sarah Jane added. "Hard to know your son through all of that growth."

At this moment the new Missus Brewster gave a slight tap on the door as she pushed into the front room with several bundles in her arms. She walked over to the table. "Here's all right?" and put the parcels down. She then collapsed into the grandchair. "I'm not much of a sailor. It's good to climb onto something solid." She took the pins out of her bonnet and removed it, showing black, shiny coils of hair, pinned into place like a little crown over her pert face. "I'm an Irving from New Brunswick. My given name is Mary Jane but I consider double-barrelled names an affectation." She gave the older couple a sweet smile. "I would appreciate it if you could bring yourselves to call me Mary."

There was a small moment of silence. Sarah Jane took her son by the hand and led him to one of the lesser chairs, pulling him down into the one beside her. "You, Watson, sit on the blanket box. As soon as Stanley comes up from the ship, have him get some more firewood from the shed so we can make it all comfy and cosy for our prodigal son . . . and his delightful companion, Mary." She put both of her hands around her son's hand. "Tell us, dearest, all about your adventures, starting with how you met your wife and what she was doing in a seaport town."

### Next Morning

"Where's your father, Stanley?"

"I didn't see him, Ma."

"Run out to the biffy and see if he's there."

"Sure will, Ma."

Stanley shucked on his sea jacket and boots and slipped out the side door, whistling a cheery tune.

"You hush up, Stanley. The young couple are still abed."

Stanley smiled back at his mother. "Time they got up, Ma."

Sarah Jane gave her younger son a stern look.

"Yes, Ma. I'll be more quiet."

Sarah Jane could hear the floor creak overhead. "Oh, well. You're probably right, son. It's time they got up anyway." She pulled the door shut and went about her business at the kitchen stove. She experienced a sense of unease when Stanley came back into the kitchen, alone.

"He's not at the outhouse, Ma. Nor at the shed."

William came into the kitchen looking particularly refreshed and content. "Whatcha lookin' for, Ma?" he asked, scratching his belly.

Suffering from what had now become a feeling of dread, Sarah Jane didn't answer. Instead, she went to the front window and looked out over the harbour. She gasped. In a firm voice she said, "Get your woman up, William. We will need blankets. Have her bring them to the shore." She was moving quickly to the door. "Stanley, run to the beach! *Pelican* is in the shallows. It's overturned. I think I see your father. Move, son!"

## *Endnotes*

[1] It was from Eric Brian Brewster that I was able to confirm that Watson Brewster was captain of the *Sarah Jane* from the 1870's through to 1908.

[2] According to Helen Brewster, Mary Jane was "a tiny woman who always wore a long skirt and big button shoes. She was old-fashioned."

## Chapter Seventeen
## The Promise

*Summer 1908*
*Baxters Harbour*

"Where are you going, sweetheart?"

William Brewster, his hand on the latch, turned to face his wife. He was struck anew with the beauty of this woman who had completely won his heart.

"I thought I might go over to Mother's." *I'm sure enough glad I went to the extra expense to put in them pine panels. With the pale wood behind her, her shiny black hair and alabaster skin bein' struck by the morning sun, she looks like a goddess.* He felt a surge of pride in what he possessed. *I have a beautiful woman in a beautiful new house.* "I thought there might be somethin' that needs doin'." He experienced a surge in his loins as the familiar pout formed on her cupid lips. "I wouldn't be gone long," he suggested, hopefully.

"You might think of my needs before you go off to see about your Mother's."

"Oh, yes, Mary." He stepped back into the kitchen. When she extended her hand, he took it with great expectation. "What would you want me to do?"

"I need you to go to Canning for me. Missus Borden was telling me she had a quilt pattern." With her free hand, she caressed his blond beard. "Do you know that you have streaks of brown in your hair?"

William leaned into her hand. "Yeah. Brewsters have blond hair when they're children. I guess I'm not a child any more."

"You know I'm not good at making quilt patterns. Missus Borden was kind enough to offer . . ."

"And I meant to sit a spell with Pa. He's been tryin' to tell me somethin.'"

Allowing the disdain she felt to show in her voice, Mary said, "I suppose he was a great story teller. Too bad he can't talk much, now."

"He was tellin' me about his ship that was lost off Halifax. Yesterday he said he would have gone down with his ship but God spared him. His bein' allowed to live was part of some sort of plan. Pa made some promises to God in return for his life."

"Really!"

"Pa thinks him falling into the harbour last November was a warnin' that there's not much time to keep his promise."

"A warning?"

"I don't know. He got tired of tryin' to talk and Ma sent me packin'. Told me to come back in the morning when Pa is most fresh."

Mary smiled at her husband. "You run along now to your Mother's. I can wait for my quilt patterns. It's only June and we won't need quilts until . . ."

"Naw! I'll go to Canning. Is there anything else you need?"

"Surprise me. You know I am always so very grateful when you bring little surprises home."

\* \* \*

Sarah Jane wiped the drool from Watson's chin. "I think someone is coming, dear." She got up and looked out the front window. "Yes, it's William. He must have been with Stanley because they are coming up the road together." She went back to the grandchair and tucked the blanket around her husband. "Mustn't get a chill, my pet." She hummed the tune to the hymn "Jesus Loves Me" as she patted his hair into place. Noting that one of his arms had slid down by his side, she put it back in his lap. She was still humming when the two men came through the door. She remained by her husband's side, raising her voice to be heard over the shuffling of the feet on the pine floorboards.

"Good afternoon, boys," she said with a touch of irony in her voice. "I thought you might have come by earlier in the day, William, but we are pleased to see you at any time." When the elder son didn't respond, she walked into the kitchen where she could see their faces. She asked, "Spending a little brotherly time together this morning?"

"No, Ma." If Stanley understood the byplay between the mother and William, he didn't show it. "Didn't have time for it," he said. "Me and Jack and two of the boys had to go out and get some traps for Mister Eaton." Stanley slipped off his jacket and threw it over one of the clothes pegs near the door. He scuffed off his sea boots and dashed past his mother and up the stairs, two at a time. "Gotta get cleaned up! Told Ella May to expect me in the forenoon. She's been awaitin' since then."

The thumping and banging overhead brought a smile to William's lips. "I suppose he'll be the rest of the day over at the Porters doin' whatever chores will put him in good stead with Ella May's father."

"I suppose." Sarah Jane inclined her head toward the front room. "Your father is still up. I know he has been looking forward to seeing you."

William strode through the door and gave a hearty greeting. Inwardly, William was shocked by the deterioration in his father's condition. He suddenly realized that his father was dying. William dragged one of the small chairs over so he could sit next to the ailing man. "You wanted to talk," he said without any preamble.

Watson struggled with some words. He sighed and gave a despairing look at his wife.

"He wants me to explain his promise to the Lord."

"Is that what you want, Pa?"

Watson worked his mouth, inclining his head, slightly.

Sarah Jane continued, "The Lord gave your father back his life. Your father never forgot that gift. Any time there was opportunity to give to another soul in need . . ." She stopped because Watson was trying desperately to say something.

He finally blurted, "N-no!"

"What do you want me to say, my dear?" Sarah Jane put her hand on her husband's wrist. "You don't want me to mention . . ."

"Fambly. Only fambly."

Sarah Jane nodded her head in agreement and, without hesitation, began again.

"When your grandfather took a new wife and departed Nova Scotia, he left very little behind. Certainly he left nothing for his children, Watson included. However, Watson had been at sea for years and had some money put by."

"Like me," William said with no little pride. "I built a fine house here at the harbour, eh?"

"Well, Watson dowered his sister. He gave money to his two brothers, which left him just enough to build this little house where he has set a fine Christian example for you boys."

"And that you did!" William leaned forward and squeezed his father's limp hand. "You certainly kept your end of the bargain, old feller," he said in a jovial manner. "You certainly did."

Watson said something that sounded like "Wetter." Sarah Jane understood.

"One time, years ago, a letter was delivered that we believe was intended for your grandfather. It told of a large sum of money that had been sent for W. Brewster to claim and use in remembrance of Samuel Brewster, the dissenter preacher who lived over near Port Williams." She hesitated as she looked into her husband's face to reassure herself that he wanted her to proceed. She must have seen a "yes" in his eyes because she went on, "We claimed the money and planned to build a church here, at Baxters Harbour."

"You didn't build the church."

"No, we didn't."

"You used it to buy a third of the *Sarah Jane.*"

"More than a third."

Stanley had been standing at the bottom of the stairs. He entered and joined the silence that had filled the room.

Her voice just a whisper, she recounted some of the troubles that had earned the *Sarah Jane* the reputation of being a hard-luck ship. "We came to believe the Lord was telling Watson that he should make amends. We always believed that someday, somehow, we would make the money and build that church like we should have done in the beginning."

Stanley spoke. "And father thinks the Lord made him fall into the harbour? That's twaddle!"

"Instead of giving, we took." She looked into the eyes of her younger son. "The letter was a sign that Watson should have heeded. We should have built a memorial to the dissenter preacher like the letter said."

"A church?" both sons said at the same moment.

As if in pain, Watson Brewster moaned a single word, "Dy-ing!"

Sarah Jane took one of her husband's limp hands in hers and held it as she explained, "Your father is . . . dying. He needs to know if . . ."

Watson took his father's other hand in his. "You'll be with us a long time yet, old timer. I know it. You can build the church yourself. Me and Stanley here will help you."

Watson closed his eyes, letting his head fall back onto the pillow.

Sarah Jane stood up. "Your father will rest now. Come back tomorrow, if you like."

William remained seated. "We will build your church, Father." He leaned forward, putting his lips close to the dying man's ear. "You can count on us to keep your promise, Father."

Watson Brewster opened his eyes. If he could have smiled he would have.

Sarah Jane patted Watson's shoulder. "There, dear. It's all taken care of." She made guiding motions to her sons with her hands. At the door she said, "They'll be back tomorrow and we'll all talk about the church."

## Chapter Eighteen
### The Family

*Summer 1912*
*The Cemetery at Pereaux*

They stood around the grave, the men dressed in black suits, uncomfortable in their stiff collars, and the women, some covering their hair with scarves but all of them sombre-looking in their dark clothes.

"This isn't a funeral." Sarah Jane smiled. "Today is the fourth anniversary of the death of Watson Brewster but I haven't called you together to mourn his passing. He was a good man, a fine husband, and a caring father, and although we miss him, I asked you to come here for other reasons. I wanted to discuss family matters and I wanted Watson to hear it first—from me—and that's why we are meeting here at his graveside."

Mary Brewster stepped closer to her William. Sarah Jane couldn't help but notice how Mary grasped the crook of her husband's elbow while, with her other arm, drawing her children closer to her side. The children, Joseph and Chester, were accustomed to such maternal gestures of control and responded as the mother expected them to; they stood as close to their mother as space allowed.

"You all know Thomas Ells." Sarah Jane gestured to the tall, robust man standing off to one side, who now, somewhat self-consciously, joined her by the side of the grave. "I want you to know that Thomas has asked me to marry him. After giving it much thought, I have agreed and will become his wife." She waited for several heartbeats for some reaction. *They are either too stunned to react or already knew about my plans,* she thought. *Oh, well, in for a penny, in for a pound.*[1]

Sarah Jane thought she would begin with her sister-in-law—Auntie Emm, as William and Stanley knew her. "Susan Emmeline Blenkhorn."

The startled woman blurted, "Yes, Sarah Jane."

"I have mourned the loss of your brother these last four years. Do you have any observations about my planned marriage?"

"Jacob and I wish you well."

"Thank you."

Joseph Brewster didn't wait to be asked. "We all wish you well, my dear."

"I can't imagine what took you so long, Thomas." Charles and Julia Brewster pushed forward and gave personal congratulations to the couple. It was noticeable that neither of the sons, or their spouses, said much. If they had opposing thoughts, they kept them to themselves.

When the talking had died down a little, Sarah Jane spoke to the departed. "Watson, I love you but I have to get on with life. I hope you understand."

"He understands, my dear." Emmeline put her arms around Sarah Jane. "He was a good, Christian gentleman who would want the best for his loved ones."

"Thank you."

Thomas Ells cleared his throat, seeking to get the attention of the family. "We should go back to the house where there's food and drink waiting for us."

Watson's brothers and sister pleaded that they would visit another time because it was late and they had a long way to go before dark.

* * *

Later, at the little Baxters Harbour house, the immediate family gathered to drink to the health of the new couple.

The toast barely out of the way, Stanley was the first to speak up.

"We have some unsettled business, Ma."

"Yes, we do," she sighed as she put down her drink. "We should get it done."

Mary Brewster was quicker off the mark. "My William gave a dying man an undertaking to help build a church at Baxters Harbour."

"Yes, he did."

"William was merely trying to make a dying man more comfortable with his going. It didn't mean . . ."

Sarah Jane caught her son's eye. "What did it mean, William?"

William turned his glass around and around in his hands, not looking anywhere but into the bottom of the glass.

Again, it was Mary who spoke up. "He didn't mean to take from our resources, the food and the clothes from the backs of our three children—your grandchildren—to satisfy a promise given to a dying man—a man who would never know if it were done or not."

"As I remember it, William told his father . . ."

Stanley leaned forward; Sarah Jane stopped to allow him to speak. "We can't build the church, Ma," he said. "That's the beginning and the end of it."

Sarah Jane fell silent.

"And, Ma," he continued, "where are you and Thomas going to live?"

Thomas Ells cleared his throat again. "Sarah Jane will come live with me," he announced after he had gotten everyone's attention.

"You can have this house, Stanley. You and your children can continue to live here." Sarah Jane looked over at the other son and added, "Watson would have done it that way; you already have a home, William."

Mary Brewster's eyes crackled with the fires of indignation. "How can you say that? It's not fair!"

The family was surprised when William contradicted his wife. "The matter of the house is settled, then."

Mary wasn't deterred. "What about the schooner?" she persisted.

"The Brewster share of the schooner remains with me, the widow of Watson Brewster." Sarah Jane saw the protests forming on the lips of her boys so she quickly raised her hands. "I plan to sign a paper dividing the Brewster share of the schooner equally between the three of us." So there could be no misunderstanding, she restated her intentions. "The schooner share will be divided equally between Watson Brewster's widow and his two sons."

Ella May, Stanley's wife, stood up. "My children are beginning to fuss," she said. "I must get them off to bed, so if you will excuse me, please." As she made her way to the staircase, she passed by close to the Widow Brewster. She stopped and kissed Sarah Jane's cheek. "We wish you the very best, Mother. You have been most fair in all of this and we appreciate it . . . even if it doesn't sound like it at the moment."

In the long silence that followed, the people sitting in the kitchen could hear Ella May shushing and clucking to her children as she got them ready for bed.

## Endnotes

[1] Most of the information about the Watson Brewster family was provided by Helen (Brewster) Fancy. If Aunt Helen didn't know, she told me where I could go to get it. However, I didn't have much information about the latter days of Sarah Jane. From information filed at the Kings Historical Society by Eric Brian Brewster, I learned that Sarah Jane married Thomas Ells.

## Chapter Nineteen
## Disaster

*Late Fall 1913*
Sarah Jane *off West Bay*

Jack Eaton watched the entrance to West Bay fall astern as the *Sarah Jane* continued on her way to Windsor. He glanced at the captain's profile, the chin set in a more determined line than usual, and asked, "We're not goin' to check for messages?"

"There's never any."

"Your father always stopped for messages."

"That was my father."

"And we're not goin' to take on a pilot?"

"I know the course."

"But your father always said . . ."

"That was my father, Mister Eaton."

"Aye, captain!"

Stanley's bearing softened right away. "Look, Jack, don't make a big thing of this." He squeezed the other man's shoulder. "You know we're still havin' the same bad luck we've always had with this ship. We're six days late for Windsor," Stanley cast an eye at the western horizon, "and by the looks of it, we might not get into Windsor before that storm hits." He released Jack's shoulder. "If we have to duck in somewhere, that will make us another day or two late." He gave his Mate a rueful smile. "By the time we get there, even our loyal furniture maker might have given up on us." He shook his head, "I just don't have the time to fool around with West Bay and pilots and such. I just don't have the time."

"Aye, Cap'n."

Taking another measure of the western sky, Stanley grimaced. "Lay on more canvas, Mister Eaton. I want us past Cape Split before we have a change of wind."

They were well into Minas Basin, coming abreast Kingsport, when Jack spotted the approaching lipper. He raised his arm. "Lipper! Lipper comin' from the port!"[1]

315

"Helmsman, ease off! All hands! Make ready to lower the mainsail!" Stanley ran to the port rail and studied the edge of the ripple that was rapidly approaching his ship. Behind it he could see the surface roughness of the sea. If they were caught under full sail, on a starboard tack, and with the obvious severity of the weather overtaking them, they could be in serious trouble, maybe even be capsized! Stanley realized that there wasn't enough room in the channel to turn to port and, even if there was room for such a manoeuvre, a schooner was usually turned so that the bow, sometime during the turn, was pointed into the wind. When the bow 'passed through the wind,' the sails would luff (become slack) and the crew could handle the sheets and use the pressure of the wind to move the sails to their proper position. If Stanley tried a turn to port, the schooner's stern would pass 'through the wind' (instead of the bow) and the wind would catch the back of the sails with such force that masts could be snapped off or the vessel capsized.

"Helmsman, starboard hard!" He ran to the wheel to give the helmsman a hand with the turn. *Sarah Jane* resented the rough treatment; she heeled, hard over, the crew hanging on, waiting for the luff so they might reduce sail. To the beleaguered captain, the choice was stark: turn into the wind, luff the sails, and get as many of them down before the lipper struck them from the wrong side, or continue the turn until *Sarah Jane* could sail into the lipper on a safer heading but be carrying too much canvas for the storm conditions.

Stanley grunted with the effort as he assisted the helmsman to manoeuvre the ship. He could see the bow was turning, turning—now no longer heading upstream but pointed at the channel buoy. *We'll never make it,* he thought. *The storm will hit us broadside before we can get at the sails. We will be bowled over. Sarah Jane* kept turning—now past the buoy and aimed at the beach—then the Kingsport pier. *The Kingsport pier!*

"Ease up, helmsman! Ease, I say!" Stanley cast a desperate look over his shoulder; the rough water was closer. "Belay taking the mainsail down," he shouted. "Starboard fenders and ready your lines, starboard!"

The crew did as they were told. The men, who had been preparing to lower the mainsail, secured the halyards and raced to the right side of the ship, where they readied the lines that would be used to tie the ship to a pier. There was concern—no, there was fear—in their eyes. Their ship was racing toward land, the large, indestructible pier looming larger and larger in their view. They couldn't see the lipper, nor gauge the destruction it would cause if the lipper's wind and rough water caught them and wrenched *Sarah Jane*'s sails across the deck, perhaps snapping the masts off with the force of their movement. The crew did as they were told; they readied their lines.

"Ease, helmsman."

As the helmsman eased up on the helm, allowing the bow to move slightly to the left, it became apparent to the crew that *Sarah Jane* would just miss the end of the pier.

"Steady, helmsman. Jack! Jack, be ready to drop the mainsail on the luff!" He turned and directed his next order to the two sailors at the stern. "Get a stern line on the end of that pier. Don't miss!"

"Prepare the stern anchor." Stanley took a moment to guess the distance from the end of the pier to the beach and the depth of the water. "Give the anchor a hundred feet. Snug her at one hundred."

The pier was about ten feet away on their right when Stanley gave the order, "Starboard hard!" *Sarah Jane* began her turn which would bring her alongside the length of the pier. The storm struck, pushing her even harder into her turn. She heeled over, further and further; so far that one of the men on the starboard lines lost his footing and fell overboard. The other sailor threw his line, trying to snare the end of the pier. Anchor cables were singing as the anchor was released, that sailor trying to guess the hundred-foot mark. When he jammed the cable, would the block hold?

Suddenly, *Sarah Jane* righted herself. She was in the lee of the pier, protected enough so that the wind no longer filled

her sails but travelling along as if she were in the free and clear
of the middle of the Bay of Fundy.

Jack Eaton dropped the mainsail. He made no move to
the other sails nor did he seek shelter from the impending
impact; he could see the big rocks at the edge of the beach that
were used to anchor the wooden pier. *Did the captain see them?
How in the name of God would they stop in time?* He moved
quickly when he heard his captain's next order.

"Haul on that foresail! Back her!"

A grinding, tearing noise told the crew that the anchor
had been blocked. The drag on the stern brought the bow
around to the right, hard up against the pier. Fenders were
being crushed with the force of the contact, but that was what
fenders were for.

"Make fast the bow!"

The anchor cable snapped, the cable whining as it
whipped through the air. No one was hurt but the ship's prow
began to move out again; however, the cable at the bow had
been secured and the movement stopped.

*Sarah Jane* had arrived at Kingsport.

The storm was all around them but the crew were too
busy responding to the cries from their shipmate floundering
in the icy water to pay much mind to the weather. Besides,
with a ship's captain like Stanley Wayman Brewster, the crew
of the *Sarah Jane* weren't much concerned with a bit of
weather.

*Three Days Later*
*Windsor*

Captain Brewster surveyed the bales and cases filling the storage shed and lining the pier. He felt smugly satisfied with what
he saw. "There are some advantages to being the last ship of
the season, eh, Jack?"

"Oh, there could be another ship; maybe, maybe not, but
they can't take a chance on it. They all want to ship with hard-
luck *Sarah Jane.*" He sniggered.

"What's so funny?"

"I bet there's stuff in there from the tannery."

"Hadn't thought of that." He stroked his jaw as he had a fleeting thought, but cast it aside. "Naw! I'd like to leave 'em in the lurch—refuse their cargo—but that wouldn't be smart."

Jack nodded his head in agreement, while saying, "Your Pa wouldn't leave 'em in the lurch." By the look on Stanley's face, Jack regretted saying it, immediately.

"You're right! And I am not my father. I will take their cargo, not for Christian reasons but for business reasons. Start the loading. I want to be well out into Minas Basin before ebb tide."

Half-way through the loading, Jack confirmed that the tannery had given them the largest consignment ever.

\* \* \*

Within sight of Cape Split, the weather turned sour. The wind changed and *Sarah Jane* ended up tacking back and forth, making little headway.

"We could always go back to Kingsport, spend the night until the wind changes."

Stanley shook his head. "You're always thinking about your pecker, Jack. You should get married and then it wouldn't seem so important."

"She's a nice little widder-woman." He gave his captain a broad wink. "If you take us into Kingsport, I might get to know her well enough to propose. If you think I should get married, you'd be helpin' me make up my mind."

"We aren't goin' into Kingsport, Jack. We would be workin' against the outgoing tide."

"Even so, the wind is with us, Captain; if we make for Kingsport we could be there in an hour at the most."

Confident in his seamanship, Stanley responded, "No, even with the wind the way it is, we will make it out onto the Fundy before dark." With great conviction he added, "But the wind will come 'round so that it helps us."

Within the hour the wind dropped off and, as the sun went down, fog closed in on the *Sarah Jane*.

"Sound the horn, Jack."

Jack put the foghorn to his lips and blew a mighty blast. They waited for the echo.

"Over to starboard, Cap'n. I heard the horn bounce off somthin' solid."

Stanley rubbed his chin. "Could be. Work the rudder. See if you can turn the ship."

Having no point of reference, the sailors weren't sure that their waggling of the rudder had much effect in turning the ship to point one way or the other.

"All right. Give her another blast!"

There still seemed to be an echo from the right.

"Just like the last time."

"Yeah, there's nothin' over there. Just a ghost echo."

"Give a blast every few minutes."

"Aye, Cap'n."

After a while, Jack's lips got sore and Stanley took the horn. He pursed his lips and, after a couple of tries, managed a good solid blow. Almost immediately there was an echo.

"There! We're close to something."

What they had thought was an echo was followed by a second note and then a third.

"My God! That must be another ship! Someone else is blowin' a horn!"

"Or someone on the shore. That could be Scots Bay over there."

Stanley felt a chill up and down his spine. "If that's Scots Bay over there, we are under Cape Split."

Whoever it was on shore gave another couple of blasts.

"Try a hail!"

Jack cupped his hands to his mouth, "Ahoy!"

There was a reply, "Ahoy! What ship?"

"*Sarah Jane* out of Baxters Harbour."

"Are you under sail?"

'Yes, but we have no steerage."

"Get your boats out. Pull away from my voice. The tide will be takin' you onto Cape Split shoals. You'll go on the shoals unless you get your boats out and pull your ship away from here."

"Launching our boat now."

"Keep sounding your horn. We will bring rowboats to help."

Stanley's reaction to the stranger's suggestion was, *Sarah Jane is a small schooner as schooners go, but thinking we can pull her out of danger with the* Pelican *is* . . .

Jack Eaton confirmed his captain's thinking when he said, "I suppose we could give it a try."

The *Sarah Jane* crew stopped whatever they were doing to listen to the distinct sounds of waves breaking against rocks.

"Launch *Pelican!*"

"I feel a breeze!"

"Forget the breeze! Hurry with the *Pelican.*"

The mainsail moved, ever so slightly. The smallest of breezes would move them away from there!

The *Pelican* was in the water and lines had been passed to the bow of the ship. There was no discussion as to which way to row; the breakers were very close now.

Jack was blowing the horn, the rest of the crew were in the *Pelican,* and Stanley was at the helm.

Stanley closed his eyes. In a quiet voice he said, "Lord, I need some help." He opened his eyes when he heard some splashing coming from the direction of Scots Bay.

"Sound the horn, Jack. Maybe they can get here in time."

It was then the *Sarah Jane* touched bottom for the first time. Both men felt the shudder as the ship's keel grazed something.

Jack looked to his captain for orders.

Stanley saw the pleading look but there was nothing he could do. There would be a breeze to save them, or there would not. The boats would arrive before *Sarah Jane* struck hard, or they wouldn't. It was all beyond him and Stanley Wayman Brewster knew it. He began to pray.

"Lord, You have helped us Brewsters before. I need you to help us again. Please don't destroy this little ship. She's all we got and . . ."

*Sarah Jane* struck hard, throwing both men to the deck. From the *Pelican* were cries of anger and despair as the cables attached to the stricken ship pulled the *Pelican* under, leaving the crew thrashing around in the cold water. Fortunately, the Scots Bay rowboats were close and they fished the men out of the water. They were taken to Scots Bay where they spent the night.[2]

Stanley and Jack stayed on the stricken ship. They watched, helplessly, as *Sarah Jane* fell over onto her side as the tidal water receded, the salt water flooding the hold.

In the morning, the Scots Bay people came back, bringing *Sarah Jane*'s crew, dry and rested. By comparison, Jack and Stanley looked in pretty bad condition, but Stanley refused the invitation to leave the ship. Instead, he suggested that the would-be rescuers join him on the schooner. They gathered on the wall of the deckhouse as being the only level place on the schooner.

"She can be floated off," Stanley asserted.

The men nodded their heads in agreement. "There's a lighter in Scots Bay. We can have her here once the tidal bore passes. Your schooner might re-float, more or less level, but first you'll have to go around and open every bung and hatch and let the water out, at least as much as you can. Then before the water comes back, seal 'em all up again and hope she lifts off."

Charles Brewster from Scots Bay slapped at his thigh. "Might as well get to it!"

Another of the rescuers held his hand up, cautioning the men to wait. "Who's gonna pay? The lighter will cost. Our time is a cost." He looked around into the faces of the Scots Bay men. "It's all well and good to fish these boys out of the drink, dry 'em off, and give 'em a night's lodging, but this is work. Who's gonna pay?"

Charles Brewster, from Scots Bay, ran his fingers through his grey hair. "This captain is family. He's my nephew. If you won't do for my kin, what can the Brewsters of Scots Bay expect from their neighbours?"

Three days later, *Sarah Jane* was towed to Kingsport where she remained over the winter while repairs were made.[3]

Although it was never mentioned, it was unlikely the Brewsters would have the money to pay for their share of the costs incurred from the mishap. Without much discussion, Nathan Eaton offered to underwrite the cost of putting the ship back into service.

Stanley's reaction, on behalf of the family, was, "We weren't meant to have that ship. The Lord tried to get our attention, time after time, but we wouldn't listen. I accept your fine offer, Mister Eaton. We'll sign over the Brewster share of the schooner."

Jack Eaton got to know the Kingsport widow and married her.

In the spring, Captain Stanley Brewster sailed *Sarah Jane* into Baxters Harbour. He gathered up his belongings, went ashore, and never again set foot on the schooner.

On that afternoon, Stanley walked up the hill, waving to his gaggle of precious souls: Gladys Rose, George, Lester, Elsie—poor little Harris had died of the mumps just last month but he was probably there in spirit—and his pregnant sweetheart, Ella May.[4] He spread his arms wide, taking as many of his family into his embrace as he could. He leaned forward and whispered into his wife's ear. "It's time, my dear."

Ella May gave her husband a smile. "Time for what, Stanley?"

"Time we built that church for old Samuel Brewster, right here at Baxters Harbour." Stanley released his hold on his kin and stepped out where he could survey his house and fields, nestled as they were against the side of North Mountain. "This here is the Paradise he was lookin' for."

Ella May handed the baby to Gladys Rose and slid in under Stanley's arm, where she cuddled against his sturdy frame. "It's home."

"And this is where we belong—all of us—the livin' and the dead. We shouldn't have to leave here for church goin' and baptizin' and such." He hugged his wife. "We shouldn't have to take our dead way over to the cemetery in Pereaux."

"We can stay here at Baxters Harbour."

"North Mountain."

"We belong here at North Mountain," Ella May agreed. "As you say, husband, we'll build a church."

## Endnotes

[1] The edge of an area of surface roughness moving across the water is called a lipper. It is a good indication of a change of conditions behind the edge. A lipper can be as insignificant as the spray of waves breaking against the bow of a ship or a sea that washes over the deck.

[2] Eric Brewster relates that the *Sarah Jane* ran aground on the shoals off Cape Split.

[3] The *Sarah Jane* was towed to Kingsport (1910/1911) where repairs were made. The financial burden of the repairs and loss of cargo, probably forced the Brewster family to sell their interest in the *Sarah Jane*.

[4] "Harris died with the mumps at nine months old. His mother, Ella, kept a small package of his effects for the rest of her life. It contained his dresses and shoes. As hard as times ever became, she didn't use the clothes for subsequent children." As related by Helen Brewster and recorded in *My Family Story* by Bill Smallwood.

# Chapter Twenty
## The Church

*Thanksgiving Sunday 1921*
*Baxters Harbour*

"It doesn't look like he's coming." Nathan Eaton took his gold watch from his vest and snapped it open. He studied it, carefully, as his companion took a couple of steps into the bright sunlight and stared up the Baxters Harbour Road in the direction of the top of the mountain.

Stanley shielded his eyes, continuing to stare up the hill. "I passed word that we would expect him. I said we would delay our meetin' until two pm so's he could finish with the Thanksgiving service in the valley." He turned away from the road and looked up at the church's spire. "I suppose I could ring the bell, sorta to hurry him along in case he's up the road a ways, talkin' to somebody or other."

Nathan shut his watch. He patted it away in his vest pocket and smoothed the material over his paunch. "I don't think he's going to be here, Stanley."

"What time did you say it was?"

Visibly irritated, Nathan drew out his timepiece again. "Two twenty. He's late enough for me to believe he's not coming."

Both men could hear the children squalling inside the church.

"I suppose we should go back in and tell them the Reverend isn't going to be here."

Stanley shook his head. "Let's go back inside, Mister Eaton. I will look after things from here."

Nathan gave a surprised look but followed the younger man back into the church.

Stanley hesitated at the vestibule. He put his hand out to stop Nathan. "Isn't it beautiful," he said. He cast his eyes at the vaulted ceiling, taking pleasure in the richness of the dark oak and of the perfect wood joins the men of Baxters Harbour had made. He let his eyes fall to the simple pulpit. *Someday it will be more ornate but for now it's just fine*, he thought. He whispered to Mister Eaton, "This is Thanksgiving and we have so much to give thanks for. The preacher should have been here."

Nathan whispered back, "Probably, that's why he didn't come. He wanted to be with his own folk on this day."

"With the valley people."

"Yes, I guess so."

"Take a chair, Mister Eaton." Stanley pointed at one of the pressed-back, wooden chairs. "Join your family." Without waiting to see if the older man would take a seat, Stanley strode to the pulpit. He hesitated before he ascended the steps but then did so resolutely. He raised his arms as he had seen the preachers do. "Brethren," he intoned, and then, in a more normal voice and wearing a bashful smile, he said, "friends and family. This here is Thanksgiving Sunday and the Reverend couldn't make it to North Mountain to be with us, and yet we have so much to be thankful for that I thought we should talk to God ourselves."[1]

The baby in his dear Ella May's arms let out a loud squawk. The congregation tittered but were obviously intent on what Stanley had to say.

"We don't have no hymn books yet. We meant for them to be here for our very first service in our church but, like the Reverend, they didn't show up." He made a lifting motion with his hand. "Let's all stand and sing one of the hymns that all the children will know; just the first verse 'cause it's all I know." He hummed a note. "Join right in if'n you don't want me to do a solo." Stanley Wayman Brewster began to sing in a beautiful baritone and the congregation raised their voices as well.

> Can a little child like me
> Thank the Father fittingly?
> Yes, O yes! Be good and true,
> Patient, kind in all you do;
> Love the Lord, and do your part;

Learn to say with all your heart,
Father, we thank Thee,
Father in heaven, we thank Thee.

The congregation sat down.

Stanley made a clapping motion with his hands. "That was right some good!" He pointed at the ceiling. "It's a good thing your daddies, brothers and uncles did a good job on the roof, 'cause you almost lifted it off!" Then he leaned on the pulpit. "I don't have a sermon to preach nor a psalm ready to read but the Lord knows I am grateful for His bounty." He extended his arms. "Just look at this wonderful building! Built on Schofield land, with community money," he inclined his head toward Nathan Eaton's chair, "and the skills of the best ship builders on the whole Bay of Fundy." He paused and then raised his voice. "We dedicate this church to you, Lord."

"Amen, amen," the people of Baxters Harbour said.

The man in the pulpit beckoned to his wife. "Ella May, would you please stand?"

Without hesitation, Ella May Brewster rose, babe in her arms, and faced the front of the church.

"I'm sure the Reverend would have baptized our youngest, if he had been here. Maybe he will, another time, but for today, Ella May, would you please introduce our daughter to the Lord?"

Ella May held her child up, shoulder high. "Lord, this here is Helen Freda Brewster. Helen is sister to Gladys Rose, George, Lester, Elsie, Glendon, Girvan, Myrtle, Leander, and Elaine."

As she mentioned each name, the child stood up with the mother.

"And Lord," the mother continued, "you have dear Harris by your side."

"Amen, amen."

Stanley motioned for the congregation to rise. "We will close today with the first verse and the refrain of another hymn we all know."

And they sang:

"Just look at this wonderful building!..."

Will your anchor hold in the storms of life?
When the clouds unfold their wings of strife;
When the strong tides lift and the cables strain,
Will your anchor drift or firm remain?

Stanley stopped singing to listen to the words of the refrain that were being raised to the Lord.

We have an anchor that keeps the soul
Steadfast and sure while the billows roll

*Through the years, the Brewsters were pilgrims,* he thought, *always searching for sanctuary.* Through his tears of rapture he saw that the sun's rays were streaming through the windows, turning the blond heads of his children to gold. *Oh! God! Thank you! Now, here, in this church, we have finally found refuge.*

Steadfast and sure while the billows roll;

*We have our church in memory of that early Brewster, the one they called the dissident preacher, who was present in Nova Scotia . . .*

Fastened to the Rock which cannot move,

*And Brewsters will always be here, in this Paradise by the sea.*

Grounded firm and deep in the Saviour's love!

"Amen."
And the congregation replied, "Amen, amen."

## Endnotes

[1] According to Helen Freda (Brewster) Fancy, "He was a beautiful singer and loved to sing the hymns at the Baxters Harbour Church. He was very religious all his life. In fact, he was the driving force behind getting the Baxters Harbour Church built and gave the occasional sermon when the Reverend couldn't make it."

*Addendum*

Today, Baxters Harbour is bleak in a picturesque sort of way. The Church is still there, by the side of the road, overlooking the harbour and standing guard over the Brewsters in the cemetery.

The closest Brewster family lives up the Baxters Harbour Road, near the old Leander Brewster place. One of the sons, Leon, lives there now.

Helen (Brewster) Fancy, the baby at the end of this story and the lead character of a later book, and Eric Brewster, another son of Leander, live and breathe the Brewster history; the information they made available was a great help with this novel.

(Sadly, Helen Brewster died after those words were written.)

And finally, children of the rest of the Brewsters of this story, scattered all over Europe and North America, send money to keep the old church in repair—you remember, the Church that was built to remind us that a dissident preacher named Samuel Brewster was once present in Nova Scotia.

MEMBER OF SCABRINI GROUP

Québec, Canada
2005